Airborne

Julian Morris-Haaker

ISBN: 1546340602
ISBN 13: 978-1546340607

3

Contents

Chapter 1: Flight

"Siphero," the father shouted, but his voice was drowned out by loud grinding sounds, sparks flying from welding equipment, and a roaring engine. Siphero was finishing his own invention, the Wing Armor.

"Siphero! Turn that damn machine off!" Siphero turned off the welding torch and lifted his shield mask to reveal his brown-eyed, scarred, sweaty face.

"What do you want, Pops?" He rose from his workbench and turned off the generator.

"Will you stop messing with your stupid pipedreams and help me finish the prototype?" His father appeared before him, a potbellied man a foot shorter than his son, nearly bald and reeking of engine oil and alcohol. He wore similar attire to his son—an apron, a fireproof vest, slightly worn trousers, and leather gloves.

"All right, Pops, all right." Siphero rolled his eyes and put down his equipment. "But on the condition that I can finish this thing here. I'm almost done."

"Sure, whatever." His father exited the room and Siphero followed. Upon exiting his workshop, he filled his lungs with the fresh oxygen of the mountainous terrain in Jormundgard, the tallest mountains in all of the lower realm. Siphero's workshop sat on a ridge overlooking a waterfall where the water spray caught the light to produce a beautiful rainbow show. He followed his dad over to a platform with seats attached to whirling gears and heavy chains that spewed steam every now and then. They took their seats, bolted themselves down, and waited a couple seconds until Pops pulled a lever. Within ten seconds they raced up the side of the cliff on the steam lift's rail system. Siphero closed his eyes because this part always made him queasy.

They reached the top, where the lift locked in place, and they disembarked the lift. They walked along the long outcropping ledge, which resembled a massive runway. There were piles of old and discarded machine parts from decommissioned airblades routinely delivered to this airfield.

"Check the mana catchers while I go on ahead, OK?" His father turned without a reply, leaving his son to the job.

Siphero huffed away, gritting his teeth while he mumbled curses to himself about all of the work he did while his father drank booze and farted around.

He hadn't gone far when he came across a few devices in the shape of drums, silver wisps flew straight into the open hatches of the massive batteries, and silver energy pulsated inside the cylinders.

He checked a few of them and saw they were filled to the brim. He walked over to a shack filled with similar batteries. He swapped them out and carried three of the mana-filled batteries over to his father's workshop.

Right before he entered the workshop, a massive gust of wind nearly knocked him off his feet.

"Dammit," he said, "the wind is never this strong at this point in the day." He looked at the clouds above his head and saw a break in the cloud cover. He caught a glimpse of sunlight and saw two large birds fly through the white blanket. He didn't give it another thought as he collected the batteries and entered the workshop.

"What kept you?" Pops said as he did final checks on his prototype.

The inside of the workshop was filled with these "prototypes" Siphero and his father had been working on for years with funding from the inventors' guild of Salvagon. The main prototype had a pointed nose, two long wings sticking out at the sides, and a dorsal fin. It was fifteen feet long, with brown and black paint slapped across it, the driver's seat placed in the middle. Its cockpit required pilots to lie on their bellies as they worked the controls with their arms and legs. To Pops, this was his pride and joy, a breakthrough in Terran technology that would become the greatest of game changers. His father loved it more than him. Siphero knew why Pops brought him along: because he was a daredevil pilot with mad skills.

"So, ya old grease monkey, what do I have to do to get back to my own project?" He set the mana batteries down, picked up a toolbox, and walked over to the airblade's engine.

"Nothing," Pops said, "it's done."

Siphero dropped his toolbox, and a small pop sounded. A mana battery started leaking. "You brought me all the way up to tell me it was done? I just wasted thirty minutes for you to tell me it's done! That's it, I'm out of here!" He shouted so loudly his lungs nearly gave out. He walked a few feet toward the hanger doors when Pops stopped him.

"Wait, Son." Pops cut him off with three powerful strides. "I brought you up here 'cause I want you to fly it."

Siphero stopped, meeting the gaze of his desperate father. A wide and mischievous smile spread across his face as Pops regrettably said, "Oh Winged, no."

The next moment, Siphero rushed off to a closet, where he donned a full aviator suit equipped with a breathing mask, ballast tank, helmet, and visor.

"OK, I'm ready, Pops," he said cockily. "Let's see how fast I can break her." He jumped into the cockpit and lay down in the piloting position while Pops shut it over him like the lid of a coffin.

"Before you go breaking my baby," Pops said, stroking the wings tenderly, "I want to do a system check."

"Why wait, Pops? I'm sure you've done it a thousand times." Siphero hit a few switches and fired up the engine. The mana batteries thrummed with energy.

"OK, OK, you can go already." Pops laughed. "Now just remember, those mana batteries will give you a few hours if you push the engine, but casual flight will yield more time. I'll check in every now and then, so she's yours for the time you have. Take care of the airblade, my Paragon."

"Great." Siphero shut his visor. He looked out the screen of the canopy and began the engine start-up sequence. The airblade slowly wheeled out to the flat mountaintop as blazing torches of mana served as guiding posts for him to take off. "Time to soar in the big wild blue."

He revved the motor, increasing the mana feed into the engine and producing thrust, propelling the airblade forward. Siphero manned the controls and soared into that amazing sky.

"It's flying; it's actually flying!" he shouted into his shortwave radio, with a very eager and excited Pops answering him back.

"Well what did you expect, fly guy? I didn't put my heart and soul into it for nothing, now did I?"

"No, you did not, Pops," Siphero returned while he leaned left and right, did a few barrel rolls, and various other aerial maneuvers. "It handles like a dream."

"Good, 'cause, boy, that there airblade is going to be yours from now on."

Siphero stalled the engine and went into a nose dive while he whooped with excitement at getting his very own airblade.

"Shut up before you damage the radio with your ecstatics. Now go and enjoy it. I'll have dinner ready when you get back. Just remember not to take it past the cloud cover. You don't want to fall out of the world, do you?"

"Yeah, yeah, no Winged, no worries." Siphero went silent, leaving Pops to laugh heartily into the receiver. He flew off into the cloudscape of the Edge Mountains.

After an hour of just goofing off in the air, Siphero decided to cut the clouds with the wings of his airblade. His boredom vanished when he saw a bright light in the shape of bird heading in his direction. A few seconds later, it was flying next to him, wing to wing.

"Huh," Siphero huffed, "where did you come from, fella? Are you the answer to my boredom?"

He watched the bird do a barrel roll when he did one, and an idea popped into his head.

"Try to keep up," he said, putting the airblade into a swift dive. He pulled out of it in a split second, dodging a mountain in the process. He looked around for his follower and watched as it slowly caught up to him, riding his wake.

"A little slow, but you're OK. Now let's see how advanced your skills are." He poured more juice into the engine and accelerated forward into a dense valley with tight turns and even closer calls. He pulled a lever that retracted the wings of the airblade, ducking and weaving through the narrow valley, scratching the airblade's shell only slightly. As he exited, he put the wings into their original position and circled the valley to see if his buddy made it out. Sure enough, he saw the light trail of the white bird as it bobbed and weaved through the canyon, joining him above it.

"Ha-ha, you are a natural," he said curiously. He pulled up, gaining altitude until he came aloft and allowed his friend to catch up.

"Well, you've proven you're quite stubborn, so how about we slow it down a bit?" He checked the fuel gauge and saw he still had over two hours of flight time left.

He slowed the mana feed to the engines until he reached a comfortable cruising speed. Casually flicking the controls, he banked back and forth repeatedly but slowly as his friend mimicked his every move. He climbed and rolled into a falling turn and repeated this at least three more times. He ducked and swerved leisurely, then flew into a barrel roll as his friend mirrored him. They parted midflight, rolled again, and flew back to a stable altitude. Again he climbed into the sky, doing a continual barrel roll, while he saw the white bird fly past him and then return to a cruising speed. Then he joined his companion at the pinnacle of the Edge Mountains, where he was treated to an amazing sunset, a rare occurrence in Jormundgard, which was usually shrouded in clouds.

The sun touched the tall peaks of the Edge, and its rays shone right at the pair as they flew toward it, nearly blinding them both. When he regained his eyesight, Siphero saw what he thought was a hand touching the wing of his airblade, and in place of the white bird, he saw his childhood stories materialize before him. He was flying with a Winged, one with pearly wings.

Chapter 2: Dance

The sun rose beautifully as it shone through a stained-glass window in the late afternoon of another day. The room was painted snow white, with dignitaries and nobleman hanging in portraits. A bed with elegantly woven quilts stretched across the mattress onto the floor where two massive white wings protruded from beneath the covers. The being under the sheets awoke, and two feet planted themselves on the soft wooden floor. The wings flapped a few times to gain some lift and raised the person into the air as she hovered over to a mirror. The reflection in the mirror was a woman with silver-brown hair flowing over her shoulders and down past her waist until it rested an inch above the floor. Her face was tanned with a few cuts and bruises. Green colored irises and indigo colored retinas stared back at her. She wore a full-length pale gown, and she grabbed the hem and swished it around in the mirror.

Suddenly one of the portraits on the wall came off of its mooring and slowly floated over to her. The picture was of a woman with gray-colored wings, gray hair, and a white-and-black gown with a white apron stretching over the top half. The image shifted as the figure began to move and itch its face, blinking and adjusting its hair until it spoke.

"Great suns do favor you, Lady Awesha," the picture said. "Your father has summoned you; he is waiting in the Vapor Halls."

"Of course, Yern," Awesha said, stretching her arms, legs, and wings in all directions. "I will be there in ten glimpses of the sun. Tell him I am coming."

The picture bowed with respect as its wings folded around her. "As you wish, my lady." The portrait stopped moving as it flew back to the wall and came to a rest on its mooring.

Silence filled the room. Awesha then snapped her fingers, causing ten baby-like creatures with wings called Cherubim wearing butler's clothing to materialize from thin air. They surrounded her and waited patiently for their orders. One of them came forward and bowed to Awesha, wearing the same attire of the other butler except he had a black top hat with a feather in the side.

"How do you wish to dress today, Lady Awesha?" asked the lead Cherubim. "Elegant, martial, or flight?"

"I'm not sure, Nerv. How about you surprise me?" she said, stretching her wings, arms, and legs in front of her attendants.

"Excellent choice, my lady," Nerv said as he directed the other attendants, who began swirling around her in a blinding light. A few seconds later, they dispersed, and Awesha's attire had changed. Awesha was wearing thick black boots with heels, a green, red, and purple dress, cut down the front, exposing her legs, where she wore long, polished pants, and a scabbarded sword rested on her belt. Her upper body showed a full bodice, while her shoulders and arms were covered in long sleeves of chainmail and pauldrons. Her hair was braided into a ponytail of long curls, an assortment of flowers holding it all together. Her wings were coated in a protective cloth of silver colors, which made them sparkle beautifully.

She turned a few times in the mirror, drew her sword, inspected it, and sheathed it again. She posed a few times to inspect her figure; otherwise, she thought it was a wonderful selection.

"Marvelous, Nerv, simply marvelous."

The butler blushed, as did all of his subordinates. "You are too kind, my lady, as always. Will there be anything else, Lady Awesha?"

"No Nerv, that is all. Please tell the rest of the Cherubim in the house I wish for them to have a welcomed day." She came to rest on the ground and walked to the doors, which opened as she stepped toward them.

"Thank you ever so much, my lady." Nerv disappeared into thin air with a respective bow, followed by his associates.

As Awesha exited her room, she entered a pearl-white hallway with massive chandeliers hanging from the ceiling and several blue-flamed candles. She took a left, strolling through the lonely hallways, past the rooms of her mother and then her father. Birds of different colors flew above her while Cherubim flew past carrying towels, food, and even special oil canisters in different directions. Nerv flew by and offered Awesha a bottle of sky water and a freshly baked pastry filled with fruit and cream. She graciously thanked Nerv, which filled him with adoring pleasure.

She finished her pastry and bottle of sky water and another Cherubim came to retrieve her dishes. Then Awesha approached a set of fifty-foot doors leading to the Vapor Halls, which opened in response to her presence.

The inside of the Halls was a massive ballroom with dark clouds drizzling a light rain. The water felt great on her skin. Then she saw her father and mother talking with several other Winged and their guards at a table. Her father and mother both wore clothing suited to their position. He wore long robes and polished armor with a long staff, and she wore a full ball gown and carried a scepter in her left hand.

"Dreadful news, simply dreadful," her father said as he looked at a map and crossed out a section with a black-inked quill. "Are you certain? Have there been any changes in their activities?"

"No, Lord Recril," said one of the guards. "They remain as they are, only the disturbing sounds have somewhat ceased over the past arc of the sun. They are up to something."

"Damned Terrans," her father said, massaging the temples of his forehead, anxiety heavy upon his face. "You are all dismissed. Return to your posts and await further instructions."

"But, my lord," several of them said. Some guards flew toward the doors and saluted Awesha as they passed.

"You are dismissed," Recril repeated, shouting. They exited the halls in a huff of anger.

Her mother, Ulmafe, took out a fan made of ornate feathers and began fanning herself while her husband continued to inspect the map.

"Graceless savages," her mother said. "What have those Terrans been doing, other than violating our peaceful lives with their incessant and destructive sounds?"

Awesha coughed, which announced her presence to her father. He smiled and invited her in. When she was near the table, Awesha folded her wings and hands around herself in a respectful bow. "The clouds part ways to your brilliance, Father and Mother."

"May they part ways for you, my dear," her father responded. "Now, Awesha, we have important matters to discuss. We can't leave this any longer. You must pick a suitor for your bonding ceremony."

Awesha's expression soured, and she turned away, her wings obstructing her face from her father's view. "We've been over this already, Father. I do not wish to give myself to any of your chosen suitors. They do not see me as an equal!"

"You have no choice in this matter," her mother said, hovering near her. "You are past the age where you must initiate the bond. If you don't do it in the next few weeks, your magic will betray your body and you will die. I was hoping for the Bond Scrivener Weeslon to bond with you. He has such beautiful wings and comes from good breeding."

"I don't care, Mother. I don't care if I die, but I will not initiate the bond with a complete stranger, especially Weeslon! I will only do it for the one I have chosen."

"You will form the bond today," her father boomed. "If you do not, then I will confine you to your room. You will not leave until you agree to form the bond with Weeslon."

Shock pierced Awesha's heart. Her father and mother were quite serious. "No…no…if you do that, please, don't take my freedom from me." She stormed out in anger, busting the doors open into the main atrium as she flew toward the doors of her house, tears flowing from her eyes. Awesha's affinity manifested; her magical will slammed the doors open, and the village of Skyspire came into view.

Skyspire, a small Winged village well-known for its magical arts but distant enough from the rest of Winged civilization to be considered autonomous, spread before her. The village's superiors were charged by the ruling party of the Winged Empire with watching out for any Terrans that might enter their territory and with monitoring any changes in their behavior. This is what brought Awesha and her family to the edge of civilization in the village of Skyspire. The proximity to the unknown world of Jormundgard piqued Awesha's curiosity.

Awesha flew past many guards, Cherubim, and workers making improvements to her parents' house and on toward the entrance to the village, where she stopped at a sky fountain and wept quietly to herself. She stayed there for a little more than an hour until one of the guards returning from an expeditionary flight joined her.

"Lady Awesha," the guard said, "is everything all right?" This guard was elderly with wings of white, gray, and black, a long gray beard, and wrinkled fingers.

"Greven, sir," Awesha wiped away her tears and stood upright in a more graceful position as she faced him. "I'm sorry for bringing you from your post. I will return to my home."

Before she could go, Greven gently held her shoulder, stopping her from going on. "Let me guess," he said. "Your father and mother brought up the issue of the bond again?"

Awesha nodded sadly as she covered herself with her wings. "Yes, Greven, but they said they would confine me to my room indefinitely if I don't agree to bond with Weeslon today."

Greven grew angry and slammed his foot on the ground, a small tremor rumbling beneath his feet. "Forgive me for saying this, but your father's crossing lines in forcing his own daughter to bond with a complete stranger. I'd tell him as much if it wouldn't cost me my post."

This made Awesha giggle a bit, and she picked herself up and walked with Greven. There were guards dozing at their posts and others playing a game of flying bones. They welcomed them both as Greven shared the news with the men and women under his command who displayed equal amounts of anger and disrespect for Awesha's father. Awesha reassured herself of her anger for her father and smiled in gratitude for their sympathy.

"Before you go and live a miserable life, do you want to go on a Terran patrol with me?" Greven offered to Awesha.

She brightened up at the mention of an inspection. "You mean it, sir? May I join you?"

Every now and then the guards of Skyspire would perform a routine patrol of the world below them, of Jormundgard. They would observe a couple of Terrans who had taken up residence below their mountain village, no more than a thousand feet below them.

"Certainly, Lady Awesha." Greven clapped her on the back. "My men promise to stay quiet about this."

They passed by the guards holding vigil at the gate, where Greven nodded to them and they whistled nonchalantly as they passed by. As soon as they had left the gate entrance, they reached a massive cliff where Greven fell, letting his wings catch the wind. Awesha followed his lead.

"Just make sure once we get down there," he said in the roaring wind, "to keep out of sight. Remember to hide yourself."

"Yes, sir," Awesha's affinity surrounded her body in an aura of light that changed her outward appearance into that of a large white bird.

During their dive, the clouds parted beneath them and a friendly air current caught them and brought them to a small overhang, giving them an impressive view of the Terran camp. They spotted the two Terrans below, and Greven removed his satchel and unfurled a scroll for taking notes. Awesha caught a glimpse of one of the Terrans carrying some strange objects into a building. Greven began jotting down a description of his appearance: brown hair, scars, brown eyes, broad shoulders, girth, and burned hands.

Then Awesha froze; she saw the Terran looking right at her. For some reason she couldn't move. Her heart was racing in her chest.

"Is something the matter, my lady?" Greven looked to see Awesha breathing heavily, her cheeks glowing a rosy red and her wings fluttering.

"That Terran…he saw me," she said after a moment.

"Not likely, Awesha. To them we're just of couple of birds."

They remained on the ledge for a few more minutes, taking note of loud grinding sounds, lots of yelling, and then a loud roar. After the noises had subsided, Awesha saw a large object roll out of the structure to the long stretch of lighted land.

"What in the endless sky is that thing?" Greven asked in a hushed tone.

"I do not know, but it appears this bird…thing is meant to fly," Awesha said, with curiosity.

"Fly, that thing? That's ridiculous. It couldn't possibly…fly—" Greven stopped short when he saw the metal bird roar into the sky without flapping its wings once. They watched it do a few loops and spins while rushing past their ledge, its speed breathtaking.

"This, this is important news!" Greven exclaimed. "The Terrans have never been capable of this. The village elder must be informed immediately."

He spread his wings to fly, but stopped short when he saw Awesha remain still where she was. "Lady Awesha, we must go or risk exposing ourselves."

Awesha did not move from her spot. She was mesmerized by the clunky metal bird that flew with such grace and speed. Then she said, "I'm going to follow it. We need more information. We don't know what else it is capable of."

Greven pondered the idea and reluctantly agreed. "All right then, but I'm going to strengthen the distortion you created." Using his affinity, Awesha felt a surge of energy surround her. The white bird aura glowed stronger. She thanked him and took off from the ledge to follow the metal bird.

"Be safe, my lady, be safe," he said as he ascended to Skyspire with news of the Terran machinations, dreading what Recril or Skyspire's elder would do with the news.

Awesha flew for an hour looking for the bird, with only the faint smell of burning air to lead the way. Then suddenly, as she broke the cloud cover, she found the bird riding the updrafts. It was as if this loud, rude metal bird was inviting her to join it.

"Ah, there you are," she said as she flew close to the wings of the bird and held her place next to it. "You are an interesting specimen." While she inspected its length from head to tail, it shot forward with incredible speed. She saw it enter a dive, which she followed closely, mirroring its flight path. It dodged mountain cliffs and made last-second swerves to avoid crashing. She caught up to it, a little out of breath.

"So you're the daring type," she observed. "If you think you can outfly a Winged, show me your best." She watched as the bird tapered off into a narrow canyon, and mimicked the bird's actions of tucking in its wings and maneuvering through the tight crevices as she followed her crazy friend. She came close to scratching her wings a few times, but her affinity aura kept her safe.

After the chase ended, the bird slowed, allowing her to rest from the exhausting flight. Both of them rode the gentle air currents. "Your skill is equal to mine, my friend." She frowned as she looked down to the clouds, a tear rolling down her cheek. "I wish I could form my bond with you."

Awesha felt a strange pulsation ripple through her body and a stream of consciousness flood her mind. Images formed in her mind of what the bird was thinking about doing—graceful maneuvers and acrobatic feats. This invisible cord connected her to it, and a strange feeling of happiness overtook her.

"You wish to dance? I would love to."

She mimicked the actions of the bird as it performed several complex turns, parted from it, twirling with amazing grace she had honed over years of skydancing with her family—themselves a fleeting memory. As she twirled with the bird, she felt more thoughts flow into her, many of which were incoherent and hard to understand. But she felt the warmth of them too. The dance ended as she and the bird did a spinning twirl into the sky and drifted upon the winds.

The sun began to set as she moved closer to the bird and touched its wing with her hand and found it was cold to the touch. Oddly, tears flowed down her cheeks again. Feelings she had shut deep inside her came flowing to the surface. And then she thought back to her father's threat and his plans to perform a kind of business transaction with her as the bargaining chip. She cursed under her breath, damning her fate and wishing to change it forever.

Her thoughts began to thin out, the inside of the metal bird became transparent, and a set of eyes were staring back at her. The eyes belonged to a person she had been taught to fear from childhood in stories of demons. A Terran was watching her from inside the metal bird.

Chapter 3: Encounter

Siphero's shock at meeting a flesh and bone Winged hadn't worn off when he saw an equal amount of shock in her eyes. Then he saw her faint while flying. He dove underneath the canopy and aligned himself right beneath the Winged and caught her in his arms. While he did so, he looked around for a landing zone on one of the many mesas of the Edge Mountains.

"Hey, can you hear me? You're going to be OK, just hang in there," he said reassuringly.

He aimed the airblade for a suitable mesa with a long stretch, long enough for an airblade to land. With one hand, he deployed the landing gear and with the other, held the Winged close to him. The airblade crash landed and slid across the mesa until coming to a rest. When the dust settled, Siphero climbed out of the cockpit, carrying the Winged girl in his arms.

Siphero set her down and raided the Paragon's supply cabinet to find a few rations, some water packs, a flare gun, flint and tinder, and a sleeping roll. He made a small campfire and lay the Winged down on the mat as he checked her for injuries, finding a singed section on her right wing. He realized he'd accidently burned her with his heated engine exhaust. Despite the burn, the wings were warm to the touch, and he was surprised at how soft they were. His inspection of her wings came to an end as he felt the edge of cold steel against his throat. Siphero's eyes met the Winged's. There was a fierce glow in them; she was pissed. He backed away slowly as she rose to one knee and continued to glare at him, despite the pain in her wing.

Darkness covered the campsite as the sun set, and the lower stars began to shine in the night sky. For two hours, Awesha held Siphero at sword point, Awesha readying to strike if the Terran made even the slightest move. During those two hours, she looked him over to see he was a scruffy-looking Terran with glowing brown eyes that could have belonged to Winged. She also saw he had some girth, an unfit Terran riddled with the scars of manual labor. Siphero, on the other hand, stared at her beautiful indigo eyes and felt at peace.

"Excuse me," Siphero said, "can I put my arms down now? They're getting tired."Awesha felt a strange tether toward this Terran as he spoke those words, making her feel at peace around this total stranger. Satisfied with this she sheathed her sword and calmed herself.

"Greetings," she said in a clear voice. "I acknowledge your existence." She bowed before Siphero, who lowered his hands.

"Uh…hi…" He strode forward with his arm extended, to which Awesha instinctually knocked him to the ground with her affinity, prompting Siphero to curse angrily at her.

"Hey, that freakin' hurt," he shouted at Awesha. "I was just trying to introduce myself." In an instant he froze. A flash of information entered his mind, and he knew the Winged's name. A chill of joy came over him.

"Your name is Awesha." He paused. "Wait, how do I know that? I shouldn't; I just met you."

At the same time Siphero said her name, thoughts entered Awesha's mind—the same pulsation she felt earlier assaulted her again, and she knew his name too. "And you, Terran, are known as Siphero, correct?"

Siphero's surprise escalated as he sat on the Paragon's wing and puzzled over how they knew each other. "Can you read my mind?"

Awesha let out a small giggle at Siphero's statement. She had overreacted. "I am sorry, Terran, for the trouble I have caused you." She spread her wings for flight and jumped a good five feet into the air. She flapped her wings desperately to gain altitude, but stabs of pain shot through her wing with every flap, causing her to fall.

"Hey, are you OK?" Siphero asked, drawing closer.

"Stay away from me, damned Terran." She drew her sword and kept it pointed at Siphero.

"Don't move. Your wing is badly burned from my airblade's propulsion. If you try to fly, you'll only open up the wound more." Siphero moved closer despite Awesha's hostility.

She wasn't going to let a dirty Terran touch her again, especially this one. Then, another flash entered her mind, and she saw what his true intentions were. She fought for control of her sword arm as she saw it lower against her will. When Siphero was within breathing distance, she looked away while he inspected her wing.

Siphero's inspection yielded results. "Hm, the burn is large, but the rest of your wing will be fine. You just need bandaging and some rest." He went back to the Paragon and found a medical kit, hoping it had what he needed.

For some reason, Awesha understood what Siphero was doing as he took out a pot and poured water from the canteen into it. While he went to look for the flint and tinder to start the fire, she used her affinity to create a spark to ignite the gas fire beneath the pot, causing the water to boil. He returned to see the fire already burning, so he moved to boil a few bandages in the pot until they were nice and hot. He removed them and approached Awesha's wing.

"This is going to sting a bit. Do I have your permission to proceed?"

"You may assist me," she said, bracing herself to endure the pain.

"If it helps, hold my hand so that you can bear it." Siphero offered his hand to Awesha. Again she found her body acting of its own accord. "OK, here we go."

As Siphero pressed down with the hot rags, Awesha gripped his hand tightly. It was the most she had ever felt in her life. During the bandaging she felt more images flowing into her. She realized they were coming from Siphero, his memories and experiences were flowing into her. Several were warm, happy memories, and others were bitter experiences from the cities of the Terrans. But one memory made tears come to her eyes. An image of a young boy watching as a woman in front of him was vaporized into droplets of water and air. It made her want to scream. This memory was a tragedy to watch, but as it slipped away, she saw only auras of burning fire.

"Your life…is beautiful," Awesha whispered to herself as tears rolled down her cheeks and Siphero bandaged her wing.

"There we go. It should heal without getting infected, just so long as you don't go flying." He packed up the medical kit and went to let go of Awesha's hand, only to find her grasping his tightly.

Siphero turned to her. "Uh…are you OK?" He met her gaze as he tried to wrestle his hand free. "Can…I please have my hand back?"

"You are my other half," she began. "You and I have bonded."

"What are you talking about?"

"My people have a ceremony that children who have come of age must go through. It is how we determine our life partners."

"Life partners!" Siphero exclaimed. "We're engaged? I've only just met you. I don't think I'm ready for a long-term relationship!"

Awesha grew stern as she raised her hand, creating an invisible barrier over Siphero's mouth, silencing his rants.

"Now please," she said, "let me explain." She went into detail about the ritual, her father's forcing her to bond with someone against her will, her snap decision to join a patrol and fly with him through the mountain peaks of the Edge.

As Siphero heard this, he tried to comment, only to find his voice muted.

When Awesha explained that her people could use affinities to channel the mana in their bodies for any number of purposes, his eyebrows raised and narrowed as he pointed to his mouth. She undid her spell, and Siphero spoke his peace.

"I guess I understand now," he said, "but what happens if a Winged doesn't initiate this 'bond' thing?"

Awesha grew silent as a tear rolled down her cheek. "If we don't initiate the bond, then the mana in our bodies will suffocate us from the overflow."

"So what you're saying is, when a bond is forged, the mana in both of their bodies stabilizes and saves them?" He paused, feeling a strange tingling sensation run down his spine. "What happens when a bond is initiated with a Terran?"

"Who knows?" Awesha said. "A bond between a Terran and a Winged shouldn't even be possible."

"Well, we know now." He checked his wrist and saw it was already the middle of the night on his timekeeper. "It's pretty late; we should get some sleep."

While he put out the fire, his arms began to itch. Siphero scratched them, but the itch became painful, and the pain only got worse the more he scratched. He fell to the ground, gripping his arms, as Awesha knelt next to him.

"Why, why is there so much pain?" he said between strangled breaths.

"Siphero," she gasped, "can you hear me?…Siphero…"

Siphero continued to wrestle with his arm until the pain wore him out, and Awesha's image flickered as his vision went dark.

Chapter 4: Anew

As dawn stretched across the mesa, Siphero awoke to find Awesha sleeping soundly next to him, one of her wings wrapped snugly around him. He tried to get up, but the pain in his body had not fully subsided. Her feathers were so soft and warm that he could feel himself dozing off again.

Feeling his movements, Awesha's eyes shot open. In one swift motion, she unfurled her wing from around Siphero, jumped to her feet, and brushed the dirt from her clothes.

"May the suns favor you, Siphero," Awesha said, with a bow. "I hope you are healing well." She brushed her hair back and smoothed out the wrinkles in her clothes.

"Uh, yeah, I guess," Siphero said. "The pain is gone at least." He rolled up his sleeves to check his arm, only to see a horrifying sight: his veins were no longer blue but cycled between every color of the rainbow.

"Deep drake shit! What happened to me?" He showed his arms to Awesha. Her curiosity peaked as she stroked Siphero's wrists. She felt the same thrum of power she felt in her wings, and her exhilaration increased.

"You have mana in you." She placed the palm of her hand against his cheek to confirm her theory. "You…a Terran…have an affinity."

"Really?" Siphero scratched his arms. "I wonder what exactly that means." He strode over to the Paragon's toolbox to grab a blowtorch. He wanted to make sure his airblade could fly. Suddenly, the toolbox opened up and a blowtorch flew into his hand. "Whoa, how did I do that?"

"You really do have an affinity," Awesha said, smirking.

"Huh, no kidding." He then thought about checking the wings of the Paragon for damage, only to find them open instantaneously. "I wonder what else I can do!"

"Siphero, wait." Awesha grabbed Siphero's arm to stop him. "If you really have an affinity, I need to confirm with a test." She held out her hand and whispered a few words. As she finished, a ball of energy materialized in her hand.

"That's neat."

Awesha whispered the words again, and the energy dissipated. "It is a test all Winged use to determine their elemental affinity. My affinity is to mana, which is connected to all affinities."

"So what do I have to do?" Siphero held out his hand like an eager student.

"Simply repeat these words: 'Show me myself.'"

"Show me myself," Siphero repeated after her. He waited for a few seconds, and nothing happened, so he repeated them again with more force. He then felt a painful thud as something hard smacked him upside the head.

"What the heck was that?" He and Awesha found that one of Siphero's tools had hit him.

"You have an earth affinity," Awesha said, intrigued.

"Really?" Siphero looked at the ground and repeated "Show me myself," but none of the rocks budged. Another of his tools collided with his back moments later. "I think I'm going to have to reevaluate your guess. I think what you mean is I have an affinity to metal."

"Metal? There has never been a metal affinity," Awesha pondered. "The only affinities that come close are earth or fire." She then drew her sword and held it perpendicular to Siphero. "Attempt to take my blade from me with your affinity."

Siphero did as he was told. He stuck out his hand and focused all his will into pulling the sword from her grasp. Awesha felt a small tug on her sword and felt it struggling to get free of her grasp, but she resisted his pull. This continued for one minute until Siphero collapsed to the ground, exhausted from using his new ability.

Awesha knelt next to Siphero and gave him a warm smile. "You did well for the first Terran to use magic, but if you wish to become a master, you must train for several years." She offered a hand up, and Siphero took it.

Exhausted, he walked over to the Paragon, wolfed down a couple military rations, and then drank a whole canteen in just a few seconds.

"So what now?" Siphero said, offering Awesha a ration. "Are we stuck with each other now that we've bonded?"

"Possibly, but am I truly a burden to you?" Awesha sat a couple feet away from Siphero on the Paragon and looked up at the thick layer of clouds that lead to her world, to her home.

"A burden? Maybe, but from what you told me about your parents…you could stay with me," Siphero offered, blushing a little bit at the suggestion.

The thought of staying with a Terran made her laugh with excitement. "I thank you, Siphero, but are you sure I wouldn't be an inconvenience?"

"You are the first person I've met who didn't think I was pathetic or useless, so in that sense…I like you. You also said it yourself; you don't want to go back to your parents."

She thought about the offer for a few minutes while Siphero prepped the Paragon for flight. "I agree to your proposal, Siphero."

"Then we have a deal." They met each other's gaze for a moment before breaking off.

"Well, that's taken care of. Do you want to meet Pops?"

Awesha looked confused. "Who is this Pops?"

Siphero laughed heartily as he put his breathing mask back on. "He's my dad. He's a little too obsessed with his inventions to care about me, but he has his moments."

"Very well, Siphero, I will trust you, but be wary. My own father will be watching your camp, and he is someone you do not want to cross."

"Then let's stop horsing around," Siphero said, before closing the hatch to his airblade. He tossed a small device to Awesha.

"What is this?"

"It's a communication piece," he returned. "Stick it in your ear, and you can speak to me even when I'm flying. Just push the button on the side, and you can speak to me whenever."

He fired up the engines and checked the fuel gauge to see that his mana batteries had refueled themselves overnight. He strapped himself in, fired up the engines, and took off from the top of the mesa. When he came to a comfortable cruising altitude, Awesha joined him. He saw that the bandages on her wing had fallen off. She had made a full recovery.

"How's the wing?" Siphero said into his earpiece.

Awesha brought her hand to the piece and said, "It's never felt so good before. I believe our bond is to thank for this."

"That's good. Let's get going to the Air Wastes."

"The Air Wastes?"

"That's what Pops calls the upper reaches of the Edge Mountain Range. It's where we scavenge for parts from old, derelict airfortresses that crashed into the mountains."

He led the way to his father's workshop while Awesha rode his air wake. The airblade felt to Siphero like an extension of himself because whenever he thought about maneuvering the Paragon, it would maneuver without his interaction. It felt like his piloting ability had doubled. They flew in silence for nearly an hour until Siphero started asking questions about the Winged lifestyle, their culture, and even the advances of their civilization, which she answered to the best of her knowledge. She told him of a life in the clouds, of magnificent palaces glittering in the sunlight, flying continents, skywhales, leviathans, and skimmer drakes. She even mentioned the Winged Empire power structure, of how the king and queen were chosen. In return for her part, she asked Siphero many questions about Terran lifestyles and about some of the myths Winged had heard of Terran societies. To her surprise, Siphero debunked each and every one of the myths she asked him about.

Over their long conversation, Siphero finally saw the airfield. The landing lights were still on.

"Awesha," he said, "I'm going to land first. Make sure you stay low. Pops has a habit of being in the wrong place at the right time."

"Of course," she answered back.

Siphero triggered his landing gear, retracted the wings, and slowed the engines for descent as he activated the airbrake, and the airblade came to a stop. As he got out of the cockpit, Awesha gracefully touched down next to him. She had a pompous smile on her lips.

"Oh, don't let it go to your head," Siphero said. "Sure, you have wings, but that doesn't mean you're better at flying."

"I have no idea what you are referring to." She laughed softly to herself and waited for Siphero to get out of the airblade. "Where is your father?"

Siphero did a quick scan of the field and hangars for the potbellied troublemaker he called Pops. "I'm guessing he's...wait, here he comes now."

Sure enough Pops appeared near the communications tower as he ran up to them as fast as his stubby legs would take him. Awesha hid herself behind the airblade, tucking her wings out of sight.

Pops surprised Siphero by giving him a big, greasy, nonalcoholic hug and smacking him on the back. "Siphero, I was worried sick about you. Where the hell have you been, Son? And how was the Paragon? Did it perform better than you expected, or did it have some hiccups in the design?

"Easy, Pops, easy. It performed great, but there's someone I think you should meet." He turned to Awesha, who was concealing herself behind one of the Paragon's stabilizers, but her wings refused to stay hidden. She came out of hiding and floated the short distance over to Pops. Bowing to him, she gave Pops the traditional Winged greeting.

"Greetings, Siphero's father," Awesha said respectfully. "It is a pleasure to meet you."

Pops's eyes focused on Awesha; his gaze contained no surprise. Then Pops said in a calm but stern tone, "You're a Winged, aren't you?"

"Yes, I am."

"What the hell are you doing here, and with my son!" He pulled out a revolver from a holster and pointed it at her. Awesha sensed the hostility and drew her sword but stopped midway when the weapon flew out of his hands and floated right above Siphero's right palm.

"Son, how did you do that?" Pops was amazed at Siphero's little intervention and was even more amazed when Siphero disassembled the weapon without even touching it. The gun's pieces fell to the ground as Siphero punched Pops in the gut.

"That was unwarranted, Pops. Why did you threaten Awesha?" He stood over his father as Pops recovered.

"Son...you have to...understand," Pops said, slowly raising himself. "She's a Winged; they're dangerous aliens who have never seen a Terran before. Do you know what would happen if all Terrans knew they existed?

"I don't care," he returned. "You just tried to hurt my friend, so I don't give a damn what could happen." He stormed off toward the steam lift down to his workshop while Awesha lingered a moment.

"I…have to report this," Pops said, getting up. "The Envisioner will be told."

"I'm leaving, Pops. It's clear I'm no longer welcome here!" Siphero called back.

Awesha caught up to him and matched his stride with the gliding skips she took. "Are you all right, Siphero?" she asked, putting her hand on his shoulder. "Your father is…protective. He reminds me of mine."

Siphero took a deep breath and exhaled before speaking. "It looks like I'm in the same boat. You ran away from your father, and I'm leaving mine. We're kindred spirits, eh?"

Awesha smiled at the comment and then asked where they were going.

"We're going to my workshop. I'm packing up some of my stuff and finishing a project of mine…from the day before we met."

Her curiosity piqued as she followed him over to the steam lift, only for Siphero to realize it was at the bottom.

"Ah, great," he said in frustration. "It's going to take forever to get the lift back up here." He looked to Awesha and got a crazy idea.

"Awesha?"

"Yes, Siphero?"

"Do you think you could give me a lift to the bottom?"

She looked offended. "You expect me to carry you down…there?

"Please?"

Between his sincere plea and their bond ringing in her ears, Awesha gave in. "Fine, I'll do it, but if you fidget, I will drop you. Understood?"

"Crystal clear," Siphero said in a rushed and scared tone.

Awesha gained a foot of altitude before grasping Siphero tightly. When she lifted off with him in her embrace, she couldn't help feeling warm inside, like the bond made this moment enjoyable to her. As they descended, Siphero stayed as still as he could, but being this close to her made him uncomfortable. It took them five whole minutes to reach the bottom, but they made it safe and sound.

"You know, you're a little heavy." Awesha elbowed him.

"Ha-ha. Come on; my workshop's this way." Siphero motioned for her to follow him as they walked down a few creaking steps to Siphero's workshop.

Chapter 5: Confrontation

Siphero lifted the flap so Awesha could slip through the narrow door
with her wings. She couldn't describe what she saw inside his
workshop. There were pictures of star constellations hanging on the
ceiling and model airblades from industrial cities like Salvagon.
Piles of spare parts, oil canisters, and mana batteries were stacked
neatly in a corner, and a hammock hung from two rafters as it swung
gently in the wind. But what caught her attention were the blueprints
of inventions strewn all across one of the two workbenches in the
shop. She took one of the blueprints and unfurled it to find a design
for a bird-shaped contraption with two red eyes and a wingspan of
four feet.

"What is this?" She showed the scroll to Siphero.

"Oh, that's a drird," he said, "a metal bird that the invention
academy back in Salvagon sent to us to test and build when we got
the chance. It's supposed to behave exactly like a living bird except
this one is inanimate. Its purpose is reconnaissance or message
delivery, a slow but tireless messenger."

"Interesting, but where is the device you mentioned?"

He pointed over to a workbench. "Right over there."

She followed him over to the bench, where she saw what
looked to be a portable engine like the one she had seen on the
Paragon. This one, however, was larger and had wings almost as
large as her own attached to its back.

"You're building your own set of wings, Siphero?" Awesha
was truly awestruck to see this device.

"More or less. It's a next-generation Skelton capable of
flight, like Winged can, but it needs fuel and can't stay in the air for
long." He paused, picked up a welding torch, and continued the work
where he left off.

"How long will it take you to finish?" Awesha said, with the
time in mind.

"Don't worry; it should take me just a few minutes to do a
safety check, but afterward it needs a test flight. Also, I think I can
use my new affinity thingy to finish it the way I want."

"How will you manage this?"

"I don't know exactly," Siphero said, after welding together some of the joints, "but I think I can build things and deconstruct them if I know how the pieces fit together, like when I took Pops's gun." He resumed work while Awesha watched patiently.

After a few more minutes of making sure everything was working properly, he announced, "OK, all finished."

He took the Skelton flight pack and mounted it on his armored back while the wings retracted into a more compact form. As soon as he put on the flight pack, he flipped a few switches on the side as he and Awesha exited the workshop. The flight pack connected with his back and fully assimilated with his arm, flapping a few times while the thrusters on the pack did a routine heat up. When it was finished, Siphero flipped a second switch, and the wings opened to their full sixteen-foot wingspan.

Awesha approached them and stroked the metal wings. They were cold, flexible, and incredibly durable. She was a little jealous of them. "They're magnificent," she said, stroking the wings with her fingers, "but how do you expect to fly?"

She was cut off when Siphero keeled over in pain. She saw strange knifelike instruments from the pack pierce his skin and stab into his muscles.

She used her affinity to relieve him of his pain, but then she felt the same pain in her own body. It took a minute for the pain to subside.

"What was all of that pain?"

"That was the implanters section of the armor. It pierced my back muscles so I could deploy the wings simply by contracting my muscles." Siphero huffed the pain away as he stood upright. "It's just a little addition I made at the last minute; your wings inspired me. Winged must have incredibly strong muscles in their backs if they can stay aloft for long periods of time."

"Well you were correct, Siphero." Awesha flicked him on the forehead. "Our wings behave like a second muscle. We can remain in the sky for quite a while, but even we get tired."

"Good, because I have a favor to ask," Siphero said. "Can you teach me to fly like a Winged?"

Awesha laughed while Siphero rolled his eyes.

"Yeah, yeah, laugh it up, bird lady."

Her laughter died, and she regained her composure. "Of all the strange happenings of these two days, that is the strangest thing I have ever heard."

Siphero's gaze changed, almost pleading in his voice. "Could you please?"

"I would be honored to teach you," she said, placing her hand on Siphero's shoulder, "but I have an easier way."

Before Siphero could inquire, Awesha placed one of her fingers on his forehead and a flash of images and experiences raced through his mind, flooding it with information that made Siphero's eyes roll into his head.

"What…was that?" He got to his feet, but his wings flapped and retracted on their own. "Did you do this?"

His gaze met Awesha's. She was floating a few feet off the ground. "I merely showed you how to use your wings as if they were your own. A Winged bond can be used to transfer memories and experiences between partners."

She landed in front of him, and they stared at each other for a brief moment. Then Awesha reentered Siphero's workshop and exited with his supply pack.

"Are you prepared to leave, my bonded?" She handed him the pack, and he secured it to his armor as his wings redeployed to their full length.

"Your bonded? Why did you call me that?" Siphero did one last safety check before getting ready to take off.

"Winged refer to their bonded partners this way…whom they like." Awesha said the last part under her breath. She turned away, slightly embarrassed.

This was when Siphero put his hand on her shoulder, one of his metal wings touching hers. "For the time being, just call me Siphero, OK?"

Awesha didn't turn to meet his gaze because she was hiding her blushing face. She had never met someone who was so informal to her. "What are we waiting for then? Let us go!"

"Yes, ma'am." Siphero did a mock salute and followed Awesha to the ledge near the workshop. She flapped her wings as she flew into the air first and waited for Siphero to join her. Siphero took one long last look over his shoulder at the workshop and then back at Awesha, her brilliant smile, brownish-silver hair waving in the wind, and then he realized his time with her was going to be a new chapter in his life. So he stretched his wings and used the experiences of flying she had given him. He took a running start as his wings began flapping and the thruster pack kicked in, providing him with additional thrust.

One of two things happened as Siphero lifted off. First he flew higher than he expected and second—he screamed like a little girl as he flew through the sky. He flew past Awesha several times while he tried to remember what it was like to fly outside of an airblade. Eventually, he stopped flying like a madman and hovered in place to catch his breath. Awesha caught up, laughing uncontrollably at him. He was annoyed.

"OK, I guess I just made myself look really, really stupid, didn't I?" He scratched the back of his helmet and looked around to see what it was like flying in the wind. He took a deep breath, felt the wind blowing in his face, and exhaled. "So this is what it's like to fly like a Winged."

"You weren't doing that the day before?"

"You have to understand, all Terrans who fly do so inside of a protective shell to shield us from wind, rain, or natural conditions in the skies. This is the first time I've flown in the actual 'sky.'" He pointed to his Skelton armor as he said this, and Awesha understood.

"Why don't you follow my lead, if you are willing?" She winked at him and gained altitude. "It will be like our sky dance yesterday."

"OK, but just to warn you, I'm a terrible dancer."

"You can fly, can't you, Siphero?"

Siphero said with pride, "Of course I can. I gave you a run for your money, didn't I?"

"Then for a Winged's standards, you can dance. Just pretend it was the day before." She climbed into the air, and Siphero followed her. His thrusters left an exhaust trail behind him.

Awesha then flew in a straight line. Siphero stayed on her tail, but then she picked up more speed and left Siphero riding her wind draft, knocking him off course. It didn't take him long to catch up to her, thanks to his newfound knowledge of Winged flight. He was keeping pace for a good deal until she pulled another crazy stunt: she decelerated and picked up speed in the opposite direction. This time, however, he anticipated that move because he had used it on her the day before. She then started a corkscrew twist into the air, which he mimicked in a parallel direction until they looped back down into a sloping dive.

Awesha then spoke through her earpiece. "Why don't we head back to your father's airfield before we leave?"

"Are you sure that's a good idea?" he answered. "My dad tried to kill you."

"Don't worry about me, Siphero. I am more than capable of defending us both from your father."

"If you say so, Awesha. I trust you." At that moment images flooded both their minds as they felt the phantasmal link once again. They recovered quickly from this new flash and came to rest on a rocky ledge.

"Did you feel that?" Siphero waited for his head to clear.

"I've heard about this." Awesha caught her breath. "When a bonded pair trust one another, their senses are enhanced."

"So, what does that mean?"

"It means our senses are sharper than before. For instance, I can hear your heartbeat." Awesha put her hand on his chest plate.

"And I can smell you." He inhaled deeply. "You smell of fresh grass and pure water."

"As a Terran, you say the strangest things." She turned her attention back to the direction of the airfield and took off.

"Back at you, bird lady." He flew after her and kept pace with her flight path.

When they approached the airfield, the sky was marking the start of the early afternoon, but it was quiet; none of Pops's equipment was running. On top of it, there was a low-hanging mist on the strip as they landed on the edge of the airfield. Siphero looked around the field as he and Awesha checked the communication tower, Pops's workshop, and even the scrapyard, but he was nowhere to be found.

"That's strange," Siphero said. "It's never this quiet."

Suddenly, a loud clap of thunder shook the airfield as Siphero and Awesha made ready to combat the threat. She drew her sword and willed her affinity to create a barrier around them as they stood back to back and watched for an imminent threat. What they saw surprised Siphero but scared Awesha. It was a squad of twenty Winged descending from Skyspire. They were all well armed with swords and shields, and some carried spears while at least six wore heavier armor and carried long staffs with strange jewels on their tips. The Winged touched the ground and surrounded Awesha and Siphero, their weapons pointed at them. Then two more Winged descended from above, and Awesha saw her father and Greven slow their descent until they touched down a few steps outside of the perimeter. She sheathed her sword and got Siphero to turn and stand beside her.

The Winged with the funny-looking hammer seemed familiar to him. "Is that your father?" he whispered to her.

"Yes," she whispered to him. "If he is here then I am afraid to know what he has planned."

They watched as the guards parted for her father while Greven stayed on the periphery and ordered his guards to remain vigilant. Awesha's father drew closer until he was five feet from her. His eyes were piercing her like massive daggers reaching into her heart. She did not avert his gaze but stared back with the same intensity.

"Awesha," her father said, "where in the name of Archons have you been?" He sheathed his weapon and held out his arms to her, but she stayed right where she was, next to Siphero.

"My dear, why won't you come home? I have been looking everywhere for—"

"No, you haven't," she interrupted. "You don't care about me! All you care for is your dynasty."

"Awesha, you have a responsibility to the family to keep our heritage strong. You do not have the right to choose, just like your mother and I."

"That's because you care not for one another, but when my sister and I came into your lives, you believed your fortune had changed!"

Her father lowered his arms and scrutinized Siphero's appearance, his armor, and then his wings. He saw nothing but ugliness.

"Who is this," he asked Awesha directly, "some secret lover of yours? I will not forgive any who have ruined our family's future." Recril unsheathed his maul from his belt, the head shaped like a skull. "You will suffer my wrath."

"Wait." Awesha stood in front of Siphero, shielding him from her father. "This lover you are so intent on killing is my bonded one."

A ripple of surprise went through the guards, and even Greven was surprised. Her father lowered his weapon and fumed with anger more than before. He tried to regain his composure.

"You bonded with a dirty Compa?" he said, veins bulging on this forehead. "What has come over you, Awesha? You have shamed this family. You have shamed all of Skyspire!"

"Hold it." Siphero butted in, taking off his helmet and meeting Recril's gaze. "I don't know what kind of parent you are, but you are a terrible father to Awesha. Why can't you respect her decision?"

Her father was about to blow his top when Greven stepped to his side and joined the conversation. "What is your name, boy? And where do you come from?"

Siphero looked to Awesha, hoping for support from her, but all she could offer was uncertainty as she interlocked her fingers in his hand and held tightly. He then answered, "My name is Siphero Antolus, and I'm from a mining town in the north called Saltdeep. I was born here, in Jormundgard."

As soon as he mentioned Jormundgard, the voices of the guards filled with shock and terror at finding a Terran in their presence.

"A Terran has bonded with my daughter!" her father raged. "This is impossible. You have sullied the good name of my family, you scum of Jormundgard. I will kill you!" He used his affinity on Siphero, and he felt all the breath leave his lungs, leaving him struggling on the ground gasping for air while Recril closed the distance to deal a killing blow to Siphero's head. A clang of metal interrupted her father's swing. Greven had intervened with his own sword by forcing Recril back. Awesha tended to Siphero by undoing the spell and pushing air back into his lungs.

"You dare," Recril fumed, "you would disobey your sovereign?"

"You are not my sovereign." Greven marched forward while his guards formed bonds of magic to restrain Recril. "You came to my village and built your little palace of marble upon our soil. It does not qualify you to lead us, pretender. Guards, arrest the pretender and kindly escort him to his gilded cage."

"Yes, Captain," a guard lieutenant said as they disarmed Recril and flew back up into the cloud cover.

"Now then, I'm sure you have an elaborate explanation prepared for me, Awesha? Hm?" Greven approached as did the rest of his guards, who came to get a closer look at Siphero and his armor. Awesha had gotten him to take deep breaths and wouldn't leave his side despite Greven's insisting.

"Are you all right, Siphero?" Awesha asked in a concerned voice. "Can you stand?"   Siphero got to his knees while Awesha hoisted him up, and Greven offered him assistance. Siphero hesitated, but accepted when Awesha nodded.

"I'll say it to you straight, Awesha." Siphero took a deep breath. "Your father is a sodding bastard."

"The supposed chieftain, Recril," Greven said, "was sent here by the House of the Sangria Legion to observe you Terrans. Because of what he represented, the people of Skyspire followed him out of fear so he proclaimed himself the village chieftain. We have you both to thank for giving us an excuse to lock him up."

"Am I going to be punished?" Awesha asked. "I disobeyed your orders."

Greven laughed heartily and slapped his knee plate. "My dear, you followed my orders to the letter, but your bonding with this Terran was unexpected. How is this possible that a Terran bonded with you?" He directed his question to Awesha, but Siphero spoke up.

"I'm just as confused as you, but have you seen my Dad by any chance?"

Greven looked astonished at this and asked, "Do you mean the loud and foul-smelling little man who lives here with you?"

"Yeah, you see, it's the strangest thing. He's usually around here."

"Now that I think about it, I haven't seen him for more than a sun's arc, but my men will help you search." He called his guards together and ordered them to search for the funny-smelling man around the airfield. They flew off in small groups while he ordered two back to the village to bring word to the rest about their unusual guest to soften the panic.

Greven spent the next hour listening to the story Awesha and Siphero told him of how they met, what happened after they bonded, and even the Skelton armor Siphero was wearing. Siphero told all of what he and Pops were doing on the mountaintop and their activities over the past several months. The whole time, Greven listened with intense interest up until Siphero mentioned the Skelton armor, which he asked for a demonstration of, and Siphero was happy to oblige.

Siphero flew several feet off the ground with Awesha, and they did a few loops, tight turns, and dives until they landed together in the same spot in front of Greven. Awesha touched down with amazing grace while Siphero stumbled and tripped to regain his footing.

"A Terran who can fly like a Winged? Now I've seen everything," Greven said. "Why did you build such a contraption?"

Again, Siphero told Greven about the history of Terran flying vehicles and how they'd been trying to make smaller vehicles capable of flight. Then he said his Skelton was the only one of its kind, the apex of Terran flight technology.

"I've always wanted to fly, but it was the stories I grew up listening to of Winged which really inspired me and"—he stopped and put his hand in Awesha's—"it's thanks to Awesha that I can realize this dream."

Awesha smiled and squeezed Siphero's hand gently. Greven looked between them and smiled. "I see why the bond formed with him, Awesha. He is a misfit, like you."

A guard landed next to Greven and saluted him just as Awesha and Siphero let go of their hands out of embarrassment. "Sir, we've found the Terran." The guard paused, a little depressed, and continued. "But…he's dying."

Greven saw the shock on Siphero's face and said, "Lead the way." The guard led them to a ledge where a few other guards were inspecting hints of environmental change. As they descended, Siphero saw Pops lying there, blood running from a chest wound, a blunt trauma. He knelt down and started crying, holding the hand of his adopted father and just whining like a child. Greven asked his guards to leave them while he and Awesha stood there.

The wings on Siphero's back lowered, mimicking his sorrow. He remained this way for several minutes while he held Pops in his arms, singing the little tune Pops used to sing him to sleep with.

"Seek a brighter tomorrow, the bad days are fading fast, remember the ones you love, they are the ones who will always last," he sang those lines several times in a row before the tears left his eyes. He gently lay his father down on the ledge and closed his eyes. He got to his feet and turned to Greven and Awesha.

"I have a favor to ask you two," he said somberly. "How do Winged bury their dead?"

Greven came forward and said, "We dispose of our dead in a unique way. Are you asking us to give him a Winged burial?"

Siphero nodded, wiping the tears from his eyes. Greven whistled, and one of his staff-wielding warriors came down from the sky. This guard was a woman with dark hair and wild orange eyes, the head of her staff shaped like an owl.

"This is Querce, one of my magi." Greven said, introducing her to Siphero. "She is a songstress by trade in our village, but she is responsible for performing the sacraments of death."

Querce bowed to Greven and Awesha but looked at Siphero and then to Pops. "I observed this man many times. Would you like for your father to go through a Wind Dissolution?"

"Wind Dissolution?" Siphero looked at her questioningly.

"It's one of the many burials I perform," Querce said. "Your father's body will become a gust of air. He will ride the winds forever as a spirit."

Siphero looked at the still bloody body of his father and then at Querce. "Please, do you promise he won't suffer?"

Querce kept her gaze focused on Siphero and said, "He will not feel any pain."

"Do it." Siphero let go of his father's hand for the last time and stepped back as Querce began chanting. A circle of runes appeared beneath Pops as his body changed color to the color of water and dissolved into a small gust of wind that whipped around in the air like a snake slithering through the grass. As Querce finished her incantation, she released the gust, which flew through and caressed Siphero gently before joining the empty sky.

Siphero was still crying when he took off, heading for Pops's workshop and air hangar. Awesha caught up to see him rummaging through Pops's belongings until he found a picture of the two of them working on a Claymore's engine. Siphero took the picture out of its frame and stowed it away in his pack, Awesha watched him the entire time.

"He really was special to you, wasn't he?" She tried to sound sincere, although she could tell through the bond that Siphero didn't want to talk.

"He was, but sometimes I felt like he was trying too hard to be my father." He paused and approached the Paragon parked inside. He took his pack and threw it in the storage bins, getting it ready for flight. "I'm taking the airblade with us. He gave it to me the same day I met you. Can you tell Greven this thing isn't a threat?"

"Of course." Awesha turned to get Greven, who appeared behind her.

Siphero fired up the engines and got the OK sign from Awesha. Slowly, he wheeled it out of the hangar and onto the runway.

"I've informed them, Siphero," Awesha said into his earpiece. "They know it's you."

"All right, Awesha, thanks. Now I have one last favor to ask."

"What is it?"

He paused as he took one last look at the workshop and then toward the supposed location of Skyspire. "Lead the way."

Awesha felt a strange joy come over her. She was excited to share her world with him, the one she bonded with. She whispered in a voice she hoped only Siphero would recognize, "Follow me to a better tomorrow."

She turned in place and began ascending to the cloud cover. Greven's guards doubted Siphero's machine would actually fly. Greven watched curiously as it took off with surprising speed and laughed hysterically to see he had been proven wrong. His guards were knocked out of their gliding spots.

Siphero followed Awesha's flight path up into the sky. He would be the first Terran to ever fly above the land of endless earth. He shot into the sky at breakneck speed, leaving the rest of Greven's guards in the dust. As he pierced the clouds, he was welcomed with an amazing sight. The gleaming mountain peak of the Edge's tallest mountain was also the home to a small community of Winged living on the top. Awesha's world—he had entered the world of the sky, Stratis.

Chapter 6: Inhabitant

Awesha slowly descended to Skyspire's main square, and Siphero did a backflip right before reaching a good cruising altitude above the village. Greven and his guards reached the village's wall first and began signaling for Siphero to approach. The entire village came out to see what strange sound was screeching through their peaceful day. When they saw it was Siphero's airblade, there was a mix of curiosity and fear in the populace.

Siphero was purposefully circling Skyspire because he had never seen a village like it before. He saw that the village rested on top of the Edge's tallest mountain peak, only there was no snow at his altitude. The village had a wall that circled its entirety with towers linking them every sixty or so feet, perches for Skyspire's guards to land and for these strange magnifying glasses stationed there. Inside the village there were at least forty large huts by his count and a large palace that dwarfed all the other buildings, a hideous structure in contrast to the rest of the village. He saw several trees growing scattered around the village and what looked like winged babies wearing robes of different colors carrying objects or scrolls between the houses. When he had seen all he could see from the air, he followed the signals of the magi on the ground and brought the airblade to a hovering position as the wings retracted and he landed the airblade in the main square.

Awesha waited for Siphero to come out, but he remained inside the cockpit and wouldn't budge. The villagers inched closer as a group.

"Is everything all right, Siphero?" Awesha spoke through her earpiece.

He didn't answer at first, but after a minute he replied, "I'm scared, Awesha. How do you know they won't attack me?"

"It will be fine, my bonded. I will introduce you to them, and if you don't come out, I will rip you out myself."

"OK, OK." Siphero surrendered. "You don't have to threaten me."

The hatch on the airblade creaked open as Siphero hoisted himself out, the Skelton armor compacted, and he hopped out of the cockpit, helmet off. The Winged surrounding him were confused as to who he was, but Awesha lay their fears to rest.

"Greetings, all my friends of Skyspire," she began as she bowed to them all. "May the suns find favor with all of you."

Siphero looked among all the assembled Winged and saw smiles on their faces as they returned her praise. He learned something important about Awesha in that moment: she had amazing charisma.

"It is good to see all of you again," she said. "I have been gone a day, and yet I see you all are busy living your lives. You may all know my father has been deposed, yes?"

When she mentioned her father, the villagers hissed and cursed his name until she asked for silence.

"I have returned to tell you all I have brought with me someone whom knows nothing of Winged and carries nothing but fascination and respect for us in his heart, so please make him feel at home, the one you see before you. His name is Siphero, and he is an inhabitant of Jormundgard, our sister world below the clouds, the world of Terrans."

Siphero waved to them all as they absorbed that last piece of information about him being a Terran. None came forward until Greven, the village's guard captain, broke the silence.

"Let me be the first to welcome you to Skyspire, Siphero," Greven said eagerly.

He then bowed to Siphero by laying his wings lower than Siphero's head. His accompanying guards did so as well, including Querce, who called a gentle breeze to brush past Siphero, causing his wings to instinctively unfold to full length, surprising many of the villagers. They felt more at ease seeing a Terran who had wings. The wings then retracted as Greven dismissed his guards. Some of the Winged came forward and patted Siphero on the shoulder while introducing themselves. Siphero met a weaver, an enchanter, an alchemist, a distiller, sky fishermen, surveyors, a healer, and a bunch who were, as Awesha would later describe, "Keepers of the Wood."

The rest of the villagers were still unsure of Siphero and instead approached the airblade, poking at it with sticks to see if it was alive.

"That's enough, everyone," Greven called out. "The day is far from over; please continue to live vigorously."

The crowd dispersed, returning to their individual huts and leaving Siphero, Awesha, and Greven in the village square alone. All the villagers left except for a somewhat elderly, balding, gray-haired, well-built, and slightly scarred Winged wearing a soot-covered apron, long pants, and gloves with runes engraved in the bindings. This Winged still hung around the airblade, inspecting its shell and parts.

"Revaal," Greven warned, "please step away from the Terran's device."

"I'm sorry, Captain Greven," Revaal said. "I can't remove myself from this exquisite contraption. It truly is a work of art."

Revaal eyed Siphero and removed himself from the airblade. He flew over to Siphero and inspected the armor he was wearing as well his mechanical wings.

"I apologize, Terran," Revaal said. "I've never seen such interesting devices before in my many years alive in Skyspire. I digress, my name is Revaal, the village's shaper and smith."

"He's responsible for many things in the village," Awesha added. "He makes and repairs the weapons of the guards, their armor, and any little trinket where metal is concerned."

"What is it that you do, Terran?" Revaal was slightly taller than Siphero, but he nonetheless was eager to hear Siphero's trade.

"I'm uh…I'm an inventor," Siphero said carefully. "I can build things and fix anything mechanical."

"What is your affinity?"

Siphero was a little worried, but Awesha reassured him as he spoke the words for an affinity. As soon as he did, a chunk of metal flew toward him from someone's window and landed in his hands. Revaal's jaw dropped, and he smiled with joy to see this.

"You have an affinity for earth, just like me and Greven here. We don't have many in the village, but more are always welcome."

"Actually," Siphero said, picking up a pebble from the ground and tossing it to Revaal, who caught it while Siphero repeated the affinity words. The pebble stayed in Revaal's hand and a screw from the airblade's supply kit flew into his hand. "My affinity is only metal; I can't control rocks or earth."

"Intriguing," Revaal said, "but still I could use someone with knowledge of how to work metal. If you're looking for work, you can stop by my hut. I could always use an extra hand." Revaal took off toward his hut and resumed his work, heating and folding the metal of a blade.

"Well, now that you have a place to work," Greven said, "the next matter is where you will stay."

Awesha curled some hair around her finger. "You are welcome to stay with me Siphero—"

"That is impossible, Awesha." Greven said, cutting her short. "Your father is under house arrest for his actions. He will be sent back to the Sky Polis for the violations of his orders in a matter of days. Behind our backs, he has summoned one of his chosen suitors, he is a Scrivener."

Awesha grew serious and said, "He deserves worse."

On a side note, she asked, "Which Scrivener is coming?"

"It's Weeslon." Greven shook his head in disgust.

"Just wonderful, and what of my father?"

"Do not worry, Awesha," he said. "He will not be allowed to leave his palace for as long as I am acting chieftain, but your mother expressed wishes of staying."

"Thank you, Greven. I hope it won't be too much trouble."

"No trouble will come of it. I have spoken with the elder Jixve, and she trusts my judgment. You will instead stay in the women's guards' quarters with Querce. Which brings us back to your issue, Siphero." He addressed the inventor. "Where will you sleep?"

Siphero looked around and then back to the airblade, and an idea popped into his head. "If it's all the same to you, I can stay right here in the square. My vehicle has a sleeping roll, so all I need is a fire pit, something to sit on, maybe a workbench where I can do some work. I don't need much."

Greven and Awesha looked concernedly at Siphero as he said this, but even Greven saw he was a man of little comfort needs.

"Very well then, boy, you will have these things you require, but try not to ask too little from the ones who wish to become acquainted with you. Folks around here hold nothing back if it means they can be of service to others."

"OK, thanks," Siphero said. He hoped that he would at least get some privacy.

Greven flew away to arrange the items Siphero requested while he started unloading his supplies from the airblade. He removed his pack from his Skelton and set it down near the airblade. While he wasn't looking, Awesha snuck up on him from behind, blade in hand. She then brought it down in a quick motion before Siphero could react to her swing. He held up his hands in surrender and retreated several steps. She then started laughing as she sheathed her blade.

"What was that for?" Siphero said shakily. "You nearly scared the life out of me."

"You are weak, Siphero," she said seriously. "You cannot fight, despite being bonded to me. I expect the person bonded to me to be my equal in every way."

"I'm not gonna fight you, Awesha."

Awesha paused, a bit surprised by his comment. "You won't fight me," she explained. "I didn't expect you were a coward, Siphero. If you will not train with me, then I will destroy everything that you make, I promise you!"

"Stop, just stop, Awesha!" He shouted at her, and she knelt down to the ground and couldn't move. She tried desperately to move but found it impossible. Eventually she realized their bond was restricting her movements; the phantom link kept her in place.

"I can't move," she said. "Release me, Siphero. Release me now! I order you to do so!"

"No, Awesha. You need to put a lid on your ego. I won't become what you want me to be. And I don't know how to release you." He sat next to her, and he could see the frustration in her eyes.

Siphero took a deep breath and began. "I don't like to fight for a good reason. Terrans do nothing but fight in Jormundgard. The earth we walk on is scorched and barren thanks to our pointless wars. I've lost a lot of good friends to these because they had no other option. I lost my...I lost my...mother...to war."

He broke into tears as he said the last part. Awesha regained the ability to move, but all she did was sit next to Siphero and put her hand on his shoulder.

"What if I trained you in the art of self-defense?" Awesha asked. "I won't train you to kill, just the basics. There are few in my world who would approve of our relationship, many more would wish it destroyed. Do you not wish to protect our bond?" She held Siphero's hand and his grip tightened.

"This bond I have with you…is all I have left." He paused a moment. "Yes, I will protect it!"

Awesha smiled, and a tear rolled down her cheek as he said this. She felt a phantasmal presence around them, surrounding them with its invisible presence. Then a strange shock hit them both, and Siphero keeled over in intense agony while holding Awesha's hand. She couldn't bear his pain even though her threshold for pain was greater than his. She held onto him tightly until he stopped moving, even breathing. She called desperately for help, as lights in the village came on, but she fell silent as a great change came over him.

Chapter 7: Changed

On Siphero's back Awesha saw his Skelton pack fall off. A massive bulge appeared beneath his clothes and ripped open his aviator suit as the fleshy bulge exploded outward and a massive length of bone began growing. Awesha was terrified; she wanted to help him. She desperately tried to use her magic, but for some reason it wasn't working. Then a second length of bone shot out of his back as Greven and Querce arrived with a small contingent of guards, including the village healer and alchemist.

"What's wrong with him?" Greven shouted in a panic. "Is he all right?"

"I don't know," the healer said. "I need you to form a bed beneath him. I have some balms to remedy the pain." Greven scattered his guards to get supplies while the healer and alchemist began preparing curatives. Some of the guards used their affinities to levitate Siphero and Awesha off the ground to allow the healer to operate.

While they worked, the length of bone continued to grow and segmented off into different sections. They seemed to resemble a set of hands. The blood from Siphero's body crept up the bones, stretching between the small sections of the fingers. Its red color would be sickening to any villagers who couldn't bear to witness the gore of Terran innards. As the blood now covered all the bones, it began to harden into an extremely thick mass of flesh, and more strange masses of flesh formed over the blood and bones, forming muscle tissue. A massive surge of heat began pouring out of Siphero's back as the heat coated the massive fleshy hands, causing them to cauterize. He was still in intense pain, but it started to subside. The villagers were starting to settle down, until they shrieked in horror as they saw the airblade in all its massive size lift off the ground. It floated above Siphero and Awesha, remaining motionless.

The airblade slowly disassembled itself into its component parts: the metal coverings, the nuts and bolts, the wings, the engine, and the mana converters. Each part individually welded itself onto Siphero's massive, fleshy hands. During this part of the change,

Siphero didn't move at all. The hands then moved of their own accord, flapping up and down. To everyone's surprise, the gigantic hands on Siphero's back were not hands, but wings. Nothing like this had never happened in the history of the Winged or what they knew about Terrans.

As the transformation came to an end, the wings began to stretch and flap a few times like all Winged did to stretch their own wings. The leftover pieces of the Paragon fell to the ground, and the Skelton floated over to Siphero's back and fused itself with his new wings.

Silence fell upon the village square as all looked at the newly formed mechanical set of wings. The guards returned with their supplies while the healer applied the curatives to both Siphero and Awesha, hoping to relieve some of the pain.

Awesha felt a strange, tingling sensation as she saw the veins on her arm changing color, just like Siphero's had done the day before. She saw colors crawl up her arm, and a feeling of rapture flowed through her entire body, but then it stopped as she nearly lost consciousness. Everyone surrounding them—Greven, Revaal, Querce, and the rest of the town—marveled at the sight of Awesha's wings: they were an aurora of rainbow light constantly changing in front of their eyes. Even Awesha was amazed as her mind blacked out.

The next morning, Awesha awakened in the women's guards' quarters of Skyspire to see she was wearing her morning gown. Her thoughts of Siphero and the other night raced through her mind as she flew out of bed and fell weakly to the floor.

In a puff of air, Nerv appeared in a guard's uniform. "Lady Awesha, it is good to see you again."

"Nerv, what are you doing here? I thought you are bound to serve my father?"

The Cherubim smiled mischievously. "You are correct, Awesha. He may be the superior authority in the family, but my place is to serve you. Now that your father is under arrest, I am no longer required to serve him and can return to my original contract of serving you." He saluted to her and drew a little dagger in his chubby little hands.

"Thank you, Nerv." Awesha got a little teary. "I never thought you would be loyal to me."

"You are the most caring master that I have ever served. The other Cherubim will never know a better master than you."

Awesha was grateful to the little Cherubim, but her thoughts returned to Siphero. "Nerv, please, I need to go see Siphero. Can you dress me? Quickly?"

"As you wish, Lady Awesha," Nerv said, snapping his fingers. Awesha's gown and slippers disappeared in a flash of light, replaced by a long silver gown and high heels. Her sleeves were open silk, and her hair was woven into a long braid that stretched down her back.

"What is this, Nerv?" she said in a huff of anger.

"I am sorry, but Lord Greven has asked me to make sure you take it easy today."

Awesha gave up and walked to the door, only to see in a mirror that a strange color pattern followed her. She realized her wings had changed color to that of a rainbow spectrum.

"My...my wings." She was mesmerized by her new wings; they were so beautiful she could stare at them for hours on end. She snapped out of the trance and opened the door to exit the guards' quarters. She roamed the halls, tripping over her dress more than once. She hadn't worn one for a couple years and had forgotten how annoying they were. She reached the exit and took off from a wall perch while a few guards stopped to gaze at her wings. While she flew to Siphero's location, the villagers beneath her stopped their daily activities to observe her glittering wings.

As she grew closer, Greven waved. She saw a newly erected hut in the village square. She touched down a few paces away from the spot as Greven approached her.

"I'm sorry for making Nerv do this to you," he said apologetically, pointing to her dress. "You collapsed along with Siphero."

"You are forgiven, Greven," she said. "Just remember that I will not forget this." "Understood, my lady."

"How is he?" she asked, with concern in her voice, as they walked toward the hut.

"He's feeling better now, but he's still adjusting to his change. I don't think I would have survived his ordeal. He really is a strong Terran."

"May I see him?"

"Yes, you may." He signaled to his guards and they let her in, her wings folded on her back. Upon entering the tent, she found Siphero in front of the town's healer while a Keeper of the Wood fiddled with some bandages nearby. She saw Siphero moving his new wings in different positions to test their flexibility, strength, and functionality.

"Leave us, please," Awesha asked. "I would like some time with him."

The healer smiled. "Yes, Your Ladyship."

They exchanged looks at each other's wings for a moment until their eyes met and they started laughing. They laughed until tears started to flow.

"You appear to be in good health, Siphero," said Awesha.

"You look like you had it just as rough," he returned.

She smiled at his words. She sat on a stool near his bunk and offered her hand to him. As he took her hand, a feeling of warmth spread through them both as peace permeated the hut.

"So, are you still going to train me?" Siphero reminded her.

Awesha laughed and nodded. "I will, just not today, Siphero. Everyone wants us to rest."

"I second that, but I'm really twitchy for some reason." He scratched his wings and his back where the airblade engine was ingrained in his metal back.

"How so?"

"Have you ever had the feeling of wanting to get out of a cramped space?"

Awesha chuckled at the comment. She saw Siphero was developing the same feeling of constraint she had each morning.

"Yes, every morning when I arise, ever since I was a child. It is the natural feeling all Winged get, the desire to fly in the open skies."

"Huh, because I feel like if I stay here any longer I'm going to burn down the hut."

"Let me talk to the healer. I will see if she will allow you some flight time."

She exited the hut and had a small talk with the healer and Greven. While she spoke to them, Siphero burst through the opening, ripping the flap to shreds.

"Siphero, take it easy," Greven warned. His guards swarmed Siphero. "You've never flown with these wings, and you need time to adjust."

As Siphero stretched, his wings reached in both directions, an impressive twenty-foot wingspan, and heat began building up beneath his wings.

"If I have to stay indoors any longer, I'm going to explode."

"Well then," Awesha said, ripping the lower half of her dress off and discarding her heels, "Let us fly!"

Siphero and Awesha got close together as power began building up in his engine and a massive aura of magical energy overflowed from her wings. As their energy reached critical, they both launched into the air faster than anyone expected them to. They stayed perfectly in pace with one another as they did loops, corkscrews, barrel rolls, and an Immelmann turn and roared across the sky at speeds most Winged could barely reach. Their little joy flight continued for an entire arc of the sun until the fiery ball reached midday. Siphero started slowing down, relying on his wings to provide thrust, while Awesha slowed to match his speed, but they remained side by side. It was just like their sky dance they performed only a few days before.

"This…this is what it's like to fly as a Winged," Siphero said excitedly.

"It is a feeling I never grow tired of, the roar of the wind in your face, the quiet of the empty skies and the boundless freedom of our blue world." Awesha's wings flapped sparkles of rainbow light while Siphero's generated a wave of heat.

"I wish I could stay up here forever."

"I do too, but aren't you growing tired?"

"Actually, I am."

They touched down as the sun began to set on their third day together in the square. Upon landing they couldn't help but notice that a crowd had been watching them the entire time. They were clapping, whistling, and cheering for them.

"What is all of this?" Awesha asked Greven.

"The whole village is voicing their approval. Everyone is welcoming you and Siphero as true bonded, and the elders have agreed to this."

"True bonded?" Siphero had no idea what they meant.

"It means the two of you have been chosen by the elders to serve as our representative Skyspire at the upcoming guardian's assembly in Skyspire."

"What he is saying is," Awesha said, simplifying it for Siphero, "every community of Winged choose among them the most unique, the strongest, the wisest, or those who understand what it means to be bonded as envoys for the community or Polis. The guardians meet every year in the city of Strati Polis."

"Great," Siphero said sarcastically, "looks like our lives just got a whole lot more complicated." His wings drooped, mirroring his frustration.

"Don't worry." Awesha leaned against him. "As long as I can whip you into proper guardian material, we will outshine them all."

Awesha drew her sword from her scabbard as Siphero readied himself for the thrashing of his lifetime. They made space between them and dueled with each other, Siphero dodging her blows with a flap of his wings and countering when possible, while Awesha swung her sword with grace and determination. The crowd watched them for a couple of hours until the guards asked them to leave. However, Siphero and Awesha continued their dance of blades and fists for longer still.

Chapter 8: Training

The next eight months went by in a flash with Siphero and Awesha spending their time improving themselves and deepening their bond with one another, but it proved difficult because they were not typical students. The science of their bond was a mystery, but they both knew, given time, they would figure it out. Siphero spent his days training with Greven and the guards on how to defend himself in the skies, and it proved difficult to train him, since he disliked using weapons, but he reverted to makeshift weapons that doubled as tools. More than once he was knocked out of the sky, but he recovered quickly thanks to his wings and armor. Querce tried to teach Siphero how to use his affinity, but whenever he tried to do what she instructed, it would backfire and have the opposite effect by messing with something metallic. She gave up quickly on teaching him, and Awesha gave it a go.

Her teaching method was different than Querce's. She knew Siphero was adaptable and had excellent situational awareness. She made him use his feelings to control his affinity, and without uttering a word, Siphero began to learn. The ways he was taught to use his affinity were simple lessons all Winged learned, like how to defend against solid projectiles or using an affinity to influence substances outside of their predetermined affinity.

Whenever they dueled, Awesha defeated him easily due to her combat prowess and because Siphero got distracted by her rainbow wings, which sparkled alluringly whenever she used her affinity.

For Awesha, teaching Siphero was a new and difficult challenge. She had never taught a Terran anything about affinities. Some days she was happiest when Siphero took to the lessons she taught him and on others she was extremely frustrated when he collapsed from exhaustion or found him doing work for Revaal or for the villagers.

One day, she thought Siphero needed a break from working so she kidnapped him from Revaal's workshop and snuck him past Greven's guard detail.

"Wait, Awesha, wait," Siphero said, carrying a saddle made from the leftover pieces of the Paragon, which Awesha had instructed him to make the day before. "Where are we going, and will it take long? I have to help Revaal repair the skyfisher nets, and then I have to survey mountain mines."

"Silence, Siphero," she ordered him. "You have been working and training with the guards ever since you came to Skyspire. I believe you are deserving of a break." She was wearing regular attire made of thick leather with shoulder pauldrons, her long silver-brown hair tied into a long bun. As the weeks had rolled by, she noticed a change in her behavior: she had grown calmer and much less restless, while Siphero seemed to devote every waking moment to working, like he needed to be busy.

"But I don't need a break; I feel fine." He yawned for the fifteenth time that morning. They had walked and flown a distance of ten miles to a floating island just south of Skyspire. It was deserted except for a small ruined building and a few trees that grew next to a lone pond.

"As your true bonded, I say you must. Besides, I want you to meet a friend of mine. I haven't seen her in ages."

"Who is this *her*?" Before Siphero could finish, Awesha took a horn from her satchel and blew into it several times. After a few minutes of silence, a similarly long cry answered as Awesha smiled gleefully, placing the horn back in her satchel.

"Yevere!" She shouted the name to the skies as something shot past them faster than Siphero's eyes could track. As the object circled the area around them, Siphero realized it was a large reptilian creature, watching them like a hawk. The creature flapped its massive wings and landed several yards from Awesha.

The thing called Yevere was at least twenty feet long with gray spikes stretching all the way down to its tail like a dorsal fin. Her wings were thick membranes of skin that caught the wind and gleamed in the sun like silver. Her mouth was shaped like a crocodile's snout, with large sharp teeth protruding from its entire mouth. Siphero looked into her open mouth as the creature yawned and saw a row of teeth in the back of the mouth that looked an awful lot like Terran teeth. The last detail that caught Siphero's eye were the hind legs. They were as thick as tree trunks and had long membranes attached to them, which he believed acted like a rudder.

"So…this is the *her*?" Siphero was dumbstruck as he looked from the head to the tail at this magnificent creature while Awesha calmly walked up to her friend and peered into her massive black and green irises. Yevere then bowed to her by lying flat on the ground and licked her gently across the face.

"This is Yevere. She is a skimmer drake."

"A skimmer drake? On Jormundgard we have deep drakes, but they're a bit larger than her and can dig through the earth faster than Terran digging equipment."

"I have never heard of skimmer drakes having a relative, but this is unimportant." She pulled out a small piece of leather from her satchel and used her affinity on it until it grew into an eight-foot-long saddle. Awesha placed the saddle on Yevere's back, hoisted herself up, and used leather straps to secure her wings. After a minute of making sure it was nice and secure, she dismounted in front of Siphero.

"I want you to let Yevere to get used to your scent." She pulled Siphero by the arm, slowly dragging him to Yevere.

"I can't, Awesha. I don't do well with animals. I'm better when I'm around machines, things without a mind of their own."

Awesha stopped pulling and looked Siphero sternly in the eyes. "You don't have a choice in this matter, Siphero. If you're going to get to the Strati Polis, you will need a mount of your own." She looked over her shoulder to Yevere, whose head had lifted, observing Siphero. "She's curious of you, Siphero. Why don't you go and meet her?"

"Are you sure that's a good idea? What if I get eaten?" Siphero's nerves made his legs shake. He didn't want to end up as a skimmer drake's lunch.

"Don't worry," Awesha reassured him. "Skimmer drakes are very intelligent and don't let just anyone ride them. Yevere has been my friend ever since I was young; she knows me. Skimmer drakes can also sense things like our bond, so she trusts you half as much as she trusts me."

"That makes me feel so much better. Should I get some salt for the Siphero sandwich?"

"Go and introduce yourself." She took Siphero's backpack and shoved him in front of Yevere.

He stumbled and fell but held perfectly still when he felt the cold breath of Yevere breathing on his wings. Hoisting himself up slowly, he met Yevere face to giant snout. Yevere took a few deep breaths of Siphero and growled when she caught the unfamiliar scent of charred metal on him. In the next minute, Yevere did something that Awesha had seen her do only once. Yevere rubbed her head against one of Siphero's wings and uttered a low, soft humming sound.

"I cannot believe it," Awesha said. "She has accepted you." Awesha moved forward a short distance toward Yevere and scratched her snout. "She is ready for us to get on." "Where are we going?" Siphero asked.

Awesha flew onto the saddle, strapped her wings in, and stuck her hand out to Siphero. "We're going to the home of all skimmer drakes. We are going to Ipherim." She pulled Siphero onto Yevere's back once he had fastened his pack to an extra spot on her back.

"Why are we going there?"

"I'm taking us there because it's a long journey to Strati Polis and I can't carry you. You need your own mount, preferably a skimmer drake." Awesha tapped the sides of Yevere's neck as it stuck out its wings, caught a strong gust of wind, and jumped off the side of the island, riding the powerful winds.

"How far exactly is Strati Polis from Skyspire?" Siphero asked, with the wind howling in his face.

"Very far. Even by slipstream, it would take us at least a week to get there with Yevere alone, but I don't want to carry your lazy hide there on her back. Plus, it is customary for new guardians to have mounts of their own. Consider them a mark of acceptance. Now hold on—you are about to see why skimmer drakes are such amazing creatures." She kicked Yevere's sides, which gave her the cue to go faster. The skimmer drake zipped through the air at incredible speed, like a bullet fired from a gun. A Mach cone formed around the skimmer drake as it broke the sound barrier and entered slipstream.

Siphero screamed for dear life, only to find the wind drowning out his cries for help. They flew like this for a few minutes until Yevere dropped out of slipstream by herself and flew the rest of the way.

"We're here," Awesha said as she unfastened herself. Siphero collected his pack, mimicking Awesha as his wings caught the wind and came to a hover in the air. Yevere flew toward Ipherim and disappeared into the immensely thick fog.

"Why did we get off?" Siphero asked.

"Because if we went further, we would risk getting ourselves killed." Awesha pointed toward their destination as a thick layer of fog brought into their view a massive floating island with a range of densely forested mountains as multiple creatures, mostly skimmer drakes, flew between the mountains with food in their mouths or eggs in their claws.

"This is where the skimmer drakes of Stratis are birthed and raised. It is a sacred ground where only those deemed worthy can gain a skimmer drake as a mount. These are the floating mountains of Delvorza, in Ipherim."

Chapter 9: Outcast

They approached the Delvorza Mountain Range at low altitude to reach the base of the mountains. As they flew, they came across a ledge in front of a cave entrance, where they landed to catch their breath.

"How often is this place visited by other Winged?" Siphero asked, slightly out of breath. "We can't be the only ones here."

"One moment please," Awesha said, stopping to listen to the air. "Don't worry; we are the only ones on the island."

"You sure? Because you never know what can happen because…"

"Silence! There is no one here, and that is final!" She took off at a brisk pace into the cave, forcing Siphero to follow.

They ventured through twist after turn of the caves as water dripped from the ceiling and eyes of all kinds watched them in the darkness of the tunnel. Siphero turned on a torch and lit up the tunnel as Awesha led the way deeper into the pitch blackness. Once or twice Siphero felt the ground shake as he looked around the tunnel, but he found no origin of the tremor and continued onward.

After several minutes of walking through the dark caves, they finally found a light and exited onto a canyon ledge with an incredible view of the Delvorza Canyon, a valley covered in a densely populated forest. Then they looked at the peaks to see skimmer drakes of all shapes and sizes flying around on the mountains where their nests were. Siphero caught a glance of Yevere as she went back to one particular nest and curled up for a nap.

"So this is what Yevere calls home," Siphero said.

"Yes, it is the only place where skimmer drakes can be free," Awesha said calmly. "I only asked for her help temporarily, as the skimmer drakes are wild but loyal creatures who heed the call of those they trust and then return to the wild when we don't need them."

"You mean you turn them loose whenever you don't need them until you need their help?" Siphero thought it was an ineffective system, but what did he know? He knew how to work with machines, not animals.

"What happens next?" he asked Awesha as she broke a thick branch off of a tree near them and threw it to him.

"You must fly up to where the sun touches the peaks and wait." She took his pack from him and pushed him to the edge of the canyon.

"Wait, aren't you going to help me? What should I do if one tries to eat me?"

"That is not my problem, Siphero," she said, moving away from him. "This is an obstacle you must overcome yourself. Do not come back until you have found your mount!"

"Man, you play tough love sometimes." He laughed a nervous laugh as he turned to face the mountain range.

"This is no time to jest, Siphero. I'm being serious. If you do not succeed, then we will be the laughing stock of the guardians. The ritual is very simple; just raise the stick I gave you to the sky and one of them may come."

"Great, no pressure," he said to himself as he looked down at the dizzying heights. He leaned forward and let his wings catch the wind. He soared over the forest below him until he reached the part of the canyon range Awesha told him to go to. Siphero looked back where Awesha was to find she had disappeared. He took a deep breath, repeated what she told him to do in his mind, and lifted the large stick into the sky as the sun captured his shadow. He looked toward the skimmer drake nests to see if any were coming, but none did. He lowered the stick. He tried again—he tried several times until he felt a massive object smack him out of the sky, and the shadow of a claw descended upon him. As he looked up, a large skimmer drake with thick brown skin twice the size of his former airblade was chasing him. Its mouth was opened wide, trying to eat him as he fell out of the sky.

Fear gripped Siphero, and he begged for help. "Please, someone, anyone, help me!" He heard a loud and angry call as something shot out of the mountain range faster than even a skimmer drake in slipstream, slammed into the skimmer drake, and tumbled to the ground, wrestling with its opponent. Siphero only caught a glimpse of it as he lost consciousness.

Siphero awoke to find himself in a cave covered in large leaves like a big green blanket. He collected some of those leaves and built a fire with some stones he found. As he got a better look at the cave, he saw wall paintings of all kinds, some of skimmer drakes, some of Winged, and then some of Winged riding skimmer drakes and winged horses called avisi. What caught his attention was a picture of a creature that lacked any similarity to the others surrounding it—the being was without wings.

His wings flapped, getting him to his feet as he looked around for the stick Awesha gave him only to find a strange wooden pipe at his feet. It had no holes, was covered with carvings of gears and deep drakes, which made him think of his childhood.

"I don't believe this," he said. "I thought I'd lost this, my drake pipe." He checked the pipe for authenticity. He even recognized the letter *S* that had been carved into it by his mother when he was seven.

As he laughed and cried at seeing the pipe, he felt a tremor beneath him and looked around to find its origin. Whatever it was, the shaking ground told him that it was big. As the tremors grew in size, Siphero looked out into the darkness of the forest to see a big black shadow enter the cave.

The creature that entered the cave was at least forty feet tall, with a muscular build. Its entire body was covered in a thick, coarse fur, with spikes sticking out of its arms every couple feet. It had hands with a set of claws that looked sharp to the touch. When he looked at its head, he saw a bull's head with several horns growing out at the sides and down its cheeks. Siphero met its gaze as it stared right back at him, grew bored, and tossed a hunk of meat at his feet. It went over to the wall, where it wet one of its fingers with crushed fruit paste and began painting.

Siphero watched curiously as he saw it paint a set of wings across the picture of the being that wasn't a Winged. It then turned its massive body to Siphero and pointed with one of its fingers at the Winged with red and black wings and then pointed at Siphero.

"That's me?" Siphero asked the creature. "You painted me?"

The creature simply took more paste and pressed its body against the wall, the finished painting a representation of itself. He then walked up to the imprint and saw it looked exactly like his giant friend. Without noticing, he saw it was in close proximity to him.

Siphero then saw how far away the creature's portrait was from all the other paintings, and he realized its meaning.

"You've been here by yourself," he said aloud, "for a long time."

The beast sat down with a loud thud as Siphero looked up into its gentle eyes. The beast brought one of its massive hands around Siphero and gently embraced him and pointed to his form on the wall.

"I can relate, my friend," he said. "I was alone for a lot of my life, but I found people who were just like me. They were alone and needed someone to be there for them. I'm sure you have someone whose there for you."

Siphero heard a low whining sound coming from the beast; it was crying. It let go of him and took a large bite of the meat at Siphero's feet as he watched it from a distance. He walked to the wall and touched the paintings, and then a crazy thought came to him. He broke some of the paste off and began painting. The creature stopped eating and watched Siphero paint a long tether between its portrait and his. When he finished, Siphero cleaned his hands with one of the leaves and turned to the creature, pointing with his finger to the tether.

"Connection," Siphero said, pointing to both him and the creature. "You and me, we have a connection."

He then flew to the front of the beast and stood on one of its legs. "I don't know how you got here, but I can see that you're lonely. If you want, I can be your friend."

The creature lifted its hand from its food and placed its finger on Siphero's forehead. He felt a string of memories come into his mind. He saw the beast and how it had been alone, hunted, and almost killed many times. Then he heard a single word spoken in his mind: "friend." The creature then lowered its finger, picked up the pipe on the ground, and gave it to Siphero. It got up and placed its hand on his chest and used its finger to touch Siphero on the heart. He heard another word spoken in his mind: "connection."

Siphero could see he had made a new friend and that this creature wanted to be his friend from here on out. "Do you have a name?"

It turned its head and looked at him questioningly. He saw it didn't know its own name or never had one to begin with. He searched his mind for a name he could call his tall friend. When he found one, he uttered it aloud.

"If you don't have a name, I will give you one." He paused. "It was you who saved me from that skimmer drake. I think I will call you Stager."

Stager got to its feet and roared loudly, so loudly that Siphero had cover his ears. He realized it was a roar of happiness because Stager put its finger on his forehead and said in his mind, "Stager, friend; Siphero, friend."

It had gotten pretty late by the time a wave of exhaustion overcame Siphero. He went to sleep on his bed of leaves and found Stager had decided to sleep right next to him, its snoring shooting hot air in his direction. Stager continued to speak in his mind as it slept, "Siphero, friend; Siphero, friend."

The next morning was nice and bright as Siphero got up from bed, only to find Stager painting on its wall and munching on a large pile of berries. As Siphero got up, Stager noticed his movement and scooped up some of its berries with one of its massive hands, dropping them in front of him. He tried some of the berries and found some sweet and some bitter, but they were a good breakfast to start the day. Stager stopped painting and showed Siphero what it had done. He looked at the painting and saw that Stager had given himself wings identical in color and shape to Siphero's. As he continued to look at the detail, he noticed Stager's real back had sprouted a massive set of wings that looked exactly like his own, including a mana engine that was larger than his. The wingspan alone was four times the size of his own, a size built to carry such a big creature.

"Whoa, your wings look just like mine." He inspected the wings and found they were an exact match to his in every way.

He then remembered Awesha and how she would kill him if he didn't come on time. As soon as he got up, Stager sensed this and got down on its arms, inviting Siphero to climb onto its neck.

"You want me to ride you?" Siphero was perplexed, only to get a reassuring snort from Stager. "OK, but don't get mad at me if Awesha doesn't like you." He hopped up onto Stager's neck and held onto the horns like they were a bridle. As soon as he was on, Stager got on its hind legs and began running at a sprint as it headed in the direction of the cliff where Siphero was supposed to meet Awesha. Stager approached the cliff, it jumped an incredible distance and clung to the cliff wall with both hands dug in. It climbed up the cliff side, each and every grasp easy and quick, and Siphero saw that Stager was at home on the ground. He wondered if the big fellow could really fly.

"Where is he?" Awesha paced back and forth atop the cliff face, with Yevere waiting patiently off in the distance, tending to her young as they lazily nibbled on her or play fought with each other.

"Siphero," she said to herself, "if you don't come back in the next few arcs of the sun, I will leave you here." She brushed her wings with her hands as they glowed and attracted the attention of Yevere's babies, who flew close to her and nuzzled her legs.

Then a massive crash caught all of their attention, and Awesha could tell from Yevere's growling that it was something it considered an enemy. She slowly approached the cliff face only to dash back a short distance as she saw a massive claw dig into the cliff top and then another as Stager's horned face came over the top. Then she saw a set of wings she recognized as Siphero's. She pulled out a sword as Yevere crouched behind Awesha and made ready to pounce. As the beast climbed onto the top of the cliff, it cast its shadow over them both, until it lowered and allowed Siphero to hop off. Its wings stretched to their full length, mirroring Siphero's in every way.

Awesha readied herself as she pointed her blade at the beast, "Siphero, get away from that creature; it's very dangerous."

"What are you talking about, Awesha?" Siphero said, puzzled. "It saved my life after a skimmer drake tried to eat me."

"Then…the skimmer drakes have deemed you unworthy." She lowered her blade in sorrow. "We cannot go to the capital now, not with that *beast*. Siphero, you are standing next to a behemoth. They are a savage and feral species that kill and destroy any Winged."

"Well, Stager here isn't what you think," Siphero said, "and even if he is what you say he is, I still owe him a debt of gratitude. He's my friend."

He flew the short distance to her, the sword's edge resting right over his heart. "I'm not going to let you hurt my friend, no matter what he is." Awesha's resolve broke as she sheathed her blade, a tear rolling down her cheek.

"Why, Siphero?" she asked. "Why have you brought shame upon us?"

"I haven't, Awesha," he said. "You grew up learning about these 'behemoths' in the wrong way. I spent a night with Stager and learned he's been alone for the longest time. I gave him the one thing he's always wanted, a friend."

He took the drake pipe out of his satchel and presented it to her. "He gave me this. It's a pipe that my mother gave to me when I was a child. I think Stager is smarter than you believe. Could something so feral and dangerous make something so beautiful?"

Awesha cupped her hands over her mouth as she gasped with astonishment. "It read your memories, Siphero. It saw deep into your memories and made for you something that you had lost long ago." She walked over to Stager, who remained where it was, standing on its arms and legs as it peered down at Awesha.

As with Siphero, Stager reached down and touched Awesha on the forehead and read her memories. It only did so for a few seconds until it stopped and stroked her on the side of the head gently. It sniffed her heavily and lowered itself as their eyes met. She felt it say in her mind, "Awesha, friend; Stager, friend; Yevere, friend."

At the same time, Yevere lowered its guard and crawled forward and sniffed Stager. Stager placed one of its fingers on Yevere's back and stroked it gently, while Awesha and Siphero slowly interlocked their fingers. A smile of joy crept across their faces.

"Can you entertain one question?" he asked Awesha. "Why does Stager have wings, and why do they look like mine?"

She fought back a tear and then answered, "Siphero, a behemoth is a creature whose bestial nature is similar to a skimmer drake. They bond with only one person across their entire lives and only do so with someone they consider to be their leader. What quality do you believe Stager felt when it met you?"

"I don't know," he said. "I saw how it painted images of skimmer drakes and Winged and even a painting of itself, alone and sad."

"That is it, Siphero. It connected with you because you both sensed each other's solitude. It then read your memories and met one of your needs by serving as your mount. It grew those wings to serve that purpose. You never cease to surprise me, you silly little Terran."

After a few minutes, she released Siphero's hand and clapped in the air, getting Yevere's attention, who trotted over to Awesha and got down on all haunches as she climbed on. At the same time, Stager gently grabbed Siphero and struggled to plop him on the back of its neck. For some reason, Siphero felt the saddle he had built was on Stager's neck as he put his feet in the stirrups and buckled his wings down. Stager marched side by side with Yevere as they reached the face of the cliff.

"How do I know if Stager can fly?" Siphero asked Awesha.

"Don't worry about it," she answered back. "When he read your memories, he learned from the memories I gave and gave himself the ability to do so." She kicked the sides of Yevere, who jumped off the face of the canyon and unfolded her wings. Stager's eye met Siphero's as it hunched down and waited for a command.

"Well, I guess it's now or never." He kicked the sides of Stager, who jumped with such force from the face of the cliff, it hurtled through the air with the same speed a skimmer drake achieved in slipstream. The wings on its back then caught the wind as it became aloft and tried to adjust to the experience of flying, requiring only a few moments. Awesha flew close to Siphero and Stager on Yevere's back.

"So do we head back to the island?" Siphero asked through his earpiece.

"No," she returned, "we must fly directly to Skyspire, where the villagers are expecting us to return. I…also told them we would return with our mounts."

"Is she going to be OK?" he asked, pointing to their mounts. "They might not be able to come back for some time."

"Yevere said good-bye to her babies. She knows she won't return, but her babies are at the age where they can look after themselves. Stager has told me that he will go wherever you go, so he doesn't care as long as you remain with him."

"Well, now that that's out of the way, let's go home."

Awesha kicked at Yevere, who took the cue to enter slipstream. It flew into it with a clap of thunder. Siphero gave Stager a similar command and realized the big guy was about to flap his wings while his back engine charged. It released a massive burst of energy, propelling them forward with such speed that they caught up to and overtook Awesha and Yevere. They reached the island where they had begun in half the time from when they started and waited for Awesha and Yevere. Stager let Siphero jump down as it waited, until Awesha appeared a minute later from slipstream and landed close by.

"That was amazing," she said. "I've never seen such speed, let alone a behemoth go that fast. What did it feel like?"

"It felt like I was going to fall off." Siphero laughed heartily as he watched Stager drink from the pond with a massive hand. Yevere took a deep drink right next to Stager, neither caring about the species divide between them.

"It's amazing, isn't it?" Siphero said. "Only minutes ago they were enemies, and now they don't even mind sharing the same watering hole."

"You have our bond to thank for it all," Awesha said warmly. "Our bond made all of this possible. It builds connections deemed impossible between animals and individuals."

"No kidding." He looked at them both, took out a snack one of the villagers had prepared for him, and shared it with Awesha. They sat in silence for a few minutes while their beasts rested.

"It's time to go now." Awesha got up and whistled to Yevere, who came over in one gallop. Stager took some water and offered it to Siphero, who had it dropped on him. He was pretty sure Stager had done it as some form of mischief because he saw the behemoth showing its teeth in what looked like a grin.

He jumped on Stager as they headed toward Skyspire. It only took them a couple of minutes in the air, and they were back by the early afternoon. Something was different about the village. As they circled a few times, the villagers stopped what they were doing and watched in amazement as a skimmer drake and a behemoth flew above their heads and landed in Siphero's square, where they dismounted and assembled in front of the crowd.

"What is wrong?" Awesha asked, standing beside Siphero. "Why are you all here?"

"They are here because I have come to retrieve you, my beloved Awesha, per your father's request," a voice said. The crowd parted to reveal a well-dressed Winged with two sets of feathered wings walking elegantly through the crowd. Yevere and Stager growled at this man while Awesha watched with horror at who had come to see them.

"Weeslon," she said, disgusted. "What in the name of Stratis are you doing here?"

The Winged named Weeslon was a blond, well-cut man who could melt the heart of any maiden. He wore a long robe of fine silk and walked with a staff adorned with a raven's head. His pearl-colored wings were dressed with glittering sapphires and rubies and flapped majestically by his sides.

"Yes," Weeslon said, "it is I, your betrothed. I have come to claim you as my own."

It was then that Stager and Yevere simultaneously let out a deafening roar that sent a shiver down Weeslon's back as he tried to regain his suave composure.

Chapter 10: Challenge

Awesha was standing before one of the suitors her father had chosen: Weeslon, a Winged well-renowned for his beauty and kindness toward women. However, she knew better; she knew his heart was as cold as the deepest tundra. She looked him up and down as she continued to hold Siphero's hand tightly. Weeslon's appearance more deeply reassured her true intuition.

"You look like the nobility have treated you well, Weeslon," she mocked. "What did you have to do? Seduce all the women with promises of love and children?"

Weeslon let out a soft, warm smile, which made all the maidens in Skyspire swoon, to which Awesha lowered her gaze in disgust.

"What are you doing here, Weeslon?" she said. "As far as I can remember, I rejected your proposals and advances. I will not be made an object of your whims."

"Ah, you never change, dear, sweet Awesha," he said softly. "I have come on the request of your guard captain, Greven, to inspect a bond he mentioned is of particular interest." His eyes met Siphero's as he stared back in confusion. "I myself never thought you would form a bond with such a lowly and piteous creature, a Terran!"

He laughed in such a way that the women of the village laughed with him in a nervous and uneasy laugh as the wonder they had for him was starting to wear off.

Awesha silenced him. "What does it matter who I form a bond with, Weeslon? What matters is we both protect and cherish what we have. And besides, Siphero is a much better true bonded than you could ever be."

Siphero felt uneasy as he whispered to Awesha. "Hey, please don't get me involved in your marital affairs. It's messy business."

"You are already involved, and don't worry; Weeslon is all charm and no power." She stepped on Siphero's foot, and he yelped quietly.

"So Siphero is his name. I will be sure to engrave his name upon your wedding ring. Sky Knights, please seize that savage." Out of nowhere several knights carrying swords and shields materialized and pinned Siphero to the ground as he let go of Awesha's hand. A total of twenty surrounded Siphero and pointed weapons at both him and any who came near. They had made a mistake in the process of harming Siphero. They had forgotten there was a skimmer drake and a behemoth standing in close proximity to them.

Stager roared ferociously as it picked up the closest guard and tossed him through the air at breakneck speed and swatted a large number of guards like so many sticks of wood as they scattered into the wind. Yevere, at Awesha's command, let loose a powerful gust of icy wind from its mouth as it froze a couple of guards in place. Awesha then drew her sword as she rushed to Siphero's aid, only to be taken hostage by Weeslon himself.

"Let go of me, you disgusting man," she said, struggling in his arms. "I told you I am not yours to take."

"I don't care, Awesha," he said into her ear. "I will make you mine here and now."

Awesha felt a cold sensation as she felt a new presence entering her body. Her bond with Siphero was being tampered with. She screamed in fear as she felt Weeslon forcing himself into their bond by overwriting it with his own.

"Awesha!" Siphero shouted, still pinned by at least five guards. He reached out one free hand and called Awesha's name even more loudly. Several guards recovered from their various scenarios, immobilizing Stager and pinning Yevere. He looked around and saw their mounts couldn't do anything, but he couldn't move either well. He was helpless in that moment as he saw he was going to lose Awesha to this scum of a Winged.

Then, as he felt a strange emptiness overcome him, he saw in the darkness of his mind a chain, but not just any chain. For some strange reason, he knew the chain, as he saw his name was carved into it. He saw another cord shaped like a ribbon wrapped around his chain, where Awesha's name was written, but it began to unwrap from his chain and flew off. Siphero chased after it, but no matter how hard he tried, it stayed out of his grasp only by mere inches. His thoughts then returned to Awesha and the many moments of happiness and joy they had spent over the many weeks in Skyspire, but one memory stood out among them: one night of watching the stars in the sky.

"Awesha," Siphero had asked that night as he looked up at the sky, "do you ever wonder if there are other worlds like yours and mine out there?" He'd pointed a finger up at the stars. They were both lying on their backs on a grassy hillside, side by side, hand in hand.

"No," she had returned, "I have only ever known Stratis and feared the existence of your world. I cannot think of any other worlds but of our own."

"I know the feeling. When I first learned of your existence during our dance in the sky, I never would have thought I'd be living here with you in this little hamlet."

Awesha smiled to herself. She had found that she and Siphero were agreeing on a number of topics that they both explored equally. It was strange they agreed on anything so easily.

"But I do wonder," she said, "now that I am sharing my world with you, when will share Jormundgard with me."

"Seriously?" he said. "You would want to see the world of the ground? It's pretty dull down there, I can tell you."

"Nevertheless, Siphero, I wish to see the place you call home, this Saltdeep you mentioned."

"Well, I guess it's a fair trade—you show me Stratis and I show you Jormundgard—but we share the experience of both our worlds."

"It's a promise then, Siphero." Awesha forced him to meet her gaze. "I will remind you every day so you will never forget."

"OK, OK, you twisted my arm. It's a promise."

They continued to look up at the stars until Awesha felt Siphero fall asleep on her shoulder as she drifted off to sleep as well.

The memory flooded back into Siphero as he remembered their promise. Anger surged through his entire body as he flew after the ribbon in his mind with the full power of his wings. He flew past the ribbon until he found a hand pulling it away from him. In one powerful motion, he grabbed the hand, broke it, and grabbed the ribbon as the hand fell into the darkness. Siphero tied the ribbon and his chain together into a powerful knot, until his name and Awesha's were together. And it was then a blinding light ejected him from the darkness and brought him back to reality.

Regaining consciousness, Siphero was still pinned down by the guards. In an instant, he used his metal control to produce a powerful force, knocking them all back as he launched himself toward Awesha. He looked at Awesha to see she was emitting a rainbow aura so powerful that it forced Weeslon to let go and crumble to the ground. Their eyes met as they embraced each other. A blinding light shone from the two of them as the colors of Awesha's rainbow and the heat from Siphero's wings fused together. The light shot into the sky, forming a pillar of light as it continued to fire into the air. It then began to settle as a massive sphere formed above them in a menagerie of color. Everyone in the village stared at it in disbelief as Weeslon recovered. His amazement showed as the sphere began to take shape. He looked to where Siphero and Awesha were standing only to see they had vanished. Only Stager and Yevere remained, still batting at soldiers like pesky flies.

They all watched as the sphere of light broke open like an egg and two gigantic wings bulged out. The wings resembled Siphero's massive metal wings surrounded in a rainbow aurora. After the wings a hand wreathed in a rainbow and covered by an iron gauntlet emerged from the egg, followed by another that was much larger and better armored. The legs and upper body emerged with the right and left belonging to a female and male figure respectively, as the whole body wore a combination of light and heavy armor. At the belt, there was a sword of incredible length stretching for at least forty feet while on the right arm there was a massive round shield. There was no face, only a helmet with five long horns and two eyes staring down at Weeslon, one belonging to Awesha and the other to Siphero. In its entirety, the being stood over one hundred feet tall.

Then Weeslon realized he was the target.

"*Archon!*" he yelled. "Everyone get to shelter! Your guardians have just summoned an Archon!"

Greven came forward with his guards as they watched with bated breath for what the Archon would do.

"How is this possible?" Greven asked. "Bonded Winged cannot summon an Archon for at least another five years."

"You forget, Guard Master Greven, this pairing of a Winged and a Terran is far from normal." Weeslon called his guards together as they recovered and thawed themselves out. Stager and Yevere joined their masters in the sky, circling them.

"What do we do, Lord Weeslon?"

"Just wait and watch," he said as he strode forward and watched silently.

The Archon drew its incredibly long but blunt weapon as it slowly descended to the village square and knelt to observe Weeslon and the guards.

It then spoke in a voice belonging to neither Awesha, nor Siphero. "Their bond is unbreakable; none shall succeed." The Archon faded into light as Siphero and Awesha slowly floated down to the ground and lay sound asleep.

All in the square came forward to view their sleeping guardians, and Greven motioned forward with relief and astonishment on his face. "These two really are special if they managed to manifest their Archon this early."

"That was no ordinary Archon that they summoned," Weeslon said, calmly serious. "It is one of the Ancient Archons said only to appear to a specific pairing, a chosen pair. This Archon is none other than the legendary Hevros!"

"Hevros, an Ancient? I thought that was all he was, a legend." Greven ordered his men to calmly lift Siphero and Awesha, separating them.

"Do not separate them," Weeslon warned. "If cut off from each other during this delicate moment, you could force the Archon to manifest again, doing irreparable damage to them both."

"Then what should we do?"

"Just leave them as they are. They deserve their rest. I have seen all I needed to."

It was early morning the next day when Awesha awoke to the rising of the sun and the peaceful snoring of Yevere, her wings forming a tent above her head. She looked at Siphero and saw Stager's massive hand covering him, a smile crossing her lips. When she looked around, her clothing had changed again, to the dress she wore on the day Siphero got his wings. At first she was resistant but found she didn't care anymore. Then, she found something interesting on Siphero's left arm. It looked like a tattoo.

The tattoo was a metal gauntlet with a massive shield covering the top, in addition to greaves and part of a helm, and there was even a massive wing on it. It made her very curious about its meaning. Then she saw on her right arm another tattoo with a gauntlet holding a sword in its hand, a leg, and half a head and wing. She was shocked as the memories came flashing back to her and Siphero's summoning of an Archon; however, she was confused. Didn't an Archon manifest from two bonded?

"So you're awake," a voice said to her. Awesha's head snapped around, and jumping to her feet, she willed an orb of crackling energy to appear in her hand.

The speaker, Weeslon, was sitting on a stool with a few of his Sky Knights standing around him. They were about to draw their swords when he waved them off, and they left. Awesha did not ease her stance, but her curiosity made her wonder what Weeslon was up to.

"Ease yourself, Awesha," he said. "I am not interested in being your betrothed, despite your father's suggestion."

"You…you never wanted to," she said, lowering the energy orb. "Then why did you attack Siphero and me?"

"I was testing you and the Terran to see how powerful your bond with each other was." He paused and rested his staff on the ground. "I was just doing what Greven asked me to do, and I decided to use your father's offer of betrothal as a device to determine its strength."

"Then you don't want me?"

"Never did to begin with; besides, I don't like rough feather wings."

"So then, what do you think of our bond?"

Weeslon was silent as a smile spread from both corners of his lips. "I found it quite intriguing."

"What made it so intriguing?" Awesha straightened herself, her wings folding behind her.

He looked at Siphero and then to her. "Two things were quite apparent to me," he began. "First, I have never seen anyone who could so strongly prevent me from finishing a bonding test, let alone suspect a Terran was capable of it. And second, the two of you summoned an Archon."

Awesha was so overcome with surprise that she fell to her knees, looking at Siphero. They had summoned an Archon and survived, a feat only possible among the strongest of Winged.

"But wait," she said, "isn't it too early for this to happen? Siphero and I shouldn't be able to, not for another six or seven years."

"That is correct, but there have been very rare instances where a bonded pair under stressful and dire circumstances summoned an incomplete Archon. Even in its incomplete form, the Archon still performed the function of protecting the pair or destroying their target. These instances have given us the only look into what we believed was possible, until today."

"So our Archon was incomplete?" She then rolled up the dress sleeve of her right arm and showed Weeslon the tattoo. "Can you explain this?"

"Hm, let me see." Weeslon leaned in and examined the tattoo, recoiling in amazement. "I...I...I don't believe it."

"Is everything all right?" She lowered her sleeve and rose to her feet.

"Awesha, this is big news. This has never been recorded in our history, but you and Siphero are manifesting your own individual Archons!"

Awesha was on her knees. The surprise had rendered her immobile, and she clenched her arm tightly. "My very own Archon? That's impossible, but then, what was the Archon that appeared before we lost consciousness?"

"The Archon that was summoned was an Ancient, an Archon whose appearance signifies that a great change will take place in our world. The two of you summoned Hevros."

The name Hevros was an ancient name to Awesha, but she knew it well. "Did anything else happen while Siphero and I were out of it?"

Weeslon curled some of his blond hair. "Yes, the Archon spoke these words: 'Their bond is unbreakable. None shall succeed.'"

While Awesha puzzled over what those words meant, Siphero finally woke up, yawned, and scratched his arm. Seeing

Awesha near Weeslon caused panic to take hold of Siphero as he jumped to his feet. Awesha alleviated his worry at Weeslon's appearance as she explained why the Bond Scrivener went to such drastic lengths to test their bond. He then scratched Stager's nose as the behemoth awoke with an earth-rumbling yawn and rested on its knees with wings still draped around its master.

"So, are we in the clear?" Siphero asked Weeslon. "Do you want to attack me again just because I'm a Terran?"

"No, as much as I'm shocked to see a Winged and a Terran sharing a bond," he returned, "I am more interested in seeing how all this will turn out. I will personally head to Strati Polis and put my recommendation of you both for guardianship to the king and queen."

"But wait," Awesha said, "won't it be troublesome for us if the citizens of Strati Polis learn of Siphero's identity? The city is populated with a lot of Avia, and they have only become more prejudiced as of late."

"To Jormundgard with what they think. I just bore witness to the summoning of an Archon, which is only ever seen when a great change is coming. All of Stratis could disapprove of your bond, but they cannot stop what is to come from it." Weeslon got to his feet and summoned his guards as they placed a white robe on his back and collected his staff. Siphero and Awesha got to their feet as well, bowing to Weeslon.

"I look forward to seeing the two of you at the capital," he said, returning their bows. "May the suns and the moons favor your continued kinship."

"And may the elders be kind to your favoring of us," Awesha said.

"Yeah, it was a pleasure to meet you, Weeslon. You aren't such a bad fellow after all." Siphero extended his hand to Weeslon, and the Scrivener just stared at it.

"It's a custom of Terrans to shake hands," Awesha said to him. "I have learned it is a form of introduction and a way to forge friendships."

Weeslon smiled with absolute joy at knowing he was subject to a Terran custom. "From the old stories of Terrans, they mentioned them as vile, barbaric, and destructive. I'm glad I was able to meet a Terran such as yourself."

"Well then, be in good health until we meet again." Siphero let go of Weeslon's hand as they parted ways. A chariot pulled by a couple of skimmer drakes descended from the sky surrounded by a retinue of Sky Knights. Weeslon boarded the chariot and waved to them as he set off with his escort. In the distance they saw a large sky galleon appear from behind a cumulonimbus cloud as Weeslon boarded the vessel and disappeared over the horizon.

"I feel somewhat indifferent about our bond," Awesha said, holding Siphero's hand as one of her wings touched his.

"That makes two of us," he returned, "but you know something?"

"What, my bonded?"

"I feel excited for what's to come." He let go of her hand and placed his around her shoulder, and she did the same with her opposite arm.

"That makes two of us." They exchanged a smile as they looked into the distance to where Weeslon's ship had vanished.

"You want to go flying?"

Chapter 11: Acceptance

The life shared by Siphero and Awesha flew by in several more weeks leading up to a night in the library. They spent their time training, attempting to manifest their Archons, learning each other's strengths and weaknesses, and riding their mounts in flying training exercises. Awesha spent time with Siphero in the library of her father's mansion, where she taught him about the history of the Winged Empire and all their past occurrences—their battles, treaties, and races. She even shared her views on the prejudice within her people, who disregard the welfare of the Sila, a race of animal-hybrid Winged, and the Compa, Winged whose wings were born unfinished or with only one wing that had to be modified and repaired for use in day-to-day flight. She then continued with the introduction of a race of Winged that were subject to the disgust of all the Avia and Engria, the Wingless, Winged born without wings and who reminded her of Terrans. She then considered that is why Wingless were discriminated against so heavily; their lack of wings made them resemble Terrans, a logical conclusion.

After their introduction, she revealed that the name of Winged like her are called Avia since their wings are made from feathers and that her group were just called Winged on the hierarchy. The last race she spoke of were the Engria, Winged with wings made from energy like fire, lightning, mana, ice, wind, and even earth.

"So how many of these Engria exist?" asked Siphero, drinking from a canteen he had brought into the library. "I mean, when you speak of them, they sound like legends or heroes."

"Becoming an Engria is a rare occurrence for Winged," she answered back. "It is only given as a gift to the worthiest or occurs naturally when Winged awaken their true power. The king and queen of Strati Polis are the only ones who can give this gift. To answer your question though, there are only a few Engria in all of Stratis."

"Would you want such an honor?" Siphero put down his canteen and watched as Awesha stared off into the distance absentmindedly.

She didn't answer him for several minutes until she met his gaze and smiled. "No, I don't think I would because everyone would see me differently, especially you."

"You have to remember," he said with a half laugh, "I'm different from you since I'm a Terr—" He couldn't finish his sentence. His mouth was sealed shut with Awesha's magic. He frowned as she took her time in removing the seal.

"I don't care that you are a Terran, Siphero. How many times do I have to tell you? You and I are held together by our bond, and as long as we remain true to our promises, I will brave any storm and any world to be with you."

Siphero felt in his heart and through the bond that she meant every word she spoke. He got up from his seat and walked toward her. He offered his hand to her, and she took it with her own, interlocking their fingers for perhaps the one hundredth time. The pulse of their hearts beat at a pace in sync with one another. Their tattoos glowed indigo and silver, a response to each other's presence and a signifier of how strong their bond had become.

"If I might say, Awesha, you are the blade of our bond, a free-spirited, wild, self-righteous, charismatic, and open-minded Winged. You hate to see others suffer under the tyranny of the corrupt, to succumb to that power, and you most especially hate being restricted by any form of law that violates your code of conduct. You strike at any who would consider our bond a violation to their natural order. In your eyes, Stratis must dispose of their old traditions of seclusion and prejudice, even if such a change must be forced upon those unwilling to accept it."

Awesha felt those words wash over her like a warm and gentle wind as she let a tear slip from her eye. She leaned in, whispering to Siphero, "I could say the same to you, Siphero. You are the most unusual Terran I have ever met, the only one I know. I have broadened my horizons because of your strange outlook on life. You are a pacifist, submissive to the requests of others, and a dreamer. You are hardworking, kind, understanding, and patient. You hate to fight since you have seen the terrible outcomes of conflict, and you desire to prevent any fight where loved ones could be injured. But you hate most of all having those whom you care deeply for ripped from your life. For you, the world must learn from the errors of the past so a better future can become a reality. This is why I care so deeply for our bond, Siphero. You are my opposite in many ways, a perfect complement to myself."

At the utterance of those last words, a light began to form around their interlocked hands—a beautiful light composed of the colors from Awesha's wings and pieces of metal from Siphero's—until they let go. However, the light and metals continued to orbit as they stared at it in the darkness of the library candlelight. Awesha's mother came into the library wearing a nightgown, and Nerv appeared from a puff of clouds by accident.

"Awesha, what is going on so late in the night?" she asked as she saw the sphere of light grow in size until it was the size of one of the tables.

"I don't know, Mother," she answered. "Siphero and I were just studying when this shining light appeared."

"You shouldn't be up this late." Her mother floated over in an instant and slapped Siphero across the face. "I thought I expressed my wishes clearly. That filthy Terran isn't allowed inside the house." She looked back at the orb of light. "You have created another abomination in my household. Your Archons are coming to claim you."

"Our Archons are coming? That's good news, isn't it?" Siphero asked.

"Silence, Terran," her mother said to him. She never called Siphero by his name. She continued to speak to her daughter. "This is an important moment for you, Awesha. The moment an Archon comes to claim its bonded pair is significant since very few ever manifest themselves to do so. You've done it, my daughter. The Archon that comes for you will ensure the honor of our family."

She eyed Siphero with disgust and prayed to any of the Archons that Siphero wouldn't get claimed. The light and metals had grown to twice their original size until they were filling the library with their natural light. A knock on the door came as Greven entered with Querce, Revaal, and a couple of guards in tow.

"What is going on here?" asked Greven. "What is this blinding light?"

Revaal took a deep breath and sighed. "I know what this is." He flew forward to Siphero and placed his hand on the boy's shoulder. "Your Archons are revealing themselves, but…this doesn't happen until many years into a bond."

"Our bond is just beginning," Awesha said to them. "I can feel it; this is what I believe my Archon is saying."

They all looked at Awesha with confusion, and her mother said, "My dear, Archons do not speak to us. It must be the moment speaking to you."

"She's right," Siphero said. All eyes met his. "I can feel it too. I hear what my Archon is saying to me." He pulled up his sleeve to reveal the tattoo. It was glowing quite brightly. Something strange happened, as half of the image seemed to complete itself, and the newly finished tattoo revealed a composite armored individual with a massive shield, no wings, and a long chain wrapped around its right arm. Its head wore a helm shaped like a behemoth's head and showed two piercing brown eyes staring defiantly at anyone who stared back at it.

The same thing happened to Awesha's tattoo as the tattoo completed itself and revealed a female Winged wearing a white dress with an armored breastplate, shoulder pauldrons, gauntlets over silk sleeves, armored leggings above heeled shoes, and an open-cut dress to allow for easier movement. The woman's hair was long and voluminous as it stretched past her wings down to the base of her dress. In one hand was a metal pole as long as a sword and in the other was a scepter with a burning crest on the top. Her wings were the strangest part. One was surrounded in a rainbow aura while the other was a deep black with spikes sticking out of the top. She wore a helm shaped like a crown and had one clear stone embedded right above the forehead area. The eyes were blue like sapphires with an iris the color of rubies. They watched with a calm coldness at all who stared at them, but there was also a warmth to them.

As Siphero and Awesha's tattoos completed themselves, they felt themselves being pulled together by a powerful force. They tried to resist, but their hands interlocked beyond their control. The hands of their Archons manifested above them and so did the rest of their bodies, which were inscribed upon their tattoos. The behemoth-headed soldier and white-dressed warrior with a black wing materialized before them as their incorporeal forms became conscious and looked about the room and at their summoners. Siphero and Awesha looked at each other's Archons and felt a great insecurity come over themselves.

The eyes of their Archons then turned to the crowd assembled. Greven, Querce, and Revaal backed away as a small squad of guards formed a barricade in front of them. The Archons willed Siphero and Awesha to move their hands like a set of marionettes. They could not move on their own. They were completely at the mercy of the incorporeal beings in their presence.

"All those here before us," the Archons said together, through Awesha and Siphero's voices, "we have chosen this bonded pair to be our chosen. They represent everything we stood for during our time and continue to believe in. All who oppose their bond shall be shown the error of their ways. We are the Archons of Defiance and Sanctuary. We acknowledge this bond of a Winged and a Terran. Their bond shall shake both worlds, Jormundgard and Stratis, to their very cores."

The Archons dissolved into the air as the energy surrounding Siphero and Awesha dissipated and their power from the Archons flowed back into their tattoos. The two of them crumpled to the ground, tired but very much alive.

"These two really are special." Revaal stepped forward and put his hand on Siphero's shoulder. "Two Archons for the price of two guardians, the Council of Guardians will be intrigued with these two."

"But this is troubling." Querce stepped forward and put her hand on Awesha's forehead. "I recognize those two Archons."

"Who are they then?" Greven directed his gaze at his subordinate. "Do speak up, all-knowing Querce."

"I recognize them both from the archives I glimpsed in the Library of the Learned in the Archo Polis. The one who manifested for Siphero is Preduvon, the Great Defiant."

A ripple of shock went through everyone at the mere mention of Preduvon. They looked at one another, all except for Revaal, who smiled at the sleeping Siphero with admiration.

"Preduvon," Awesha's mother said, "the scum of Sky Polis who challenged all? That Preduvon?"

"Yes, that Preduvon," Revaal said in anger. "He was a patriot for the Sila, the Compa, and the Wingless. He challenged all who tortured, punished, and killed the lower castes. He was ruthless. Preduvon defied the orders of all around him, from the king of Sky Polis at the time to even the guards, but he never killed anyone. No matter where he went, he was shunned, beaten, and cursed by the upper crust of our society for simply being who he was. To this day he is a beacon to all of the lower castes for never giving in to the corrupt ways of the upper castes."

"He was an incompetent Wingless who didn't know his place," Awesha's mother said coldly. "The world would have been better off had he not been born."

"You don't get to make that accusation." Revaal rose in anger. "My mother and father were Wingless, and here I am with my own wings. Take back your slur, you Avia bitch."

Greven's guards pulled out their blades and pointed them at Awesha's mother, and Greven stepped in front of them.

"Need I remind you," he said to Awesha's mother, "that you are a guest here in Skyspire at the request of your daughter? I will not have you insult the Archons. You too, Revaal; do not make the situation direr."

The two turned away from one another as Querce inspected Awesha's tattoo. "I remember the Archon on Awesha's arm, but"—she paused and looked at Awesha's mother with sadness—"your daughter has been chosen by Verrencae, Lady of the Scarred."

"Verrencae," Awesha's mother said silently. "No, not my own daughter, chosen by that…that wench. Every day my daughter is becoming less like the perfect child her father and I wanted her to be, even after he ended that foul Terran…"

"What Terran?" Greven ordered more than asked. "What Terran are you speaking of, my lady?" His voice was filled with aggression as the ground shook beneath his feet.

Without them noticing, Awesha and Siphero came to with assistance from Revaal and Querce as they watched the confrontation unfold.

"The one we were dispatched by Sky Polis to observe beneath this backwater little village and have been watching this whole time," Awesha's mother said. "The one who made all of those loud noises and foul contraptions, the Terran this Winged abomination calls—"

"Pops," Siphero said, with tears and shock in his voice. Greven and Awesha's mother turned to see they had awakened. Siphero was on his knees sobbing and wailing in pain at this news while Awesha rushed her mother, holding her by the throat as her mother struggled through strangled breaths.

"Dear, please let me go," she said, begging for her life, "Your mother still…loves you."

"Silence, Mother. Don't you dare speak another word to me," Awesha said bitterly. "You do not have the right! Do you know how great the pain is I am feeling from Siphero? Do you! His pain is unbearable; it screams in my ears. And now that I know the truth, I have no love for you."

She shook her mother and slammed her against a bookcase.

"My lady," Nerv pleaded with Awesha, "please let go of the mistress; she is suffering."

"Yes, thank you, little Cherubim, keep your master safe," Ulmafe said.

Nerv stopped pleading with Awesha and turned to her. "You are not my master." He flew back to the side of Greven and saluted the guard captain. As he vanished in a puff of smoke, Greven faced his guards.

"What are your orders, Greven?" The guards awaited what he had to say.

"The blood in the upper crust of our society is twisted and oozing a blackness such as this," he said. "Arrest the woman and lock her up. She shall not leave for any reason other than to eat or take a small flight. Give her only bread and water, if she asks for anything beyond these mercies, give her nothing instead. Let her be a prisoner of her own vanity until we can get rid of her."

"Yes, sir." They saluted and turned toward Ulmafe, who was still suspended above the ground with Awesha's hand on her throat. Siphero then walked past them as he placed his hand gently on Awesha's.

"Please, Awesha, please stop." His red eyes still flowed with tears, a sign he was done mourning the memory of his beloved Pops. However, Awesha slowly lowered her mother and sheathed her sword. Then she grabbed Siphero in an embrace as she cried into his shoulder.

Siphero met Ulmafe's gaze and just stared at her for several minutes until he said, "I feel sorry for you."

"I do not need your sympathy, Terran defecation," she said in disgust.

"I feel sorry that you were bonded to such a cruel and degenerate man who lacked the ability to care for you as Awesha and I do. And now you have to live the rest of your life knowing the solitude that we both feel. Congratulations, you have just orphaned the two of us." "But Awesha still has her sister, me, her father and the rest of her family in Sky Polis. She is not an orphan."

"How can I call you family, Mother?" Awesha said through her tears. "You and Father really are perfect for each other. I hope you live a lovely life in a cage. From this moment you and Father and anyone in our family who despises my bond or Siphero's identity is no one I can call family!"

"No, Awesha, please don't," her mother pleaded. "You are still my daughter. Please just kill that Terran scum and we can be a family—"

"*You are not my mother!*" she shouted at the top of her lungs. The silence that followed told her she had made her point clear.

"Get her out of here," Greven ordered. "Don't let her speak to or make eye contact with anyone."

The guards carted Awesha's mother off as she stared into space like a doll broken from too much wear and tear.

"Nerv," Greven said, at the mentioning of his name, the Cherubim popped into existence, "inform the elder. She needs to know of this atrocity."

"At once, Your Grace." Nerv vanished before his eyes.

"Now then, you two," Greven said, "what are we going to do about that thing?" He pointed to the metal orb that continued to float above them in absolute silence, the light of the rainbow aura piercing it every now and then. Then, it slowly descended as it drifted toward Awesha and Siphero. It floated in front of them as if waiting to be opened.

They looked at each other, tears in their eyes, hands clenched, and foreheads touching.

"We should open it." Awesha was the first to speak, in a strangled voice. "The Archons chose us for a reason. We stand alone, but we will stand together as we have always done since we first met."

"I agree," he said back to her. "This bond is all I have left; you are all I have left. You are the only one I trust with all my being, all my soul, and all my future. I promise to stay with you even if our bond expires, until my life ends."

The metal orb burned brightly with light as they placed their hands on it. It shattered into a thousand pieces as light flooded the library, blinding all those present. The light faded as a pair of weapons floated down to them, a shield and a very lengthy chain rope went to Siphero while a blunt baton and staff went to Awesha, the weapons of their Archons.

"We give you our weapons and blessing to you both," a whispered voice of the Archons spoke through the silence. "Bear this new honor with renewed purpose and show the world that the principles of old are about to come crashing down around them."

They wiped tears from their eyes as the weight of this new burden eventually sank in and their new weapons evaporated into thin air. The night seemed to have become peaceful as Siphero and Awesha grew closer, losing everything except each other.

Chapter 12: Embark

It was a bright and early morning in Skyspire when Siphero, Awesha, Greven, and Querce were about to depart from the little mountain village on a direct course to the Strati Polis. Siphero and Awesha were just checking their saddlebags, which were filled with what they needed, and made sure they were fastened tightly to Stager and Yevere respectively. When they looked at each other now, there were mixed feelings of compassion and shyness. They had endured a great deal of hardship, hard truths brought upon them, their bond continually reminding them of one another's strengths and weaknesses. They always stuck together, and the villagers of Skyspire could see a blossoming of sorts growing between their chosen guardians.

Greven and Querce were going with them as guides because Siphero and Awesha had never been to the Strati Polis, and getting there was no easy task. They also knew how to get right to the palace of the Polis because they knew for a fact the Avia of Strati Polis would be well aware of the guardians attending the assembly. They always knew in advance. Plus, they wouldn't take lightly to a Terran in their midst, which could result in rioting and as much chaos as could be mustered. The two of them were going as guards of the guardians.

They were just saddling up a few of their own avisi, winged horses similar in look, color, and variety to horses used by Terrans—except these creatures had wings, much like the Avia that domesticated and cared for them. Their two avisi were called Lightsoul and Deepheart. Lightsoul was white and brown spotted across its body, with a star on its forehead. The other, Deepheart, had a silver coat, black mane, and three stripes running down the length of its head. Both avisi were beating their wings, eager to take off. They could fly nearly as fast as a skimmer drake, but they had greater maneuverability, a reason why many Winged preferred them over skimmer drakes.

They looked like an odd bunch: two avisi neighing wildly and nickering to their owners; a skimmer drake dozing in the warm sun while Awesha scratched her scales; and a behemoth sitting on his haunches, eating berries that children fed him, and tossing said children into the air so that they could gently glide down.

After their preparations were complete, they assembled in front of the crowd of guards, townsfolk, and Keepers of the Wood, who had been gathering before them. Siphero and Awesha held hands as an elderly Compa came toward them. This frail old woman was the village elder. She had short graying hair with silver streaks, and her face was filled with wrinkles. Baggy skin drooped over her eyes, but black and white eyes stuck out from under it as she smiled at them, showing her missing teeth. She looked genuinely happy. Her clothing was a basic robe with a long gown embroidered with white and silver flowers that a florist had picked out. She wore sandals with long ribbons attached to the toes and walked with a staff carved into the shape of a peacock's head that glowed with a green aura. Her wings were a sight to behold. Her one good wing was white like any other, but the other looked like a garden had taken shape. It was completely made up of flowers, grass, leaves, and tree bark, and it smelled wonderful.

She stopped in front of Siphero and Awesha and bowed to them, and they bowed to her in return.

"The suns favor you both, guardians of Skyspire," she said in a croaky voice. "It has been only a few months, and yet the two of you have become something more than just our beloved guardians."

"Thank you, Elder Jixve," Awesha said graciously. "We hope to exceed the expectations you and all of Skyspire have placed upon us." She kicked Siphero in the knee so he would say something polite, to which he grew cross-eyed.

"I thank you as well, Elder," Siphero said. "If it wasn't for your kindness and mercy, I believe I would never have been accepted into the village."

"No, no, no formalities," Jixve said to them both. "I grow tired of hearing them and want this to be a moment of celebration, not one of farewell." The rest of the villagers and guards started laughing, when Elder Jixve raised her hands into the air. They quieted down at her request for silence, and she continued her speech. First she turned to Awesha, who knelt before her, as the elder took a small amulet out of her satchel and held it before her. The amulet was shaped like two crescent moons held together by a single stone. It was carved out of a skimmer drake tooth and housed several brightly colored stones.

"You, Awesha," Jixve said to her directly, "look at you. You have grown so much since I have come to know you. I will never forget the moments when you came to me for wisdom and asked about the world outside our tiny village. You spent all your time wondering about the world below us, and now you lead a life free of restraints and laws. There is a spirit of freedom within you. Verrencae has chosen well. A daughter of exiles must adapt to a world constantly changing, as many hardships place themselves in your path. But you have someone to share them with. This is all you ever wanted in your life, child, someone to share your troubles…and joys with."

She raised the amulet and placed it around Awesha's neck as she rose, to the eruption of applause from all the citizens of Skyspire. "Awesha, Daughter of Exiles, stands before all who would welcome her into their midst. Would you all welcome her with open hearts, minds, and wings?"

"They shall remain open for all times and all days until this oath is broken by the ones with no love and respect," Querce said, speaking for all the villagers.

"Let all who speak this oath, repeat, for our Daughter of Exiles must be welcomed with open arms."

"Skyspire shall remain a place all exiles shall call home." The villagers said this with the greatest of fervor and erupted into thundering applause as Yevere roared, mirroring their enthusiasm. The cheering ended after a minute of applause and went silent as Elder Jixve turned to Siphero, who knelt down, doing as Awesha instructed.

"Siphero," she said, hugging the Terran adolescent to everyone's surprise and then releasing him, "my boy Siphero, my dear, dear boy." She stroked his cheek as a tear rolled down her own.

"Siphero," Jixve repeated, "you are such a sweet boy. After losing someone so precious to you as the one you called your father, you chose to start a new life with us, the Winged of Skyspire. After undergoing many a change, you have become a part of our family just as much as anyone else. I would even call you my grandson if I could."

"That means a…great deal to me," he said back to her. He started to cry a little as tears rolled down his cheeks, and then Awesha was trying to hide her tears, much to her own surprise.

"Enough crying, young man." Jixve snapped him out of it. "You need to act appropriately."

"Yes, ma'am," Siphero said, choking back the tears.

Elder Jixve removed a circular object from her pocket. She held it in her palm and raised it up for all to see. The object opened and revealed four directions, and Siphero realized it was a compass. It was brown and orange with a depiction of his airblade carved into it and a crystal that depicted him in a flash of images, working with and for the townsfolk in Skyspire.

"Siphero Antolus," Jixve said, "you are a Terran, the stranger from the strange world of Jormundgard, a place no Winged has ever ventured to. Yet the time you spent with us has shown me you do not need to come from Jormundgard or Stratis. You are one of us regardless of the world you once called home. Despite your age, you are a well-traveled, deeply experienced Terran who approached us with curiosity and kindness and an otherworldly desire to learn all he could about us. You may dislike fighting, but you understand the need to protect those who are precious to you. Preduvon, the Great Defiant, was a powerful and dangerous Wingless who used force to accomplish his goals, and he made many enemies on both sides of his cause. He may have chosen poorly with you, but I believe that many other Archons would realize you are an innovator, one capable of finding new solutions to old problems. The Great Defiant may have chosen you for his own reasons, or perhaps he wishes to learn from you rather than make you fight for his beliefs. Siphero Antolus, the Otherworlder, has come to us seeking a home, a purpose, and he has found it."

Jixve handed the compass to Siphero, who accepted it and placed it in his pocket. The village erupted in equally great applause as Jixve tested the resolve of the village. "The Otherworlder must brave new lands and new peoples in his constant search for experience and wisdom, and if he loses his way, what place can he return to for sanctuary and respite?"

Revaal was the first to speak. "The sanctuary that touches the heavens as a beacon of hope and new beginnings: Skyspire!"

"Then speak, all who see this Otherworlder, do you welcome and accept this Terran, this stranger of our brother world Jormundgard, into our fold?"

"The earth and skies shall remain open, and the gate shall close for our brother Siphero!" The villagers thundered an applause while Stager rose in the background, fists raised to the sky and wings outstretched as far as they could spread. Then the behemoth roared a clear and powerful roar, one of true joy.

"Venture forth into the world," Jixve said. "Siphero and Awesha, the two of you are the symbols of Skyspire. I bequeath to the two of you the titles of the Otherworlder and the Daughter of Exiles. Appear before the council of guardians not as a Winged and a Terran brought together by the bond but as equals in the eyes of Skyspire because that is how we see you, as linen cut from the same cloth, made stronger woven together."

They both rose, their bond causing the weapons of their Archons to appear before them, the shield and chain and the baton and staff, which then dematerialized into magical mist one moment later.

The crowd began clapping again. Siphero felt Awesha grapple him in a powerful hug, and then she kissed him. It had taken him by surprise, but he didn't fight her—he couldn't get out of the bear hug—and he actually had wondered why she had been biding her time. He kissed her back as the village applauded more and mirrored his surprise. Elder Jixve laughed and rolled her eyes at the two and quieted the crowd down.

"Are you two lovers done?" Jixve asked, with a mischievous smile.

Awesha let go of Siphero as he just stared at her, completely dumbfounded, while Stager caught him in one massive hand. He got back to his feet with Stager's help and felt his bond with Awesha become red hot, realizing Awesha's feelings were flowing into him. They had become quite close since he met her all those months ago, and for the first time they had become something more than friends; she had shared her first kiss with him.

As they separated, they climbed into their saddles while Greven and Querce spoke a few words with the elder. After they finished talking and had climbed onto their avisi, Greven and Querce took off first, followed by Awesha and Siphero on the backs of

Yevere and Stager. Pretty soon all Winged on the ground had taken off and were flying with Awesha and Siphero, waving and shaking hands as they offered gifts like wreaths of woven flowers and necklaces of feathers. They flew alongside them all until Greven and Querce went into a slipstream. Awesha and Siphero waved good-bye one last time as they flew off into the distance and flew into a slipstream, Awesha leading the way.

The two roared past Skyspire as they easily caught up to the others, who were in slipstream as well. They had practiced the slipstream a lot, and now the behemoth could maintain its pace with the others without overtaking them and, thanks to its stamina, it could stay in slipstream longer than a skimmer drake or an avisus could for an extended time period.

"Awesha," he spoke into his earpiece, "why did you kiss me?"

There was a long silence before she answered him back. "It was my way of saying to all the maidens in the village that you belong to me."

"Really? I didn't think anyone in Skyspire was interested in me. Plus, doesn't a bond pretty much mean I've been taken?"

"It does, but it is also a custom that those tied together in a bond do not need to become romantically involved. I watched many girls take a shine to you."

"Then thanks, Awesha," he said to her, "thanks for getting me out of that cauldron of heartbreak and romance."

"We'll talk later, Siphero," she said. "You and I are bonded. We have each other, and that is all that matters."

They continued in silence as they flew through the skies, the speed of the wind whistling through their ears.

Chapter 13: Freight

They flew for three days in and out of slipstream, allowing their mounts time to rest and eat at some of the neighboring skylands. Siphero and Awesha spent their nights talking about the formalities of the council as well as the party. Greven and Querce watched with fascination as their guardians in training learned more and more about the politics of the guardianship and its nuances. The two even began to share a mat on these nights, as they had grown accustomed to sleeping close to one another.

On the fourth day, they finally arrived, the empire of Strati Polis in their sights. A massive floating island the size of a small continent was a city of castles, walls, markets, and ship docks stretching across its entire length. They saw gigantic creatures flying through the skies at a crawl, massive animals the size of one floating island, but only a tenth of the size of the land mass that supported Strati Polis.

"Skywhales," Greven said, "they are the beasts of burden used throughout Stratis to ferry incredible loads of resources and finished goods. The Far Eastern Polis has an entire pod at its command."

"Are they docile animals?" Siphero asked. "They seem like they are in a great deal of pain."

"They are long-suffering," Greven said, "but they will only let their handler direct them. They are incredibly sensitive."

Siphero stared at one as they flew past it. Their skin was thick and coarse with a coloring of black to dark blue, with eyes the size of Siphero's airblade. On some of these creatures, buildings were placed upon what appeared to be massive saddles that were securely fastened to their backs. Siphero directed Stager to fly close to one that was still quite far from the Strati Polis. He flew right next to its massive eye, which looked right at him and blinked.

"Hey," a voice shouted to him from above the skywhale's eye. "Hey, are you done interrogating my skywhale?"

Siphero pulled up on Stager as he became eye level with the Winged who shouted at him. The fellow had no wings, a Wingless, but small puffs of steam shot out of his nose and ears at regular intervals. He wore trousers, a vest, and smoked a small pipe. He looked rather old and spoke through a few missing teeth, showing off his white beard and jade-colored eyes.

"Oh, sorry, sir," Siphero said, picking his words carefully as to not reveal who he really was. "I was just fascinated by your skywhale. I've never seen one up close before."

The Wingless softened his demeanor and smiled with pride. "You like old Corty? She's a tough old blubberer. I've been doing trade with her for several decades, and she never lets me down. Oh, sonny, what's your name?"

"I go by the name of Siphero. I'm here with my friends for the council of the guardians in the Strati Polis."

The handler whistled to himself and looked over Siphero's mount. "A strapping lad like yourself is going to be a guardian? You guys need a ride through the Rising Wind, right? Why don't you and your friends come aboard? Old Corty's taken a liking to ya."

"Really, how can you tell?"

He put his hand on the skywhale's side. "Put your hand on her side right above her eye. She'll tell you straight."

Siphero followed the old codger's directions and placed his hand on the side of the skywhale. He felt a loud vibration under his hand as it gently rumbled, and he looked at the skywhale's huge eye. The lid was half closed and her mouth had opened, producing a gurgling sound.

"She's only ever done that two other times: when she chose me as her handler and when she wanted to do supply work. The name's Losfodel. It's nice to meet you, Siphero. Now get your behemoth aboard and tell your friends too. They're welcome as well."

Awesha, Greven, and Querce came to a rest next to Siphero, staring at him in disbelief.

"What are you all staring at?" he asked. "We're still quite a ways from the Strati Polis, and our mounts are tired, so why don't we take him up on his offer?"

"Oh, that's not what surprised us," Querce said. "You made a friend out of a Wingless skywhale handler; the pure races in Strati Polis won't like this."

"Oh, to Jormundgard with what they think," Awesha said. "Siphero got us a ride to the capital, and I for one will not see this opportunity missed. He solved our issue with the Rising Wind." She and Siphero flew aboard the skywhale's saddled back, where rigging similar to that of a sky galleon was beneath them. As they touched down, the few deckhands looked at them, as one of the few behemoths they had ever seen was on their deck, as well as a skimmer drake and two avisi. Awesha, Siphero, Querce, and Greven dismounted and met with Losfodel, Corty's handler and captain.

"Welcome aboard old Corty," Losfodel said, spreading his hands in front of him. "You're all heading to Strati Polis, right?"

"That's our mission," Greven said, pulling out a small sack filled with several blue and red gems from his satchel. "We've brought with us an individual that will make those pure Avia bastards scream in shock. We will pay you for your discretion and safe transport to Strati Polis, if you will accept it."

The deckhands gathered around Losfodel as he sized them up, taking the sack and looking inside at the glittering gems. After a small chat with his boys, he held onto the bag with one hand and made eye contact with Greven.

"You have a deal, ya Avia bastard." He let loose a loud whoop, and his deckhands laughed at his comment. Losfodel tossed the sack to his first mate and walked up to Greven.

"I might have to charge you all double if you plan on keeping it a secret from me and my associates. Who is this special somebody, and what makes you think all those purebred bird shitters in their shit-colored castles will shit sapphires and rubies at seeing him and—is it him?"

He pointed to Siphero, watching as his wings unfolded from his back and then retracted. Greven looked to Siphero and Awesha, who both shrugged. Greven then went on to tell the old Wingless.

"Are you afraid of Terrans?" Greven asked in a whisper.

"Terrans? What has that got to do with anything?" He walked a small length of the deck and then back to Greven. "To answer straight, no, I'm not afraid of Terrans. I've never met one, and besides I'm more afraid of those pureblood bastards than I am of one…measly…Terran."

The gears in his brain began to turn as he connected one idea to another, and his eyes met those of Siphero, noticed how plain the boy looked, how something about him was different from the Winged surrounding him.

Then his smiled broadened. He couldn't stop smiling. His cheeks would have ripped apart if he continued, but he started to laugh as hard as he ever had.

"Boys," he said aloud, "we have ourselves a special guest today. The demon most of us learned about as whining babes is standing in our midst—we have a Terran aboard!"

His deckhands stopped what they were doing and ran up to Siphero, each one staring at him, grabbing at his hair or poking him in the face. Awesha took some offense to this, and she backed them away with a light push.

"Enough, boys, enough!" Losfodel called them off. "Get back to work, ya unwinged bastards. A Terran is on old Corty. I knew she saw something special in you," he said. "So a Terran is going into the Strati Polis, the greatest collection of cutthroat haters of the other races in all of Stratis, and a Terran is going to light this spark dust keg? I've been waiting for an opportunity like this for a long time."

"So we will have your silence then?" Greven wondered. "He is the first Terran to ever come to Stratis, and we want him to remain in one piece if at all possible."

"You've been honest with me. You didn't let your superiority define your actions and are asking me, a Wingless, for help. How can I refuse an opportunity to stick it to those motherless pureblood bastards? Of course I'll help, but I have one request."

"Which is?" Awesha said, with a hint of warning in her voice.

"You tell me all about Jormundgard," he said. "That's all."

"Can you give us a moment?" Awesha grabbed Siphero by the back of the neck and pulled him over to their mounts. Greven and Querce saw Awesha gesture for them to follow and they did so discreetly.

"This is a terrible idea," Awesha said in a loud whisper. "These men are a bunch of conniving Wingless backstabbers."

"They don't seem all that bad," Siphero said. "They aren't afraid of me, which is a good sign. If anything they seem downright curious."

"But is their curiosity the only fee?" Querce wondered.

"No matter," Greven said. "We need safe passage through the Rising Wind, and a skywhale is our best bet. They came when we needed a solution to our problem, so Awesha, be grateful to these Wingless. There are others among their number that would not let us aboard. Be thankful for Siphero because they are more interested in him than they are in throwing you overboard."

For the slow ride over to the Strati Polis, Siphero spent the better part of three hours answering the questions of the Wingless crew, trying some of their different imported teas, and getting treated to a free lunch. Awesha would fold her arms and look away from Siphero whenever he tried to make eye contact, but his conversation with the crew always made him break off his attempt to get her attention.

"So," Losfodel asked, "there is no real difference between all Terrans on Jormundgard? Does Terran society have a caste system like Stratis?"

"Well, yes and no," Siphero said. "Your place in society is determined by your value to a community based upon your skillset. Because Terrans fight in battles and skirmishes all the time, we are required to learn two of four disciplines: soldiering, engineering, piloting, and medicine. I've trained in engineering and piloting. That's what I chose out of the disciplines since I don't like to fight."

"I have a question, Siphero," a deckhand said. He had a limp in his step. "How would something like our profession compare in Jormundgard?"

"Let's see," Siphero began. "You guys basically do transportation of valuable and dangerous commodities, right?"

"Yep."

"And do you often get attacked up here in Stratis?"

"Not often, but it can happen; why? Is what we do a possible boon in Jormundgard?"

"Actually it is." Siphero smiled, and the crew matched his expression with smiles of their own. "Terran trade is one of the more dangerous professions because since my world is constantly at war with itself, our flying caravans need protection and brave freighter crews to man the freight dirigibles. It is a well-compensated profession, but only if those onboard have skills to match."

"Well, we're plenty brave," Losfodel said, "aren't we, boys?"

The crew cheered in response to their captain's challenge.

"There you have it."

They continued chatting like that for a couple more hours until Corty made a loud rumbling sound, making the avisi and Yevere a little uneasy, while Stager slept right through it as if nothing had happened.

"That's the call," Losfodel said. "Old Corty is about to cross the Rising Wind.
Everyone and everything aboard, brace yourselves!"

Losfodel's crew grabbed ahold of any rigging they could. Siphero, Awesha, Greven, and Querce got ahold of railings or ropes to tie themselves down. In another second, a powerful gust of wind, stronger than even the most powerful hurricane-force wind, swept across Corty's back as all aboard were buffeted by the Rising Wind. Cargo flapped around dangerously, and creaking sounds ran across the skywhale's whole back. Their ears popped.

This continued for at least a few more minutes until Corty crossed the Rising Wind and they were clear of the dangerous gusts.

The city itself had many massive stone structures with no protective walls, but palaces coated in gleaming colors of pearl, silver, or gold covered its vast landscape. There were academies for the military arts, economic arts and magical arts where young Winged trained for the future in their respective disciplines. As they surveyed the city, one massive palace stuck out before them, gleaming in a beautiful bronze color which made the other palaces more beautiful, but this building seemed more regal because it did not shine in amazing colors.

While Corty came to a stop near the piers which stuck out of freight docks on the outskirts of the Strati Polis, Losfodel lowered the ramp for his crew to unload the cargo. As his crew started to unload the cargo, a figure wearing a white robe and brushing shining blond hair came into view; Weeslon was walking through the docks accompanied by a small retinue of fifty Sky Knights.

"Do you know that idiot?" Losfodel asked. "He looks kind of stupid with all that blond hair."

"Unfortunately we do," Awesha said. "That is Weeslon, a Bond Scrivener. He was the one who tested my bond with Siphero."

"Ouch. How did it end?"

"We handed his ass to him." Siphero smirked.

Losfodel broke into laughter as he told his shipmates the short story of Siphero and Awesha's trial against the Bond Scrivener Weeslon. They too broke into laughter as Weeslon looked in the direction of Corty the skywhale, and then he noticed Siphero and Awesha were aboard. He whispered a few words to what appeared to be the captain of the Sky Knights, and he then whispered orders to his troops. They flew forward and took up position around the ramp to Corty's saddle deck while the crew continued to unload cargo.

Weeslon flew onto Corty's back and bowed with respect before Siphero and Awesha.

"Welcome Awesha and…Siphero," Weeslon said, a hit of disgust in his voice toward Siphero, "to the purest gleaming jewel of the Winged Empire, Strati Polis." He spread his arms before them and a minute later lowered them. "If you will please follow me, I will take you to the capital."

As they followed Weeslon and his guards, Siphero called out a question to him. "So has word gotten out that a Terran is coming to this big old birdhouse?"

Weeslon laughed at the birdhouse comment and answered, "I told no one of your arrival. I was sketchy about the details of two guardians from Skyspire."

"What do you mean by sketchy?" Greven asked.

"I simply said that a Compa was coming to Strati Polis. I didn't tell the council from what village or city you were born in though."

"I believe we owe you our thanks, Weeslon," Awesha said. "If it were not for your mischief, we might have gotten a different greeting group."

"Trust me, Awesha; they might know by now because of the behemoth flying down to the city."

They walked down the street and began moving into the outskirts of the polis, passing patrols of Winged bearing the standard of multiple crimson fists raised in unison. They spat at the feet of Siphero and knocked him to the ground. Awesha helped him up and decided to throw a rock at the back of their heads, but before she could, Greven and Querce stopped her.

"Awesha," Greven said, "let's not make things any worse for us. They might think it was Siphero who threw it."

Awesha gritted her teeth and dropped the rock. She floated the rest of the distance to catch up to them. Passing through a checkpoint, the guards bowed to Weeslon as he handed them a scroll and whispered to them while pointing at Siphero and Awesha. Again, one of them was about to spit at Siphero when his own bile blew back into his face.

"Who did that?" he said to their group. "One of you did that. Did you do it, excrement Compa?"

"I did it." Querce stepped forward. "If you spent half as much time doing your jobs as you did antagonizing the other castes, then maybe you could call yourselves actual Sangrians, and yet here you are being complete drake arses."

The anger in their eyes was rising, and one of them with a raised spear said, "Just because you are an Avia—"

"What is going on?" another Winged, one with wings that appeared to be made of fire, descended from the upper tiers and landed in front of them. He wore a long cloak over his back, triple woven drake mail on his chest, and the same went for his greaves and pauldrons.

The two guards, as well as Weeslon, immediately dropped to their knees, followed by Greven and Querce. Awesha realized who it was and forced Siphero to drop to one knee as well.

"Who is that guy?" Siphero asked, in a modicum of pain from Awesha forcing him to kneel.

"That," she said, pointing at the Winged with burning wings, "is an Engria. They are considered to be paragons of society. We are in the presence of Cortus, the military champion of the king and queen of Strati Polis."

"My lord," one of the guards said, "A dirty Compa has been nominated as a guardian of Skyspire, he cannot be allowed to enter the po—"

"You are denying guardians-to-be from entering the polis for the commencement! Such pitiful excuses for guards; all of you arise now."

Siphero, Awesha, Greven, Querce, and Weeslon rose to their feet while a small group of Sky Knights landed behind them.

"You, Bond Scrivener," Cortus said to Weeslon, "is what they say true? Are you escorting guardians into the polis?"

"Yes, Lord Cortus," he said, "I am…we were on our way when these rude gent—"

"It doesn't matter," Cortus interrupted, approaching Siphero and Awesha. "What are your names, guardians?"

Awesha stepped forward and bowed to Cortus. "I am Awesha, daughter of Recril, the Daughter of Exiles."

"And you, Compa?" Cortus said sternly.

Siphero gulped down a bit and looked at Awesha, who gave him the like-we-rehearsed look.

Stepping forward, Siphero saluted the six-foot-six-inch-tall Winged and said, "My name is Siphero, the Otherworlder, and I'm…a Compa."

Cortus was quiet for a few minutes as he inspected Siphero's armor and then his wings. He had never seen a Compa with metal wings before, let alone with one with metal everything on his wings. After what seemed like a small eternity, Cortus breathed a bit and turned his back to them, his fiery wings dying down.

"Men, call a carriage down for them," he said.

"But, sir, a Compa is with them. He can't—"

Cortus eyed them with a murderous glance and said, "They are guardians! Guardians! Anyone can be nominated to be a guardian. Do you have a problem with that!"

"No, sir," they said. "We will see to it, sir."

"Excellent," he said. "Once you're done, see to it that you never come back to this post again."

"Sir, please," one said. "I need this to feed my children."

"You're prejudiced; a member of the guard is above prejudice. You have shown you are incapable of manning your post proficiently. Now go!"

The two guards scrambled away in fear while a carriage bearing the crest of Strati Polis, two white wings surrounding a cross of roses with birds touching beaks around them. The white carriage was pulled by a team of four avisi wearing purple bonnets atop their heads beneath their harnesses. The door of it opened, and a steward beckoned Awesha to enter.

"If anyone else gives you trouble," Cortus said, "just mention me and tell them you have my permission to violate any and all rules established upon prejudice."

Cortus flew off into the sky, flanked by a large group of Sky Knights as the chaotic traffic lanes of the polis parted for their entry.

"This is where we part ways, Siphero, Awesha," Greven said. "We did our job and got you to the polis. You can take it from here."

"You're leaving us?" Awesha asked. "I thought you were welcomed, just like us."

"Actually," Weeslon corrected, "you and Siphero were given that honor; they were your honor guard."

"Do not worry about us, Awesha," Querce said. "The captain and I never dreamed we would see the capital polis with our own eyes in this lifetime."

Querce embraced Awesha like a sister would, while Greven talked with Siphero.

"You need to watch over her, Siphero," Greven warned. "Awesha is a child without a family. The only other person is her sister, Myrvah, and she is still at the Sky Polis, doing Archons knows what."

"What's her sister like?" Siphero asked.

Greven sighed heavily. "I don't know for certain. She and Awesha don't talk since they had a falling out. You should talk to her about it."

"And suffer her short fuse of a temper? No thanks!"

Awesha let go of Querce and asked Siphero, "What are you talking about, my bonded?"

"N-nothing," he said quickly.

The guards returned and approached Siphero and Awesha. "We will take your mounts to the royal stables," one said. "We apologize for our rudeness. It will not happen again."

Siphero approached the guards, who had lowered their heads, and stuck his hand out to them. "Don't worry about it. We'll get out of your way so that you can get back to your jobs." The guards looked up in surprise and nodded. They didn't expect to so readily be forgiven.

"Pleasant journeys to the two of you," one of the guards said.

Siphero waved good-bye as he and Awesha approached the carriage. The steward bowed as Awesha stepped in, but as soon as Siphero came, they shut the door in his face.

"Compa," the steward said, "are not allowed to ride in a carriage, even if they are to be guardians. You must fly to the palace yourself."

Awesha kicked the door open and stepped out.

Nerv appeared next to her and said, "My lady, we can't start an incident."

"I hate this," Awesha said. "Why is it so important for these race haters to keep us apart?"

"It is their way," Nerv said. "I don't like it either, but I have no choice since I am a Cherubim."

"It's OK," Siphero said. "I don't mind flying. Besides, I know a way around their rules."

As the steward closed the door and climbed into the carriage, he eyed Siphero with disgust. Siphero waited for the carriage to gain a little altitude, and in a quick motion, he took off and landed on top of the carriage.

"Get off, you defecating Compa!" The steward spewed a bunch of hateful words at Siphero, who had taken up residence on top of the carriage. "Get down from there or else I will call the Sky Knights."

"I'm not going anywhere," Siphero said. "I'm going with my bonded. That is, if she will join me on top?"

The steward looked to Awesha for help, as if asking if she would get rid of him. Awesha just smiled, opened the door, and joined Siphero on top as the carriage began flying through the high traffic of the Strati Polis dockyard.

The steward eventually gave up, while Nerv closed the door and spent the rest of the ride in abrupt silence.

The districts, plazas, and suburban landscapes were numerous and vibrant. Merchants were selling strange and exotic goods from all over Stratis, tradesman bartered for services rendered, scholars walked on the ground with Wingless carrying piles of books for them, and a large number of Sky Knights marched, flew, and patrolled the area for anything out of the ordinary. Many of them eyed Siphero and Awesha resting on top of a carriage but came to issue with it since they saw an Avia and a Compa sitting next to one another. A captain flew close to the carriage and addressed them.

"Pardon me, Your Grace," the captain said to Awesha, "but could you please remove that Compa scum from the carriage? He is violating the rules."

Awesha took issue with this. "I will not. He and I are guardians on our way to the palace of the king and queen. If you have issue with us, then you should take it up with Cortus."

The captain looked a little shocked and said, "Cortus…the Cortus? Please forgive me. I will tell my men not to bother you. And welcome to the Strati Polis, guardians. May the suns favor you."

He flew off without a second thought and left them on the carriage.

"He seemed like a nice guy," Siphero said absentmindedly.

Awesha rolled her eyes. She put her head on Siphero's shoulder, closed her eyes, and said, "Just shut up and be my pillow for a bit. I'm very tired."

They rode atop the carriage for nearly two hours, watching skywhales swim through the air above the polis. Street merchants flew up to them and tried to sell their wares at a discounted price, but Awesha chased them away with the threat of decapitation. She wasn't kidding; Siphero had to hold her back to prevent her from trying to smash their heads in with her baton. The same thing happened when beggars swarmed them, but Siphero reached into his pocket and took out some gold pieces, tossing them into the wind. The beggars left, chasing after the money and leaving them both alone.

The carriage driver eventually shouted to them, "We have reached the palace gates, guardians. Please disembark here. The palace guards will see you through."

Siphero and Awesha glided off the roof of the carriage, and Nerv disappeared into a puff of smoke inside it. As they gathered their knapsacks and equipment, Cortus arrived at the gate and waved them over.

"Welcome, Siphero, Awesha, to the Halls of Rulers," Cortus said, "the home of the king and the queen." They looked around to see that Greven and Querce were with them as well as their mounts. The palace itself had many ornately carved statues and several stained-glass windows in the shape of two Winged in different poses. The gates were lavishly decorated in flowers and jewels.

Large birds rested on the roosts overlooking the walls, watching for any intruders, as the gates opened for Siphero and Awesha.

Cortus reassured them. "As guardians you are given the highest honor to protect the polis you hail from, and so none are allowed to question your authority."

Awesha and Siphero looked at one another as Cortus flew toward the palace and Stager and Yevere were led to some stables.

"Please come this way," Cortus said. "Their majesties are not to be kept waiting." He led them into the palace, although after he let Siphero and Awesha pet their mounts good-bye.

They followed him through two massive doors that dissolved and then solidified as they passed through them. Inside the palace Winged servants and their Cherubim were flying around, carrying decorations, food, and clothing materials. They passed a bunch of other Avia wearing ball gowns and suits of a variety of colors, their hair decorated with jewels and flowers, medals on the men and birds resting on their shoulders. The women fanned themselves repeatedly while the men chatted them up, but they all stopped as they eyed with jealously and disgust at Siphero and Awesha and their wings. Cortus gave them a piercing look, and they returned to their conversations, whispering disgust at the appearance of a Compa.

"Do not mind them," Cortus said. "They have no respect for anyone except Avia appointed to the guardianship."

"If all they do is gossip and make people feel inadequate about how they were born," Siphero said, "then they should spend a day or so in this polis's slums. They might learn something then."

Cortus snorted at Siphero's comment. "I am in full agreement, Otherworlder. They were born into this lifestyle, with the world handed to them. They do not know what it is like to fight every day for the right to exist. I learned this, and I still get their distasteful stares."

"So then how did you become an Engria?" Awesha asked. "What were you before all of this?"

Cortus looked back and said, "I was an Avia like them. I had black wings. I was a lieutenant in the Sky Knights when the previous Engria of the king and queen of the polis died in a duel with a Sangrian. The damned race hater had no mercy for the old Engria, and so I killed that hatred-riddled avisus shit in his sleep."

"I'm sure you had good reasons for killing him," Siphero said solemnly. "You don't have to tell us if you don't want to."

Cortus stopped before two doors and turned to them both. "I feel like I should tell you. The Engria before me was an old friend, and I didn't realize until after I had killed the Sangrian that he had gifted with me his powers as an Engria. My wings erupted in fire and burned off my back, only to be replaced by wings of fire, the ones you see me with now."

"Well spoken, Cortus," a new voice said. A Winged with three pairs of white and black wings appeared before them, clothed in royal garbs of silk and golden fabrics, a crown of bronze atop his head. The being floated before them and came through the double doors, causing Cortus to sink to the ground in a humble bow.

"My lord, please, do not surprise us like that," Cortus said apologetically.

"Arise, Cortus," the king said. "I am not the king for the moment. I am without my chair of worthless respect."

Cortus rose at the command and held his hand to Awesha and Siphero as they went to mimic Cortus's movements, but the king stopped them with a raised hand.

"Please, my friends, do not bow," he said in a relaxed tone. "You are my guests and newly appointed guardians. Now, what are your names?"

"My name is Awesha," she answered. "I am known as the Daughter of Exiles."

"And I am Siphero. I'm called the Otherworlder."

The king nodded with respect to them both. "I welcome you both, Siphero and Awesha, to Strati Polis, reeking splendor."

"Uh, thanks?" Siphero did not know what to make of a king who welcomed strangers as honored guests, but he actually liked this king. Any ruler who said a throne was a chair must think being king is just a big joke.

"Your Majesty," Cortus politely interrupted, "the new guardians are very tired, and I am sure they would like to rest before the grand ball tomorrow, so…"

"Oh, of course, Cortus." The king laughed. "Thank you for reminding me. Please take them to their rooms."

The king flew off, accompanied by a group of Sky Knights who eyed Siphero with a mix of forced respect and disallowed disgust. Cortus eyed them with a warning as they passed and returned to Awesha and Siphero's attention.

"I apologize for my king's behavior," Cortus said. "He does like meeting new peoples and getting to know them, but the appearance of the first Compa guardian made him especially excited today."

"I think you're lucky to have someone like him in charge," Siphero said. "A king who doesn't have fun at what he does won't last long in the role." He put his hands in his pockets and looked in the direction the king had flown. "Believe me; those in power fall from it every day if they abuse it. And one more thing: I'm not so good with parties, especially with all those eyes staring at me."

Cortus stared at Siphero suspiciously. "You do not wish to attend the ball? The king would take it as an insult if you did not come."

Awesha stepped in before Siphero could speak. "We will come, but with your permission, we will only stay for the main ceremony."

Cortus scratched his chin for a moment and then nodded. "May I ask why you are this way about coming to an honored gathering?"

Awesha looked at Siphero, and he searched his mind to organize his thoughts the best possible way without revealing his true identity.

"When I was being educated," he began, "I was bullied a lot at my academy...they humiliated me because I was a pacifist."

Siphero and Awesha looked to Cortus and worried if that would be enough to convince the former Sky Knight. Cortus surprised them by saying, "I understand, Guardian Siphero. As a Compa I'm sure you have suffered enough."

"Please just call me Siphero." He extended his hand to Cortus, who shook it uneasily. "And thank you for understanding."

"You are welcome. Now follow me; I am sure you are tired from your long journey." He led them down a few more halls adorned with large chandeliers, past more servants and Cherubim assisting them, and up a few flights of stairs to a set of rooms. One of the doors was a rustic metal color with burn marks on its surface while the other appeared to be made of feathers with a rainbow pattern embroidered across its entire surface.

"Hey, what's with these doors?" Siphero asked Cortus. "Why does one look like a burned sheet of metal while Awesha's looks like a rainbow?"

"Oh, that. This palace is the ancestral home of every king and queen who have ever ruled over Stratis, and it has housed generations of guardians. Because so many different Winged have come through these halls, even Wingless, the rooms themselves formed a strange psychic connection with those who are meant to stay in them. I have never seen this happen for a Compa before; then again, I have never known a Compa to wield such a unique affinity like you do, Siphero."

He smiled at the fact that his room resembled his machine shop back in the Edge, complete with hammock and invention designs posted across the wall. Awesha saw that her room resembled hers back home in Skyspire, but she was even happier to see that Nerv was waiting for her in the room, wearing his familiar top hat/black-and-white robe combo.

Cortus then said, "The king has given both of you permission to roam the halls at your own discretion, but please try not to bother his majesty or the queen, as they are attending to important matters in preparation for the grand ball to welcome the other guardians."

"The other guardians are already here?" Awesha asked.

"Most of them." Cortus nodded. "You two are the second to last to arrive. Also, make sure you have the proper attire for the ball. The both of you must make a good impression on the other guardians and His Majesty's guests. I will be there, of course, so I expect nothing but the best from guardians-to-be."

"Uh, one problem," Siphero said. "I don't have any formal attire."

Cortus laughed and said, "The ball allows for warriors such as the two of you to wear armor or some sort of battle vestige. I myself don't care for the elegant silks, fabrics and finery our nobles employ in their dress."

"I certainly do!" Siphero exclaimed as he pointed to his armor.

"That will do. Just ask your Cherubim to polish it for the ball tonight so you will be prepared. Other than that, I wish the two of you a wonderful night and hope you enjoy the ball tomorrow. If you need anything, do not hesitate to ask one of the servants. They will try to accommodate your requests."

As Cortus left them to rest, Siphero and Awesha looked at each other and sighed with relief from their long journey. They smiled and held hands as they sat outside their rooms, folded their wings around themselves, and relaxed. Servants flew past, ignoring their indecent gestures, thinking they were not in their right minds. They stayed that way for a few more minutes, then they got up and looked at their rooms.

"We're here, Siphero," Awesha said. "We're here and we're together now."

"We certainly are," he answered. "Well enough relaxing, let's check this place out." He got to his feet and was about to walk off when he saw Awesha standing outside her door.

"If it's all right with you, Siphero, I think we should get some rest now." She went into her room, and Siphero was pretty sure she smiled in a way he hadn't seen before. He shrugged his shoulders and looked out the window to see the sun was setting pretty fast. Opening the door to his room, he decided it was a good time to get some rest. It would be a long day tomorrow anyway.

Taking off his armor and placing it on a mannequin, Siphero looked around the room and saw many things were like his old room. There was a workbench, his hammock, a weapons rack with no weapons on it, and pictures of him and his Pops. A tear came to his eyes, and he wiped it away. He had to be strong for Pops; that's what he would have wanted.

Looking at his designs, Siphero rummaged through his knapsack for his tools and some scrap metal but had no metal to speak of. Scratching his head, Siphero thought back to what Cortus had said about the servants. He opened his door and waited for one to show up. From around a corner a short Wingless appeared with a polished saddle and reins in her arms. She had turquoise colored hair, violet eyes, and some bleeding cuts on her arms and legs. It appeared she was floating on air because she traveled the hallways rather quickly, heading to some particular destination. She wore pant-like overalls with holes and messily stitched seams which were coming undone.

"Excuse me," Siphero asked. "Do you think you could help—"

As he was speaking, the Wingless looked in his direction and collided with the wall, dropping the saddle and reins on the marble floor. Siphero ran over to her to help her up. She blinked a few times. She was half conscious.

"Hey, are you OK?" Siphero said. "You took a nasty tumble there, what with your face colliding with the wall."

The girl regained consciousness and stared up at Siphero as he smiled back. Panic taking hold of her, she made herself into a ball and lowered her head to the floor.

"I'm sorry, my lord. I ruined the saddle. Please do not punish me!"

Siphero looked shocked at this statement and said, shaking his hands, "Whoa, whoa, whoa, take it easy. I'm not going to punish anyone, and I should be apologizing. It's my fault that you ran into that wall."

Slowly, the girl looked up at Siphero and his wings, realizing that he was a Compa. "You're...you're not going to hurt me?"

"Wouldn't dream of it, besides I like Wingless. I sympathize with people like you."

She seemed to perk up a bit and asked, "O-O-Ok, what do you need, sir?"

"I was wondering where I could get some scrap or sheet metal."

"Scrap metal...there's some in the stables. If you wait a few moments, I can get you what you need."

"Sure," he said, "take all the time you need. I'm not going anywhere. After all, I'm not becoming a guardian for nothing."

Her face lit up at the mention of that word. "You...you've been named as a guardian? A Compa has never been named to the position of a guardian. You're the first to ever receive such an honor!"

"Really? Huh, you learn something new every day here," Siphero said, but he didn't notice that his new friend disappeared with the saddle and reins down the hallway. He decided to wait for her to come back. He didn't have anything else to do except sleep, but he was too excited to sleep. He was in Winged central.

After waiting for what seemed like half an hour, he passed the time by watching his wings fold and unfold from his back. The girl came back with two others like her, with eager smiles on their faces. They too had no wings, but Siphero didn't care about that. He was staring at their hands, filled with small pieces of scrap metal of varying lengths from a few inches to two feet. He admired their commitment to helping him as he inspected the metal, taking whichever ones would work best for his little project.

"Thank you, all of you," Siphero said to them, gathering up the pieces of metal he had chosen. "This is really going to help me in the long run."

"You are most welcome," the girl said as she and her assistants bowed to excuse themselves. "Please let us know if there is anything else we can help you with."

Siphero nodded to them, carried the scraps back to his room, and shut the doors. Laying them on the work table, he rummaged in his satchels for his welding equipment, hammers, metal saws, and mana batteries. He was going to be up late working on his project.

By the time Siphero finished his project, it was nearly dawn. He yawned heavily as he put away his equipment and came back to admire his handiwork. On his workbench, standing no taller than a foot, gears turning in its stomach, small green lights for eyes and two wide wings a foot long each, was his finished little project, the drird. It was like the automen back home, but it was the first of its kind: a bird that was mechanical from the ground up. It looked up at him, preened its metal feathers, made a chirping sound that sounded like grinding gears, and unfolded its wings in front of him as if to stretch.

"OK, let's see if you work," Siphero said, outstretching his left arm, equipped with a steel gauntlet. The drird chirped again, lifted its wings, and took off from the tabletop. It flapped a few times and landed on his arm, the talons digging into the gauntlet, causing Siphero to wince in pain a little bit.

"Talons…a little tight," he said. "I'll fix that…right…now."

He took a screwdriver and adjusted the talons only slightly. The drird loosened its grip a bit and rested comfortably on his arm.

A knock came from his door. Siphero made sure his tools and equipment were safely hidden away, as he was trying to maintain a hidden identity and he didn't need to ruin it for himself or Awesha.

As he went to answer the door, the drird moved to his shoulder and went to preening its feathers. Upon answering the door, he looked outside to see Cortus and a contingent of guards behind him.

"Uh, sorry about the noise?" Siphero said apologetically.

"All that noise," Cortus said, "that was you? Do you know how many people you've kept awake with the ruckus you made?"

"Uh, no not really."

Cortus forcefully opened the door and came into the room, his guards streaming in behind him. They looked around the room and saw how Siphero lived. Some of them found it appalling, and yet others were taken in by its homely feeling.

"You…" Cortus began, "you don't live like most Winged."

"Listen, I'm sorry about the noise I was making. I just started working on a project, and I lost track of the time and had to finish it. I made this; I call it a drird."

They then all looked at the little creature on Siphero's shoulder. Most of them had no idea what it was until one of the guards used his affinity to hurl a rock at it. The drird raised its wings and hissed loudly at him.

"Hey, don't antagonize it," Siphero warned. "It's just like a regular bird, only this one is made of metal."

"I've never seen one like it before," Cortus said, "Did you make it?"

"Yes, I did."

"Huh, OK then," Cortus said, leaving the room. "By the way, don't make any more of those loud sounds, understood?"

Siphero nodded and Cortus left, his guards growling at him while the one guard threw another rock at the drird. This time the drird took off from Siphero's shoulder and began scratching at the guards exposed shoulder, the talons going straight through the chainmail. It then returned to Siphero's shoulder and hissed again.

Cortus called for his man to come while he gave Siphero the evil eye. Siphero waved good-bye and closed the door behind him, sighing heavily to himself. He had dodged another bullet somehow. Seeing that it was already dawn, he decided to check on Awesha to see if she was up and about.

When Siphero knocked on her door, Nerv opened it to speak to him. "Hello, Master Siphero, how are you this fine morning?"

"I'm great, Nerv," Siphero said. "Is Awesha up? I was wondering if she wanted to explore the castle with me."

Nerv sighed a bit and looked into the room. "Lady Awesha is still sleeping, and apparently she didn't sleep very well last night."

A loud thump came from inside the room, then what appeared to be a sword stuck out of the door. Nerv was gone for a minute before he returned to converse with Siphero.

"Is everything all right in there?" Siphero asked, "It sounds like a warzone."

"Don't worry, Siphero; everything is fine. My lady gets a little cranky when she hasn't gotten enough sleep, and she usually starts…dueling…when she is half asleep."

Siphero slowly backed away from the door and decided now was not a good time to talk to Awesha. He'd come back when she was in better spirits and less murdery. He said good-bye to Nerv and went to roam the halls of the palace on his own.

Running through the rooms and chambers revealed a great deal about the architecture to him. Many of the halls were at least fifty feet tall; a Golem could fit through with no trouble at all. The ceilings in the hallways were mostly open to allow Winged to fly in and out whenever they needed to go outside. Stairwells seemed to repel his feet when he stepped on them, causing Siphero to float down them or up with relative ease.

The morning hours of the palace made it a regular mad house, as he saw Cherubim rushing through the air at what appeared to be the speed of sound and Winged servants ferrying morning meals of rich meat and delicious fruits to their respective recipients as a chorus of impatient bells rang for them to come. Siphero saw the guards of the palace going about their business, training in an outdoor royal sparring ring, visiting the stables, and patrolling the grounds. Oddly he even saw a group of guards wearing an insignia of bloodied fists walking through the courtyard, and they seemed to be escorting someone that had a…tail? It didn't make sense to Siphero, so he made a mental note and moved on.

Siphero felt a tap on his left shoulder where the drird was, and the drird hissed loudly at the person who touched him.

"Well, that's no way to greet a friend," a familiar voice said.

Siphero turned and looked down to see a smiling Nylf staring up at him.

"Nylf, good morning," he said, with a polite bow. "I didn't expect to run into you here. Did you get in trouble last night at all?"

"No, I didn't," she said. "And thank you for your kindness. Wingless don't get a lot of gratitude for what we do around here. The purebloods consider us no better than avisi dung, and they often tell us to our faces."

Siphero gritted his teeth in disgust. "Why? What makes them think they are entitled to do this?"

"That is how society has been for a couple centuries, but I am lucky," she said, grinning. "The king and queen of the polis have been pushing for equal treatment of lower castes, but the Sangria Legion has shown they want no reform. The Grand Clerician says there is no discrimination when she allows it to happen with her permission."

They heard broken glass ring through the hallway as they looked over to see a noble was harassing a Wingless boy as he tried to pick up the broken pieces of a plate, only to have his hands stepped on and blue blood to trickle onto the floor. The sun had risen enough over the walls, and the light hitting the stained-glass windows cast a rainbow-like hue throughout the hallways.

"Just like that," Nylf said. "They always do this to us. They never...hey, Siphero, where are you going?"

Siphero ran as fast as he could to where the Wingless boy was. The noble hurting the child had two large white wings and wore a long sapphire ball gown, and there was a rather large bird resting on her left arm. It was twice the size of Siphero's drird and covered in blue feathers.

"Hey," Siphero said to the noblewoman, "the kid doesn't deserve that. Piss off."

The noble turned and faced Siphero, her face young and innocent. Siphero guessed she was in her late teens. He knew from speaking with Awesha that the life expectancy of a Winged was higher than a Terran's by at least fifty years.

"How dare you speak to me this way," she said in a pout of disgust. "Such a drab mongrel like you has no right to speak to me that way, especially one of your miserable dress and manner."

The bird on her arm squawked and took off from its perch, flying away from her. It had smelled Siphero's drird, and it was a foreign scent, which scared it.

"Oh, I'm sorry," Siphero said sarcastically. "Let me rephrase: would you most humbly piss off!"

"How dare you! How dare you!"

"Can you say anything other than 'how dare you,' or is your corset too tight?" Siphero snickered. "It must be preventing your ego from deflating due to all the air in your stupid head."

That seemed to do it. The young noble girl floated across the marble floor in a swift movement and raised her hand to slap Siphero across the face. Her hand contacted Siphero's face, but Siphero just laughed. He didn't feel a thing.

"Is that all you got? You really are a pathetic little noble, aren't you? Why don't you follow your bird. Fly away, little bird, fly away."

Siphero crossed his palms, with his thumbs touching, and flapped his fingers, imitating a bird's wings.

The girl flew away with tears in her eyes, leaving the Wingless boy alone as Nylf rushed over, wrapped his hand with some torn cloth, and helped him up.

"Now you've done it," Nylf said. "You just insulted the daughter of the Romaria family. They are a powerful family in the Polis, and you may receive a challenge of a duel from her brother. He is a skilled duelist and archer."

"Hey, it's not my fault," Siphero said innocently. "She needed to be taught a lesson. A spoiled brat is a spoiled brat."

Nylf laughed aloud and so did the boy, and they all looked around to see that some palace guards had been watching them. They noticed the guards were laughing, as if what happened provided them with entertainment.

"What are you looking at?" Nylf shouted. "Get your worthless hides in gear. Piss off, if you will!"

She said those last words with gusto. Repeating the phrase Siphero said felt especially good. The guards left, knowing full well how the king or queen did not like them slacking on the job.

"You might want to remove yourself from this place," Nylf said to Siphero. "That Romaria whelp might return soon with her family in tow. I won't say anything of what has happened."

Siphero nodded, but before he could go, the boy tugged at his arm and bowed his head. Through pained breaths the boy said, "Th-han-k y-ou."

Nylf flew through the air with her affinity, leaving Siphero alone in the hallway. Then his drird took off from his shoulder and flew through a large open window and down into a vast garden. Siphero called after it, but it didn't listen to his orders, which forced him to jump out the window and glide down four stories of palace to a magnificent garden filled with flowers of many shapes, sizes, and qualities of mana. There were even trees, about fifty or so, standing between twenty and forty feet tall. Siphero saw keepers tending to the many plants and trees, even encouraging bushes and hedges to grow into different shapes, some of which resembled the king and what appeared to be the queen of the polis. Siphero found the drird hanging around a large garden.

"I'm going to have to come up with a name for you ya malfunctioning moron," Siphero said to the bird. "Since you're made out of good quality iron and argon, I'll call you Airon."

The drird squawked at him, obviously annoyed, but the name stuck. Siphero held out his arm and Airon flew to his shoulder instead, its talons clamping down on his shoulder.

"Ow," Siphero winced from the pain. "Still too tight."

With Airon on his shoulder, Siphero went to explore the new garden only to come across a magnificent collection of flowers that shocked him. They shouldn't have been in such a healthy and lush garden. There he saw ruster petals, flowers he had seen as a child across the battlefields of Jormundgard, growing from the husks of destroyed and rusting Terran war machines. It was a flower the deep shade of the color rust, had petals that stuck out in all directions of the sun, and smelled like boiling metal. While he observed the flower, he was skeptical about how this flower had come to grow in such a garden, but his question was halted when he heard sobbing coming from a little floating gazebo.

A girl that was a couple years younger than him was sitting on a bench holding a flower in her hands, crying. Her wings were the color of silk with patches of white feathers sticking out, and her hair reached past her wings. Her face was cut and scarred, but her red eyes were quite beautiful despite the cuts. She wore a blue gown that stretched down to her feet, where heeled sandals stuck out. The most striking detail Siphero saw was that her ears were pointed in two directions, north and south.

He quietly approached her until he accidently stepped on a branch and alerted her to his position, but she made no attempt to leave. She just held her gaze for a few minutes and went back to crying. Siphero came closer until he was at the base of the gazebo and looked up to the girl. Airon squawked loudly at her, but even his guttural cry did not pique her interest.

"Are you OK?" Siphero asked sympathetically.

"Go away," the girl said.

"Oh, sorry, I just saw you crying there, and I wondered if you were hurt." He paused to see she was still crying, and resumed. "You are hurt, aren't you?"

He flew up to the gazebo and hung on one of the poles, waiting for the girl to notice him. She stopped crying long enough to repeat herself. "Go away!"

"You don't seem like you want to be alone."

After a short silence, the girl stopped crying and moved over on the bench, allowing Siphero to sit down.

"Is everything all right?" he asked again. "I know I said that before, but—"

"My lover will die," she blurted out. "He will die, and it's all my fault."

"Whoa, OK, didn't expect that to come out." He picked a better position and relaxed as he listened to her. "I won't talk. I'll just listen."

She met his eyes, and her gaze grew serious. "I cannot tell my secret to a stranger. How do I know I can trust you?"

"Well, you don't, but is there anyone else around you can talk to, other than Airon?" He raised his hands and pointed to the entire garden.

"Who is Airon?"

The drird hissed at her and made his presence clear.

"That's Airon," Siphero said, with a chuckle.

"Then at least show me yourself. Chant your affinity." She held out her hand and spoke the words of her affinity, and a bright light flickered in her hand and disappeared as soon as she finished.

"Yeah, well," he said, "my affinity is a little tricky."

"Show me your affinity," she repeated forcefully.

"OK, OK, but don't blame me if something goes wrong." He held out his hand and spoke the words of his affinity. Then with a crunch, a sword at least three feet long embedded itself in the gazebo pillar behind them and startled her, but not Siphero.

"Are you trying to kill me? Do you know who I am?" She rose and attempted to slap Siphero across the face.

However, Siphero caught her hand before she struck him and let it go as soon as she struggled. "I did warn you, didn't I? Anyway, that is my affinity, metal."

As he said that, his wings shone in the sun, revealing their nature to the girl, and she backed away in shock. "You...you are a Compa, are you not?"

"You're only half right there," Siphero said, getting up from the bench and placing his hand on his heart. "My name is Siphero, a guardian-to-be from Skyspire. I am known as the Otherworlder."

"Ah, a guardian." She smiled with joy. "Please, can you help me with my troubles?"

"Uh, sure, but why the sudden change from hostility?"

"I can trust a guardian, even a Compa for that matter. You are bound by law to obey the king and queen, and even the princess, of Strati Polis."

"A princess!" Siphero exclaimed. "You're a freakin' princess?"

The girl stretched her wings and took the folds of her dress as she curtsied to Siphero. "I am Ieava xin Roncresta, the princess of the king and queen of Strati Polis."

Now Siphero was the one who was surprised. "You're the princess, wow. I didn't think I would ever meet one in my lifetime."

"Stop loafing around and follow me, Siphero. That's an order." She took flight as she headed north through the garden, with Siphero hot on her tail. Airon flew behind him and tried to keep up as best it could.

"Where are we going?" he asked her.

"I need your help to rescue my lover," she said desperately. "He is a Sila who was taken away by the Sangria Legion and one of their agents. They took him to the dungeons to cage him like a wild beast."

"I think I saw them earlier this morning. He was definitely being dragged somewhere by ten or so Sangria Legion," he said as they rounded corner after corner, heading into the lower levels of the palace.

Ieava was silent for a moment before she replied. "The Sangria Legion believe they have the right to do whatever they want, even punish someone because they are different." She let slip a tear, which hit Siphero's forehead and dissolved. They flew down some stone steps as they exited the garden and headed toward the basement entrance to the palace and the location of the dungeons. The passageways were lit by torches of green and emerald colors, illuminating their flight down the dark corridors. As they went further in, the torches began to change colors from green to brown to orange and finally to red. They passed multiple cells with Wingless, Compa, and some perfectly deranged individuals clawing at the cell doors.

"So this guy you call your lover, are you bonded to one another?" They were getting closer to the dungeon, but then Ieava stopped abruptly and stood behind a corner. There were five guards standing around in front of a prison cell where two clawed hands held the bars and shook them multiple times.

"That's him, Guardian Siphero." She pointed to the cell. "He is there, and I sense the Sangrian agent is close by." She paused and checked the room with a spell that allowed her to see the room from the vantage point of the torches in the dungeon.

"Yes," she said, in answer his previous question, "yes, Guardian Siphero, he and I formed the bond this morning when he confessed his love for me."

"Well then, that's all we need. Let's get him out." Siphero held out his hand, remembering the feeling of manipulating the metal as he pulled the weapons out of the guards' hands and then used their armor against them, causing the four guards to bump into one another and knock themselves out before they knew what was happening. The first four were taken out easily, but the last one was able raise the alarm. Then a blinding light caught his eyes. Siphero looked to see that Ieava had given him an opportunity, so Siphero knocked out the distracted guard with a hard blow to the back of the head. Over the next few minutes, Siphero bent the metal and bound the guards and their wings together and put gags on them. As he finished, he called Ieava out from behind cover. As she rushed for the cell, she met the gaze of her lover, and they grasped hands and cried tears of joy.

"Ieava, my love," the Sila said through the bars. There was a slight purr of happiness in his voice. "What are you doing here?"

"I came to get you. I was so worried about you," she said, tears rolling down her cheeks.

"What do you think you are doing here?" a sadistic voice said. A well-dressed, fiery-red-haired nobleman about four years older than Ieava came out from around a corner, spinning a key ring around one of his fingers.

"Mervieris," Ieava said, "please let him go. He hasn't done anything wrong."

"Don't you know anything?" he said, with cold-hearted charm. "That damned Sila hissed at me. He should have minded his manners and pissed on a tree. And you bonded with him. The Grand Clerician will never approve of this union. Your family will be beside themselves with shame, and you will make enemies with the Sangria Legion." He pulled a dagger out of a sheath behind his back.

"I won't let you jeopardize your family's future." He returned it to its sheath. "Now out of my way, you wretched Compa. You shall not bar my path."

Siphero stood defiantly in Mervieris's way. As his shadow rose up behind him and manifested in the form of Preduvon, Mervieris looked at the form and backed away in fear.

"What...what kind of monstrosity are you? Stay back! Stay away from me!" Mervieris fell back on his wings as he backed away desperately, clawing to escape until a length of chain wrapped around his legs and pulled him back.

"You should be scared, little Avia." Siphero spoke in a voice that was not his own. "The hatred of millions lies behind my words. Be afraid for your very life, and pray to your false idols that you never see me again."

The Preduvon-possessed Siphero pulled Mervieris all the way back, and the noble shrieked in fear as he looked into Siphero's eyes. Then the fear melted from him, and Siphero's eyes told him just to stop, stop the hatred and intolerance; it was enough. Oddly, Mervieris understood the gesture and reluctantly handed the key ring to Siphero and got up, his expression cool, collected, and a bit surprised as he walked off and left them in the dungeon.

I would have made him beg for death's sweet release.
Preduvon's voice echoed to Siphero. The shadow sank behind him until only the light of the torches illuminated the dungeon.

Siphero turned to Ieava as he threw her the keys and waited for her to open the cell. The cell swung open, and a black-haired, silver-skinned Sila with bat-like wings exited the cage. His eyes were yellow and feral, dagger teeth revealed themselves in his smile, and clawed feet anchored his body to the rocky floor.

Ieava hugged and kissed the Sila as he kept his gaze on Siphero, the chain and the shield in his hands. Then he embraced his lover and cried loudly, growling from deep within his throat. The weapons in Siphero's hands dissolved into the air as he moved toward them, patiently waiting for them to acknowledge him.

They let go as the Sila and Ieava faced Siphero. The Sila glared at Siphero cautiously, sniffing the air around him. When he was satisfied, he knelt down to Siphero and spoke.

"Thank you, stranger, for your coming," he said. "My name is Tratiki, chosen guardian of the Sila. I am the Tireless Hunter."

Tratiki rose and held hands with Ieava. "You have done the Sila a great honor. You can be counted as one of us. May I know your name?"

"Certainly," he said, "my name is Siphero Antolus, I am a—"

"A guardian like myself," Tratiki said.

"Heh, you catch on quick," he said, surprised.

"Your scent," Tratiki said, "you do not smell like the rest of the Avia in this palace. You smell of metal and fire. I've never met anyone whose scent was so…"

"Remarkable?" Ieava chimed in curiously. One of Tratiki's large arms rested over her shoulders.

"I would say pungent," Tratiki said. "He smells like a burning forge."

"Uh, thanks, I had a bath two days ago. I'm not that smelly."

Ieava let out a small giggle but covered her mouth to hide her amusement.

"Follow us," she said. "I will tell my father of what has happened here. You have done me a great service, Otherworlder. I will see to it you are rewarded for your troubles."

"There's no need," Siphero said. The drid on his shoulder chirped loudly. Siphero looked at his wrist and saw it was already five. The ball would be starting in about two hours. "I have to go. I need to get ready for the ball. I only have two hours to…what are you doing?" Tratiki was inspecting his timekeeper, sniffing it a bit.

"Tratiki, that's rude." Ieava smacked him on the back of the head.

"Sorry, dear, I was just curious."

Then a loud humming reverberated throughout the dungeon and the entire building. Ieava and Tratiki looked at each other, panic taking over.

"What the hell was that?" Siphero said aloud.

"It is the fifth hour," Ieava said. "I'm sorry, Siphero but we have to go. We must get ready for the ball tonight."

"Heh, OK, see you later." The room became quiet as Siphero turned and found they had disappeared.

"OK." Siphero did a recap, while the drird on his shoulder continued to stay at rest. "I saw a Jormundgard flower, helped a princess, reunited a few lovers, stopped a religious fanatic, and now said lovers have vanished on me…that's a good day."

Since he still had two hours, Siphero decided to go and see Stager and Yevere in the stables. He flew and/or ran out of the dungeon and back into the vast garden, asking for directions from servants or Keepers of the Wood, who gave him directions to the royal stables.

Once he happened upon the place where the stables were, he noticed an open stadium where Winged soldiers were training through flight, magic, and sword clashes on the backs of avisi. He only looked for a few minutes and noted a rather large and elderly Winged among them was swinging a harpoon around. He seemed very skilled with such a weapon. Smiling to himself, Siphero saluted the old warrior from a distance and headed toward the stables.

Inside the stables, he saw many different breeds of avisi and skimmer drakes making noise, eating, shitting, or getting prepped for riding. He easily found Stager; the only behemoth in the whole bunch couldn't fit into any of the stalls, so they left him in an open pen happily munching on small piles of meat, fruit, and grain while demonstrating his mental dexterity by smearing the fruit into paste and using the juices to paint on the walls.

"Hey, Stager," Siphero called to him. "Stager, how you doing?"

As soon as Stager heard his voice, he turned around and lumbered forward with massive strides, startling the other animals in the stables. He got on his bottom, reached a hand down to Siphero, and lifted him up until he was face to face with him. Stager just breathed in Siphero's scent as he scratched the behemoth's chin. He started growling happily. He put down his friend and just sat there, getting a good scratch down from Siphero.

"What a unique creature," a voice said. Siphero turned and eyed the familiar silhouette of Nylf, who stood with a saddle over her shoulder, and he then noticed there were scars on the side of her face that had recently been sealed.

"Hey, Nylf," he replied. "What are you doing here?"

"I'm the stable master," she said, with a bit of pain in her voice. She put the saddle in a tack room and returned. "The king gave me this position as an act of respect and good faith toward us Wingless."

"Wait," he asked, "what's wrong? Who gave you those scars?"

"No one did," she said painfully. "It's nothing; just let me get back to work. I have a lot to do in order to get ready for the ball."

"Oh, can I help you with something?"

"Not really. You can brush down your behemoth. He won't let anyone near him." Stager heard what she said, got to his feet, walked the short distance over to them, and sat down on his butt. His movements shook the earth and made animals around him panic while a few skimmer drakes roared in challenge. Nylf handed a brush kit to Siphero, and he started brushing the behemoth's furry body, starting with the chest. The drird took up a perch on one of the awnings above their heads. Stager sniffed the drird once and let it be. It didn't smell interesting at all.

"How long have you known this creature?" Nylf asked as Siphero moved to brushing one of Stager's arms.

"Oh, a couple months. I'm the first friend he ever had." Stager growled happily and settled down, letting Siphero brush his arms, torso, legs, and finally his back. Nylf, watching curiously, disappeared for a moment and came back with a few of her subordinates, Wingless like her. She asked them to go get some water, and they returned with four buckets full.

"Siphero," Nylf asked, "with your permission, my friends and I would like to give your mount—Stager was it?—we would like to give him a bath. He kind of smells like a skimmer drake's arsehole."

Stager opened his eyes and looked down at them, then lifted an arm to smell one of his armpits. As if a gust of wind had swept through the stables, animals left and right clawed at their noses, trying to get rid of the horrible scent, and a few stable hands fell over clutching their noses. Siphero and Nylf recoiled from the unbearable smell.

"Cover your armpit before we all suffocate," Siphero ordered.

The big guy did so and then looked at all the destruction his scent had wrought. He smiled a big, toothy, guilty-looking smile as if to say, "Oops."

"Yeah," Siphero agreed, waving his hands in front of him, "he definitely needs a bath. Stager," Siphero said to the behemoth, "Nylf and her nice friends are going to give you a nice bath. Don't cause any trouble for them, and they won't trouble you, understood?"

Stager touched Siphero's forehead, and Siphero smiled. "All right, he's all yours, Nylf. Take good care of him."

"Thank you, Siphero," Nylf said. "We promise he will have the best care."

Siphero left them to clean up his smelly behemoth, and the big guy roared happily and jumped a few times when they scrubbed his unmentionables. Siphero roamed the stables a couple times, petting a few of the animals that would let him get close, until he came across Yevere, who was in a spacious pen all to herself, from which she called to Siphero. He came up to the stall and scratched the skimmer drake on the nose.

"Hey, Yevere," he said softly, "are you doing OK?"

The skimmer drake called happily and nudged Siphero gently. The drake was doing a lot better, and a friendly face seemed to have cheered her up. He scratched her one more time on the snout and left her to her own devices. He felt another vibration rumble throughout the stables. Six long rumbles, and Siphero realized that meant six o'clock. He checked his timekeeper, and it was exactly that. He only had one hour left to get ready for the ball.

As he was leaving the stables, a few Sky Knights carrying their training equipment dumped them in the middle of the stables in front of a stable hand and ordered her to pick them up. She did so only to get kicked in the back and fall onto the armor, denting them in the process. The knights laughed at the Wingless as she tried to get up, only to get hit in the back with a blunted practice sword.

"Get up, Wingless scum," one said. "You are going to pay for that until you grow back your wings. Oh wait, you don't have any wings!" They all laughed while the girl tried to get up, only to be knocked down again. Other stable hands with and without wings just minded their own business, mostly because they were afraid of getting involved.

Siphero watched in shock but felt himself moving toward the group not of his own accord. Preduvon was making him do it, and Siphero understood.

Your friend needs our help, Preduvon's voice said. *Are you going to watch as these spineless cowards oppress someone?*

"No," Siphero whispered, "but I'm not going to hurt them."

Then let us resolve this peacefully.

Siphero approached the Sky Knights, surrounded in a shadowy aura and a rather large shield and length of chain. The animals in the stable grew quiet as they watched Siphero approach the knights. The stable hands watched Siphero's aura cast long shadows toward the Sky Knight trainees.

The Sky Knights turned around and saw Siphero/Preduvon's form coming toward them. A few of them took a step back.

"Cease and desist," Siphero said. "You white wings do not have the right to dominate those subservient to you. Leave her be, and I will not harm any of you."

"Harm us?" one guard said, laughing. "We are going to harm you. Uh, who are you, Compa scum?"

"I am Siphero Antolus, chosen of the Archon Preduvon, the Great Defiant!" The shadowy aura of Preduvon solidified around Siphero, and a couple of the knights backed away in horror. Many of them grew up listening to scary stories of the Great Defiant. To see their fears incarnate before them was enough to remind them of their childhood fears.

"The Great Defiant is an Archon, and he has a chosen! Fly away; get away from him!" Half the guards left while the others picked up their weapons and surrounded Siphero.

"The Great Defiant is an Archon, ha!" one said. "It will be a privilege to kill you, Compa scum." Two guards rushed Siphero from the sides, and the chain wrapped around his arm flailed in the air like a rope, knocking the two guards back and disarming them. Their swords hung in the air in front of Siphero as he bent and broke them into metal balls that flew toward the two downed guards and knocked them out. Only four guards remained. One rushed him, and another launched a fireball at him. He deflected the fireball with his shield, wrapped the chain around the sword arm of the other, and flung him at the other knight. They both got knocked down, but they couldn't get up, as a skimmer drake had decided to sit on them both, pinning them to the ground. Siphero looked over, and a couple stable hands were helping him. He nodded his appreciation to them.

The last two guards watched him cautiously as one told the other, "Get Cortus. He'll kill this monster." Before the one chosen to carry the message could fly away, the chain wrapped around his leg and pulled him at neck-breaking speed back to Siphero, where he made contact with a shield bash. The last knight got to his knees and begged for his life.

"Please, spare me, Great Defiant," the knight pleaded. "I promise to never punish a Wingless or Compa, I swear on the wholeness of my wings."

As the knight had his head down, the aura around Siphero faded, and he knelt down. He placed his hand on the knight's shoulder and the knight looked up, quite surprised and speechless. He did not expect mercy or even kindness for his actions.

"I'm glad we could reach an understanding before this got out of hand." The knight rose and looked around the stables as he saw numerous stable hands wielding shovels, rakes, and pitchforks, prepared to fight him if he should change his mind. They all looked at him defiantly, and this last knight appeared to have some common sense after all. He acknowledged he had been defeated. Finally, he looked to the Wingless on the ground and breathed a sigh of relief. He picked up one of his men by putting his arm over his shoulder, while the others picked themselves up and left the stables.

"Watch your back, Compa," the knight said. "You're taking residence in a leviathan's nest."

His men left with him, some dented and bruised, but all still able to limp away. Siphero slouched to the ground, where he panted for breath. Stable hands helped up the girl who had been hurt and carried her over to a bale of hay. They cleaned and patched her wounds, nodding and thanking Siphero for what he did, while some tended to a few scratches he had received. Many of the stable hands showed their gratitude to Siphero by shaking his hand and telling him their names and even said he was welcome anytime.

After a few minutes of meeting and greeting the Wingless he had helped by defending them from the malicious Sky Knights, Nylf came over, covered in behemoth, and smelled like a walking, talking armpit.

"Thank you, Lord Siphero, for what you did," she said. "As a guardian to be, you proved you are better than the Great Defiant in every respect of his name."

"You're welcome," he said, "but I just couldn't stand by and watch. It's not in my nature to fight, but that wasn't fighting. It was righting a wrong."

"Then I will speak for all the workers here when I say that you and your behemoth are always welcome here. You are a friend of Nylf, the stable master to the king and queen of Strati Polis." She placed her hand on her heart and bowed, as did all the other stable hands.

Siphero looked at the sun, saw it was about to set, and realized he was going to be late to the grand ball. He booked it out of there, waving good-bye to everyone in the process, and headed back to his room. One approach he took was flying straight through an open window at top speed, roaring past servants as they wondered what happened. He made it back round to his room in record time. As soon as he was in, Nerv popped in and bowed to Siphero in the same getup he appeared to Awesha in.

"Hello, Siphero," he said, "are you ready for the ball?"

"Uh...not quite," he said. "Is my armor ready?"

Nerv snapped his fingers, and Siphero's armor appeared in front of him. Before Siphero could put it on, Nerv snapped his fingers again, and the armor magically appeared on his body over his regular clothes. Siphero looked at himself in a mirror and was pleased with how shiny the armor was. His wings unfolded from his back, and he posed a few times, causing Nerv to roll his eyes.

"Thanks, Nerv, you really are a lifesaver."

The Cherubim laughed and bowed to him. "It has become my full-time job to make you somewhat presentable."

"Hey, I can be presentable when I want to."

"I quite doubt that. Anyway, Lady Awesha is waiting for you outside the door. Shall I tell her you are ready?"

"Sure, go ahead, but could you tell her to wait a few minutes? I'm going to just do something quickly."

"All right, Siphero." Nerv disappeared in a puff of clouds and left Siphero to himself.

Siphero looked around and wondered where the drird was. He whistled a few times out the window, but no response came, and no drird appeared.

"Shit," Siphero said to himself. "Where could it have gone?"

He looked out at a tree and thought he saw it, only to see a bird with bright colors disappear into the sky. He felt another rumble go throughout the palace, seven rumbles this time. It was time for the ball.

As he exited his room, his jaw dropped when he saw Awesha standing outside his door in her new getup. She was wearing her traditional white dress with flowers woven into it with the front cut open, showing her silk and armored leggings and heeled boots. Her hair was curled and shone with a brilliance he had never seen before. The silver in her brown hair seemed to glitter. Her wings caught his attention. The rainbow aura seemed to have settled in her wings, as each and every feather was a solid color of the rainbow.

She smiled as she looked at his armor.

"Before we say how well we look, let me say I'm sorry— mmm..."

Awesha smothered him with a kiss, silencing him. She released him softly and waited for him to extend his arm to her. She twirled in place while he recovered. She seemed to be genuinely happy, although his bewilderment did little to help him.

"Shall we?" she said as she grabbed Siphero's arm and held it with both of hers. They took off toward the grand ball. As they approached the ballroom, they saw a line of Winged and Wingless standing alone or with their partners. He soon recognized Ieava and Tratiki, who waved them over.

Ieava was wearing a red gown, fully covering her legs, with green ribbons decorating it. Her hair was tied back in a bun, with snowflake-shaped earrings in her ears. On her arm, Tratiki was dressed in loose leather pants and an animal-skin shirt, a skimmer drake scale drawing across his hide like a shoulder sash. He wore a crown of teeth and had tied his black hair back to show off his savage regality. They looked like complete opposites, but anyone who told them that was ignored. They did not care one bit.

"Awesha, it is so good to finally meet you," Ieava said. "My father told me all about you, and Siphero, I thank you for helping me with my...problem."

"You are lucky to have him as your companion," Tratiki said. "He is an honorable and caring Compa."

Awesha whispered to Siphero softly, "What did you do today?"

Siphero mouthed that he would tell her later.

As they waited outside the massive double doors, two Cherubim slowly opened them, and light streamed through. Siphero and Awesha waited in the back of a long line of nobles as it slowly became smaller. Once it had gotten to Ieava and Tratiki, a voice on the other side of the doors announced their presence to all within the ballroom. "Princess Ieava, guardian of Strati Polis, the Lily of Light, and Tratiki, guardian of Silacorlis, the Tireless Hunter."

They stepped through the doors to massive applause as Siphero and Awesha waited at the doors. Siphero was very nervous, but Awesha quieted his heart by kissing him softly on the cheek.

"Don't worry, Siphero," she said. "We have braved much since we first met; a couple of nobles will be nothing."

"If you say so," Siphero said, "if you say so."

She smiled beautifully for him, and he felt so much more at ease. He stopped sweating like a waterfall.

Then as a servant called them forward, a voice announced their presence. "Now the last guardians to grace us with their presence: the guardians of Skyspire. Awesha, Daughter of Exiles, and Siphero, the Otherworlder."

Applause erupted as they walked through the doors and into the light. Their bond burned like a star in the night sky.

Chapter 14: Acknowledgment

Siphero had lived in the death-inducing slums of Salvagon and the dizzying heights of the Edge and soared in the skies of Stratis with Awesha after getting his own wings. None of that had prepared him for what he saw in the ballroom of the Hall of Rulers. The sight made him cry with disappointment.

As he and Awesha walked arm in arm into the grand ball, there were Winged in lavish ball gowns, gleaming suits of armor and princely suits at serving tables or in the air. Wings of every color appeared before them and flapped gently in the air above them, and all of these Winged were clapping with enthusiasm that was either forced or genuine.

The ballroom was beautifully built and furnished, and there were massive golden chandlers hanging from the ceiling being periodically relit by Cherubim as they burned out. The ceiling itself was at least two hundred feet tall as stained glass glinted in the moonlight, creating beautiful images on the marble floor that seemed to dance with the participants. Servants and Cherubim flew between the tables, replenishing the appetizers and alcoholic beverages as quickly as the guests consumed them. The ballroom stood out on a balcony that looked out upon all of Strati Polis, shining in the starry night like a beacon. It was an amazing sight to behold, Awesha thought, but Siphero thought it was a waste of time and money.

They followed a servant that led them to a table in the center of all the tables, where Ieava, Tratiki, and about five other guardians stood. Siphero saw Weeslon standing in a corner watching them all, and he waved to them both. The other guardians standing near the table had glasses or plates in their hands, and they eyed Siphero and Awesha curiously, scrutinizing them and each other.

Then a whistling sound echoed throughout the entire ballroom. A flash of light exploded like a firecracker, blinding everyone in the ballroom for an instant. Near a set of thrones, the king and queen of Strati Polis stood before them. As they took to their thrones, the king spoke first. He had changed from his long robe from earlier to a suit of armor with a long green and white cloak draped across his back. He wore a helm that was both a metal helmet and a crown, as spikes stuck out of the top, but it gleamed with jewels colored a clear crimson.

The queen wore a magnificent purple and crimson ball gown embroidered with feathers and jewels. Her hair was treated and made into long curls that formed a bouquet of flowers upon her head. Her face was like that of a young woman, and yet she seemed to be much older than she appeared. In addition, her black hair, piercing silver eyes, and full red lips made almost all the men in the court lust for her, except for Tratiki and Siphero, who remained oddly immune.

He thought it over and came to a conclusion. His bond with Awesha had become so deep that women he would be attracted to became unattractive when his thoughts wavered from her. Another conclusion he had was that he only saw Awesha as beautiful because even when he stole glances at her, she still caught his eye every time. To him, Awesha was the only person who truly mattered.

The king raised a glass to all his guests in the ballroom, and they did the same. "Welcome all who could come to the thousandth meeting of the council of the guardians. It has been so long since this magnificent tradition was started, when unique and powerful individuals from every part of Stratis come to gain the acknowledgment of their guardianship. This is a time-honored tradition of ours, and I am pleased to acknowledge to the guardianship of our first guardian." He paused for a moment as he looked at the table to see which of the guardians deserved their title and finally picked the first one.

"Tratiki of Silacorlis, please step forward," said the king.

Tratiki heard his name and flew away from Ieava's side toward the king, where he dropped to one knee and folded his wings around him. He remained in this position a while longer until the king asked him to rise.

"Tratiki, the Tireless Hunter," continued the king, "do you swear by all your people represent, to serve Stratis to the best of your abilities, to maintain their gentle ferocity, and safeguard your fellow guardians? Do you swear?"

"I do, Your Kingship," he said. "I swear by all the moons and all of Silacorlis who chose me as their guardian, to serve the people of Stratis, even to the day I shall die!"

"Then rise, Tratiki, the Tireless Hunter, a fully realized guardian of Silacorlis!"

The king applauded along with some of the people in the audience, mostly Sila who had come to support their chosen guardian. The king then summoned the other guardians to his presence one by one. First a half-bird, half-woman Winged with wings on her arms and talons for feet, dressed in tribal robes and stones, a Sila as well. After her was a blue-haired teenaged boy with a long staff in the shape of a trident, black and white wings, and pieces of skywhale attached to his cloak and armor. Then came twins, both of them girls, dressed in long robes embroidered with flowers and their black hair tied back into buns as they walked side by side, their hands held at shoulder level.

The last of these initiates was a gray-haired, much older looking man in heavy armor with a large harpoon holstered across his back. Oddly, this man had no wings, and yet all of the Winged in the ballroom feared him when they said his name. When he looked at Siphero and Awesha, he nodded with respect to them but winked at Siphero specifically. He had seen Siphero walk by the arena earlier. He walked toward the king and queen, saluted them, and was royally acknowledged as a guardian.

Finally, Ieava was called forward, where she bowed to her parents, the king and queen. They embraced her like two loving parents would a much-loved child. Siphero felt bile explode from his throat. A painful memory had surfaced in his mind.

"Ieava, we are so proud of you for wanting to become a guardian of Strati Polis," the queen said. "The people will follow you, for you are an example of purity that all of us wish to follow."

She bowed to her mother and father and flew back to Tratiki in the midst of massive applause from all of the guests. She smiled and waved while some guests quietly commented about her terrible choice in a bonded mate. Tratiki snapped his gaze at them, and they recoiled in fear. He had heard them quite clearly.

"Awesha, Daughter of Exiles," the king said, "please step forward."

Awesha let go of Siphero's hand, flew to the king and queen, curtsied before them, and awaited their acknowledgment.

"Awesha, you stand before us as a chosen guardian of Skyspire. Alas, a village does not have the right to name a guardian. To remedy this oversight, news of your naming to guardianship has reached your home of Sky Polis, as have the treasonous deeds of your parents, and they have been disavowed of any wealth to their name. However, the council in Sky Polis has decided to name you as its guardian. Will you accept this?"

Awesha was surprised, and tears filled her eyes as she nodded her approval to her king. "I accept it with all of my heart, my king."

"Rise, Awesha; rise and be known as the Daughter of Exiles to all of Strati Polis."

Awesha rose, and there was a thunderous applause from many of the people in the room, especially the other guardians, and especially Siphero. He was so happy she had been named the official guardian of her home city and that they had backed her in this regard. As she returned to his side, she laughed and cried with joy while Siphero embraced her for the accomplishment.

"Siphero, the Otherworlder," the king said seriously, "please step forward."

At the mention of his name, the people began roaring with protest, calling Siphero a dirty Compa and many other terrible insults. The king and queen silenced them all with a very loud and powerful thunderclap that shook everyone out of the air.

"Order," the king roared at the top of his lungs, "I will have order in this hallowed hall! All are equal in the eyes of its king!"

As Siphero stepped forward, he saw the angry gazes of the nobles glaring at him. He felt like they were going to stab him in the back.

Out of nowhere, the elderly man with the harpoon applauded for Siphero, as did a couple guards in the room, including the pampered Mervieris and Weeslon, much to his surprise.

Siphero approached the king on the ground, walking the whole way, and yet the king waited patiently for him to arrive. He bowed to the king and awaited his judgment. Would he be named a guardian, or would his Terran nature be revealed?

"Siphero," the king said aloud, "you come before us under the illusion of being a Compa."

Siphero held his breath. He hoped the king hadn't realized what he really was. He was dancing a razor edge between the truth and lies.

"As you heard before, Siphero," the king said, "you cannot be a guardian of Skyspire, but I believe a break in tradition is in order. You are not like other Compa; your wings are artificial. Pray tell us, how did this come to pass?"

Siphero searched his mind for the best possible lie to answer to the king's question. He couldn't tell the truth and be found out. He then decided it would be best to just say what came to mind.

"Your Majesty," Siphero began, "these wings of mine"—they unfolded from his back, and feather after metal feather gleamed before the entire assembly of nobles and guests. They were in awe of how every facet of his wings gleamed a chromic color. "I was originally born a Wingless in Skyspire, and no one respected me because of my lacking wings. It was a cruel hand I had been dealt in life, so I tried to remedy my plight. I made the wings that you see before you."

Silence fell across all in the ballroom, and then laughter broke out among many of the nobles, that Siphero would say something so stupid and pathetic.

The king silenced them all with another thunderclap. His anger was aimed at each and every one of them.

"Absolutely unforgivable," he said. "You think it is amusing to slander the words of a guardian? You all disgust me. A new guardian, a Wingless who just wanted to fly, how can you belittle a people who stand beside us as our equals, day in and day out! As king, I will acknowledge him as a guardian, but as the laws dictate, there must be others to support this decision, at least seven among us. Who will support my decision?"

No one stepped forward in the ballroom, but the silence was broken when Awesha stepped up, as well as Ieava and Tratiki, who shouted their approval.

"We wish for this to be so," Awesha said, for the three of them.

Then the guardian with the harpoon stepped forward and said in a deep voice, "I, Gargran, Storm Rider of the Stormlands, do so acknowledge this Wingless not as a guardian but as an Engria."

Silence permeated the Hall of Rulers. The king stood there with surprise upon his face. He had never thought such a declaration would be made, and there was already murmuring and planning among the nobles to "remove" Siphero from the hall.

"I will support this decision."

All eyes snapped to the queen as she collected her gown and stood before them all. "I believe there has never been an Engria with metal wings. Tell me, young Siphero, how did your wings come to be?"

Siphero breathed a sigh of relief. This was something he could explain more easily, and he didn't need to stretch the truth any more than he already had.

"Your Ladyship," he said, "I was testing my skills against a fire affinity in aerial combat. While we were dueling, I took a powerful blast to the back, where the wings were located, and he seared my flesh around my metal wings."

There were a few gasps—this even made Mervieris cringe, as he had been responsible for his fair share of burning flesh.

"And so after a few weeks' rest and generous healing from Skyspire's healers and alchemists, I found my metal wings had permanently been burned to my back, but it wasn't all bad. People considered me one of them, and Wingless looked up to me from then on. I now have a place in Skyspire as a Wingless who had found his wings through horrible disfigurement."

The silence had returned to the hall. One soul finally broke the silence.

"I will acknowledge him as an Engria, the Engria of Metal," Cortus said as he descended from the upper parts of the ballroom. Many nobles gasped at hearing one of their paragons say this, but their disputes would fall on deaf ears.

"Why do you choose to support this decision, Cortus?" the king asked.

"My Lord," Cortus said in a bow, "This Wingless assisted your daughter in rescuing Lord Tratiki from the clutches of some overzealous Sangrians. I believe it is time a new Engria was chosen."

The king smiled and laughed, and then looked around the room for anyone else. Then a hand raised from Weeslon.

"What do you have to say for this decision, Bond Scrivener?" the king asked Weeslon.

"Your Most Gracious Majesty," Weeslon said, "when I performed the test of bonds on Awesha and this Wingless, he proved their bond could not be broken by my hands. I believe we could learn much from him, and so I believe Siphero must be given acknowledgment for being the first in all our history to prevent a Scrivener from breaking a bond."

"Well spoken," the king said. "Is there anyone else who would accept this guardian?"

"I will accept him," another voice in their midst said as a being came from the upper levels, surfing the wind with her feet. It was Nylf, the stable hand who had spoken this endorsement.

"Ah, Nylf," the king said, smiling. "How do you fair this evening…"

The king trailed off when his eyes caught the sight of Nylf's face, arms, and legs. They were marked with half-healed scars, stitched wounds, and bandaged fingers. An aura of white and black energy surrounded the king as his wife attempted to calm him with the press of her hand on his arm.

"Who did this to you, Nylf?" the king asked in an angry calm. "Who, pray tell, was so impulsive as to hurt one of my confidants!"

The king looked around the room at the nobles and then at the guards, whose expressions changed from those of pride to those of fear and horror.

"That is not the point, My Lord," Nylf said as she bowed to her king. "This Compa is one of us. He selflessly defended my stable hands from the prideful wrath of the Sky Knight trainees. He is kind, compassionate, and merciful. He is a far better Wingless than I have courage to call myself."

The king and queen stared, eyes wide, at Nylf and then at Siphero. Then the garden-variety nobles started to aggravate the crowd into hateful frenzy toward Siphero again. Again, the king silenced the nobility who were acting in particular bad taste that night.

"Please continue," the king requested, "and would all nobility who have acted disgracefully please leave for the evening? You are not welcome here. Cortus, please escort them from the hall."

"Gladly, milord," Cortus said.

"My Lord," Nylf said, waiting for the disgraceful nobles to leave, "Siphero was at the stables during the day where the white-wing believers came in and demanded for one of my associates to pick up their weapons and armor. As she was fulfilling her duties, they began kicking and beating her for simply doing what you requested of me and my fellows. They even went as far as calling us Wingless slime."

The king gritted his teeth with anger, while the queen held her husband at bay.

"Siphero intervened but did not harm a single one of my attackers, much." She smirked at that mentioning, and the guards looked away, their pride wounded.

"He has the respect of all who work under me; he even has my respect. I wish to call him a friend of mine."

As the king's anger subsided, he smiled defiantly at all the nobles and raised his hands to Siphero. "Rise up, Siphero," said the king. "Rise up as one of us. Not as a Wingless or as a Compa but as our newest guardian, the Engria of Metal!"

There was applause from the other guardians, as well as from some nobles and guards, and even Mervieris supported this choice, clapping softly.

When Siphero flew back to Awesha, Tratiki, Ieava, Mervieris and Gargran, the Storm Rider of the Stormlands, they mobbed and congratulated him. Awesha then kissed him again for joining their ranks, a fitting reward.

As the excitement died down, the king raised his hands to them all. "Now, everyone—guardians, honored guests, guards, and servants—let the festivities begin!"

Chapter 15: Incarnation

As the festivities started, Awesha and Siphero lost track of time as they participated in dances, games, gambling, and the feast. It was all new to Siphero and familiar to Awesha, but she cared not for his unfamiliarity with these rituals because it allowed her the opportunity to teach him the complexities and ridiculous nuances of etiquette. Dancing was perhaps the hardest affair since Siphero could not dance elegantly, so he just flew around the ballroom like he and Awesha did when they first met, and those watching them could not understand what they were doing. Siphero met many of the lords and ladies who had remained in the ballroom. They bowed before him and recognized him as an Engria.

Toward the end of the feasting, Siphero sat out on the balcony by himself, looking out to the city below them, reflecting on all that had happened to him over the course of those long months.

The sound of wings and clicking heels landing aroused him from his pondering. Upon looking, he saw the queen of the polis standing behind him, waiting patiently for an audience.

"Your Majesty," Siphero said, and dropped to one knee, "I didn't know you were there. Please forgive me for not noticing."

"Please, rest at ease," she said, with a smile. "Engria are considered on par with any king or queen. They are representative of that which makes our world of Stratis unique." Siphero dropped his guard and went back to looking out to the city below the palace.

"Are you enjoying the view?" she asked sincerely. "It is one of the finest views in all of Strati Polis."

"Not really," Siphero said bluntly.

This caught the queen by surprise. "Are you not pleased with the view? How could you possibly be displeased with—"

"It's not that," he said. "I just don't like going to these fancy parties. I prefer being down there." He pointed down at the city, where a hundred thousand bustling lights flickered and danced with each passing second. "Down there, that's where real life is. I think the best view is when I can sit on top of a building and look at all the people living their lives to the fullest, braving the harsh lives they have been given, laughing with their friends—that's what life is like for me."

The queen remained silent, then spoke. "Do you consider our lives to be too restrictive?"

"With all due respect, Your Majesty, I wasn't born into this way of life. I had to fight claw, tooth, and nail for where I am today. There were no easy victories, no promises fulfilled. I had to pay my way with flesh and blood, metaphorically speaking. Besides, everyone here, the nobles, the servants, the Cherubim, and the guards, you all live inside a gigantic birdcage. It's not a life I could be happy living."

The queen smiled to herself, turned, and reentered the ballroom. "Go and live your life with your freedom, Siphero, chosen of the Great Defiant."

This made him jump. How had she figured that out? He never said a word. He summed up that Winged are simply more perceptive than he gave them credit for. He continued to look out upon the city until he was visited again.

The sound of chainmail boots clanging upon the marble floor woke him up, when he came across Gargran approaching him. The Storm Rider saluted and moved next to Siphero, looking out to the city.

"This lifestyle isn't to your desire, is it Otherworlder?" Gargran raised an eyebrow as he sipped from a canteen of liquor. He offered some to Siphero, who politely declined.

"You're right about that," he said. "All this wealth and beauty makes me sick to my stomach. How can they be so happy when there are Wingless, Compa, and Sila suffering at their hands?"

Gargran spat over the balcony railing, the big lougie landing upon a noble's neatly combed hair. The noble panicked, looking to see if perhaps a bird had pooped on his head.

"It is considered a sport in Strati Polis," Gargran began. "And in any polis where there is a majority of white-wing zealots. They believe they are entitled to inflict suffering upon Wingless specifically. They get a considerable high from doing so."

"Those rich, arrogant bastards!" Siphero slammed his fist against the railing and broke part of the stone, surprising Gargran, who looked at Siphero with renewed interest.

"How would you like to do something a bit more exciting than insult imaginary nobles?"

"What do you have in mind?"

Gargran grinned as he jumped off the balcony and landed with a massive thud in the gardens below. He signaled for Siphero as he flew in the direction of the training ring the Sky Knights used for sparring.

Just then, Awesha appeared behind Siphero and startled him. "Where are you going, my bonded?"

"I…uh, I'm going to the sparring ring the Sky Knights use for training purposes," he said nervously.

"What are you going to do?" They saw Tratiki coming toward them, with Ieava clinging to his arm.

"Sheesh," Siphero said, "why don't I just tell the whole friggin' castle!"

"Don't be silly," Ieava chimed in. "They wouldn't care what you would have to say, Engria."

"So then let's go," Awesha said. "Come on, to the training ground we go."

Awesha was the first to jump off the railing, Tratiki and Ieava right behind her. Siphero rolled his eyes and jumped over the balcony railing to follow them. Once he descended to the ground, Ieava motioned with her hands from about twenty yards away to follow her. Siphero followed her signals and slowly caught up to the three of them, who had already arrived at the arena.

There was already a small gathering of guards sparring with one another in the ring and some Sky Knights dueling with Gargran. He beat each one singlehandedly. He was like a metallic storm with a harpoon jutting out in each and every direction.

When they joined the sparring guards, they left the arena and joined their comrades in the stands, leaving Gargran without an opponent.

"Ah, you decided to come," Gargran said. "Who among you would like to be my next opponent?"

There was silence among their ranks until Awesha raised her hand and flew into the ring, her clothes magically changing from her ball gown to her sparring clothes, a light chainmail tunic and trousers, with her metal baton in hand. The guards in the stands started laughing, placing bets on Gargran, some saying that Awesha was out of her league. Some of them even rubbed bruises that Gargran had given them in the previous duels.

"Would you allow me to be your opponent, Storm Rider?" Awesha asked, raising her baton and assuming a fighting stance.

"Yes," he said with fervor, "a worthy opponent only need present themselves to me. Only one rule exists: if one of us takes to the air, the fight is forfeited, agreed?"

He pointed his harpoon toward Awesha and made ready for combat.

There was much disgust for that rule, but Awesha agreed nonetheless; they began.

Silence passed over the whole field until the two clashed with one another, Siphero and the others cheering her on. Metal clanged as Awesha parried all of his strikes, while Gargran thrusted and cleaved to no avail. While she used her wings to dash to the left and right, Gargran threw his harpoon, only to will it to return to his hands whenever he missed.

Once, Awesha almost took to the sky, but instead she leaped back and allowed her wings to carry her a short distance to safety. Gargran didn't mind this because he immediately closed the distance with no difficulty. They continued for another minute until Awesha kneeled in defeat, and Gargran sheathed his harpoon.

"Well fought, Daughter of Exiles, but you must train more. I have been around for over one hundred years. I have hunted many of the largest game in the Stormlands. It is not easy for anyone to wear out a well-trained Storm Rider in a fair fight."

"I will, Storm Rider," she said, exhausted. "It has been a pleasure." She flew out of the arena, still wearing her combat clothes.

"Who is next among any of you drake whelps? Who can I test myself against?"

A hand raised, Tratiki, who spoke. "If it would not trouble you much, Storm Rider, may Siphero and I test each other in your stead?"

Gargran smiled and left the arena with one mighty step, while Tratiki stood in the arena wearing his tribal armor of drakescale over a layer of chainmail, waiting for Siphero to join the fray. Siphero looked at Awesha, who pushed him toward the arena.

"I want to test your strength, Siphero," Tratiki said. "You seem like a capable warrior."

"OK, just don't go crazy on me."

"No guarantees, Siphero," Tratiki said as he fell to one knee, growling in pain as all watched his body begin to change. First his hands turned into massive claws, his upper body resembled that of a lion, and his wings doubled in size. He grew fur over his entire body until he was three times his original size and in the shape of a massive flying lion.

"A Silacon," Gargran said. "This is the form only the strongest of Sila can acquire once they have become adults." He turned to Ieava, who was smiling with admiration. "This is the one you bonded with?"

"Yes," she said, "and all should be afraid of his magnificence."

Siphero, who was staring down a lion with wings, felt a tad bit creeped out, but he held his ground because he knew that it was just sparring for fun.

He wants to fight? the voice of Preduvon whispered. *I do not fight Sila, not for fun.*

"Kinda beside the point here," Siphero said to Preduvon.

I will not help you in this fight, Siphero.

"A lot of help you are." Siphero made the shield and chain materialize in his hands as he circled the Silacon. Tratiki lunged a few times. Siphero leaped out of the way and swung the chain, cracking it like a whip, keeping the Sila at a distance. Then out of nowhere, Tratiki breathed in deeply and roared so loudly a shockwave formed, causing Siphero to get knocked against a wall, dazing him. As he got up, Tratiki pounced on him, causing Siphero to roll to the side, using his wings to take to the air and wrapping his chain around the lion's paw, a bad idea.

Tratiki wrestled the chain to the ground, pulling Siphero toward his open jaws. Siphero saw the jaws and fired his thrusters toward the direction of Tratiki's mouth with his shield extended outward. He slammed into Tratiki's face with a loud clang as the lion was knocked out and reverted back to Tratiki, dozing, with a big, swollen bump on the side of the head but very much alive.

Ieava just shook her head and laughed at what happened to Tratiki. He got up and landed next to her.

"Oooh, that's gotta hurt," Siphero said as he rejoined them outside the ring. "Sorry about that, Tratiki."

"Do not worry, friend Siphero," Tratiki said, his bruise being tended to by Ieava. "I lose myself in my Silacon form. I have only so much control over it. I hope I did not startle you."

"Oh, it's not like I would be afraid of a giant flying lion trying to kill me!"

They all laughed, and Gargran clapped them both on the shoulders and congratulated them. "Both of you are very much greenhorns, but you both bring new strategies and tactics to the battlefield. Keep up the practice, and always continue to re-create the way we fight."

Just as they were enjoying their company, a massive beam of light shot up into the sky from the ballroom. The echoing vibration was back, only this time it was vibrating constantly, echoing a loud and annoying sound, like a siren. The guards around the arena panicked as they started swarming the palace, and a large number of them immediately formed a guard around Ieava.

"What's happening?" Ieava asked one of the guards. "What's going on?"

"Milady," one of the guards said, "the Sangria Legion are attacking the palace; they have broken into the ballroom."

Ieava's face erupted into panic. "Mother, Father!"

Ieava took off from where she was and headed straight for the ballroom, Tratiki and her guards hot on her tail.

Siphero and Awesha looked at one another and nodded, and they took off with Gargran toward the ballroom.

"We're under attack," a guard screamed at them. "The king and queen need the assistance of any and all able bodies to reinforce them, immediately!"

As they reached the ballroom, there was a big hole in the ceiling, and the smoking bodies of many servants, Cherubim, and guards strewn across the floor. The king was standing outside the pile with Cortus and the queen while they were surrounded by many Sky Knights and magi wearing white and red standards and banners with a bloodied fist as their sigil, the Sangria Legion.

The twin guardians were held in magical bindings, the blue-haired one was kept at bay by a whole squad of Sangrians, and a pile of their slain brethren lay on the ground. The bird-winged lay on the ground, her blue blood staining the floor as she bled out. As the others reached the king, queen, and Cortus, Ieava's guards set up a defensive perimeter around them and pointed their weapons outward like a spiked wall of lances and shields.

"What's going on here?" Awesha asked. "Why are all these Avian here, spilling the blood of their own?"

They are the purebloods, rising up to slay the ruler they deem a traitor, a voice said.

Awesha looked around the area and realized it was a voice she recognized. The voice of Verrencae, Lady of the Scarred, was calling to her.

She felt sick as she bent over, her wings sheltering her, but Verrencae's staff appeared in her hands.

The enemy's number swelled to several hundred in the ballroom. some wore armor, and others wielded staves and wore robes. The rest fought with anything they could get their hands on, like pitchforks, swords, and spears. The entire Sangria Legion was mismatched with the addition of noncombatants joining their numbers.

You must protect the exiled, Awesha, Verrencae said in her ear. *Protect them, protect the one you treasure deeply.*

Her body pulsed with pain as these words were repeated in an echo.

"No, I want to fight," she said. "Siphero doesn't need my protec—" She doubled over from more pain until she finally gave in.

"Awesha," Siphero exclaimed, rushing to her side, "what's wrong?"

Awesha rose beside him and held his hand tightly. The bond between them was woven so firmly that they could feel what the other was thinking.

Then, the strangest thing occurred. Time froze for Awesha and Siphero as they looked around the room, shocked at the full carnage that had been wrought by the Sangria Legion. Two beings appeared before them; two beings wreathed in a golden light, came to greet them as Awesha and Siphero watched with wonder and confusion as the silhouettes became more familiar to them. The ones standing before them were beings that were always pestering them to do what needed to be done, their Archons, Verrencae and Preduvon.

"Children," Verrencae said to them in a clear voice, "You are at a precipice. The Sangria Legion knows of your bond and of your identity, Siphero."

"A Winged and a Terran, together," Preduvon said, with a laugh. "Who would have thought this would spark such hatred and upheaval in the Strati Polis? The barriers that have kept the worlds apart are beginning to decay."

"What do you mean, Verrencae, Preduvon? What is the meaning of this?" Awesha looked around as small spirits began to float away from the other Winged in the time-frozen ballroom. Siphero saw them too, but wondered the same as Awesha about their purpose.

Their Archons approached them and knelt down. Then Siphero and Awesha felt their arms move toward Preduvon and Verrencae outside of their control. A symbol burned into the back of their hands and up their arms, a ribbon and a chain linked together.

"I remember this," Siphero said, in surprise. "I remember the ribbon and the chain."

"Very good, Siphero," Preduvon said. "These are the items that represent the link of the bond between the two of you."

"But what does it mean? Why the ribbon for me and the chain for Siphero?" Awesha asked.

"The bond," Verrencae said, "your bond specifically has never happened before; it is an anomaly to all Archons."

"To answer your question," Preduvon added, "you are represented by a ribbon because you are Winged, Awesha, and Siphero is a chain because he is a Terran. It is the difference of your lives."

Preduvon and Verrencae rolled up their sleeves to reveal a tattoo in the shape of a ribbon and a chain tied together, bound together in a beautiful helix.

"Your bond is so powerful that it has drawn the attention of the King of Archons. As of this moment, your bond is causing a great power to grow within the both of you. This power is the power of the Incarnates, a great and powerful race with unimaginable abilities." Verrencae stroked her arm as the ribbon rustled and flew in different directions. Preduvon touched the chain on his arm, and the chain peeled off of his skin. The two links flew together and tied a beautiful knot of ribbon and chain, the symbol of a strong and beautiful bond.

"Your bond has infected us," Verrencae said. "Your ideals, desires, and love have flowed into us, and now we are bursting at the seams. We have been summoned by our king, and he wishes to know of your bond."

"But who are these Incarnates?" Awesha said. "We need your help now more than ever, so why are you leaving us?"

"Do not question our intentions, Daughter of Exiles," Preduvon said coldly. "Our master has called us, and we must heed the call. Our aid is limited; we will come when it is absolutely necessary, so continue to exist, continue to survive."

They stopped and looked around the room as the spirits in the frozen time began to materialize. These other Archons were of warriors, magi, kings, queens, peasants, and even priests. All of them stared at Siphero and Awesha, and yet they looked through them at the same time. None smiled or shouted with anger, but all just watched with calm and quiet.

"Our king's attendants have assembled," Verrencae said. "Time grows short; we must leave now."

A portal opened up behind them at the foot of the throne as all the assembled Archons drifted through the portal, passing by Siphero and Awesha just enough to acknowledge them. Just as the Archons stepped through the portal, they turned to face Siphero and Awesha. Some of them bowed to the two, some laughed with joy, some screamed in fear, and others just ignored them and drifted through the portal.

Only two turned to face them as they flew through the portal, a king and queen who looked too much like Ieava's parents. Their looks and clothing were so completely similar that they could not be any different.

The Archon versions of the king and queen held hands, much like Siphero and Awesha did, and spoke a single phrase: "We acknowledge the bond of a Winged and a Terran." They were then sucked up into the portal, as were Preduvon and Verrencae, the only words echoing off their lips "Save as many as you can."

Siphero and Awesha reached after their Archons as they flew through the portal. The king and queen of the polis were Archons, but what did that mean? As time began to return to normal, tears flowed down their cheeks, an unbearable sadness had gripped them both. They felt something terrible was going to happen.

Then, time unfroze as the guards surrounding them began to move at a quickened pace. Weapons were trained on them as their attackers formed a barricade around them all, on the ground and in the air.

All of a sudden, the bodies of the queen and the king crumpled to the ground, Cortus bending over trying to shake them awake. It was then Awesha and Siphero realized the king and queen they saw as Archons were in fact the real king and queen, but they were so overcome with sadness that they could not tell Cortus the news, let alone Ieava, who would be devastated.

"All of you stand up," Gargran yelled to the rest. "The string puller is about to make his appearance. I'm sure he has a lot to answer for."

As he said this, the Sangrians began parting ways as an individual wearing a long robe fluttered across the ground. As the one in charge came into view, Cortus looked up and reeled in shock—it was his true bonded, his wife.

Chapter 16: Usurpation

"Grand Clerician," Cortus said, with betrayal in his voice, "what is the meaning of all this!"

The Grand Clerician, a modest woman of excellent bearing, had jet-black eyes with hair the color of ivy that stretched all the way down her back. Her lips were pure white, and her ears bore earrings with the symbol of the bloody fist the soldiers bore as standard. The oddest part about her was that she stroked her stomach occasionally, where a rather large bump protruded, her pregnancy.

Whenever she smiled at the men and women bearing arms beside her, they would close their eyes or do the best they could to focus on the task at hand.

"Cortus, my love," she said, with a soft but harsh tone, "you must get away from those infectious half breeds before they ruin your wings."

Cortus stood his ground as his aura burst into flames and rose higher. The other guardians had rejoined the many of them in the center, but they were worn out and drenched in sweat. As they all looked around the room, the Sky Knights on the outside joined the ranks of the bloodied fist and took up arms against the ones they once served.

"Jieti, my true one, what have you done?" Cortus was on his knees as tears rolled down his cheeks like a waterfall. If he admitted defeat, Cortus did not say it, but the morale of the other guardians was beginning to decline.

"You shall address me as the Grand Clerician, my one Cortus. The people of Strati Polis have grown tired of the king's many sins. He embraced the Wingless scum and Compa defects as equals and allowed them to infiltrate all corners of the palace. This uprising, as you may see it, is merely the voice of the people, the pure Avian who seek to cleanse the world of all mongrels born impure."

The soldiers in the room screamed a battle cry, as if this was an unspoken agreement between them all, an army of zealots with a religious leader, a mother no less.

"This is despicable." Tratiki raised his voice. "You would wipe out the Sila as well? Do you know how much suffering your nightmare will bring?"

"Silence, Sila scum," Jieti said. "You have no right to speak here! Be crushed underneath our righteous cause!"

She signaled to a soldier with a long lance, who rushed forward and was about to impale Tratiki, when a large length of chain wrapped around the soldier and sent the lance flying until it impaled a wall. All recoiled to see Siphero had intercepted the lance and forced the weapon to fly away. Siphero stepped out, holding up a large round shield, and smiled defiantly. More soldiers tried to rush him, only to be knocked back in a large cleave as Awesha intervened, using her staff to summon a large pulse of energy that exploded in front of the Sangrians, driving them back. The rest of the soldiers recoiled and watched with fear and disgust as the two made more room for the other guardians, giving the soldiers still protecting Ieava and the others time to regroup around Cortus.

"Get up, Cortus." Gargran slapped some sense into him. "Your wife just killed the king and queen. Do you really want to betray their trust?"

Cortus said nothing. He remained where he was and looked at his hands.

"Cortus, my dear," Jieti said, "the child is kicking." She stroked her stomach, which awoke Cortus from his stupor. As he rose he rushed forward on his wings and moved closer to his wife. Sangrians parted for him to pass, and their morale grew as their military champion seemed to be joining their cause.

"Is she happy?" he said, in a soft breath, as he placed one hand around his wife and the other on her stomach. "Is our child well?"

The attitude of Jieti changed from sternness to softness as she reassured her husband and whispered a few words into his ears. At first he was shocked, but the words sank in as he turned and faced the guardians in the middle of the crowd.

"Guardians," he began, "by the order of the Grand Clerician and the military champion of Strati Polis, lay down your weapons and surrender for cleansing. All must comply. You have no choice."

The guardians looked at one another in confusion, but the twins and the one with the trident complied as they lowered their

weapons and knelt in front of the soldiers. A couple of Sangrians
drew in close to skewer the surrendering guardians, only to be
knocked back by Awesha and her affinity. They picked up their
weapons and rallied around Ieava and Tratiki while Ieava's guards
continued to protect her.

"Don't surrender!" Awesha screamed. "Don't give in to these
purist zealots! They will kill you all if you just give up!"

"Awesha, child," Jieti said in a motherly voice, "you are an
Avia too. Don't you see the truth in our cause? A pure and better
world is possible only if the spawn of the unworthy are wiped clean
from Stratis. If only you'd kill that disgusting Terran, you shall
regain your former glory as one a part of the Bugieros family."

The other guardians were confused and surprised—a Terran
was among them? Siphero was scared. How had the Grand Clerician
discovered his identity? He looked around the room and found
Weeslon had been captured and bound by the Sangrians, and his face
bled fiercely.

"No," Siphero said to himself. "He was forced to tell them."

Awesha looked at Siphero and then at the sword at her belt,
the sword her father had given her, the one passed down through the
many generations of her family. She unsheathed it and threw it at the
feet of Cortus and Jieti. What she said next surprised and offended
them both. "I will never join you. Eat shit!"

Gargran joined the line of men protecting Ieava, and he
impaled soldiers with his harpoon as Ieava chanted her magic and
blinded Sangrians with an intense light. Tratiki shifted into a half-
Winged, half-Sila form where he darted around the room, slashing
soldiers in two or knocking archers out of the sky. Then, on the
balcony on the upper ballroom floors, archers began jumping off,
immolated in flames, their wings burnt to a crisp. A figure appeared
on the balcony, Mervieris, who glided down with blade staff in hand
and joined the guardians in the tight circle.

"Mervieris," Ieava said, "what are you doing here?"

"Fighting these purist radicals," he replied. "Also repaying a
debt to your Engria friend there." He lit a few soldiers on fire as they
flew around in the confusion and panic.

"You may have become an enemy of Strati Polis for your
actions," Ieava said as she chanted another spell to knit the flesh of
Tratiki's wounds and heal a few of her guards.

"Well, between the two sides, I prefer to fight for those fighting a stupid opponent." His comment goaded a couple soldiers to attack him, only to be knocked senseless by Siphero's shield.

"Then it's good to have you here." Siphero clapped him on the shoulder as he bashed another soldier in the head.

"We cannot hold them for long," one of Ieava's guards said. "Please, Tireless Hunter, protect our lady. She is the only surviving heir to the throne; she must survive at all costs."

"What are you talking about, Galius?" Ieava said. "You're coming with us."

"I am sorry, my lady," the one called Galius said, "but you know we cannot. We must teach these stupid zealots a lesson."

Ieava tried to protest, but Awesha touched her shoulder and discouraged the action, as the guards had made up their minds.

"Survive," Ieava said. "I order you as the future queen, survive!"

He nodded to Ieava and turned his attention back to fighting the Sangrians. He became wreathed in flames as they engulfed his armor and weapons, plunging headfirst into the multitudes of the Sangria Legion.

"We need to get out of here," Awesha said as she pulled a whistle from her pocket. Gargran, Ieava, and the other guardians followed suit and made a calling sound. As luck would have it, a whole stream of creatures crashed through the ballroom windows and appeared in front of them. An albino skimmer drake, a gigantic armored skimmer drake, a blue one, and two avisi appeared before them and made a massive clearing around those who summoned them, breathing fire, clawing, roaring, and swiping at any foolish enough to get close. Then after they came, Yevere and Stager came crashing through, with Nylf riding on Yevere's back, clinging for dear life.

The soldiers watched in horror as Stager and Yevere appeared but were particularly fearful of the behemoth. The riders mounted their creatures as the skimmer drakes poured different elements of fire, ice, or acid into the Sangrian ranks, creating a temporary barrier. Stager let out an ear-shattering roar that made many soldiers cover their ears and others crumple over stunned, a very demoralizing roar.

As Siphero and Awesha climbed onto their mounts, the others took off through the opening they had created. The wind roared in their ears as they took off, with Mervieris riding behind Gargran and Nylf with Yevere. Tratiki morphed forms just quick enough to catch a ride with Ieava.

Their escape into the open sky was illuminated by the bright stars, but they only had a few moments' respite before the zealots took to the air on avisi and a couple of skimmer drakes. Off in the distance, a sky galleon circled the palace and changed course to intercept them. Below them, the different districts of Strati Polis were up in flames as the Sangria Legion moved through each one, pillaging and burning the impure to the ground with a powerful bloodlust.

"They're hot on our heels," Mervieris called out. "They'll overtake us pretty soon."

They had no idea where to go or of an escape plan, until Siphero felt a warm wind, a wind he hadn't felt for several months, the wind of a familiar person. He smiled as his uncertainty vanished and a voice spoke in his mind. He pulled out his compass and saw it point northwest; that was their way out.

"This way," he called out, "everyone, follow me! We're going to go to slipstream."

"We can't all enter a slipstream, Siphero," Ieava said aloud. "If we do, the zealots only need to catch up to us later."

"Stager and I will lead the charge," he said to them all. "His slipstream is the fastest of them all. Follow us in the slipstream for three minutes and break formation. You all got that?"

There was total silence in the group, but Awesha spoke aloud. "Do as he says; it is the only plan we have at the moment." The silence continued until heads started nodding, and Siphero had all the approval he needed.

"OK, Stager." He whispered words of encouragement into the behemoth's huge ear. "I need you to slipstream like you did before and cut us a path to the skies ahead. You can do it, my friend."

Those words were all the behemoth needed, and he let loose a very happy guttural cry and entered a slipstream as it lit up the night sky with a blazing light. The others were amazed by this magnificent sight, but Awesha directed them to follow the slipstream as she went first, then Ieava and Tratiki, Gargran and Mervieris, and finally the other guardians. They shot through the air, leaving behind some very stunned and amazed zealots. They tried to enter slipstream only to fail terribly.

Chapter 17: Reinforcement

They roared across the sky, Stager leading the charge as the rest rode the accelerated slipstream at normal speed. They continued like this for only a few minutes, stopping abruptly in an open spot. The stars illuminated the night sky and the moon was almost as bright as the sun. Stager stopped because he was tired and flew lazily in the air while everyone else caught their breath.

"That should put some distance between them and us, at least for a day or two." Gargran brought out a star glass and stared up at the night sky. "From our position, I would say we are eight hundred miles from Strati Polis, a good distance."

They flew in silence for a few more minutes while Stager rested in flight. The behemoth was tired, but the others could tell he was actually quite happy. Before they flew any further, Siphero asked them all for silence as he listened for something. Awesha came closer to him on Yevere and wondered what he was trying to listen to.

"What is it, Siphero?" she asked with concern. "We need to press forward. The Sangria Legion will catch up to us if we linger here."

Before she could finish her sentence, the clouds below them parted as a massive, shadowy shape emerged. It was made of metal, Siphero could tell. The object took the form of something that he recognized—but never thought he would see in Stratis. It was an airfortress. The massive airship was larger than a skywhale and weighed much more than that. Its decks were lined with passengers, who looked up into the sky or out toward those flying in the air. Several large cannons lined the ship's decks while gun crews manned turrets and pointed them toward Siphero's group. A giant door opened from the inside of the airfortress, revealing a host of Claymores and Sabers resting in the hanger, immobile. As the ship breached the clouds nose first, it came to a rest and held its position right next to them. On the nose of the ship, several soldiers formed a shield wall with large letters above them that said *Legionnaire*.

The hanger of the airfortress lit up like the night sky as a set of lights began to flicker inside, the signal reminding Siphero of the landing procedure of airblades and fortresses back home in Salvagon.

"Don't worry, everyone," he said to them all. "They're friendlies. They're inviting us aboard."

"But that thing is the size of a skywhale. How do we know it won't eat us?" Mervieris was looking nervous.

"Well, do you want to hang out here in the air and wait for our mounts to run out of energy? The alternative is we land on the ship."

He turned to Awesha, who was puzzled but eager to get out of the air. She nodded to him as they turned their mounts toward the airfortress, following the flickering lights. The rest waited a moment only to resign themselves to follow. As they entered the ship, they touched down in a clearing between all the Claymores and Sabers. A number of armored soldiers, wearing some kind of strange external armor over their bodies, came forward from every direction and surrounded them. They were armed with ballistic, energy and incendiary weapons.

Then at the order of an invisible leader, all the Terrans holstered their weapons as their leader came through the crowd. The being stood at least seven feet tall, wearing armor similar to his soldiers, but from behind him protruded one massive silver wing and a metal one. He wore a long sash across his shoulder that held many capsule grenades on it. His hair was the color of sapphires, and one of his eyes was an emerald color while the other was a deep brown. He was scarred heavily on his arms and forehead, but he wore them proudly.

This being before them all was unmistakably a Winged, and yet he appeared to be at home among Terrans. To their surprise, he smiled and raised his hands to them all, and the soldiers exited as quickly as they entered.

"Welcome, friends, welcome all, Winged, to the great *Legionnaire*." This Winged looked at all those in his audience to see if they were guarded against what he might throw at them.

"Please, friends, you are safe here. There is no need to be on guard." He took out a long sword like weapon, which Siphero saw was a mana blade, and he dropped it in front of them all and held his hands up in surrender. "Perhaps if one among you would please come forward, we could discuss the situation."

They all turned their back to the Winged and faced one another, deep in discussion on what to do next.

"He's honest about his intentions," Siphero began. "If he meant us harm, he would have done so by now."

"But, but these are Terrans," Mervieris said. "They can't be trusted. It doesn't matter if they come in peace; we will leave in pieces."

"Stop your bickering, Mervieris," Gargran said. "This fellow is offering us shelter, and I suggest we accept it."

"Oh, I'm the one bickering now."

"Will the two of you silence yourselves?" Ieava held a hand between them. "This is not the time to be arguing." She tried to stop a tear from flowing down her cheek, but Tratiki wiped it up and held his loved one closely.

"I don't know about this," Gargran added in. "I've never seen Terrans before, let alone this vessel of theirs. I believe we should stay."

"He's right," the young child guardian said between them. All heads turned to him as he surprised them by breaking his silence. "Look" he said, "not to state the obvious, but we must trust in their hospitality. Siphero got us here, so I believe he should be our intermediary."

"Very well, then, go on, our intermediary," Mervieris said in a huff of anger. "Go and intermediate."

Siphero turned and approached the leader of the ship's crew. Awesha followed him as she held his hand tightly, reassuring him of her trust in him.

"Uh, hello there," Siphero said. "My name is—"

"Siphero," the captain said. "Do not worry; we know all about you, my friend, and your true bonded one." He turned to face Awesha and did the traditional Winged bow and greeting to her.

"May the suns find you worthy of our assistance, Lady Awesha," he said humbly.

Siphero stared speechlessly at the captain while Awesha returned the greeting in her own way. She looked at Siphero, and her own amazement mirrored his own.

"How did you know my name, our names?"

The captain smiled as he turned and beckoned the rest to follow him into the ship. "Have no fear, my friends, this ship is stocked with food and bedding for your beasts. You may let them roam in the hanger. They will not come to any harm."

The others jumped down from their mounts, said their good-byes, and left them to hang around the airblades, where many just plopped down on the cool metal floors and fell right to sleep. Mervieris, Nylf, Gargran, Ieava, Tratiki, the blue-haired boy, and the twins followed Siphero and Awesha through a bulkhead, down some corridors, past an armory, and up a lift or two. The captain led the way without any difficulty, his metal wing and organic one folded around his back like the wings of the others. Oddly enough, the bulkheads, doorways, corridors, and even the lifts had been made to accommodate Winged, which they all found strange.

The captain finally came to a stop as he opened up a bulkhead, which lead to a very spacious and roomy lounge with couches, chairs, and beds that were bolted to the walls, and a table filled with foods similar to Winged cuisine lined the table. As they all settled in, the captain called to their attention one important matter.

"Now that you are all settled in, I wish for you to remain here for a few minutes. A special guest of mine wishes to meet all of you, so please try not to wander up to any of the passengers, as they are not accustomed to the appearance of Winged yet. Please just remain here. He will answer any and all questions you may have."

"What is your name?" Gargran asked the captain, his hand on his harpoon. "We must know of the one who came to our aid."

The captain smiled and answered in kind. "My name is Drenex, commander of the *Legionnaire*."

With that, Drenex left them to their own devices, closed the door behind him, and went to retrieve this "guest" he mentioned.

As the guardians took seats and rested, Mervieris went over to the table, took a large plate of mixed foods, and began eating, spitting out food he didn't like.

"Everyone," Siphero said. They stopped what they were doing to listen to him, though Mervieris was still munching on food. "I have something important to tell you."

He took a deep breath, and Awesha nodded for him to proceed. "I'm a Terran."

Shock ran through the group. Ieava, Tratiki, the blue-haired boy, and the twins gasped, but Mervieris just laughed, food coming out of his mouth.

"You, a Terran?" he said. "That is the funniest thing I have ever heard. How can you possibly be a Terran…"

He looked at Siphero and found he was dead serious. Mervieris slowly stopped.

All eyes were on Siphero, a thousand questions running through each of their minds. The blue-haired boy spoke first.

"Then tell us, Siphero, how are you a Terran and yet you have wings? Let us hear your reasoning. I, Octavio, would like to hear this."

Siphero sighed relief and sat in a chair while the others took up seats.

"Where do you want me to begin?"

"Summarize for us your life," Octavio said simply.

"OK, my name is Siphero Antolus, and I was born in the town of Saltdeep in Jormundgard's Midwestern province. It's a mining and farming town; it produced raw salt and the occasional shipments of titanium ore."

"You were born a peasant?" Ieava asked. "I never met someone who was born at the lowest parts of society."

Tratiki growled at Ieava, "I was born down there as well, Ieava. Be more respectful."

"My apologies, Siphero. Please continue."

Awesha shook her head in disgust. A princess had no place judging someone based upon their upbringing. She would know; she hated her upbringing.

"All right," Siphero said, "when I was about seven, my town came under attack from some strange beings clad in a foreign crimson armor. They rained fire from the sky and even destroyed most of the village…and—"

"What else?" Gargran said, pausing to assess Siphero's state of mind. He saw Siphero was crying softly to himself. "Is this a particularly painful memory?"

Siphero nodded, took a deep breath, wiped away the tears, and continued. "Their leader…killed my mother."

Everyone in the room gasped. Awesha placed her hand on Siphero's shoulder. "He's only ever told me once. Jormundgard is a world of never-ending war kept in check by powerful armies."

"How barbaric," Mervieris said bitterly. "You come to Stratis and tell us you dislike fighting in a world of war. You are a pathetic excuse for a Terran and an even worse Engria."

Before Siphero could retort this insult, Mervieris found a pair of twin daggers underneath his throat. He looked down and found the twins were within an inch of slicing his throat wide open.

"You are not worthy of speaking that way," they said in sync. "You know not suffering, you know not intolerance, nor do you understand the fear of death. The Far East has all of these, and we, Xhe-Zhe, were born into its hardships."

They withdrew their daggers and returned to their seats. Octavio motioned for Siphero to return to his description of himself.

"Where did I leave off? Oh, right. I was accepted into Salvagon's military academy, where I majored in engineering and piloting. That's why I'm so good at fixing things."

"So that's why you made that metal bird of yours," Nylf said. "You can make things."

Siphero snickered. "Well, I don't mean to brag, but yes I am very good at building and fixing machines, even modifying them."

Awesha rolled her eyes and slapped him on the head, getting him back on track.

"I graduated from there, along with five of my best friends, who were oddballs like myself. I don't know what they are up to now, but I'm sure I'll find out if I ever go back. Anyway, after graduation, the Envisioner, the General of Salvagon, sent me and Pops, my adoptive father, to the Edge Mountain Range. For the next two months, Pops and I built, tested, and refined the designs the Envisioner occasionally sent us, with our last invention being an airblade, the fastest one ever, capable of carrying a single pilot."

Awesha stepped forward and finished the story her true-bonded was telling them all. "It was then that I met Siphero, when I was spying on him, and this is how I bonded with him."

A lot of them nodded. This had cleared a lot of uncertainty they had about the formation of such a strange pairing.

"What was Siphero like when you first met him?" Ieava asked. "Was he brave, strong, handsome?"

"None of the above, unfortunately," Siphero said, chuckling. "I'm sorry, princess, but she didn't find her prince. She became bonded to a loser like me."

Gargran, Octavio, Tratiki, Nylf, and the twins, Xhe-Zhe, chuckled at this. They found it amusing that Siphero would belittle himself in response to such an important event.

Awesha drew her baton and clubbed Siphero twice, gently, on his head.

Siphero rubbed his head in response to the new pain while Awesha berated him. "You are not a loser, Siphero. I will admit that I was less than pleased to have bonded with a Terran such as yourself, but now that I am with you here, I am glad it was you. You are the most considerate, compassionate, driven, and understanding person I have ever met."

They smiled at each other for a moment, and Awesha continued. "Of course, my parents denied my bond with Siphero, and my father…killed his adoptive father without a second thought."

More gasping occurred while Ieava looked from Awesha to Siphero, but she saw no animosity toward each other in their eyes. They only saw the two of them grip their hands tighter out of concern for one another.

"After that," Awesha said, "my father was expelled from Skyspire, and we were chosen by two of history's most defiant Archons, Preduvon the Great Defiant and Verrencae, Lady of the Scarred."

Now this surprised the likes of Ieava, Octavio, and Mervieris, but it delighted Tratiki, Xhe-Zhe, Nylf, and Gargran.

"The Great Defiant chose you, Siphero?" Nylf asked. "That's spectacular. I never thought he would become an Archon, let alone Verrencae becoming one as well. They hold a special place in the hearts of all Compa and Wingless. They died in the defense of those they promised their lives to."

"It's true," Tratiki said. "My leaders feared and respected Preduvon. They even traded and helped take care of the Scarred under Verrencae's care. The two of them are important in the lives of all Sila. You have no idea how important they were to the lower castes of Stratis."

"Now you tell us," Siphero said. "Even I don't know so much about Preduvon or Verrencae. They were really that important?"

"Yes," Gargran said. "It's been over twenty years since they died, and they are still missed. I knew Preduvon when I was younger. He was like a brother to me. He was always so angry, difficult, and short tempered, but he was someone who would stick by your side no matter the number of enemies or how powerful they were. He stood up to everyone, and I mean everyone."

"That's about all there is too it," Siphero said. "I got my mount, Stager, I grew bones out of my back one night, and…"

Awesha shivered a bit, while the others wondered what that meant, until Siphero briefly described it to them. But when Siphero mentioned Awesha's change, her rainbow wings, all of what Siphero said left their minds.

"Awesha trained me and helped me get ready for the guardianship, and then we came here, but you have to understand why I hid my true identity. If I had told anyone in Strati Polis—"

"They might have killed you on sight," Octavio said abruptly. "That would have been their most correct course of action, specifically the Sangria Legion."

"And that's how I'm here telling you my life story," he said. "Now, do you mind introducing yourselves? I only know your names, so do you think you could tell us more about each of you?"

The unnamed guardians came forward, one by one, bowed to them all, and introduced themselves. The young boy went first, lowering his trident. "I am called by my people and my faith Octavio, the Faithful Enlightened. I am a monk from the remote church state of Archo Polis, the home of all the history of Stratis and the Archons."

"So your people are record keepers for the Winged Empire?"

"Yes, and so much more." He paused and smiled a childish grin. "You are confused why a child such as myself was named a guardian, despite my age?"

Siphero laughed in an embarrassed tone, as did most of the others. "Can you blame me?"

"Not at all, but I was named to guardianship by the head archivist more as a way to get rid of me rather than as a position of honor."

"Gee," Siphero said with sorrow, "I really don't know what to say to that."

"Then say nothing. It is easier to listen than it is to speak, is it not?" Octavio turned to the twins, who faced the rest of the company. "Now who might you two be?"

The twins stepped forward, bowed to them all, and introduced themselves, the whole while performing actions in perfect synchronization. "We are called Xhe-Zhe, the Twice-Born. We are from the far eastern continent of Stratis, the Far Eastern Polis, birthing ground of the skywhale, the richest nation of trade and mercantile practices in all of Stratis. We ourselves are from a well-renowned theater and family, the Jeweled Garden of the Jade Drakes."

"I have heard of this," Gargran said. "This theater is well-known in the Stormlands, a place for weary travelers to rest their souls and enjoy the bounty of beautiful women and their graceful dancing."

"We thank you, Storm Rider. Your people have always visited our theater and have traded with us graciously." The twins again bowed and did a little twirl for all the watchers, mesmerizing them with their beautiful dancing.

They instantly stopped as Gargran stepped forward and introduced himself to them all. "I am Gargran, Storm Rider. My home is deep in the Stormlands, a desolate place constantly bombarded by a never-ending storm."

"How do you and your people survive there?" Ieava asked. "It must be impossible for anyone to live there."

Gargran laughed heartily as the air around him crackled and popped with flashes of lightning around his wings.

"We survive," he boasted, "because we are the strongest warriors in all of Stratis. We have leviathans, wild storm drakes, skysharks, and the occasional skywhale, and we even tame them the hard way. We do this with no more than the weapons we wield and the affinities in our blood."

"That makes sense." Siphero hunched over as he listened with interest. "But you mentioned back at the ballroom that you were a hunter. You bragged about it a lot."

The others nodded a great deal to this, and Gargran just grinned wildly at them all. "It is true; I am a hunter. It is the trade in that part of the world. It is a dangerous life, but never dull, and I was named to guardianship for having the most skyshark kills. The other hunters in Storm Polis were always jealous of my achievement, and to this day they use my accomplishments as a driving force to succeed in the hunt."

"That is an amazing way of life," Tratiki said, "but you would enjoy the Sila life just as much."

"After all of this is resolved," Gargran said, "I may take you up on that offer."

"Now, now, everyone, aren't you forgetting that you wish to hear of Jormundgard from our friend Siphero here?" Octavio pointed out the reason for their conversation.

"All right, all right, I'll tell what it was like." Siphero started, and over the next few minutes, he described Jormundgard to them, taking sips of water to keep his throat moist. He started with his hometown of Saltdeep and then moved to the different parts like the Rusted City, an abandoned city filled with buildings falling apart. Once he got to Salvagon, he described its wide cityscape, how every citizen was trained in the use of different armors like the ones they say the soldiers were using on the *Legionnaire*, including the strange metal skeletons they used. Siphero included how it was necessary since war was so common between Terrans on Jormundgard that just in case a city or town was invaded or taken over, the citizens were given value to a battle so meaningless slaughter would be minimized. As he drew to a close, they asked him a myriad of questions.

"All Terrans are trained in the art of battle," Gargran started. "That must be an incredible achievement for your people."

"Yeah, but it makes handling criminals a troubling procedure."

"But are there not Terrans who dislike this system in Jormundgard?" Ieava asked. "Surely they must live outside of the larger cities' influences?"

"That's actually quite true, Ieava. They live in caravans or camps and make a living as scavengers, raiders and pirates. Then there are the pacifists, like myself." His gaze turned to Tratiki, who scratched his chin.

"What about the military might of a battle-hardened soldier?" Mervieris butted in. "There must be soldiers mightier than those in this flying tub."

"There are, but they are the elite of the elite, and they are also the most dangerous. You see, when it comes to battlefield strategy, Terrans prepare for everything. They prefer versatility over specialization. The greatest weapon they ever created was the Iron Giant, a hulking war machine—"

Before Siphero could explain any more, the door to the lounge slammed open, and a small group of soldiers marched through, carrying projectors as they escorted an elderly man in a blue and white robe with armored pauldrons and chest plate. The gentleman was completely bald, with one white eye and a mechanical one. He walked with a staff made of turning gears and cogs that constantly whirred and grinded. Strangely, he had wings upon his back. One was a pure white while the other was bat-like. He was the special guest of the *Legionnaire*.

Drenex came in behind this old man and bowed before him. "Let me introduce one of the leaders of our organization, which seeks to safeguard against hostilities between Winged and Terrans across both our worlds of Jormundgard and Stratis. The eye that long foresaw the inevitable struggle, the hand that strode forth to establish a secret peace with the Terrans of Jormundgard and watch over the future of events to come—"

"Rekusolus," Octavio said in amazement, "the Teller of Doom."

"Ah, so one of you knows of me," Rekusolus said. "This will make it easier to explain our circumstances."

Rekusolus cleared his throat before he spoke. "As your friend the monk from the Archo Polis has said, I am Rekusolus, and I am one of many leaders of the True Allegiants, an organization that stands vigil in preventing the inevitable conflict between Winged and Terrans."

"Preposterous," Mervieris said. "A Terran and Winged alliance? It is the most absurd claim I have ever heard. The ground dwellers would never agree to such a partnership; they are too barbaric."

He regretted that statement as soon as Siphero and Awesha turned their attention to him, as did Ieava and Tratiki. Mervieris slunk to the back of the lounge, where he stuffed his mouth silently.

Rekusolus continued. "As I was saying, the enlightened fools in the Archo Polis said the same thing about my insights. I was exiled for 'continuing to spout blasphemous claims about the future of the Winged Empire,' so I decided to take matters into my own hands. Fifteen years ago, I left the world of Stratis and descended upon Jormundgard to seek an understanding with any Terrans I could gain an audience with."

As he spoke, the entire group listened to his story, and no one interrupted unless there was a break in the conversation. Siphero and Awesha were surprised themselves to hear of a Winged making contact with Terrans.

"The one disadvantage I had was that I did not know what happened when a Winged enters Jormundgard. For you see, in order to make the crossing between worlds, the benefits you gained in one world must be forfeited. Upon entering Jormundgard, I lost the use of my wings. I was shocked as I watched them vanish from my back, but I still retained the use of some of my magic. The part of Jormundgard I had entered was known as the Diseased Abyss, where Terrans deposit all of the waste and sludge their highly civilized cities produce."

Siphero remembered that area of Jormundgard. "I know that place. It's the most polluted quagmire in all of Jormundgard."

"Correct, boy," he said. "There, a collection of Terrans found me and took me in, and that was where I met Drenex. Not all Terrans are monsters; there are some who live in relative safety and only fight when they have been threatened."

He took a deep breath as he continued. "A few years later, I met up with a general who was quite open to any and all information regarding Winged. The strangest thing happened when I introduced myself as a Winged."

The room grew silent when Rekusolus paused for dramatic effect.

"This general believed me, any and all information I shared with him. He shared his concerns on how Jormundgard might erupt into another major conflict because its present leadership teeters on the edge of civil war. When I proposed we form an alliance, he agreed, and from then on I have served as a guide and one of the leaders of the True Allegiants."

Ieava interrupted. "How is this possible? Winged and Terrans working together? Surely there were Terrans that wanted nothing to do with you."

"You are correct, orphaned princess," Rekusolus said to Ieava, "getting more Terrans to join us was difficult at first. Most Terrans are civilians or engineers that have served in an army, but what they want most of all is safety, security, and a good cause to fight for, which is almost impossible to find in Jormundgard. Upon discovering that we offered all of these, Terrans around the world began joining us. we have agents in almost all Terran cities. The True Allegiants are at least a few million Terrans strong."

"I have a question," Gargran said, raising his hand. "How many Terrans occupy all of Jormundgard?"

Rekusolus smiled. "You would be surprised, Storm Rider. Their number is several times larger than all of Stratis. Octavio, by the elders' last count, how many Winged exist in all of Stratis?"

Octavio reached into his satchel and pulled out a journal and flipped through a few pages until he came to a set of pages lined with numbers. "We did a population count about two years ago, but we found the population of Stratis is over seven million, eight hundred forty-five thousand, eighty-seven. That figure includes all the major poleis and all castes."

Ieava, Tratiki, and Mervieris were impressed with that number, but Mervieris was a little worried. "How large is the population of Terrans in Jormundgard if you were to use the same characteristics, including all major cities, villages, and backwater communities?"

"The total number of Terrans is always in flux, as they are dying and more are born every day, but I know this for certain," Rekusolus said. "There are over one and a half billion Terrans in all of Jormundgard across all of its provinces and territories."

Everyone in the lounge gasped, Ieava fainted, Nylf mouthed her surprise, Gargran whistled, and the twins fanned themselves. Octavio crunched the numbers and came to the conclusion of how many Terrans there were to Winged.

"That means they outnumber us at least two hundred to one," he said. "They could invade Stratis and wipe us out without a second thought."

"That is correct," the Teller said. "It is for this reason that the True Allegiants exist, to recruit, train, and help any Terrans that are sympathetic to our cause. Over the last fifteen years, it has been a race against time to garner as much support as we can to try and dissuade, distract, or divert the attention of the other generals of Jormundgard away from the frontier of Stratis. It appears from what Drenex has told me about your recent dealings with the Sangria Legion that our window for preventing a war from breaking out is fast approaching."

Drenex stepped forward and said, "So now that all of you have been informed of the situation, I have an offer to make to you all. Will you join the True Allegiants?"

The offer caught the group off guard, but they were keenly aware they had nowhere else to go.

"What's in it for us?" Ieava asked. "Can these Terrans meet the demands of serving Winged royalty?"

Drenex eyed her angrily. "The first thing you should know once you join us is that the person you were before does not matter in the True Allegiants. All that you once were—titles, former jobs, castes, place in society, and privileges—will be cast out. You will start with a clean slate and be assigned work based upon your skills and merits. Either you have useful skills or you are dead weight. There is no such thing as royalty in the True Allegiants. It serves no purpose except to show that someone is superior to another based simply upon birth.

"I'm liking this already," Nylf said. "Do you have a place for Wingless in the Allegiants?"

Drenex turned his attention toward Nylf and smiled. "Wingless are considered more akin to Terrans that anyone else. Nylf, is it? You are already one of us."

"All right then, I want in," Nylf said immediately. "I don't care what you throw at me; I want to join."

"Absolutely not," Ieava interrupted. "You served my mother and father, which means you must serve me, Nylf. You are honor-bound to serve."

"I will not serve you, Ieava," she said to the princess. "I served your parents, but I do not serve you. Find another to alienate for your own amusement."

Nylf marched right up to Drenex, ripped off the symbol of the king and queen, threw it at the feet of Ieava, and was escorted through the bulkhead to a room of her own by Allegiant soldiers.

"Anyone else?" Drenex asked. "If you do not wish to join, you will be treated as guests until we can transport you to a friendly polis who can 'tolerate' your stay."

The lounge was silent until the twins stepped forward. They removed their badges of honor they had been given to mark their title of guardian and handed it to a Terran soldier. They were escorted out of the lounge. Next, Gargran stepped forward and did the same, followed by Octavio and Tratiki.

Ieava was frightened that Tratiki was leaving her. "Tratiki, why are you joining these barbarians?"

"Ieava, my dear," he began, "these Allegiants are offering us shelter and a way to strike back against the Sangria Legion. They killed your mother and father. I want to make them pay for this. Aren't you angry with them at all?"

Tratiki approached Drenex and imitated a Terran salute. "I would like to vouch for my true bonded. May she stay in a room with me?"

Drenex pondered for a moment and agreed to the offer. "I understand how important it is to have a true bonded, so she may stay in your room instead of in the guest quarters."

Tratiki bowed his head, grabbed Ieava's hand, and dragged her forcefully out the door.

The only ones still in the room were Siphero, Awesha, and Mervieris, the undecided ones.

Drenex approached Siphero and said, "How about you, boy? Do you want to join us?"

Siphero kept looking from Awesha back to Drenex. He had a hard time deciding. "I don't know. Do you have any place for a pacifist?"

Drenex laughed at Siphero's statement, the reaction Siphero expected.

"Of course we do," he said. "A great deal of our forces are pacifists. They understand, however, that the only way for them to remain safe and secure is to fight. What skills do you have?"

"Well," Siphero began, "I graduated from Salvagon with expertise in engineering and piloting—"

"Wait a minute. You graduated from Salvagon? You mean you're a Terran?" Drenex asked.

"Um, yes, sir, I thought that was apparent."

"But you have wings. If you're really a Terran, what town or city in Jormundgard are you from?"

"Saltdeep. I lived there until I was seven, and it was nearly destroyed…"

Drenex went slack-jawed. He seemed to mumble his next sentence. "What is your name, boy? Your full name?"

"Siphero Antolus, sir."

"Oh dear," Rekusolus said. "Oh dear."

Drenex seemed to drop to his knees in sorrow, tears rolling down his face as he cried with joy. Siphero watched as the Winged with a composite wing reached his hand out toward him. Awesha felt Siphero's memories flash through her mind: a burning town, a white-winged Avia fighting against a knight wreathed in flames while a small child was shielded from a ball of fire by a woman, only for her to burst into flames and disappear into water vapor.

"Siphero," Drenex said. "You…you have your mother's eyes."

Shock crept over Siphero, and Awesha was hit with a flood of memories.

"How did you know my mother?" he asked, completely puzzled. He then looked into Drenex's eyes and he felt something familiar. The memory of the white-winged Avia's face flashed in his mind.

Chapter 18: Traumatism

Awesha awoke in a strange place, a bedroom fit for a small child. The room contained a wooden and metal bed that rocked from side to side at regular intervals. On the walls were screens that flickered with pictures of people performing daredevil stunts on airblades as they flew past skyscrapers. Above the bed were models of airfortresses, Claymores, Sabers, and stars that seemed to hover in the air by themselves. A window from the room overlooked an entire town surrounded by tall, thick mountains.

"What is this place?" Awesha asked, fluttering to her feet.

"This is my room," a little boy said in front of her. "Who are you?"

Awesha looked down and saw the child. She thought he looked an awful lot like Siphero, with scruffy brown hair, brown eyes, and a bunch of freckles on his face.

She knelt down and asked, "Hello, little one, what is your name?"

The boy looked up at her and said, "I asked you first, you should answer first."

"My name is Awesha," she said. She realized that this child was a lot like someone she knew.

"Siphero Antolus Dreamen," a voice called to him from another room, "it's time to get ready to do some farm work, my little dreamer."

The speaker came through the open door, and Awesha made a guess as to who it was: this was Siphero's mother.

"Please, Momma," the young Siphero said, "can't I just help fix the airblade engines?"

"No, little dreamer," she said, "do you remember what I always tell you? Opportunity…"

"…is open to those who have the skills," little Siphero recited. "Fine, Momma, but can my friend come with us? Her name is Awesha."

Siphero's mother looked up, and her eyes met Awesha's. "Oh, I didn't see you there. Do you mind coming with us? Siphero has so few friends in Saltdeep; he's happier to fix things than he is helping me."

Awesha didn't know how to answer, so she just nodded, and Siphero pulled her by the hand out of his room, through the kitchen, and out the door.

Siphero's mother followed them. Awesha quickly examined her out of the corner of her eye and learned a great deal. She was a short woman with worn hands, beautiful green eyes, and brown hair cut short with streaks of gray tucked in over her ears. Her clothing was simple: oil-stained overalls with black pants and closed-toed sandals. She wore some old worn steel body armor over her chest, arms, and legs.

Upon exiting the kitchen, the town of Saltdeep opened up before them as Siphero continued to drag Awesha down the hill, past mining crews riding on trucks, tractors hauling crops that had been recently harvested, and houses decorated with different colored pieces of metal sheets that had been rigged as makeshift protection.

While walking, Awesha had tried to use her wings, only to find they were not upon her back. This made her panic a bit, but she realized she must be witnessing one of Siphero's memories. She was dreaming.

Once at the bottom of the hill, Siphero let go of her hand and ran off to help some farmers lift crates of food that were ready for shipping onto transport rigs. Straea, Siphero's mother, came down and handed her a flower.

"You are very beautiful, Awesha," she said. "I hope you will take good care of my son. He's goofy, stubborn, and gets into trouble all the time. He will never betray your trust."

Straea passed Awesha and waved good-bye. Awesha tried to chase after her, but the landscape changed before her. She was now standing in a small forest, with Saltdeep at her back. Looking around, she saw Straea and ran after her. Young Siphero was riding on her shoulders.

After following them a short distance, they came upon someone meditating underneath a small waterfall. Awesha ducked behind a tree trunk and watched as Sstraea set Siphero down, letting him run up to the person underneath the waterfall.

As soon as Siphero was close enough, he called out, "Papa, Papa, we brought you some dinner! Won't you eat with us tonight?"

The one called Papa opened his eyes and came out from underneath the waterfall, picked up Siphero, and spun him around in a circle. Awesha couldn't help but notice two stitched wounds on his back. She assumed it was a unique injury. Upon closer examination of the person Siphero called Papa, she realized there was an uncanny resemblance to Drenex, the commander of the *Legionnaire*.

"So you're the one who is bonded to my son," Papa said to Awesha. "You are his family now, the one he cherishes above all else."

Before she could react, the scene changed again back to Saltdeep. It was already night.

Awesha walked around the town for a few minutes. It was pitch black, and she was calling for Straea and Siphero. She was cut short when a flaming rock came crashing down on top of a house. Then a whole barrage of flaming rocks rained down from the sky as beings appeared in the sky, flaming-red wings and blood-red armor. Citizens in Saltdeep rushed out of their houses, clad in armor and holding projectors as they fired up into the sky, felling a few of the fiery demons, but the citizens fell quickly. Everyone in the town was slaughtered and set on fire. Awesha tried to fight back, but she had no weapons, and when she tried to pick up a Terran projector, her hand went right through it. The attacking warriors ignored her as well.

Then from among the forest, a being shot out of the woods at lightning speed and slew soldier after burning soldier. On the ground, a lone woman carrying a child came running out of a house. The flying warriors in the air saw the woman running on the ground, and a soldier broke off from the main group to pursue the woman. The woman ran, crying out desperately for help as the flying soldier knocked her over and caused the child to go rolling out of her arms. The woman crawled over to the child and stroked him gently to stop his crying. She got on her knees and spread her arms to act as a shield.

"I won't let you take my child, you monsters," she said.

"You know not how important that child is," the warrior said in a deep voice, "I will take your child and raise him as my own."

"You cannot have him!" Straea pulled a pistol from her belt. "I will die before you even touch him!"

She fired a few rounds at the warrior, who dodged out of the way of the shots and grabbed Straea by the throat. The warrior smiled maliciously as Straea's body began to dissolve before her, starting with her feet and continuing up. She started to panic, but then she saw little Siphero watching her dissolve into nothingness. She stopped panicking and stared straight into the eyes of her attacker.

"You will never have my son," she said. "You will never have the opportunity to know what it is like to be a mother. The day you die, I hope that is the greatest regret you have." As her face dissolved, all that was left behind were her clothes, which the soldier lit on fire and cast aside. As the warrior approached the child, it sheathed its sword and removed the helmet to reveal a woman with fiery hair and crimson-colored lips.

She smiled lovingly at the small boy and reached out her hand.

At that moment, Awesha regained the use of her wings and held her baton and Siphero's shield in her hands. She rushed forward at blazing speed and slashed at the woman who had killed Siphero's mother.

"You will never have him," she said coldly. "He is not yours to take."

The memory faded. Awesha stood in front of little Siphero, who was still crying and asking for his mother. As the world crumbled into nothingness, Awesha approached the little boy and held out her hand to him.

"I promise I'll be there for you, Siphero," she said. "I promised your mother and father I'd be there for you."

Awesha awoke in a cabin, the rhythmic hum of the engines running through the entirety of the *Legionnaire*. As she rose from the bed, she saw Siphero sleeping in the corner. She smiled and remembered how he was always faithful to her. She got up and found she was wearing the long white gown she had worn when Siphero flew with his wings for the first time. Her hair had been undone and let hang across her back. She hated wearing this dress, but it reminded her of how much Siphero meant to her.

"Oh good, you're awake." Gargran appeared in the doorway.

"How long have I been asleep?" she asked Gargran.

"Only a couple days, Awesha. But you've got to see this machine, it is massive…"

Awesha's attention drifted over to Siphero, who was still sleeping soundly in the chair.

"He never left your side, you know," Gargran whispered. "Two days you were out, and he has remained here all this time. I wonder though, what were you dreaming of?"

She remained silent. She couldn't put into words what she had seen. It was too painful for her, too painful for Siphero. She had seen his childhood ripped away from him by those murderers. Who were they? This made her think of her own sister and wonder if she would ever see her again.

Gargran departed, leaving the door open for another to enter. Drenex came through and sat in a chair closest to the door, adjacent to Awesha's bed.

"How are you doing, Awesha?" he asked. "Well, I hope."

Awesha met his eyes, and she could see he was more concerned about Siphero than for her well-being.

"You're Siphero's father, aren't you?" Awesha said. "You are Dreamen."

Drenex appeared shocked for a moment, then nodded. "That is correct."

Awesha rolled up the sleeve on her left arm and showed him the ribbon and chain tied together.

"You are a Winged like me," Awesha said gently. "You were true bonded with Straea, Siphero's mother. I am true bonded to Siphero."

Dreamen touched the tattoo and smiled. He removed the armor on his bicep, rolled up his sleeve, and showed a faded tattoo of a blue ribbon tied together with a chain.

"I never thought I would see another one of these marks in my life," he said. "Tell me, what was it like bonding with my son?"

"It was wonderful, and yet," she began, "foreign. When I first met him, I thought he was a giant metal bird. My parents wanted me to become bonded to a Bond Scrivener, and I wanted to escape their arranged marriage. When I bonded with Siphero, I regretted it at first. But now that I am here, in his world of war, I am happy that my bond formed with him. He is the only person in my life that I cherish."

Dreamen smiled. "So you're in love with my son?"

Awesha blushed and her rainbow wings shone brightly. She tried to hide her embarrassment, but it was all the proof Dreamen needed.

"Why the secrecy? Why did you call yourself Drenex?" Awesha asked him.

Dreamen got up, paced a bit in the room, and then said, "I was afraid once my wife died at the hands of those monsters, I exiled myself. I have carried this sin of mine for eighteen years. I abandoned Siphero in his hometown when I should have raised him myself."

Awesha dropped her gaze and focused on Siphero's tattoo of their bond. "I saw his past, I saw what you did to the enemy, and I saw you leave. It's not your fault. I will tell him when he awakens that you love him."

Dreamen nodded in appreciation. "Thank you, Awesha. I had my doubts about you, but you are quite honorable. You have my blessing."

"What?"

"My blessing," he repeated. "Is it not customary for a father to give his blessing to a potential suitor? I am well aware of Winged family traditions, but nearly twenty years with Terrans has taught me tradition can get you killed."

"I can't picture myself as Siphero's wife right now," she said in a flustered manner. "We're at war and I don't know what tomorrow will bring."

"I know, but he loves you. My son has fallen in love, and I want him to be happy. That is why I joined up with the True Allegiants. This is why I fight, to make a world where people like Siphero can live without the fear of war."

Dreamen nodded good-bye and exited the room, closing the door behind him.

"Is he gone?" a now-awake Siphero said.

Awesha snapped her attention back to see Siphero laughing at her. Her blush turned scarlet as she reached out with her affinity and pulled him by the feet out of his chair and let him dangle in the air.

"Hey, let me go," he said. "This isn't funny, Awesha."

"And you think listening to your father say I could marry you is?"

"Yeah…I can see how that is unexpected."

He continued to dangle, trying to get free, but he had no luck. So he folded his arms and directed his attention to Awesha.

"Awesha," he asked sincerely, "do you love me?"

Awesha's eyes snapped open, and she focused her gaze on Siphero. She had always been taught that for Winged bonds were necessary for survival, not for romance. Winged who didn't bond risked suffocating on an overabundance of mana in their bodies. But Awesha couldn't deny that her bond with Siphero had evolved into something more.

She smiled as a tear rolled down her cheek. For the first time in her life, she was overcome with true happiness.

"I do," she whispered.

Chapter 19: Rekindling

A couple days passed aboard the *Legionnaire* without much incident as it traveled along its set course, Silacorlis, the homeland of all Sila. This destination was decided upon because Tratiki had suggested this. The House of Feral Beasts needed to be told of the Sangria Legion's traitorous deeds. Rekusolus agreed to this as well. He explained the mission of the *Legionnaire*, to form alliances with any and all Winged who wanted to prevent a future war with the Terrans.

Each of the *Legionnaire*'s new crewmembers settled into their roles aboard the airfortress. Nylf joined the Allegiants as a recruit and quickly started learning the ways of Terran warfare, a much-deserved change from her previous duties of sucking up to corrupt and prideful nobility. Gargran became a fighting instructor to Terran soldiers, teaching them what he knew about Winged strategies and tactics in battle. The twins, Xhe-Zhe, spent their time cooking in the galley, learning from the mess hall cooks, and entertaining the soldiers onboard the ship with their beautiful dances. Mervieris spent most of his time alone in the guest quarters. He was still undecided over whether he wanted to join the True Allegiants or not. Tratiki shared information with the Terrans onboard the *Legionnaire*, telling them anything that might help them once they arrived in Silacorlis. Ieava spent most of her time in Tratiki's quarters, waiting for him to return, or in the company of Rekusolus, being taught the importance of her situation and how she was now the only legitimate heir to the throne.

Ieava hadn't had time to properly mourn the loss of her parents, and she was still distraught.

Siphero and Awesha spent those days learning more about the True Allegiants, their goals and their future plans for Stratis and Jormundgard. Octavio was with them the whole time, learning all he could from Rekusolus, as he had wished to assist the Teller of Doom in any way after learning of the inevitable war and seeing firsthand how far the white wings of the Sangria Legion were willing to go. In return, Siphero and Awesha shared any and all information they could recount with Rekusolus and Dreamen, the father Siphero had forgotten. They spoke of being chosen by the Archons Preduvon and

Verrencae, the disappearance of their Archons, and of Ieava's parents becoming Archons themselves.

"The king and queen became Archons?" Rekusolus said. "The Sangria Legion will run rampant now that they are gone. Tell me what happened to them."

"They disappeared through a portal," Siphero said, "with Preduvon and Verrencae saying the bond between us must survive."

"As did Ieava's parents," Awesha said. "Before they left, they said they acknowledged the bond between Siphero and I."

Rekusolus's eyebrows rose, but he remained silent for at least another few minutes to reflect on it. "That is an amazing statement there."

"What is it, Rekusolus?" Dreamen was sitting on a lounge chair adjacent to Awesha, his wings draped over his sides.

"Don't you see? The king and queen, right before they left this world, gave their Archonic blessing to these two. The bond between them is considered precious to those who live on. This is excellent news."

"What do you mean?" Awesha asked. "Are the Archons not manifestations of the emotions and feelings of those who act as our spirit guides through life?"

"No, my dear, the Archons are not empty husks that answer the call of their chosen. They are actually the echoes of Winged whose very ideals and beliefs were too powerful to die, so they live on as incarnations of their own purposes."

"So our Archons," Siphero said, "Preduvon and Verrencae, continue to exist because of what they believed in?"

"You are only half correct, Siphero. Those two were chosen to become Archons for they represented the feelings of the downtrodden, the oppressed, and the discriminated who were preyed upon by the Avia. If anything, most Winged who form the bond pray they are not chosen by either of them, but for the both of you to be chosen individually truly makes your pairing special."

"Did you and Straea ever manifest an Archon?" Siphero asked his father.

Dreamen was silent as he scratched his head in anguish. He spoke after a minute of silence. "We did, but I didn't expect it to happen since we were in Jormundgard. I didn't even think an Archon would make an appearance. The Archon who appeared when our bond was formed was Hevros, the Broken-Born."

Rekusolus and Awesha jumped out of their seats in amazement at the mentioning of that name. They returned to their seats after a few seconds, but Rekusolus was the first to speak.

"Hevros…that Hevros, but he has only ever answered the call for individuals who have changed the very nature of the bond. Why would he appear for you and your former wife, a Terran?"

"It was because she was a Terran that he came. When he first appeared, I was shocked to see him, as was Straea. She had never seen an Archon before. In his own words, he said that the potential for the bond had expanded, that now Terrans can form bonds with Winged."

"Wait, wait, wait." Siphero stopped his father. "You mean to tell me the reason why Awesha was able to form a bond with me is because you and mom formed the first bond possible between Winged and Terrans?"

"When you put it that way, son," he said, "you're welcome."

Awesha smiled, and Siphero rolled his eyes and huffed one word: "Great."

"Then back to the matter at hand." Rekusolus turned his attention to Siphero and Awesha. "The bond between you is incredibly strong. If the Sangria Legion discover your bond, the Grand Clerician will use it as fuel to drive the fires of her war."

"She already knows," Awesha said gloomily. "Somehow during our skirmish at the palace, she said a Terran had infiltrated the palace of the king and queen. Someone told her of our bond, and she used it to whip the zealots that follow her into a large enough frenzy."

"Now that the king and queen are dead, the Sangria Legion will surely follow her destructive plans." Rekusolus paused for a moment and noticed that Siphero and Awesha's fingers were interlocked. "Why are you two holding hands again? It's the third time today that I've seen you do this."

Siphero and Awesha looked down at their hands and were shocked to see their hands were gently interlocked, the tattoo of the ribbon and the chain glowing brightly on their arms. They let go, and the tattoo faded.

"We didn't mean to do that," Siphero said. "For some reason it just happens when we least expect it."

"I do not mean to intrude upon your personal lives, but how deeply have the two of you become bonded with one another?" Dreamen looked over at them.

"I'm not sure," Awesha said, surprise in her voice. "Sometimes I see flashes of Siphero's memories. I can feel his pain, his joy, his sadness, even his breath when I am far from him."

"Then that is our proof." Rekusolus twiddled with his staff for a few seconds. "The bond the two of you share is continuing to blossom and grow. I heard, Siphero, that you thwarted a Bond Scrivener's attempt to break your bond. Is that right?"

"It's true," Siphero said. "Is that normal?"

"No, it isn't," Rekusolus exclaimed. "Bond Scriveners exist to test a bond, to push it past its limits. It is the ultimate test of faith and love between bonded partners. To think you caused a Bond Scrivener to fail in his duty must have scared him beyond belief. But I am curious about what your Archons said, 'Your bond must survive.' I don't know what that means, but I believe your bond is unlike any other that exists in both our worlds, so it stands to reason that your bond will continue to strengthen as you meet new challenges and overcome them. I believe your bond will guide you on this long journey."

Siphero and Awesha let their hands touch again, and the tattoo glowed brightly. They left the room while Dreamen and Rekusolus discussed what to do next with Octavio, who had been waiting patiently outside the door.

"So what are you going to do now, Awesha?" Siphero asked her in the hallway. "I'm headed down to the hanger. Rekusolus has asked me to do something."

"I will go to my room. I'm tired from having that discussion." She yawned, kissed Siphero on the cheek, and walked in the direction of her room. However, just as she was about to enter one of the bulkheads, she felt herself turn around and return to Siphero.

She took Siphero and herself by surprise when she held his hand, stopping him from leaving.

"Uh, Awesha, are you OK? Do you think you could let go of my hand?" He tried letting go, but her hand stayed bound to his own.

She was attempting to move her fingers, and for some reason they would not obey her.

"I can't; it's like my hand has a mind of its own." They continued to try and let go for at least a few more minutes until they just gave up.

"Well, this is a fine mess," Siphero said, annoyed. "I never thought our bond would do this to us. Why don't we just go to the hanger? I promise I'm only going to be down there for about an hour."

"Fine then," she agreed. "Perhaps by that time we'll let go."

They ruffled their wings, and headed in the direction of the hanger. They talked for a few minutes about some of the annoyances their bond had caused them along the way.

"Why do you think this is happening to us?" Siphero said off the top of his head. "It feels like it is forcing one of us to do something."

"Certainly, how can we have time to ourselves when we are forced to always be together?"

A twinge of pain ran through both of their hands, and they recoiled from it. Then they looked and saw the ribbon and the chain on their arms glowing brightly, the two tying themselves together tightly. In an instant, the two were embracing against their will, their wings locking them together.

"Great, this is just great." Siphero fidgeted to get free.

"I, I can't move," said Awesha. "The bond must be doing this." She then felt a burning on her arm, and she saw the ribbon gaining the links of the chain from Siphero's arm. She tried to let go, but they both saw their arms were changing. Silk braided armor was beginning to encase her hand while metal was growing on Siphero's.

They both felt hot and sweaty from the intense feeling the bond was instilling in them, but they were soon able to let go of their hands. Upon release, their bodies obeyed them, and they fell to the ground, very much exhausted.

"Siphero," Awesha said, getting to her feet first and helping him up but avoiding touching his hand.

Siphero came around in a few seconds. "The damn bond did it again, didn't it?"

"Yes, but what has it done this time?" They both inspected their arms and saw the tattoo of the chain and ribbon had disappeared, but it was etched onto the wardrobe change each of them had experienced. They then looked at the rest of their clothing to see if there were any other changes.

"Uh, I think I'm going to head back to the hanger," Siphero said hastily, and darted through a bulkhead.

"Right, I'm going to my room now," Awesha said, going in the opposite direction.

As they parted ways, the force of the bond tried to pull them together again. They struggled to resist, and this time they broke free, heading in the directions they intended.

Siphero panted, his breath escaping him as he just ran the whole way to the hanger, dodging crewmen and his friends. Once he got to the hanger, he saw engineers inspecting the machines and arranging a pile of spare parts on the side. An engineer came up to him, saluted, and gave him some tools.

"Good afternoon, sir," the engineer said. "How do you fare?" He saw that Siphero's arm did not match the rest of his clothing but kept his mouth shut.

"Well, you guys know, never a dull moment for a Terran."

"Indeed, sir. Are you ready to begin your work on the airblade?"

"Definitely, but I don't need tools. Just stand back and watch."

This is what Rekusolus had asked him to do: begin assembly on as many of the new airblades that he and Pops built as he could. They would be the first generation of Paragons to enter service. Siphero had shared with the Teller of Doom that Pops had completed the prototype, and it had outperformed its specifications. Now Rekusolus wanted Siphero to get them built and retrofitted by their engineers for aerial warfare. At first, Siphero wasn't thrilled about making weapons, but his father reminded him he was not there to make weapons, only make devices that could keep his friends safe. Airblades would be equipped by their engineers.

"You aren't responsible for the lives or the deaths of any who choose to fight," he remembered his father saying to him, "but you are responsible for increasing their chances of surviving so they can return to their families."

He took a deep breath, placed both hands in front of him, and began working his magic. The spare parts on the ground floated in the air as Siphero manipulated them with his affinity. He made pieces go together, taking the procedure in steps, the engine being the first piece. Soon after, he began assembly of the cockpit, the wings, the stabilizers, the exhaust, and finished with the main body. The last part of the job was ensuring the pieces would stick together. After making sure any and all lose bolts and nuts were properly tightened, he fused them together. He had done it. He had constructed from memory a complete copy of his airblade, the Paragon. One little addition he had made was a seat and railing right above the cockpit.

The other engineers stopped their work and watched Siphero manipulate the metal in constructing the Paragon. The engineer who had met Siphero inspected the machine, tested the wings and thrusters, and even turned the engine on. To his surprise, the airblade worked exactly as Siphero thought it should.

"It's working. A new airblade has joined the *Legionnaire*!" The engineers cheered as a couple pilots in training came to see Siphero's handiwork, clapping enthusiastically.

"You've really done it," one of the pilots said. "You've added another blade to the armory."

"True, but what class of ship should it be called?" Siphero asked.

The pilot that spoke scrutinized the airblade from head to stern and then looked at the cockpit. Scratching his head, he said, "It's small and compact, with wings that retract. I can see it being able to glide quite easily and—what is this on the back?" He pointed to the seat and canopy on the Paragon's back.

"Oh that. It's something I thought of off the top of my head. It's just in case in the coming days we end up working alongside allied Winged. They are skilled aerial combatants; we only know how to fight other Terrans. We are not prepared to fight enemies who are born in the skies. The only advantages we have are our speed, firepower, and versatility."

"What about the Winged on those creatures?" an engineer said, pointing to the skimmer drakes, avisi, and the behemoth, Stager, in the far corner of the hanger, munching on bales of hay, meat, or fruit.

"Well, that's the thing," Siphero said. "Not all Winged can get a mount, and those creatures are more meant for travel." He then explained how they can enter a slipstream and that they can go a lot faster when doing it, using his own experience to describe what it was like.

Many of the crew were surprised with this news and factored it into their questions. "So which of the beasts we see here should we really worry about on the enemy's side?"

Siphero looked between the animals, and he came to a conclusion. "The real threat you have to worry about are the skimmer drakes, which are vicious and have the added ability to breathe fire, ice, or other elements. They're just like the deep drakes back home, homicidal and extremely foul tempered."

A lot of them nodded, remembering their mixed experiences with the deep drakes. None asked about the behemoth, but they knew from meeting Stager that they could work in peace around him, and the big guy would actually help by moving machines when he was asked to and get food as a reward.

"So then back to the seat," the pilot said. "Is it meant to show our progressive cooperation for allied Winged?"

"Yes, that is correct," Siphero said. "They can't fly as fast as us, but we need to show we are thinking of assisting them, an unexpected mutual cooperation. Besides, they can use magic, and if they are onboard, they just might assist in your defense."

Engineers nodded, knowing that this was a good idea, but the pilots thought this was questionable. "How do you know we can trust these birdbrains?"

Siphero looked at the soldier and said, "I trust them, and if you haven't realized, I am kind of like one of them. The one thing you should remember is that they are just like us. Their wings, traditions, and magic are the only differences. If you think they are inferior or disgusting, guess what? There are Winged who hate Terrans and would love to see us all dead. They tried to kill me a couple of times. Even within the Winged Empire, they discriminate against, torture, and kill their own kind, just like Terrans. If you think that way, then you are no better than them at their worst. So I ask this: be the first ones to trust them because the trust has to come from somewhere. Show them you are willing to fight by their side, and they will trust your intentions at the very least."

The engineers applauded, and the pilots in training nodded. Crewmen appeared in the hallway, joined in briefly, and dispersed, going back to their duties. Word spread throughout the *Legionnaire* of the Terran who was a Winged.

"Then, sir," said the pilot, "as more Winged join the True Allegiants, we shall try. We will attempt to trust the Winged."

"But what of the airblade?" the first engineer asked. "What class should it be named?"

More spoke up, questioning what it should be called. Siphero thought over it long and hard, and the answer came to him as he explained the roles of the other airblade classes.

"As you all know," he began, "the Claymore is the flying fortress of a squadron. It's job is to carry ordnance, soldiers, and weaponry to target. It is also the most heavily armored of them all, making it the slowest."

He flew over to a hanging Saber and placed his hand on it. "The Saber is the protector of the Claymores, as it requires a smaller crew to pilot them, making it a more capable hybrid airblade. It can dispatch ground targets with ease and is excellent at dogfighting. Since it is our most advanced airblade, it has served as the workhorse of our military."

Then he came to a rest next to the airblade he built. "Then there's this thing, the one Pops and I built, rest his soul. This one is faster than the others, highly maneuverable, and requires only one pilot. A first for airblades is that it has retractable wings, meaning it can fit through tight spaces and relies upon the shifting of body weight for maneuvering. Since it is the smallest, it has the least armor and can pull off some crazy maneuvers. It is a dogfighter's dream."

"So what is its name?" an engineer said.

"Simple," he answered. "This airblade is the tip of the spear, the first in and first out. It is our Spearhead."

The soldiers nodded in agreement. The pilots liked being the first ones into the fight, and it gave them more to brag about.

"We will begin construction of more Spearheads," an engineer said. "We will also add your modification to the Sabers and Claymores. Friendlies might appreciate hitching a ride at speeds most of them would never dream of reaching."

"Good, because I need a short break. I'll help you guys out in a bit." He left the hanger right after he stroked Stager on the arms and head. He also paid Yevere a visit, who licked him and went back to eating. As he exited the hanger, Mervieris, Ieava, Tratiki, Gargran, Nylf, and Xhe-Zhe were standing outside. They had been listening to his speech about Terrans trusting Winged.

"What are you guys doing out here?" he asked them.

"Oh nothing, we were doing nothing," Mervieris said, before Xhe-Zhe both kicked him in the knees.

"We heard your speech of trust, trust for us," Xhe-Zhe said, "and we are joyous to know you trust us."

"When we first came onboard," Gargran said, "I was afraid we would be fighting another battle against an unknown enemy, but now I'm taken by the idea of fighting alongside an ally as fierce and experienced as Terrans. It's a dream come true for a warrior like me."

"They are capable warriors, skilled workers, and driven individuals," Tratiki said as he scratched his arms. "I've never seen such unquestioning cooperation before."

"You have even convinced me," Ieava said. "If I ever regain my parents' throne, I would agree to a peace treaty between Winged and Terrans."

Then before Siphero could comment on their revelations, they all bowed or curtsied to him. He chuckled to himself and bowed to them in return as they departed, heading to their individual cabins. The only person to stay behind was Nylf, who stuck around for a few minutes.

"There is something that I want to tell you," she said shyly.

"What is it Nylf? Is there something I can help you with?"

She took a deep breath and said it proudly. "I am now a full-fledged member of the True Allegiants."

"That's great news," Siphero said enthusiastically. "You are now an honorary Terran. How does that make you feel?"

"I…I feel like a great burden has been removed from my back," she said with hope. "The goals of the True Allegiants must be told to all Wingless. They would join in a heartbeat. They would gladly join a cause like this if it meant permanent liberation from oppression. We would be slaves no more!"

"Hell, you aren't! But, Nylf, you need to understand. Terrans sometimes face oppression too, from other Terrans. I don't want you to join the True Allegiants thinking you will be completely free of oppression."

Nylf glided along the ground using her affinity. There was joy in her glide as she slowly left. "Siphero," she said over her shoulder, "I don't care. Anything is better than watching one's parents die before you just because they are considered inferior."

She left Siphero standing in the hallway with a concerned look his face. "I hope you don't have any regrets, Nylf. I'm sure you've had enough of those to last a lifetime." He finished his break and went back into the hanger, where he set to work overhauling all of *Legionnaire*'s airblades with his modifications, getting them ready for a battle he knew was coming.

Chapter 20: Realization

Awesha returned to her cabin after that strange moment with Siphero. Her left arm was still transformed. It baffled her; how could this have happened? No matter how many times she tugged and pulled at the silk and armor on her arm, she couldn't rip it off. She gave up as she sat on her bed, only to see Nerv pop up next to her, wearing his little guard outfit again.

"My lady," he said with a polite bow, "is something the matter?"

"Yes, Nerv," she replied. "Can you do something about this thing on my arm?"

Nerv took a look at her arm and snapped his fingers. Nothing happened. "Odd, that should have done something."

"Do you think you could just give me something to cover it up?"

"Not to worry, my lady." Nerv drew in the air a shape, and a brown leather cloak appeared and fastened itself to her shoulder, covering her left arm.

"Will there be anything else, my lady?" Nerv was about to disappear into a puff of steam when Awesha held his arm.

"Please don't go yet, Nerv. Can you stay for a bit? I need someone to talk to right now. Someone other than Siphero."

"Would you like some tea, my lady?"

"No thank you, Nerv. I don't want any distractions."

"Very well, my lady."

Nerv materialized a chair and sat down, poured himself a cup of tea, and gave her his full attention. She began talking about all the things that had been happening to her: meeting Siphero, forsaking her family, becoming a guardian, witnessing the death of the king and queen of Strati Polis, fleeing the Sangria Legion, and coming aboard the *Legionnaire*. The one thing she had the hardest time explaining were the moments she found herself fretting over Siphero or wondering how she truly felt. Nerv did not question a single thing she said. He only listened while taking periodic sips of his tea.

"Then what is it you are worried about?" Nerv asked after a few minutes. "What is it that makes you not yourself?"

Awesha folded her arms around her legs, and her wings folded around her. "I don't know, but I'm scared almost all the time when I'm not with Siphero. I wasn't afraid when I stood up to my parents and disowned them or when I faced the treachery of the Sangria Legion. It goes against my nature to feel this way."

"Milady, if you want to solve your predicament then you must remember who you are. You must show as much courage in love as you do in battle."

"You know what's strange?" She snapped. "I hate so many things about him. He is a cowardly little pacifist, he goes out of his way to help people, he never follows the traditions of the Winged, and he has a hard time standing up for what he believes in. He is so nice it infuriates me. I can't stand it."

"Milady, do you think you are having these feelings because you are afraid of losing Siphero to the war that is to come?"

Awesha paused. "I guess I am."

"You have survived for so long without a companion because of your independent spirit," Nerv said. "I've seen Siphero, and he tells me you are always on his mind too. His only major flaw is that he cannot share his feelings when he is focused on his work. In my time with both of you, I have noticed he does all he can to stay by your side. And the work he does, his coldness as he prepares for matters of battle, it is his way of protecting you. He will always work if it means he can protect his bond with you."

"Thank you," she said as she rose from her bed and glided towards the door. She paused long enough to look back at Nerv over her shoulder. "I must be there when he needs me."

She left her room and flew down the hallways, passing her friends and crewmembers, who got out of the way of her wings. She apologized as she flew until she stopped outside of the hanger, where she saw Siphero working, covered in grease and engine soot. He was at home in his element.

Her arm underneath the brown cloak began to glow as she saw the chain and ribbon glow warmly. She saw Siphero stop doing his work and turn around to meet her eyes. He appeared to be in better spirits. They met halfway in the hanger. The engineers continued their own work while Nylf assisted them with Siphero's modifications. Gargran was there as well, schooling Terran soldiers on many different tactics and giving them practice for defending against affinity users.

"Hard at work, my true bonded," she said warmly.

"You know me," he replied, "I can't seem to keep myself clean." He scratched his armor where his tattoo was, like he was trying to scratch his own skin. Awesha grasped both his hands with her own. She wanted his full attention.

"Don't ever change, Siphero, because I love you just the way you are. A Terran with a Terran heart, mind, and soul. I cherish you the most."

Siphero was blabbering a little bit when he spoke. "Now you got me tongue-tied, Awesha. I feel the same way. I want you to be the one who picks me up when I feel like I've fallen. The Winged girl who knew nothing about me, accepted me for everything I was. I accept all that you are, all that you will ever be, I will accept it all, Awesha. All your flaws, mistakes, consequences, and imperfections are what I cherish.

They embraced each other in a tight hug, tears rolling down their cheeks. Out of nowhere, the ribbon and chain on their arms began to glow again, except this time the light engulfed the two of them, blinding everyone else in the hanger, causing them to stop what they were doing and shield their eyes.

The silk on Awesha's arm slowly spread across her shoulder, changing the color of her cloak to a pearl white, and the rest spread over her upper body and down her leather clothes and boots. Her clothing turned into a gown with skirt cut open, draped around armored leggings and white armored boots. Her hair was tied back behind a silver circlet, which covered her forehead and ears, while her hair hung over her back in a long ponytail. The rainbow aura that usually surrounded her wings became emblazoned upon them like a painting. Her wings were also covered in a similar silver armor. She was amazed at her new appearance, but she stared at Siphero and saw his changes were just as surprising.

The armor on Siphero's right arm started to grow. It crept up his shoulder, getting thicker as it went. Within minutes, the new armor engulfed his entire body. His boots became armored, and magnetic locks appeared beneath the boots, anchoring him in place. The wings on his back transformed as they froze in place and formed flight stabilizers. The engine on his back became a part of the armor and grew in size. As it slowly grew, a second thruster appeared alongside the first. His armor continued to thicken as he felt his body engulfed in a thick sheeting of the stuff. His helmet changed as well, to one with a reflective visor, complete with breathing apparatus. The last touch was a skull that appeared on the armored shoulders, with gears for eyes, and behind it was a shield very much like Preduvon's.

As the light dissipated, those within the hanger slowly approached them. Awesha and Siphero inspected themselves and each other, the great changes brought about by their bond. Soldiers and engineers came forward and inspected them, as did Nylf and Gargran, but they were stopped by the appearance of Rekusolus and Dreamen in the hanger doors. They had been watching and waiting for the change to finish.

"Simply magnificent," Rekusolus said to the two of them. "This is the seed your Archons were talking about." He approached Siphero and Awesha, to see Siphero had grown two feet from all the armor he was wearing, while Awesha's wingspan had grown as well by a similar measure.

"What does this mean?" Awesha asked. "Are we stuck as we are?"

"Because if we are, I really want to know how I'm going to the bathroom," Siphero said, struggling to get his helmet off. It wouldn't budge. He tried willing it, and the visor around his face slid back.

"There must be a way," Rekusolus said, deep in thought. "How did the two of you come to have these forms? What did you do?"

"Not much," Siphero said, gasping for air.

"We only said that we loved and accepted each other for what we were, nothing else." Awesha blushed a tiny bit, and her wings folded around her.

"Aha," the old Winged said, "Aha! That is the solution. The both of you accepted one another, so the bond rewarded your ultimatum. Simply face one another and renew the promise."

They both nodded as they faced one another and held hands, the bond awakening to their touch. Awesha went first. "I cherish you as you are."

Siphero went next, saying, "I accept you as you are."

Their bodies were engulfed in light as it blinded everyone again. It slowly dissipated and showed Siphero as he used to be, his wings and armor normal.

Awesha's armored dress was gone, but her rainbow wings remained, as did the circlet upon her head.

"True Allegiants," Rekusolus shouted as engineers, crewmen, and soldiers assembled themselves before him. Nylf and Gargran were wearing a sigil of the True Allegiants-a coat of arms with a metal gear, a rifle and a Winged's wing with different feathers representing the different races of Wingless, Compa, Sila, Avia, and Engria. Beneath the cross arms was an armored hand and a bare hand holding the other in a tight embrace. This was the symbol of the True Allegiants.

"All who serve the cause of True Allegiants," Rekusolus said, "I introduce to you our champions: Awesha, Daughter of Exiles, and Siphero Antolus Dreamen, the Otherworlder. They are the symbol the True Allegiants stand for and will always stand for: trust, respect, understanding, and camaraderie. The bridge that connects our worlds! The bridge that connects us all!"

The speakers rang with the voices of all the Allegiants aboard the *Legionnaire*: "Truly, Allegiant, truly Allegiant, truly Allegiant!"

Chapter 21: Strategy

Violent flashes of memory awoke an angry and frightened Tratiki, who was sleeping in his cabin with torn bedsheets, ripped pillowcases, and an animal skin rug in tatters surrounding him. This was why a Sila did not sleep in someone else's room, like Ieava's; he couldn't hold still long enough. This morning, however, was different because he could feel the hairs on his back stick straight up, his animalistic senses firing off randomly, and he could taste the cold iron of blood in his mouth.

He exited his quarters and knocked on Ieava's door with one of his hairy arms. His room was next to Ieava's. They considered it a good idea not to sleep together since a lot of unwanted harm might come from doing so.

"Ieava, my love, wake up." He continued to bang on her door. "I smell death in the air. I fear the worst for Silacorlis!"

The door opened, and Ieava came out, brushing white hair out of her eyes and trying to stay awake. She was not a morning person despite being a princess. This was just not one of her better moments in the day. As she looked at her lover, she placed her hands on her hips and gave him an angry look.

"Tratiki," she said half asleep, "if it is important, can you please come get me sometime later? I need to sleep."

"Ieava, please, this is urgent. I had a vision of my polis. It needs assistance; we must get—"

Before he could finish, the *Legionnaire* shook with a violent thrash as everyone lost their footing. Ieava fell forward onto Tratiki, and he caught her and helped her regain her footing.

"What in Stratis was—?"

Sirens began ringing throughout the *Legionnaire*, and a voice came over the communicators. "Attention, all hands! The *Legionnaire* is under attack. I repeat, under attack. All personnel report to your battle stations. All Winged and guests report to the command wing. Rekusolus requests your presence!"

Ieava and Tratiki feared the worst as they donned their martial clothes and rushed through the hallways of the *Legionnaire*, dodging crewmen and soldiers going to their assigned stations, while they found Mervieris, who decided to join them on the mad dash to the bridge.

As they rounded corners and took shortcuts, they finally reached the command bridge, where fifteen Terrans were assembled, manning instruments and equipment, checking readings, circulating orders, and bracing for impending hits. On the bridge, Ieava and Tratiki saw Nylf, Gargran, Siphero, Awesha, Octavio, and Xhe-Zhe arrived in suit, before Rekusolus and Dreamen.

The deck looked out onto a large view of the upcoming battlefield, Silacorlis. Tratiki was frightened, as he had seen the very same thing in his dream. Sky galleons were sailing over the clouds, firing magical projectiles at a magical barrier, which constantly cracked only to regain its strength. Dozens upon dozens of Sila rode beasts similar to his own Silacon form. They clashed with Winged soldiers who had an insignia of a crimson fist and a cross guard of two white wings on their armor. The Sangria Legion had the support of Sky Polis.

"It's the Aerial Fleet of Sky Polis," Awesha said in anger. "My own home has joined the cause of the Grand Clerician!"

"This betrayal is strange," Ieava said. "I feel sorrow for you, Daughter of Exiles, but who is leading them?"

"Give us a visual of the flagship," Rekusolus ordered the Terrans at the equipment. They manipulated their equipment and instruments until a zoomed-in picture of the flagship appeared, and Awesha's breath was taken away as she saw who was onboard.

"No, no it cannot be," she said fearfully. "This cannot be true."

"What is it, Awesha?" Siphero and Mervieris asked her.

She regained her composure, her fear replaced with disgust. "It's my father. He is commanding the Aerial Fleet alongside Vice Admiral Sorice."

Rekusolus's eyes lit up with surprise, and he smiled cynically. "So the race hater has decided to show his true colors."

He paused for a minute until Tratiki came forward and bowed to Rekusolus. "Please, Teller of Doom, my home is being threatened, and my people are to be exterminated by the Grand Clerician and her forces. I beg of you, please help Silacorlis, and I will negotiate with my people directly on your behalf."

Rekusolus turned to all who watched him. Then he looked at Tratiki and said, "This ship is filled with men and women, Terrans, who have families back on Jormundgard. They signed on with the True Allegiants because they wanted to protect their loved ones from a threat beyond their regular comprehension and they were willing to align themselves with those from an entirely different world to fulfill their mission. The question I ask you is this, Tireless Hunter, would you fight alongside complete strangers and put your life in their hands as they risk theirs for your sake? Can you trust us?"

All eyes were on Tratiki as Rekusolus waited for an answer. "I would trust Siphero with my life before your Terran soldiers, but I will fight with them if it means saving my people."

"Excellent answer, Master Tratiki," Rekusolus said, with a chuckle. "All hands, make final preparations for combat. The *Legionnaire* is entering battle. All pilots and soldiers get to the hanger; this is not a drill."

Terrans throughout the *Legionnaire* began running around frantically, fulfilling Rekusolus's order for battle, carrying armor, ammunition, or necessary supplies to where they were most needed.

Rekusolus then turned back around to Siphero and Awesha and said, "I have an important job for the two of you. I need you both to take out the Aerial Fleet's flagship. Cut off the head of the army while our main battalion shores up the Sila defenses and keeps the Sangrians busy."

Awesha was silent for a moment, looking at the ground in calm reflection. "You want me to kill my father?"

"The two of you are our most powerful soldiers," he said. "We just don't have the armaments to take out the fleet on our own. All we can do is drive them out. If you have reservations about attacking your father, then I can assign Gargran to—"

"I will deal with him," Awesha said coldly.

"Are you sure, Awesha?" Siphero asked.

"Yes, I am."

"Very well then," Rekusolus said. "Get to the hanger immediately. We are about to make our presence known to both the Sila and the Aerial Fleet. Neither side has seen a Terran airfortress before, so the brief moment of confusion will force Vice Admiral Sorice to reevaluate his strategy."

Siphero and Awesha rushed down the hallway to the hanger, and Gargran, Nylf, and Mervieris followed after them.

Tratiki and Ieava took up the rear as they barreled through the hallways down to the hanger, where a large platoon of Terran soldiers were standing in line in front of Dreamen, all covered in battle-grade armor, toting automatic, tesla and pellet-spray weapons. Behind them were at least ten Claymores, thirty Sabers, and, surprisingly, twenty-five Spearheads all ready to go. Next to the airblades were all the animals participating in the battle: Yevere, Stager, the armored skimmer drake, and the albino one, all of which had been outfitted with makeshift armor sheets.

The guardians joined the ranks of Terrans, where Dreamen was giving them all the battle plan. "Listen well, True Allegiants, the battle being fought out there is a battle of extermination. The same thing will happen to Terrans if we allow it to continue, but we are the vanguard for both our races; we will stand against this war of purification!"

A war cry rang from all of them as he said this, even from Tratiki, the Sila who had requested them to help. He looked at them all, and he felt honored to know these strangers would be helping him but responsible for them at the same time.

"Now," Dreamen said, "Claymores crews, you are responsible for making landfall on Silacorlis. You will be transporting the Clippers to the polis, where they will be dropped off and provide anti air support. Claymores will then engage the Aerial Fleet while Sabers provide escort. Spearheads will escort Siphero and Awesha as they head toward the flagship. Once they are close, dive bomb the enemy and break off the escort to assist Sabers in tightening air support. Tratiki…"

The Sila met the gaze of Dreamen and responded, "Yes, sir?"

"You and Ieava will fly to Silacorlis before us all and make contact with its leaders. Tell them we are coming to render aid to them and make sure they do not accidently fire upon us. Gargran will act as your vanguard. The *Legionnaire* will remain concealed behind the cloud bank and will only enter combat as a last resort."

As Terrans filed into their assigned airblades and the guardians climbed onto their mounts, giant machines rolled onto the hanger floor, where they became attached to the Claymores. These were the Clippers, giant artillery cannons that were a deterrent against large targets like airfortresses. They were also common in gaining air superiority. They were four-legged machines with two large guns on their backs, firing mechanisms, and two options for ammunition: flak or concentrated mana lasers.

The doors began opening up, and Terran crewmembers stood in front of all airblades and mounted soldiers, waving to them with torches. Then, Ieava, Tratiki, and Gargran took off first, with the Claymores in tow, carrying the Clippers on their backs. The second to take off were half of the Sabers available. The others would have to wait until they made landfall with Silacorlis before they could take off.

Ieava and Tratiki were riding on her albino drake as it rode the winds through the skies toward Silacorlis. As they got closer, they could see several of the ships were fighting the main forces from the front of the island, but there were none facing the back of the island.

"Is there anything the matter, my love?" Ieava asked. "Are you not happy these Terrans have offered their aid?"

"No, Ieava," he responded, "I am, but how are we going to convince the Alphas? They are too stubborn and prideful to accept help from strangers. They would fight and die with the forces they have before they accepted help from strangers."

"Then give them no choice but to accept your aid," Gargran said behind them. "Even brutes know that life is preferable to death."

The Claymores were catching up to them, the Terran subcommanders signaling to the others to remain in formation. The Sabers kept close, acting as both eyes and ears to the heavies.

Silacorlis's size was amazing to behold. The entire flying continent was covered in a dense forest. A couple of mountains surrounded the middle, and a large, clear blue lake covered its center. As they all gained altitude, they passed over the lake and began circling right above Silacorlis's main city and port. Tratiki signaled to the others to remain there while he, Ieava, and Gargran went down to the city.

As they descended, enemy Winged soldiers saw the three of them closing on the magical barrier that served as a protective shield for the city. Ieava, Tratiki and Gargran skirted the shield a few times until the Sila, who were sustaining the barrier with their mana, noticed the new group flying by. Then, Tratiki riding shotgun on the albino drake's back, let out a loud and fierce roar from deep within his throat. This identified him to the Sila as one of their own, and the defenders created a small hole in the shield which he, Ieava, and Gargran flew through. The hole immediately closed behind them.

Landing inside the city, Tratiki and the others noticed Sila were running back and forth carrying wounded, weapons, magical remedies, and parcels in a mad dash to defend against the Sangria Legion's attack. Each of them had different wings in the shape of birds, bats, insects, butterflies, and drake wings, although they saw a bunch of Compa wings among them. The fortress where they were located had many walls, magnifying turrets, shield towers, and a central spire. No soldiers came to surround or hold them prisoner, as all Sila were focused on fighting in the battle. No guards were needed because they knew a Sila was among them.

Shortly afterward, a Sila with brown and black spotted wings wearing a suit of leather and chain armor, with a set of tusks on his shoulders and toting a long bladed staff, approached them. He had a scar across one of his red eyes, and sharp teeth protruded from his mouth.

As he dashed forward, he and some of his men growled to Tratiki, and he growled back. They pulled their drakes into cover while Gargran, Ieava, and Tratiki followed him toward the central spire. When they got to reasonable shelter inside a makeshift bunker, he turned around and growled again.

"Please, brother," Tratiki said, in a growling voice, "control the beast. I need to speak to your Alpha."

The scarred soldier calmed down to speak. "My apologies, brother, those damned Avia have been battering us for hours. Our Alpha is dead."

"Then let his soul run forever free. Who is your new Alpha?"

The soldier stood at attention before them and made his authority known. "I am—Weltrox, the temporary Alpha."

Tratiki looked him up and down, sniffed him, and knew for certain. "You are indeed an Alpha. I am Tratiki, and these two are Ieava and Gargran, and we have come to render aid in whatever way we can."

"We need all the help you can muster," Weltrox said. "Our Omegas are too foolish in thinking we can win this battle with the forces we have available." He scanned some maps of their region where the ships were positioned and the other cities of Silacorlis.

"How did this come to happen?" Ieava asked.

"Silence, wench," he roared at her. "Mates may not speak!"

Tratiki roared at Weltrox, who backed off a little bit. "She is my bonded. Back away, Alpha, I am the Tireless Hunter, the guardian of Silacorlis!"

The Sila in the war room turned and were kneeling before Tratiki, Weltrox included. No growls were emitted, and only whelps of mercy sounded from them.

"Forgive me, Tireless Hunter," Weltrox begged. "I knew not who you fully were. You outrank even me. Please forgive us."

Tratiki let his anger go as Ieava held his hand in comfort. She shared his pain in knowing he had a part of himself he wished he could forget but knew was necessary for the moment.

"All Sila," Tratiki ordered, "clear the debris from the main courtyard as fast as you can, and when I say, open the tip of the protective shield."

"Tireless one," a Sila wearing a blue robe said, "if we leave it open, the enemy will be able to take the fortress. Their troops will invade us."

"No, they won't," he returned. "Please trust me! Do this, and I promise you a miracle will occur!"

A group of at least a hundred Sila and Silacon began hauling the wreckage from the main courtyard, at least two miles in diameter and filled with splintered wood, broken stone, and scattered or discarded weapons. It took them a little over twenty minutes to clear the field, and Gargran and Ieava watched with wonder at how fast the Sila followed the orders of their commanders and then at Tratiki, who seemed to easily strike fear into those he ordered.

Once they were done, Weltrox kneeled before Tratiki. "It is done, my guardian," he said. "What are your next orders?"

"Open the shield when I say to," he answered. He then pulled out a flare projector, something one of the Claymore crews had given him, telling him to fire it toward the sky.

He pointed it into the sky and fired it, and a small flare flew up to the tip of the sphere and exploded inside, scaring all of those within. They were scared, so they ignored the order Tratiki gave for opening the shield. He repeated the order with a growl. He wasn't going to let his new allies down now that they had committed themselves to the war effort.

Then from up in the sky, the Claymores transporting the Clippers upon their backs went into a steep dive and flew right into the open shield hole, flying right past the attacking soldiers, who, in their brief astonishment, let the massive transports slip past them. All ten Claymores made it through the barrier, to Tratiki's surprise, with only a few scratches to their hulls.

The Clippers were dropped off next to the Claymores, and the artillery pieces planted themselves in the ground and pointed their massive cannons at the ships attacking the city. Terran soldiers started unloading from the Claymores, carrying communication equipment, ammunition, guns, and medical supplies toward one of the shelters where Tratiki, Weltrox, Ieava, and Gargran were standing.

"Who are these beings?" Weltrox shouted in scared curiosity. "Wingless have come to our aid?"

"No, Weltrox," Tratiki said, "these are not Wingless; these are Terrans."

The Sila who had been wondering who these soldiers were, upon hearing they were Terrans, became fearful and transformed into Silacon, stopping the Terrans in their tracks.

"*Stop!*" he shouted in a loud roar, causing all Terrans and Silacon to meet his gaze. "This is no time to let your fears dominate you. You are abominable Sila to dispute the orders of your guardian. Hear me now. These Terrans are here under my request. They have the power to destroy our enemies. If we don't trust them, we shall all die! Now will any test my authority?" Silacon growled angrily and backed away, allowing the Allegiants to continue their work as they constructed shelters for the Claymores, a command center in some abandoned buildings, and a weapons depot. While they worked, Gargran assisted the men, doing what he could to help. Slowly, some of the Sila came forward in their Winged form and helped by following Gargran's directions. When all was done, after an hour of work under the constant bombardment of magical fire, the Terran field commander in bronze-colored battle armor reported to Tratiki.

"Sir," he said, "the Clippers are ready for combat. What are your orders?"

Tratiki eyed the closest ship above the city. Sila and Silacon were engaged in battle right above their heads. "Aim for that ship, and give it whatever you've got."

"Yes, sir," the sub commander said. "All right, men, you heard him. Light the bastards up." He shouted orders as Clipper crews began lining up the cannons toward the closest ship. The Sila in the air seeing the cannons didn't know what to make of them, but magically they had received the message that they were allied artillery. Once the cannons were locked on target, ammunition was loaded, and systems were readied, they awaited firing orders.

"Fire, fire, fire!" the sub commander ordered. With a loud clap like thunder, two beams of purple energy pulsated out of the Clipper cannons toward the ship and cut through the ship's hull like it was nothing. The ship took a massive hit to its wings and hull as the beams cut right through the ship like a giant sword swipe. It burst into flames as the Winged aboard abandoned ship, trying to avoid Clipper fire, while the Sila picked off the enemy in the air. A second volley from the Clippers destroyed the command deck, thoroughly annihilating the ship and anyone onboard.

All the Sila in the skies roared a triumphant battle cry, while the Saber squadron began attacking a ship adjacent to the one going up in flames, trying to render aid. The Sabers flew too fast for the zealots to keep up or even put a dent in them. Within seconds, the airblades cut through the zealot ranks. It only took one more Clipper volley to finish off the second ship.

The Clippers stopped firing, as they had used up half their mana charge, and switched to explosive shells. The ships left in the Aerial Fleet began to pull away slowly, the Sila pressing the attack.

"Sir," the sub commander said to Tratiki, "the Clippers are nearly out of energy. We will only be able to provide anti air support now."

"All right, my friend," he said, "do what you need to do, but make sure your Sabers assist the Sila."

"Don't worry, sir. We know the ways of war; we will keep them safe."

He turned to Ieava and asked, "Will you assist me in battle, my love?"

She came close to him and kissed him on the cheek. "Your battles are my own, as are your pains, your pleasures, and your prejudices. I am bonded to you, until the death."

She drew her staff and was about to call to her albino drake when Tratiki changed shape into a Silacon right before her. As a giant winged lion, he was clad in armor of a ruby and sapphire combination, and his wings were now covered in a similar coating. He faced her in his Silacon form and then turned to the skies.

Let me serve as your mount, he said through their bond. *I will be the beast that leads to our victory.*

"Yes…you will, my love." She climbed onto his back with a soft beat of her wings. Sila soldiers in the courtyard heard Tratiki roar. They answered his roar by entering Silacon form as flying wolves, cats, gorillas, and bears, and Sila who couldn't transform grabbed weapons and climbed onto the backs of Silacon. Once again he roared, reared up, galloped forward, and took off into the skies, and those able to fight followed him into the air, clashing with zealots in the skies.

Never waver, my love, he said through the bond, *and trust in our friends…"*

"For they have pledged their lives to end our war." She finished his sentence. They were meant for one another; this was apparent.

Chapter 22: Blitz

The bay doors of the *Legionnaire* shook as the wind whistled through the hangar. Terrans and Winged were geared for battle— fingers shook nervously on controllers, animals snorted and pawed the ground impatiently—but the only person who showed no signs of tenseness was Nylf, the first Wingless to join True Allegiant. In truth, she was happy to be a part of a movement that held so much regard for all the lower castes, the Sila, Compa, and the Wingless. All her life, she had searched for a purpose other than being subservient to Avia or any who said she was the scum of Stratis. She only ever met two people who showed her kindness, the now dead king of Strati Polis and Siphero, the Winged Terran. When she saw the corpse of the king, she thought her life was over. She thought she would never again find fulfillment in her life. She came with Siphero because she saw him as a beacon, another person whose kindness and inspiring nature reminded her of what the king stood for.

She was onboard one of the Spearheads, the airblade that Siphero had created with the canopy modifications. The Terrans had treated her like one of their own, caste differences didn't matter to the crew of the *Legionnaire*. As she came to learn, the crew had been taught a great deal about the caste system of the Winged Empire, and many regarded it as a cruel and disgusting hierarchy, words that made her smile with satisfaction.

As Nylf settled in to her seat, she checked the equipment a Terran soldier had given her: a communication device, a set of Light Armor, a semi-auto rifle, a few cartridges, and a motor blade. This equipment didn't seem like much to her, but she had practiced multiple times with the armor and the lead projectors, even the motor blade, finding them effective weaponry despite her affinity for wind magic. Being a Wingless meant she could not fly like a regular Winged could, but she had been blessed with an affinity for the wind, which allowed her to fly just as well as any Winged could, perhaps even better.

"Hey, Nylf," a voice said on her earpiece, "Cadet Nylf, are you ready?"

The voice belonged to the pilot of the Spearhead. She didn't know his name, but she knew that he would be her wingman. This one had an emblem of a burning vulture painted right above its cockpit.

"Y-yes, I'm fine," she said nervously. "Is there anything else I need to do?"

"Nylf, what's the matter?" His voice was concerned. "Are you afraid of the battle?"

She snapped back to the moment and responded rudely, "Oh, shut up, Terran. I don't know what to think!"

"OK, sheesh," he said, "there's no need to be so rough. I thought you were chummy with all of us."

She immediately regretted what she said and replied, "I'm sorry. I'm not used to kindness from others. As you know, Wingless are considered the lowest of all Winged."

"Yeah, that's just pathetic of those Avia bird shitters. What gives them the right to do that to their own citizens?"

"They believe it is their birthright to declare themselves superior to all Compa, Sila, and Wingless. Don't Terrans do this as well?"

The pilot thought long and hard before answering. "Sure, Terrans do this to each other all the time; it's a part of our lifestyle to outcompete one another, but that doesn't exist here in the True Allegiants. All Terrans here feel the same way. This is the defining message the Teller of Doom decreed to us. It was the founding law of our group. You won't find a single Terran here who didn't have trouble accepting the existence of Winged."

Nylf laughed at this for a few seconds until she quieted down. "I'm happy to be here" was all she said.

"Well, it's good to have you here," he said. "After the battle, do you want to talk over a couple drinks?"

She didn't understand what a couple drinks had to do with the battle ahead, but she had heard from Siphero it was meant as a gesture of friendship between Terrans.

"Certainly," she whispered back. "I'd be happy to."

"That's swell," he said. "The name's Urvnic, by the way."

Before she could answer back, sirens started blaring in the hangar. She saw Siphero and Awesha approach the hangar doors atop their steeds.

"All right, Allegiants," Siphero said on all their coms. "Phase one has just been completed; Ieava and Tratiki have succeeded in putting a dent in the Aerial Fleet. It's our turn to take the pressure off them and put the hurt on the Sangria Legion. The fate of all Silacorlis rests upon us."

"The fate of all Sila depends upon your actions in this battle," Awesha said. "The first battle to change our fates starts with us, Winged…"

"…and Terrans," Siphero finished.

"As we join together and push back these murderous zealots, we will not let their deeds go unpunished!" The entire fire team shouted hoorahs of confidence across the coms, answering the aligned call to arms with thunderous agreement.

Siphero and Awesha faced the doors as they both said, "We fly together!" As they said this, Stager grew armor similar to Siphero's, and Yevere's hide thickened with a rainbow-like aura of protection.

All left the hanger. Beasts went first, Sabers came second, and Spearheads roared out from behind, circled the *Legionnaire* once, and joined up in an aerial formation. Nylf and Urvnic took up the rear. A Saber flew in front of them and a Spearhead flew on either side. They were all flying at a speedy pace when Siphero relayed the orders Dreamen had given to them earlier.

"Just to remind you all," he said, "all Sabers and escorting Spearheads will assist the Claymores and Sabers engaged in combat. The rest will assist Sila soldiers in the air. Just make sure you show them that you're friendlies like Tratiki showed you. Remember, if you make the engines roar every time you assist a Sila, they will acknowledge the assistance, and then you can fight side by side without any trouble. Awesha and I will keep the attention of the flagship and neutralize the commanders."

He paused as he and Awesha made eye contact and nodded encouragement to each other. "True Allegiants, fly fast and fight fiercely." Just as he said it, the Spearheads and Sabers took off ahead of them, shooting directly toward the enemy and allied forces, speeding ahead as Terran dogfighting erupted in front of them.

Ships were on fire as the zealots tried desperately to save them, and Clippers cut through one ship at a time with their powerful cannons. A Claymore or two had been knocked out of the sky by magic fire and crash-landed on Silacorlis. Sabers were assisting Sila who had been knocked off Silacons by giving them a lift, and Sila were even aiding Terran soldiers who had engaged their parachutes. The casualties for the zealots were racking up; they'd been caught completely off guard by the Terran war machine. Terran casualties were kept to only a couple men and women. It was apparent to Siphero and Awesha in the theater of war that the True Allegiants were a well-trained group of soldiers, adept at aerial combat and controlling the battlefield.

"This frightens me," Awesha said. "The True Allegiants are a superior fighting force to the Aerial Fleet. It may become a slaughter if we cannot force them to retreat."

"You want to save the zealots, even your father?" Siphero was confused. She had disowned her father from her family, but here she was taking pity on the enemy, who originally wanted to slaughter the Sila.

"I care nothing for my father, but Sorice is an honorable war leader who cares a great deal for the safety of his soldiers. If he is here, I can only imagine the pain he is experiencing in watching the actions of my father's folly. We only need speak with him to come to an understanding, and he may withdraw his soldiers."

"That's a big maybe, but it's worth a shot." Siphero agreed wholeheartedly. He disliked the carnage of war, but even he knew trying to stop a battle once a faction had committed was almost impossible. "Let's try to convince him."

They directed their mounts to fly directly toward the flagship. Yevere and Stager both wrestled their riders' control, but they settled down as they headed away from the carnage of battle.

Nylf was riding onboard Urvnic's Spearhead, protecting it with magic while he fired upon zealots and harassed the crewmen onboard the sky galleons. They flew too fast for arrows to hit them, and magicians couldn't focus long enough to restrain the airblade. Other Spearhead and Saber pilots were doing all they could to keep the flying ship crews off balance and on guard. The strategy was working brilliantly. Nylf could tell as she rode past that soldiers and magicians were abandoning ship faster than they could keep them together. The only downside was, she saw airblades had a finite amount of ammunition for their weapons, similar to how Winged had a finite amount of magical energy. So she did her part to assist Urvnic by striking down zealots with wind projectiles or making them easier to hit by restricting their movement.

"There's a Sky Knight right behind us," Nylf said at one time. "He's carrying a Sila lance!"

"What's a Sila lance?" Urvnic asked. "Is that bad?"

"It is a magically crafted weapon specifically meant to slay Silacon."

"OK then, that is bad. Hang on tight."

Urvnic pulled a sharp 180 turn on the Sky Knight and forced the knight on his avisus to follow, without much success. The avisus could not keep up as it huffed with exhaustion. They then faced the knight as Nylf used the wind to knock him of his mount but caught the Sila lance and stored it in a compartment.

"The spoils of war." Urvnic laughed.

They flew off into the sky, where they were joined by two Sabers, a Claymore, and three Spearheads. A radio message came from the Claymore, rallying all of them.

"Listen up, troops," the voice on the radio said. "The *Legionnaire* wants our group to drive the remainder of the Aerial Fleet away from Silacorlis. How are you all doing on ammunition and fuel?"

All pilots sent mixed messages of more fuel than ammo or vice versa, but Urvnic and Nylf were the only ones to report they had three quarters of both, much to the surprise of the others.

"Pilots with more fuel than ammo will resupply with this Claymore, while pilots with low fuel will refuel at the munitions ship sent out from the *Legionnaire*, then all resupplied ships are to rejoin the fight. Urvnic and Nylf, you have been instructed to be the eye in the sky. You know your orders, now move!"

The Saber pilots with low fuel flew back toward the *Legionnaire* while the Spearheads docked with the Claymore to regain some fuel and arms. Urvnic gained altitude while Nylf surveyed the area, watching the deadly dance of battle from a safe vantage point. It felt like the battle was miles away from where they were, and they engaged in conversation while watching the battle play out.

"Those damned zealots are getting hammered," Urvnic said, with haunting delight. "They don't stand a chance against Terran ingenuity."

"I agree," Nylf said. "Those murderous Winged are getting what they deserve. Die, you oppressive monsters! Die!"

Urvnic was a little surprised by her joy at seeing the zealots die, but it didn't bother him much. They flew around near the Claymore.

"Attention all Terran forces." Tratiki's voice came from the radio. "The Aerial fleet is in retreat except for the flagship. All forces in the city are clearing out the invading zealots, the Clippers are nearly out of explosive ammunition, and Terran soldiers have been evacuated to our position. We have orders to chase the remaining enemies out of Silacorlis's airspace."

The Claymore leader then spoke on the radio. "OK, you heard the Sila guy. Let's chase those bastards out of here!"

Urvnic and Nylf rejoined the formation, while another Claymore, distant Saber, and Spearhead pilots rejoined their little squadron and flew toward the retreating Aerial Fleet. A total of nine airblades comprised the group, the four Spearheads, including Urvnic's, two Claymores, and three Sabers flew in formation toward what was left of the Aerial Fleet, a mere four ships, some on fire or falling apart, while others were getting ready to accelerate into slipstream. Oddly, a few Sila soldiers had hitched a ride aboard the Spearheads and Sabers as they sped toward the ships, already aware of the orders Tratiki had given.

As they gave chase to these ships, a small contingent of Winged soldiers took flight to defend the ships as they escaped, but they were cut to ribbons as Sila unleashed magic upon them and the Sabers and Claymores aimed for a ship that was already on fire. They took it down with little difficulty and moved on to the next. While the one they shot down was burning, it had provided them with enough of a distraction to cover the remainder's retreat, and they accelerated into slipstream and disappeared in a clap of thunder.

"Let them go," the Claymore leader said. "They've had enough."

All airblades broke off pursuit and headed back toward the flagship, the massive vessel that began to dock with the city, except for a few avisi and skimmer drakes taking off and going into an immediate mass slipstream.

"That's curious," Urvnic said to Nylf. "The flagship surrendered, and most of its passengers have retreated; I wonder what happened."

"Awesha and Siphero," Nylf happily concluded, "that's what happened."

They flew with the rest of the squadron back to the *Legionnaire*, which had emerged from behind the cloud cover and approached the continent of Silacorlis.

Siphero and Awesha approached the flagship on what appeared to be a suicide run as magic projectiles bounced off them while arrows and rocks, some burning, battered them. Stager even caught some of the harder projectiles and threw them back at the flagship, scattering the crewmen at the impact sight. Yevere spat ice projectiles at some of the crew, and one even got impaled on a mast.

The ship they approached was as large as a skywhale with six tall masts, each at least eighty feet tall and one hundred magnifying turrets sticking out both sides of the ship. In addition, Winged onboard flew between masts as they let go and tied up sails, but the sight of a skimmer drake and a behemoth scared the crew and caused them to hide below deck. Sky Knights and battle mages came to the deck as Siphero and Awesha touched down their mounts. As they dismounted, their mounts roared fiercely, breaking the spirits of any weak-hearted soldiers, who backed away in terror. Slowly, Siphero and Awesha approached the guards, their Archon weapons manifesting in their hands.

Some Sky Knights charged forward only to get knocked aside by Siphero, Awesha, or Stager, while Yevere froze them solid.

Again, soldiers tried to stop or kill them, but each of them ended up as their fellows, either knocked out cold or frozen solid. They could not stop Siphero and Awesha's advance, despite having superior numbers.

"What are you doing, you Winged cowards? Push them back!" The voice came from the helm area—it was Awesha's father.

"What a surprise, what an absolute surprise," he said. "The honorable daughter returns, and the Terran scum has a pet." He glided down from the deck with another accompanying him, were both clad in golden armor, just like their wings, but neither glinted in the suns. Awesha's father carried a helm at his side, a gold and silver helmet, the mark of an admiral of the Aerial Fleet. The one to his side was none other than Vice Admiral Sorice, a man past his prime with wrinkles all across his face and partially graying hair. His face was scarred across the cheeks with long dark marks, and his expression was troubled as he looked from Siphero and Awesha and back to her father.

"So you've come to die, little Terran defecation? What a surprise—now seize him!" None of the men onboard made any attempt to capture Siphero, either because they were too scared or they had seen it was impossible to do so.

"What are you standing around for? Capture the Terran!"

"Wait, Recril," Sorice interrupted. "I don't believe they are here to fight; they have come to negotiate with us—"

"No excuses, you old broken crow," Recril said. "Now order your men to capture them, or I will resort to other means!"

"No, Recril. The Grand Clerician may have named you to the admiralty, but I am still the superior commander."

Recril stomped his foot but smiled at the old admiral's decision. "Thank you for your treachery, Sorice. I see you have outlived your days." He pulled out his favorite maul, and Siphero could see it still had traces of blood on it, which made him angry. Awesha could feel his anger as she saw her father's intention to kill the honorable Sorice.

"We will stop him," she whispered. They reached out their hands, pointing them toward the maul. Recril felt the maul fly out of his hand and hover before them. He tried to summon it in his hands, but it would not come to him.

"Give me back my weapon," Recril shouted with disgust. "Give it to me, you ungrateful bonded demons!"

"Be silent, Father!" Awesha shouted. "Now hear me, those loyal to Sorice. My father just attempted to kill your beloved admiral. If you have an ounce of honor in you left, know that we are not your enemies, but we seek to end this battle without further bloodshed. Your true enemy is the one standing before you—have at him!"

Heads turned to Recril as fear and despair began to creep in, but upon turning to Sorice, he received a punch in the gut as the old man glided down to his men, who stood in rank around their leader.

"Listen, men," Sorice said, with authority. "Your orders are thus: expel the treacherous zealots and their leader from my ship. Free the *Vigilant!*"

A roar from Winged soldiers, Sky Knights, and battle mages loyal to Sorice went up as they approached on the deck and from the air. Members of the Sangria Legion swarmed out from below deck only to be grabbed by Sorice's crew and thrown overboard, where they were susceptible to airblade fire.

As soldiers began to surround Recril, he backed into a corner, and yet there was no fear in his eyes. A maddening smile spread across his lips as he saw ships cut to pieces around him by giant mana lasers and Terran airblades cutting Sangrians to ribbons.

"Did you think I would not expect this betrayal!" he shouted. "Did you think I am a fool to think I could not control you? I have a contingency."

A door opened next to him, and two beings emerged from the room. The first was a woman clad in a black dress and armor. Her hair was as dark as tar and a murderous smile accompanied her blue and onyx eyes. Black roses were woven into her hair. Next to her stood a man covered in white leather and chainmail armor, with short, curly blond hair down to his neck. His eyes were the most beautiful marbled gray, and his expression was calm and seemed to compliment his partner's wicked demeanor.

Awesha recognized the woman, and she felt weak in her stomach at the sight of someone she knew. Her knees buckled from underneath her, but Siphero caught her.

"What wrong, Awesha? Speak to me," Siphero said, concerned.

She was speechless for several seconds, but she then shouted to the men around her, "Run, all of you, run! That is my sister, Myrvah, and Sleghis, her bonded one. They are the Revelers of Slaughter!"

All Winged soldiers knew that name. It was a name to fear, like a waking nightmare or your most terrible memory. Before they could back away, a pulse of black and white magic rippled through the twenty troops nearest to the Revelers, causing them to dissolve into ash.

"Oh, it is so good to see you again, my Awesha," her sister said. "You've finally found yourself a bonded one, a weak little Terran. I wonder what his blood looks like upon my—"

"Now, now my lovely Myrvah," her partner said, kissing her on the cheek, "we mustn't defy your father. Can we please at least cut off his arm or something, dearest Father?"

Recril laughed with utter madness as he kicked the piles of ash that used to be men and women under Sorice's command. "Do whatever you want, my lovely ones; kill them all, flay them alive. They are nothing but traitors in the eyes of the Grand Clerician."

"Yay, Sleghis," said Myrvah. "Papa says we can do what we want. Why don't we start with the little Terran over there?"

"Agreed, my dear," said Sleghis. "His blood will be so beautiful to watch, flowing from his body like a river."

"Oh, I love rivers."

They flew from the deck, and the shadows of their black and white wings scared the rest of Sorice's men, who backed away. The Revelers began to gather energy before them as their black and white magic fused into a massive spear and hurtled toward a few stragglers of Sorice's men. The men couldn't scatter, but that wasn't necessary, as weapons fire intercepted the spear and it dissipated into bits of energy. An airblade roared across the deck, bringing with it an incredible draft, a friendly Saber pilot had seen them in trouble and came to assist. As it flew away, the Revelers pierced the metal of the airblade, and it exploded before them.

The Revelers were delighted at the sight of a destroyed enemy vehicle. They approached Siphero and Awesha.

"No," he yelled, "don't you dare hurt these men and women! Your fight isn't with them; it's with us."

An aura of rainbow light began to form around Awesha while a chrome-colored one surrounded Siphero. Awesha looked at him, scared and terrified, but she saw the dread upon Siphero's face. He was even more frightened than she was.

"We can't win against them," she said weakly. "They will kill everyone. The Revelers of Slaughter are feared for this reason.

All Winged fear them, not even the Storm Riders would go up against them. We will lose everything, our lives, even our bond."

She then felt Siphero's kiss upon her cheek as their individual auras intensified. "I'm just as afraid as you are, Awesha, but I'm more afraid of losing what we have gained. We have bled together, lived together, and grown to know one another. You are my pillar in life, our bond is my anchor to Stratis, and I cherish it. I don't want to lose anyone else close to me. I've lost too much already."

Then the memories they had made flowed into her as she felt his warmth, his hope, his fear, the sincerity of his words enter her body. She remembered everything they had done together and all they still had left to accomplish.

"How could I forget?" Awesha said, relieved. "You and I are meant to be together. The most defiant of Archons treasure our union. The king and queen of Stratis even approved of us right before they died. We owe to them, and to everyone we have met, to survive."

She picked herself up as she held Siphero's hand, her resolve reawakened and strengthened, and they became encased in light, like before on the *Legionnaire*.

Sunder the lies of this world, a voice whispered— Preduvon's.

And awaken Stratis to your potential, Verrencae whispered.

The rainbow light exploded outward as Siphero and Awesha emerged in their Archon forms, Siphero as the armored Terran and Awesha as a rainbow winged heroine, with weapons in hand.

Their forms surprised Sorice and his soldiers, but from glimpsing at them, he felt renewed purpose. "All men and women, retreat to Silacorlis, abandon the *Vigilant*, now!"

Soldiers departed from the ship quickly, as crewmen followed, carrying belongings and any weapons they could muster.

The deck was cleared as both parties stared each other down. Myrvah and Sleghis made their weapons appear before them. Both carried knives of ornate and serrated designs, true to their titles as Revelers of Slaughter.

"Awesha," Siphero said through his helmet, "you have no qualms about fighting your sister?"

She picked a battle stance with her baton as she focused on the crazed and crooked smiles of her sister and bonded one.

"I am resolved to defeat my sister," she replied. "She cannot be allowed to continue her slaughter unchallenged."

"I don't want anyone else to be hurt today by these twisted children." Siphero unholstered his tesla rifle, a weapon of lightning his father had given him to neutralize, not kill, any who would stand in their way.

"What are we waiting around for, my love?" Myrvah pouted. "I want to make them bleed the rivers of blood."

"Just a moment, my sweet, sweet lovely," Sleghis said as he looked to his father-in-law, who nodded cynically.

"Cut them into pieces, my lovely little monster," Recril whispered.

In a flash of dark light, Myrvah rapidly closed the distance with her sister as she slashed with her curved knives. Siphero intercepted six consecutive slashes with his shield while Awesha took to the air and unleashed a volley of energy bolts at her sister. The bolts hit but did nothing to slow down Myrvah as she flew straight up, summoning more magical knives as they floated around her and began slashing faster than Awesha could parry or dodge. She felt herself pulled out of a barrage of blades by Siphero as they flew together, trying to outrun Myrvah, but she was keeping pace with them. They scattered as Siphero fired bolts of lightning from his rifle, which bounced between the many knives surrounding Myrvah. At the same time, Awesha unleashed energy bolts on her, but Myrvah did not move an inch.

As the smoke settled around her, Myrvah laughed hysterically, and her knives became wreathed in her black magic. Each of them launched from around her in all directions like rain drops in the sky. Siphero and Awesha dodged or blocked the hits while they regrouped with one another. Myrvah was bleeding from the face, neck, and legs; her hysteria only seemed to increase the rate she was losing blood.

"We need a new plan!" Siphero yelled. "Her defense is too strong!"

"We need to hurry," Awesha said. "She's starting to bleed out."

"Then let's knock her off balance."

Siphero and Awesha both whistled as loud as they could while knives and black magic projectiles flew past them. In an instant, Stager and Yevere took off from the deck of the ship, grabbing them from the sky and planting them in their saddles. They gained speed as they circled Myrvah, who was just watching them with an even more deranged look of madness upon her face.

"Come back, Sister," she said, "come back and play with me." Her knives flew out again toward Siphero and Awesha, who rolled out of the way. Then in a split second, a knife flew past Awesha and planted itself in her saddle. She pulled it out, and as she glanced over it, a premonition came to her, one of her sister's face.

Chapter 23: Sanctum

The chaos of the war's theater melted away around her, Awesha found herself floating in a dark and empty void with Siphero by her side, the link between them showing as a thick and unbreakable cord.

"What is this place?" Siphero asked. "Why are we here?"

Awesha looked around the void where her sister's face once was but saw nothing as she and Siphero flew in deeper. In the blink of an eye, a cage appeared before them, bound with chains and ropes. Inside the cage Awesha could make out the shape of a girl wearing a familiar black dress. She floated closer to the cage and examined her sister, who was curled up into a ball and crying silently to herself. Blood seeped from the gashes in her body; she even started to cry blood.

"Myrvah," Awesha said gently through the bars into the cage.

Her sister stopped crying for a moment, and toward the bars of the cage, she recognized Awesha's face.

"Awesha? Awesha, is that you?" Her sister cried blood tears of joy at seeing Awesha's face. "It is you, Sister. I've missed you so much."

"I'm here, Sister. I'm here to get you out." Awesha tried to spawn her baton, but nothing came.

"I cannot leave here, Sister. I'm trapped by that demon, Sleghis. He did…terrible things to me." She brushed her arms and legs, scars of black and white pulsed all over her body like an infection had overtaken her.

"He…he did this to you?"

"Father allowed him to. He cut part of my personality away and harvested the person you are fighting. That is not me!"

Awesha became and angry and impulsive. "How far is our father going to go to fulfill his twisted legacy? First I disobey him, and then he does this to you. He must be stopped!"

Myrvah looked to Awesha's left and saw Siphero's armored form. "Who is that by your side?"

Siphero hovered forward and introduced himself. "Hello, I'm Siphero. I'm half Terran and half Winged. Pleased to meet you. I am also bonded to Awesha." He gripped one of Awesha's hands tightly as he had always done, and she found comfort in this.

A chill ran down Myrvah's spine as she tried to digest this information. "Sister, you bonded with a Terran? That shouldn't be possible. I thought Terrans only existed in the stories our parents told us as children."

"Yes, Myrvah, Terrans do exist. Siphero is my other half, and our bond is incredibly strong."

Siphero felt the darkness around them beginning to close in, signaling they didn't have much time left.

"We are going to get you out of here, Sister. We are not giving up on you!"

Awesha began trying to pull the chains off the cage, but it was harder than expected to remove them. The darkness grew slowly closer.

"Please, Sister, I can't lose you to this. You are too precious to me. Leave me to this oblivion." Myrvah withdrew to the center of the cage and curled back up into a ball.

"Sister, don't give up."

Two hands grasped the bars on the cage; Siphero tried to pull the bars open with as much power as he could muster. Awesha was surprised by his desire to help, and she continued to rip and tear at the chains.

"Just leave me," Myrvah begged. "You cannot break Sleghis's hold over me. I tried to fight his control, but nothing came of it. I am broken. My pieces lay scattered and cannot be put back together."

"Don't give us that," Siphero shouted. "We aren't giving up on you. You are going to be free whether you want it or not. So stop sounding so damn depressing and help us!"

Myrvah glanced up, and as she stared into Siphero and Awesha's eyes, she saw hope and unflinching stubbornness. She smiled as she wiped away a tear. "You two really are alike." With renewed hope in her, Myrvah grasped for Siphero and Awesha's hands as they held tightly. The shackles on Myrvah's cage began to dissolve, the cage cracked open, and the chains disappeared. As the void filled with light, it reached each and every dark corner of the void.

In place of the dark and brittle prison was a meadow filled with flowers, waterfalls, and sparkling rainbows glittering in the skies as mountains floated in the distance. In the center of the field was Myrvah, only her appearance had changed since being released from the cage. Her clothes matched her attire in the real world, except they had a blend of white over her skirt and the upper bodice. As her hair flowed down her back, white roses from the meadow were placed next to the black ones, enhancing her beauty even more. Her wings appeared to have changed appearance as well, the feathers blending their colors to create wings that were both black and white, the feathers woven together.

Siphero and Awesha floated down and approached Myrvah.

"Myrvah," Awesha asked, "are you all right, Sister? You look…different."

Her sister opened her eyes to the world that surrounded them all. She smiled as tears flowed down from her eyes. The darkness inside her had receded and returned to its rightful place. The sky lit up like the night sky; stars in great numbers illuminated the ground as twin moons shone above them.

"It's amazing," Siphero said. "It's just like the brief patches of night we glimpse back home in Jormundgard."

"You mean this part of the world?" Myrvah pointed behind them as this part of Myrvah's world seemed to be joined by another. The world was a simple sphere in the sky that dissolved away to reveal a world of metal cities, flying machines, and lands filled with rusting war machines reclaimed by nature. Myrvah's world became small beneath them as Awesha and Siphero floated on air next to her, and they watched the two worlds mesh together with Myrvah's paradise.

"That's…that's Jormundgard, my home, but how is it here?" Siphero watched as this world merged with Myrvah's and made a resounding thunderclap.

"We have another world about to join us." Myrvah pointed to another sphere, which collided against both Siphero and Myrvah's worlds. This world was filled with an endless sky, one with floating islands, flying beasts, and ships sailing on clouds.

Awesha said, "This is Stratis…this is how I see it, but what is it doing here?"

"These are replicas of what your minds envision Stratis and Jormundgard to be." Myrvah pointed to both of their worlds as they collided, destroying the boundaries protecting them.

"The worlds are fusing," Myrvah said in astonishment.

"Into what?" Siphero looked from her to the light as it dissipated.

The sight surprised them. Stratis, the world of the sky, and Jormundgard, the world of the ground, had fused together to form a new world. A world where the sky and ground reached one another, and there was nothing separating them, no impenetrable barrier to speak of. This world had two layers of land, where the mountains floated in the upper atmosphere and large continents floated above what appeared to be oceans and lakes on the lower section. On the lower half, mountainous regions touched the sky and even came close to the floating mountains. Both sections had lush forests, mountains gushing lava, swamps, and creatures of varying sizes flying or marching across the landscapes.

"Hey, I recognize some of those cities on the planet," Siphero pointed out. "That's Salvagon, and that's Terminus Dominus, the capital of Jormundgard. I can also see the Rustlands and even the Diseased Abyss."

Awesha could see on the flying continents some of the cities as well. "There's the Sky Polis, the Strati Polis, and I can even see Skyspire."

This is the true vision of the world you live upon, a voice echoed to them in the void.

"Who are you? Show yourself!" Awesha drew her baton, while Siphero stood at her back.

You cannot begin to fathom how long I have waited, the voice said. *The ones who have breached this world's lies have come to my domain.*

It was then Siphero recognized the voice. "I know who you are. Show yourself, Hevros."

Awesha and Myrvah looked out into the starry sky as a hearty and kindly laugh rung throughout the starry void, and lights appeared all around them, lights that revealed themselves as the spirits of Archons that once existed on Stratis. Awesha and Siphero recognized two of them as being Verrencae and Preduvon, their defiant Archons.

Verrencae and Preduvon, however, were no taller than Awesha and Siphero. They flew in close upon a chariot of stars and came to a stop before Siphero and Awesha, beaming with pride.

"Look at you two," Preduvon said, no longer a whisper of nothingness, an actual embodied voice. "You're not exactly yourselves now, are you?"

"If anything," Verrencae added in, "Awesha, you have become much more beautiful. The love in your heart is showing."

Awesha blushed heavily at that comment, which made her rainbow aura intensify in color and brilliance.

Preduvon slammed his weapon against Siphero's shield, which made a loud clanging sound.

"It's good to see you again, Preduvon, but why are you here? Why are all of you here?" Siphero regarded all of the Archons in the space.

Hevros, the Archon all other Archons, bowed before approaching Siphero and Awesha. Preduvon and Verrencae knelt to their leader, slinking away to the far corners of the void.

"You are here," Hevros said.

"Why did you summon us, gracious Hevros?" Myrvah asked from behind them.

The great Archon turned to her and nodded with respect. "You deserve to know this, Sister of Awesha. Your sister and this hybrid have manifested the power of an Archon in physical form."

Myrvah did not understand this revelation, but when she looked at Siphero and Awesha, she saw a certain power emanating from them.

"How did this happen?"

Hevros pointed to an empty space of the void, where images began to flash, drawing the attention of all Archon spirits. The images were familiar to Siphero and Awesha: the moments when they first met, bonded, kissed, accepted each other, realized hard truths, and finally accepted each other's existence.

"Never in the existence of Winged and Archons has there been a union between Winged and Terrans, or more specifically, the birth of a child who carried in them the essence of a Winged and a Terran. That child is you, Siphero, the child of Dreamen and the Terran woman known as Straea. A child with Terran flesh but the blood of a Winged running in his veins."

"But how did they attain these forms?" Myrvah was still unsure what he meant.

"It was the bond. It is what awakened them to their potential."

"That makes sense," Siphero said. "When I first bonded with Awesha, I experienced incredible amounts of pain, but I realize now that the dormant Winged part of me awakened." He pointed to his wings, which extended outward.

"Awesha," Hevros said, "the bond formed between the two of you awakened the blood within Siphero, the magical blood of a Winged. The gift of magic that existed within you flowed into Siphero through the bond."

"How do you explain the wings?"

"His wings came later, but to surface, it required the two bonded to reach a deeper understanding of each other. Once that hurdle was reached, the magic in Siphero's blood manifested them into a possible form."

"Then what about my rainbow aura?" Awesha asked.

"This aura is Siphero's gift to you, an aura measuring the intensity of your love for one another. Because it is difficult for you, Awesha, to show your feelings for those you cherish, the aura speaks your true feelings for you."

Awesha blushed again heavily, remembering all the moments she had felt feelings of attachment for Siphero. While she did, the aura around her wings reached a more beautiful hue, shining light like an aurora. Her heart beat faster, and her chest tightened a little.

"Awesha," Verrencae playfully said to her, "your love is showing."

Upon realizing, Awesha couldn't stop them from shining even brighter from the embarrassment. She then felt the tug of a hand in hers, Siphero's hand.

"You don't have to feel embarrassed," Siphero said in a comforting tone. "I think it's lovely you're able to show this much love for someone like me. Sometimes I think I don't deserve it."

Awesha could feel her heart slow down, and she became comfortable as she leaned on Siphero's arm and the aura around her returned to normal.

"There is your proof," Hevros said. "Our gift to the Winged has transcended our original designs. The gift has grown to include Terrans, and even hybrids."

Hevros spoke to all Archons in the assembly of the void, who all wondered and appeared troubled until two Archons from among them came forward. Siphero and Awesha immediately recognized them and bowed. They were the now-deceased king and queen of Strati Polis.

"Your Majesties," Awesha said respectfully, "I feared we would never see you again."

"Please rise," the king said. "You do not need to bow; you are all honored guests here."

"Who are they?" Myrvah asked. "How do you know these Archons?"

"Sister, they are the former rules of Strati Polis. They died, thanks to the revolt led by the Grand Clerician and the Sangria Legion. Their ideals allowed them to continue to exist as Archons."

Before Myrvah could react, the king spoke up again. "How is my daughter, Otherworlder? Is she doing well?"

"She is doing better," Siphero said. "She is fighting in the battle against the Sangria Legion, those zealots who killed you and the queen. She is on Silacorlis with a contingent of Terran soldiers called the True Allegiants, a Winged and Terran alliance."

The king and queen bowed their heads with relief, but hearing the news of their daughter accompanying a battle made them worry.

"Don't worry," Siphero said. "She is in good hands."

"Does she miss us terribly?" the queen said. "Is she still mourning us?"

"There were some nights when she cried, but as time went on, she strengthened her bond with Tratiki and with us. She still cries, but that is because she knows she could lose the new bonds she has forged."

The king and queen smiled with delight as tears rolled down their eyes. "Please tell her that we are proud to have been her parents."

Both of them drifted off to the far corner of the void as the Archonic spirits began to disappear one by one until Hevros, Verrencae, and Preduvon were the only ones remaining in the void.

"This power you have cultivated," Hevros said, "it is a power that Winged, Terrans, nor Archons can use. Only you can wield it. I beg you; use it wisely."

"Due to this development, we Archons have consulted one another and have decided to leave it in both of your capable hands." Verrencae curtsied to them both.

Preduvon was the last to speak. "But we require one thing from you both: a promise. A promise that you will share this power with those you deem worthy. With those you trust and with those who have formed a bond."

Awesha and Siphero looked at one another in surprise, but they knew what the Archons asked.

"We will share this power with those who can be trusted to safeguard those we wish to protect." Awesha stood firm in a salute before Verrencae, who returned the salute in kind.

"And to give those who have formed the bond a chance to bridge the gap and protect a lasting peace between Winged and Terrans." Siphero slammed Preduvon on the shield as a bit of payback for before, and the Archon smiled with admiration.

"Before you all leave," Hevros said, "you must know these zealots you fight are being directed by a mysterious force, an unknown enemy who wishes to see all the unworthy perish before them—a collection of supernatural beings I call the Incarnates."

They were all shocked, but Siphero and Awesha understood there was an enemy behind all the machinations of the Grand Clerician, Recril, the Sangria Legion, and their suicidal, pureblooded feud for slaughter.

"The Incarnates are the reason we Archons exist," Hevros said. "They have come to claim this world as their own. They are false gods without form or substance who seek to be made whole any way they can, even if it means destroying civilizations."

Awesha was fearful at hearing this, while Siphero thought the Archon was spouting nonsense.

"The Incarnates," Awesha gasped, "they are behind the slaughtering of the king and queen?"

"Yes, the very ones. They are fighting a battle of immortals on the planes of our world, and we are losing. The best we can do is give you the opportunity to strike back, or else we may lose the war of many worlds."

"You've got to be kidding," Siphero said, "the Incarnates? I've never heard of them. The real enemy we have to worry about is all of Jormundgard. Once the Terrans of Jormundgard's many factions discover the existence of Stratis, there will be little the True Allegiants can do to stop their combined advance."

"Jormundgard is not our problem, young Siphero," Hevros said. "Only you and Awesha can settle the affairs of both worlds and unite them for the greater war to come."

"What do you mean by a 'greater war to come'? Is the war we are fighting now not that greater war?"

"I have said too much. You need not worry yourself with this. We will continue our crusade from our side of this conflict. You two must focus on settling the matters of your worlds. Only then can I tell you the truth of the world."

The darkness in the void began to crack as bits of light started to filter through.

"We are out of time, Hevros," Preduvon warned. "The Incarnates have breached the Sanctum. They need to leave now!"

"Please be safe." Verrencae hugged Awesha and Myrvah. "You are like my long-lost daughters from ages past. Survive, please, at all costs."

Preduvon winked at Siphero before disappearing in a shimmer of light. Verrencae followed, pulling her wings about her, and disappeared in a similar fashion.

Hevros was the last one left. "The odds are stacked against you in the battle to come. Share what we have said with those you trust and be careful of the one called Mervieris."

Hevros caused a massive explosion within the Sanctum, which ejected Siphero, Awesha, and Myrvah back into the real world. They disappeared from the sight of the true enemy that would have ended their existence.

Chapter 24: Alliances

Awesha and Siphero regained consciousness alongside Myrvah upon the grassy plains of Silacorlis outside of the capital. Myrvah had returned to her normal self, the mental restraints Sleghis had placed on her had disappeared, and she laughed sincerely for the first time. Their mounts, Stager and Yevere, were huddled around them, standing watch and waiting for their masters to awaken.

Siphero was the first on his feet. He saw his Archon form had dissipated, as had Awesha's. She was the second one to get on her feet, and she helped her sister up.

"Myrvah, are you all right?" she asked cautiously.

Her sister opened her eyes, and she met Awesha's gaze. She immediately embraced her sister, tears flowing from her eyes. Their mounts rose and squealed with happiness. Stager got scratched behind the ears by Siphero, and Yevere, purring with affection, licked Awesha on the face.

"Sister, I'm so happy to be free of that foul man's hold. His mind felt like it would crush me into nothingness."

"Don't worry, Sister; you're safe with us now."

"Us?" she asked. "Who is this man with us here?"

Awesha felt suspicious. How could her sister not remember? They were in each other's minds only moments ago. She let go of her sister and stood next to Siphero, who had been listening to them the whole time.

"Siphero," she whispered, "it's as if my sister has no recollection of what transpired when our minds were linked."

"Yeah, that is weird, but right now we have to rejoin the *Legionnaire*."

They agreed and were about to climb on their mounts when a Spearhead flew close to them, and a being glided to the ground upon summoned winds. Nylf.

"Nylf," Siphero inquired, "what is the status of the battle?"

"There is excellent news, Siphero," she answered. "The battle is won, the Sky Polis Aerial Fleet is retreating, the monsters Sleghis and Recril are in custody, and Vice Admiral Sorice has regained full control of the *Vigilant* with his forces."

Siphero and Awesha let out a cheer as they embraced, holding each other closely.

"We did it, Awesha! The disaster of Silacorlis is over."

"This is the first victory of Winged and Terrans, a great victory indeed."

Nylf asked for their attention again. "Siphero, Awesha, Rekusolus wants all soldiers and airblades to regroup with the *Legionnaire* as it docks with Silacorlis."

She turned to face Myrvah, sensing she was herself again. "You are welcome to join us if you wish, Myrvah."

Myrvah, upon hearing herself regarded in a casual nature, snapped and retorted angrily, "It's Lady Myrvah to you, broken Wingless scum. If you cannot speak to me as your superior, then do not speak at all."

Before Myrvah could strike at Nylf with one of her knives, she felt the knife in her hand fly out of her grasp, while Nylf knocked her off her feet and stood beside her, Myrvah's cold and hateful eyes staring up at her.

Nylf let out a spiteful laugh that angered Myrvah even more, while Awesha walked over to her sister.

"Awesha, please help me. Make this Wingless pay for striking me, an Avia—"

"Be silent, Sister. Nylf hasn't done anything to hurt you. In fact, you deserved that for what you said. Nylf is like a sister to me, and I would protect her with my life."

"No, Sister, please," she begged, "I can't get along with a…Wingless. Father would never approve of it."

"You don't need to worry about Father. He can't harm us anymore, and neither can Mother. We are free of their machinations."

After hearing those words, Myrvah's face became blank for a minute. Then, she looked up at her sister, Siphero, and Nylf. She appeared older in her looks, like she had when their minds were connected. As she got up, her wings came to rest behind her as the familiar white and black pattern appeared on them, and her senses returned.

She blinked a few times and met their gazes. "I'm sorry for my manners just now. My memories hadn't fully returned, so I apologize to you, Nylf, for my behavior." Myrvah turned her attention to her sister. She was relieved to see her sister for the first time with her own eyes.

Siphero felt an awkward silence fall over them all, and he clapped his hands. "OK, I think we should head back to the *Legionnaire*. Nylf, please send word to my father and Rekusolus that Awesha's sister is safe with us."

"At once, Siphero." Nylf fired a flare into the sky as she glided up to a certain height. The Spearhead Urvnic was piloting slowed down enough for her to hitch a ride and then flew off at top speed.

"What an odd contraption," Myrvah said. "Are we going to this *Legionnaire* to meet with someone important, Sister?" She then turned to Siphero, who was about to get onto Stager's back when she approached him.

"Thank you, Siphero," Myrvah said, her brilliant eyes peering into his.

He nodded quickly and climbed onto Stager, but there was a sharp pain in his right arm. His bond with Awesha was keeping him honest.

"Sure, you're welcome," he said back. "Anything to help."

He climbed onto Stager's back while Awesha took her place atop Yevere, and Myrvah joined her. They took off in one giant beat of wings and soared above the grasslands and back toward the main city of Silacorlis, where they saw the *Vigilant* was docked right next to the *Legionnaire*. On their flight over, Awesha and her sister had a wonderful chat as Awesha brought Myrvah partially up to speed on what had happened.

"That is amazing, Sister," Myrvah said, after a respite. "You formed a bond with a Terran who has Winged blood in him. How lucky are you?"

Awesha smiled back at her sister. "Siphero is the best and strangest part of my life since I met him several months ago. We've been together ever since I disowned Mother and Father."

"So has he confessed to you yet?" Myrvah asked, with a hint of mischief in her tone.

Awesha was silent for several seconds, listening to the rhythmic beat of Yevere's wings before she answered. "Yes, he has."

Myrvah went silent and looked down at the landmass of Silacorlis. "Oh, I am happy for you, Sister. You always seem to beat me at everything. Battle, getting a mount, pleasing our parents, even forming a bond, you've always been my better."

Awesha understood her sister's plight. "I believe you should know, Sister, that father wanted me to become bonded to Weeslon. He didn't approve of my bonding with Siphero. Father killed someone who was close to Siphero, and even Mother approved the deed and didn't tell me."

At hearing this, Myrvah felt shame and hatred toward her father and mother. "We truly have treacherous parents. How will we ever recover from their machinations?"

"By putting an end to the conflict that they are intertwined with somehow. I'm not too worried, Sister, as I am bonded with Siphero. His father has become like a parent to me, and he may to you as well."

"Who is this father of Siphero's? Is he not a Terran?"

"What should it matter if he is a Terran? I have found Terrans to be trustworthy and hearty comrades. Siphero was once a Terran, but now he is one of us as well; he is a hybrid of sorts."

Myrvah came to a realization. "Then that means his father is a—"

"His father is a Winged, Dreamen, the commander of the *Legionnaire*."

"That Dreamen, the former Herald of the Grand Clerician? The one who went missing in Jormundgard twenty-five years ago!"

"Yes, Sister, that Dreamen."

She hugged Awesha closely, feeling amazed and relieved that her sister had found another group of loving individuals to call family. She felt a strange tingling on her arm. Myrvah looked down to see a black and silver ribbon tie itself into a bow upon her arm and ingrain itself into her skin.

"Sister?" she asked.

"Yes?"

"We are bound once again. Our family bond survives."

Awesha knew what she meant, and smiled. The bond continued to surprise her.

They flew the rest of the way in silence until they were right over the main city of Silacorlis, The Savage City.

As they descended toward the ground, they were flanked by
Sila and Silacon clad in elegant and well-polished armor, who acted
as their honor guard, bearing banners with the symbol of an animal
claw and a circle depicting animals, predator and prey, the standard
of the Sila. Upon their final approach to the city, Siphero, Awesha,
and Myrvah saw a massive crowd of Sila, Silacon, Winged from
Sorice's *Vigilant*, and Terrans standing next to their airblades and
Clippers, while the crew of the *Legionnaire* stood on its multiple
outer decks, waving and cheering to them as they landed safely in
the courtyard.

When they landed in an open grassy stretch among the many
ruined houses and towers, they dismounted, with their Sila escort
walking beside them. Stager and Yevere stayed behind, watching
their masters stride past the assembled Sila, Avia, Compa, and
Terrans. The Winged population cheered and threw wreathes of
flowers toward them as a sign of praise. They walked past the
grateful masses toward a group of ten individuals dressed in armor
and tribal garbs with animal hide, feathers, decorative tusks, and
flowers adorning their clothing. There were six men among them,
two Silacon, and two women.

Siphero and Awesha caught a glimpse of Tratiki and Ieava
standing among those in this number, wearing the royal attire they
had worn at Strati Polis. They waved to Awesha and Siphero until
they came to a set of stairs that went up to a balcony, where more
familiar faces were waiting for them. At the balcony Siphero and
Awesha saw Sorice, Rekusolus, Dreamen, Xhe-Zhe, Mervieris,
Gargran, Tratiki, Ieava, and Octavio. Myrvah went to stand with
Dreamen and Rekusolus.

One of the men from the group of ten Sila came forward. He
was much taller than the rest and wore a robe made from a brown-
skinned skimmer drake hide and armor made from the same animal's
scales. Atop his braided gray and brown hair was a crown made of
bones, teeth, and tusks, while his face was heavily scarred and one
eye was gray in the retina. He was much older than the others in his
group, but he his wingspan was nearly the full size of a skimmer
drake, though one of his wings was mostly bone with only a few
feathers.

This giant of a man stood over Awesha and Siphero by at
least a foot, but his eyes were gentle and experienced. A man like

this had seen a lot of fighting in his time and had been marked because of it.

He opened his mouth and a loud roar resounded among the populace, and the Sila and Silacon answered it back with roars of their own. When the man spoke, his tone was light but venerable.

"People of Silacorlis, warriors who fought to safeguard The Savage City and all of its citizens, as your Omega Alpha, I congratulate you on fighting and dying to save those you cherish!"

The crowd roared again, the Sila and Silacon roaring the loudest because their king was honoring their sacrifice and commitment to their homeland.

"Long have the Sila and Silacon stood claw to claw and arm to arm against the tyranny of the murderous Avia of the Sangria Legion who tormented our kin and young ones with their hierarchies and superiority. Today, this all changed when we drove them back, their ships burning, their spirits crushed, and their blood falling like rain into the open sky. This day, they will no longer bring us to the edge of oblivion!"

The Sila cheered much louder. The Omega Alpha had the ability to inspire an entire country, and he did so by playing to their strengths and reinforcing their triumphs.

"But today, our victory would not have been possible if not for one of our greatest warriors, our Tratiki, the Tireless Hunter, who came to our aid upon the wings of an albino. The daughter of the great king and queen of Strati Polis fought for us in this battle. It is with the deepest of regrets I must say the murderous zealots of the Sangria Legion have killed the king and queen. They have rejoined the great cycle!"

Upon hearing this news, men in Sorice's army, the citizens of Silacorlis, and even Myrvah erupted in fear and agony at this news. The Omega Alpha raised his hands, and most of the crowd went silent, allowing him to continue.

"I understand many of you are fearful for what is to come, but the ones who killed the king and queen, the minions of the Grand Clerician and now the Aerial Fleet of Sky Polis, are the ones who must fear us! The true miracle that was visited upon us was the appearance of the supposed demons we had been taught for generations were our enemies, the demons of Jormundgard, the Terrans!"

It was then the Sila erupted in applause and turned to pilots, soldiers, and crew of the *Legionnaire*, the members of the True Allegiants who were present among them. Many roars of appreciation and honor went up for them as Terrans returned the praise with a mass salute. The Omega Alpha asked for silence, and the excitement died down.

"And now on this momentous day, we honor those responsible for averting an even greater disaster and redeeming our enemies. Today we honor Awesha, Daughter of Exiles, and Siphero, the Otherworlder."

More excitement came from the crowd as a little girl carrying two wreathes made of flowers, feathers, bones, and plant vines came forward to her leader and knelt presenting the wreaths. The Omega Alpha picked up the first wreath made mostly of flowers, feathers, and vines to place upon Awesha's head. She dropped to one knee to accept the honor.

"I give this wreath to Awesha, the courageous daughter who fought against her own kin and redeemed her sister from the tyranny of her father, an incredibly selfless act. I bequeath to you the rank of Sigma Alpha, the enemy of our enemies will become our kin from this day forward, and your sacrifice will not be forgotten."

The crowd applauded loudly to Awesha's honor, but she remained kneeling. The little girl handed the second wreath, made of pieces of scrap metal, tusks, and woven vines to her leader. Like Awesha, Siphero knelt to receive this honor.

"I give this wreath to Siphero, a Terran with the blood of a Winged running through his veins. He exists as an enigma to us all, but it was he who nonetheless fought our enemies and opened our eyes to the existence of Terrans. We now know there are Terrans who are willing to fight and die for our kin, and they are worthy of our praise. I bequeath the rank of Sigma Omega to Siphero, the first hybrid of both our worlds."

The Omega Alpha signaled for them to rise, and the crowd applauded again in one final burst of excitement. All leaders, soldiers, and citizens recognized Awesha and Siphero as the heroes of Silacorlis.

"With our heroes honored," the Omega Alpha said, "I have one last motion to decree. The leader of the True Allegiants and I have been in talks. I am pleased to tell you that we have reached an agreement. A storm is coming, my beloved Sila and kin, a storm the likes of which we have never seen before, one that threatens our very existence. But fret not, my people, because from this moment forward, the Terrans of the True Allegiants, the Winged under the command of Vice Admiral Sorice, and our very own cities of Silacorlis have pledged to form an alliance of all free peoples and those who would fight against the forces of the Grand Clerician and the Sangria Legion. Starting today, we start the reclamation of Stratis with our own hands and wings. We fight as the Demon Allegiants!"

Then all the Sila in the crowd roared at the top of their lungs, so loud it made their previous roars seem quiet in comparison. Sorice's troops and the Terrans had to cover their ears in response just to keep themselves from going deaf.

"This is how the Sila honor promises," the Omega Alpha said to Awesha and Siphero. "They roar as loudly as they can to tell all they are committed to their promise until they die."

"That's some loyalty," Siphero replied.

"But hopefully they won't have to die to keep that promise." Awesha smiled at their loyalty; however, she hoped they wouldn't needlessly be put in harm's way.

The roaring ceased as the crowd parted and began meeting with Terrans and allied Avia at the docks. A large number of Sila were moving throughout the northwestern part of the city, preparing festivities, decorating the roads, and wearing elaborate garb and dresses.

"What are they doing?" Awesha asked. "Is that some sort of celebration going on over there?"

The Omega Alpha looked in the direction Awesha was pointing and said in response, "It is a special celebration we Sila hold to commemorate important moments in our history. It is called the Feral Dance, a festival as old as our ancestors when they hunted, told stories, and danced in celebration of life and death, of battle and victory, of love and birth. Please attend, please. I will be greatly dishonored if you do not go."

The Omega Alpha was so kind and insistent that Awesha and Siphero gave up on their ability to say no. The leader then walked off with Dreamen, Rekusolus, Octavio, Xhe-Zhe, Gargran, and Sorice to talk of the formalities to make the alliance official. Myrvah bade her sister farewell as she went to speak with Dreamen about joining the True Allegiants.

Tratiki and Ieava came up to congratulate them, and Ieava embraced Awesha as if they were related, while Tratiki and Siphero shook hands. They were happy to see each other, even after such a long and grueling battle, but Tratiki and Ieava could tell something was up with Awesha and Siphero.

"Siphero, Awesha," Ieava inquired, "why are you so withdrawn from speaking with us?"

"It's not like the two of you to do this." Tratiki showed the same worry. "Something bothers you; I can smell it."

Siphero and Awesha looked to one another and nodded.

"We need to speak with the two of you, Nylf, and Mervieris. We have news, straight from the lips of Hevros, the Archon of Siphero's father and mother."

Ieava's face drained of color, while Tratiki's hairs stood up on the back of his neck.

"Did…did you say Hevros?" Ieava gasped. "Your father and mother manifested Hevros as their Archon? That's impossible! The legendary Archon rarely appears before anyone. How did this happen for a Winged and a Terran?"

"Well then, that's because," Siphero added, "I am the first hybrid born in Jormundgard. Now can we please stop with the surprised looks? I'm sure Hevros is a great Archon, but we have important news to tell."

"Very well," Tratiki said, "we will meet back on the *Legionnaire* in a few hours, but for now let's enjoy the Feral Dance!" Tratiki changed into a Silacon right before their eyes, Ieava climbed onto his back, and they flew off in the direction of the festival.

"Do you think it can wait?" Siphero asked. "They've had a long day, and I'm sure they could use a break."

"No, it cannot wait." Awesha fumed. "The enemy we had been wondering about for days is now known to us, and you want to wait! I still wonder why you and I can remain bonded."

"What do you still wonder about?" A familiar voice popped up. Nylf had gotten the drop on them again, except this time she was riding on the back of Urvnic's Spearhead. They had landed in the middle of the square as some Sila from the battle came to inspect the machine. As she hopped off the back, Urvnic opened the cockpit hatch and jumped out, saluted Siphero, and struck a casual pose as he took a big swig of water from his canteen.

"Siphero, Awesha," Nylf said respectfully, "what is wrong with you two?"

"Yeah, what's up? Your wings caught in a bunch?" Urvnic snickered, but as soon as Nylf gave him the cold shoulder, he went silent and took another sip of water before handing it off to Nylf. She took a quick drink and handed it back to him.

Then Awesha and Siphero saw an invisible tether forming between the two of them, a gray line attached to their arms closest to each other. It was with this realization that Awesha asked them both, "Nylf, the funny man called Urvnic, are the two of you bonding?"

Nylf gasped. She looked down at her arm and saw a small piece of a tattoo forming on her right arm, the beginnings of what appeared to be the shape of half an airblade. Urvnic had no idea what a bond was, but he looked at his left arm and saw the other half of a Spearhead on it.

"OK, I don't remember getting that tattoo," Urvnic noted, "and I have gotten a lot of tattoos."

Nylf felt shocked and amazed. She was forming a bond with a Terran, much like Siphero had with Awesha, but she wondered how it would be different because she knew Urvnic was pure rotten Terran.

"What does this mean, Awesha? Is it going to be painful? Am I going to be shunned? Will I be ugly?"

"Calm down, Nylf." Awesha comforted her. "Nothing of the sort will happen. It didn't when I was with Siphero. I'm somewhat sure you will be fine."

While Awesha sat down next to Nylf at a fountain, Siphero leaned against Urvnic's airblade. Urvnic offered him some water, and Siphero nearly drained the whole canteen. He pulled out a few more from the storage compartment and offered them to Awesha and Nylf.

"So what's this bond thing?" Urvnic asked Siphero. "Is it some sort of mating ritual these birdbrains undergo?"

"Something like that, but let me ask you something. How do you feel about Nylf? What I mean is, do you love her?"

Urvnic drank quietly for a few seconds, letting the question sink in before he answered. "I wouldn't say that I have those kinds of feelings for her. If anything, you know how old I am. I'm at least six years older than her and three years older than you. I feel like I want to do something important for her. Perhaps it's this bond thing, or maybe I really do want to help her."

Siphero looked over at Awesha and saw she was embracing a crying Nylf, comforting her as a mother would a child. "You're right, Urvnic. When I first bonded with Awesha, all I wanted to do was find my way in the world with her by my side. Slowly, I came to accept Awesha and truly care for her as she has for me. And now I admit to you I wouldn't have fallen in love with her if not for our bond. It was the best thing to happen to me after Pops died at the hands of that Recril."

Siphero spat on the ground at the mention of that name, and Urvnic spat too. "I heard about that. I'm truly sorry Siphero. But how can you still have feelings for that Awesha over there? Isn't she the daughter of Recril?"

"That's the important part, Urvnic. She may be his daughter, but she didn't have a hand in it. When she learned her father was responsible, she nearly killed her own mother. She settled for disowning her parents, which she did right in front of her mother."

The doubt on Urvnic's face disappeared, and he smiled and leaned forward. "I take back what I said. She's all right in my book."

"Do you promise to stay with Nylf? She's had a rough life so far at the hands of the damned purists, nobility, and race haters. And now she wants to throw her life away fighting for a noble cause."

"Certainly," he promised. "I can understand her. I had a rough life too until I joined the True Allegiants. And now here I am with the most defiant organization in two worlds, making alliances with beast people, rogue birdbrained soldiers, and a motley crew of Terrans and Winged. We might actually beat these bird-shitter zealots, but who exactly is this enemy you were talking about?"

Awesha and Nylf had rejoined them at that moment. Nylf was less flustered, and she appeared to be smiling.

"About that, you two are going to think we're crazy." Siphero sighed heavily. He explained what happened to him and Awesha during the battle with Myrvah and Sleghis, about their encounter with Hevros, the explanation given to them about their unique power, and how Hevros revealed to them the real enemy, which was keeping itself well hidden. When he got to the part about the Incarnates, Urvnic interrupted him.

"Whoa, whoa, whoa, the Incarnates? What are the Incarnates? Are they that musical group that has been touring around Jormundgard? Is that who you mean?"

"What? No, no way, what the hell do you think we were talking about?"

Urvnic held his hand over his mouth and laughed hysterically, but he saw the seriousness in Awesha and Siphero's eyes. They weren't joking around.

"Sorry," he said, "it's not every day you hear about a group of unknown enemies who are trying to kill everyone."

"But still," Nylf pointed out, "I've never heard of these Incarnates. Could they be the ones driving the actions of the Grand Clerician and her Sangria Legion forward?"

"Why haven't you told Rekusolus or your father yet?"

Siphero shrugged, and Awesha stroked her hair. They had their reasons, but they wanted Urvnic and Nylf to be the first to know.

"We have a gift for you," Awesha said to them both. "A gift that the great Hevros entrusted to us to share with those deemed worthy by our standards."

"We feel the two of you should be the first recipients of this gift." Siphero and Awesha joined their marked arms and tried to draw upon the energy of the Incarnates within themselves.

In moments they were interfaced with the energy. It was brimming with power, a power that lacked the strength to level a mountain, lacked the ability to manipulate others. It was a different kind of power, one that grew and changed, evolved, and flourished with time. Like planting a seed, watching its growth progress, and seeing it nurtured, until a strong and healthy tree has grown in its place.

The power of the Incarnates responded to their wish and materialized into a crystalline sphere that hovered in front of them. Then it fractured and a tiny piece broke off, enough to fit in the palm of the hand.

When they opened their eyes, Awesha and Siphero realized that shard was clasped between their linked hands. It was small, pulsated with warmth, and sparkled with a rainbow light. It then left their hands and flew closer to Urvnic and Nylf, who for some reason had interlocked their hands. Siphero and Awesha saw their eyes focus intently on the light. They looked around to see if anyone was watching, but it seemed everyone was ignoring the strange event of the floating energy sphere. There was an odd silence around them as time seemed to slow.

Nylf, loyal friend to the deceased king of Strati Polis and Siphero Antolus, a voice resonated from the sphere, *do you accept the gift of the Incarnates, to discover the truths of this world and to protect the one you hold dear?*

"I accept," she said willingly. "I accept this responsibility."

And do you, the voice said to Urvnic, *Urvnic of the Demon Allegiants, one who has fought for the generals of Jormundgard, do you accept the gift of the Incarnates, to brave this conflict and live this life with the one you cherish?*

"I do," Urvnic said, tears flowing into his eyes. "I won't let death take me yet."

The sphere shattered in place, and as the energy from it flowed into both their arms, their shared Spearhead tattoo became whole.

The scene around them dissolved as Sila brushed up against them while carrying festival supplies, and loud roars came from Sila arguing with Terrans. Then Urvnic and Nylf fainted, and Siphero and Awesha rushed to assist them.

"Hey." Siphero patted Urvnic's cheeks. "Snap out of it; get up."

"Nylf, can you hear me? Please awaken." Awesha was by Nylf's side, trying very hard to awaken her friend from her stupor.

After a heavy groan from the both of them, they leaned forward and groggily got to their feet with the support of the airblade behind them. Siphero and Awesha observed that the whole time they hadn't let go of their hands, just like when they first bonded.

"Ugh," Urvnic groaned. "I feel like I got hit by a Scrap Rig."

"I feel just as terrible." Nylf held her forehead, but when she looked down at her hand, she saw that the veins on her hand glowing a light bluish color and that Urvnic's veins had a strange grayish hue to them.

Urvnic followed her eyes down to his hand, and his face matched Nylf's surprise.

"Well, you don't see that every day," he said. "What the heck is going on with my arm?"

"I have the same question. Awesha, Siphero, what does this mean?" There was worry in Nylf's voice, but while she was on the verge of panic, their friends just smiled back at them.

"Congratulations, Urvnic," Siphero said, clapping softly. "You now have the gift of magic."

"And to you, Nylf, you now know everything about Urvnic."

Urvnic and Nylf looked at their hands and then at each other, and Nylf blushed quite heavily while Urvnic turned his attention to Siphero.

"Gift of magic? Are you pulling my leg or something?"

Siphero smiled and put out his hand, as did Awesha, and they both spoke the familiar words: "Show me myself."

A small chunk of metal, probably from a Sila's old battered armor, flew into his hand. In Awesha's palm, there was a sphere of arcane energy swirling like a vortex. Urvnic stared with open eyes at both their palms, and his jaw dropped. He looked at Nylf, who held out her hand and repeated the same words. In her palm a small gust formed and churned, wrestling to be set free.

Urvnic stuck out his own hand and also spoke the words, putting all his energy into what he hoped would be an amazing power. "*Show me myself!*"

They all looked at his hand, but nothing happened. Urvnic repeated the words again and again, but still the magic in his veins would not make itself known.

"Ah, dammit, I really thought I had it," he vented, "and here I went and got all excited for it. I looked like an idiot doing it."

The others sighed. What had gone wrong? Urvnic put his hand on the fountain, but he fell over into the water. Nylf tried to grab his other hand to help him out, but her hand slipped through his fingers. Siphero and Awesha both gasped with delight. Urvnic had magic, just not the kind they had expected.

"So you still think you don't?" Siphero said, with a smirk.

"Yeah, yeah, yeah, laugh it up, metal mouth." Urvnic spat water out and climbed out of the fountain. "So I can lose my grip, whoop-de-do."

Siphero had a thought. "Awesha, can I borrow your sword?"

"Of course, but what for?"

"I have a theory, but whatever you do, don't stop me."

"What's this about having a science-y theory all of a sudden? Wait, what are you going to do with that sword?" Urvnic looked over as Siphero swung Awesha's sword at him.

"Don't man, I'm too pretty to die." Urvnic panicked, sticking out his arm in an attempt to block the blow.

The sword hit right into his arm with a loud clang and bounced off, denting the blade.

Nylf stared at his arm, the same as Awesha, Siphero, and a few passing Sila. Eventually, Urvnic opened his eyes and stared aghast at his own arm. The part of him that was his forearm was a completely different color, almost completely a reddish-black color.

"Un...unbelievable." Urvnic gasped. "What...what does it mean!"

"It means," Siphero said, summing it up, "that you can control the natural state of your body."

Urvnic stared with disbelief as his arm returned to normal, inspected the fleshiness, and then tried to touch the fountain. He felt the stone's cold surface like he always could until he decided he didn't want to, and his hand passed right through it.

"I don't think I'll ever get used to this." Urvnic frowned. "It's a little creepy."

"It suits you," Nylf said. "It's like the wind, light and unbound but powerful and reliable."

He smiled at her compliment and then turned to Siphero and Awesha. "Am I going to get wings like you?"

Siphero shrugged, but Awesha answered for him. "I don't think so. I know more about his situation. Siphero was born with a Terran mother and a Winged father, but after he bonded with me, the Winged side of him surfaced and compensated for his lack of possessing wings. The magic in his veins manifested a set for him, and it was not a pleasant affair."

"What do you mean by 'not a pleasant affair'?" Urvnic asked.

"It's like having your back ripped open while your bones grow, and it smells like burning flesh as a bunch of mechanical parts weld themselves onto your flesh to create a set of wings." Siphero touched his wings, showing Urvnic how they were a part of him and how he could still feel the pain of the grisly transformation.

"Well, that pretty much sums it up." Urvnic looked up at the sky. "So what happens next?"

Siphero was about to speak, but Awesha interrupted him. "I need my beloved here to celebrate with me. I suggest the two of you do the same." She dragged Siphero toward the festival grounds while Nylf and Urvnic just stood there with stupid looks on their faces.

"Do you want to go flying for a bit?" Urvnic couldn't help but say that. He didn't much care for flying, but it felt amazing to do it with someone, and it might as well be with the one he was beginning to bond with.

"I'll race you." Nylf smirked wildly at him. "To the end of Silacorlis and back."

She took off from her location, riding the wind she commanded. Urvnic couldn't help but notice that she left the ground at the same speed a Sabre could fly at cruising speed.

"Oh, you picked the wrong person to challenge." He grabbed his flight gear, buckled into his Spearhead, and took off from his location, knocking over a lot of aggravated Sila. He roared across the sky, trying to catch up with Nylf. On the side of his Spearhead a new image had appeared, without him even noticing. It was a vulture with streaks of fire under its wings facing a small sparrow. This was the result of their bond, the third bond formed between a Winged and a Terran. Urvnic and Nylf flew together, strangers from different worlds, sharing the skies.

Chapter 25: Stratagem

The festival was in full swing with the Silacorlis heroes Siphero and Awesha dancing in the city square amidst all the celebrants. Overhead, Nylf and Urvnic raced through the skies. Tratiki and Ieava were dancing as well and they seemed to be having the most fun of anyone there. Gargran was drinking with the old soldiers of the Silacorlis army and Sorice's men, starting bar brawls just for the heck of it. Xhe-Zhe were dancing to the rhythmic music, causing many a man to stare with hypnotized expressions. Octavio didn't attend the festival. He was with Rekusolus and Dreamen, negotiating the final pieces of the alliance and tying up loose ends with the Omega Alpha.

Sorice attended these peace talks with his lieutenants, staking his claim to the alliance.

"Much still needs to be done," Sorice said, "but my men and the Vigilant will join the Demon Allegiants in the fight to take back Stratis from these damned zealots."

"And so will the clans of Silacorlis," the Omega Alpha said. "The white wings have always sought to destroy us, but now they want to wipe us out. They want a war, and the Sila will commit all we have to their annihilation."

"There is something to consider here," Rekusolus said. "We have pieces on the board that can aid us in bringing about a decisive end to this war."

"My son." Dreamen gritted his teeth. "You want to use him and Awesha as weapons of war!"

"We have no choice," Rekusolus said. "The Grand Clerician will not let us idle. Even as we speak, she is sending invasion forces to all outlying settlements to recruit those who fit her desire for perfection while the rest are exterminated."

Dreamen went silent. He knew the risks, but he had just reunited with his long-thought-dead son, and now Rekusolus wanted him to fight a war he had no reason to be a part of.

The Omega Alpha broke the silence. "Before we can unleash our full forces, we need time to rebuild, strengthen our forces, and bring more factions to our side."

"Yes," Rekusolus agreed, "the other three poleis are pieces that must be dealt with. If any of them were to fall, our chances for victory would decrease."

"The only polis we truly need to be concerned with is the Far Eastern Polis. If they are taken, then we might as well hope for quick deaths." The Omega Alpha crossed his arms, examining the map of Stratis. The Far Eastern Polis was the most distant city of all.

"They have enough economic power to sustain the zealots for several years if it is ever captured," Sorice said. "Perhaps we could ask for the aid of the Xhe-Zhe. They could provide us with a way in."

"Perhaps, but that leaves the Storm Rider clans in the Stormlands and the Learned of the Archo Polis." Rekusolus examined the polis that was his home for many years, dreading to see it fall to those who would steal the secrets of Stratis. "We must consider our next move carefully."

"Consider what?" Gargran stumbled into the war room, smelling terribly of alcohol and someone's blood. He looked like a painting had been disfigured by an artist and was about to be lit on fire.

"Oh, it's the old Storm Rider who left his people," the Omega Alpha said cynically. "Go back to drinking, and let those responsible for our victory decide what is best."

"Lay off, pup," Gargran barked. "You all say you need to get to the Storm Polis; I'm your best bet to get there."

"You? What could an old drunkard looking for one last bit of glory do by getting us through the Stormlands?"

"How about I shove my harpoon up your—"

"That's enough, both of you." Sorice intervened. "Now Gargran is correct, as much as we refuse to accept it. Only a Stormrider can make the journey in and out of the Stormlands. But the question remains, Gargran. What would the Demon Allegiants gain from assisting the Storm Polis?"

Gargran took a sip from his alcohol and smiled. "The Storm Polis can offer you…the Horn of the Storm Beasts."

Everyone in the war room went silent. All eyes were on Gargran as he shared with them this legendary object.

"The…the Horn of the Storm Beasts," the Omega Alpha mumbled. "That is a legendary artifact said to…"

"…allow the wielder to call to his or her aid the king of all leviathans, the Skyeater." Gargran finished the legend.

"That is incredible." Rekusolus gasped. "With such a prize, we could surely win." He considered it a moment but looked back at the table and reconsidered.

"It's too much of a wild card," Dreamen said. "We need soldiers, magi, ships, and resources. A legend won't help us win a war."

"It is our legends we cling to for hope though," Gargran stated. "If you won't consider it, then at least let me take a small contingent of men. All I ask is for a chance to pursue this as an option. Even if I fail, we may still gain the assistance of the Storm Riders and their powers. They may be small in numbers, but their fighting prowess is legendary, and they are always spoiling for another battle to add to their legends."

Rekusolus and Dreamen spoke among themselves for a couple minutes, the others watching to see what they may say to either protest or support this lofty goal. When they were done, they moved apart and faced Gargran.

"Very well, Gargran, we approve your suggestion. We will grant you a platoon made up of Winged and Terrans, handpicked by Dreamen and Sorice. You may also take Nylf and Urvnic; they need experience in battle. Will this suffice?"

"It certainly will." Gargran saluted with appreciation. "I can leave tomorrow, if that will work."

"We are in agreement; you are dismissed," Rekusolus said as Gargran turned and flew out of the war room.

As he left, the others looked at one another, thinking they had just sent Gargran on a fool's errand.

"Are you sure we can trust that grizzled old Storm Rider to succeed in either affair?" The Omega Alpha clasped his mug and drank deeply. "I apologize for my lack of faith, but Storm Riders are not known for distinguishing truth from legend, especially their own."

"Remember, honorable Omega Alpha, any who would oppose the Grand Clerician and her army of zealots are in danger of their wrath. We have the responsibility to at the very least give them enough time to prepare themselves against the inevitability of destruction."

"Well said, Teller of Doom," Sorice agreed. "I will select men to brave the Stormlands."

Sorice ordered his lieutenants back to the *Vigilant*. They left the war room, leaving Sorice, the Omega Alpha, Dreamen, Rekusolus, and Octavio to speak among themselves.

"Now we must speak about the inclusion of Jormundgard in our deployment strategy." Rekusolus was the center of attention as he explained his point. "When the True Allegiants came to Stratis, we came through a weak point in the impenetrable cloud cover that corresponded to the coordinates where we met Siphero, Awesha, and the others. If the generals of Jormundgard discovered any of the weak points in the clouds and ventured through, they would flood in to claim everything as their own, and a fifth great Terran war would begin."

"I thought you represented the Terrans of Jormundgard," the Omega Alpha said. "You mean to say there are as many factions on Jormundgard as there are on Stratis?"

"Yes, and many more; they are just as greedy, hungry for blood, and controlled by an unquenchable thirst for conquest and claiming the spoils of war as their own. However, there many factions like us, the Demon Allegiants, who seek a resolution to all future conflicts, but they fight among themselves, unable to rally behind one specific solution."

"That is troubling," Sorice said. "So how will we deal with these rogue factions and potential allies in Jormundgard?"

"Awesha and Siphero will be going to Jormundgard and assisting the True Allegiants based in Salvagon, and Dreamen will accompany them." Rekusolus paused to let the plan sink in.

"Rekusolus," the Omega Alpha said grimly, "those two are the most important pieces on the board you so mentioned. If they were to leave, then the Sila would lose their beacon of hope, the two who put an end to Recril and Sleghis. They performed the impossible by bringing the Avia Myrvah back from beyond the brink of insanity. My people look up to them. We cannot let them go. They would lose their heroes."

It was then Rekusolus broke into warm laughter. It was unexpected for him to do it, and they all looked at him with puzzled expressions.

"Venerable Omega Alpha," Rekusolus said, and caught his breath, "your people already have a beacon. Your guardian and the daughter of former king and queen of Stratis, Ieava."

The Omega Alpha grew angry at the suggestion of Tratiki, throwing his mug at a pillar and growling, "You dare suggest that mongrel become the hope of my people? They would rather eat their own excrement than follow him into battle!"

"Please, my lord, I beg your forgiveness. We are not aware of his origin, but we suggested he take this position because he and Ieava are deeply in love. Their bond is very strong, and she holds strategic importance to the future of Stratis."

The Omega Alpha vented his frustration and composed himself. "It was wrong for me to snap at his name. Tratiki the Tireless Hunter is a Wildborn, a Sila born one in every few thousand. His birth mother was a Sila, but his father was a full-fledged Silacon. His birth is the result of his father's abuse of his mother."

As the Omega Alpha finished, the room went silent, and the leaders around the map table stared into space, wondering how best to deal with this information.

"So what you mean is," Sorice said, "Tratiki's birth was a mistake; he is the result of a Silacon forcefully impregnating his mother."

"It is a crime punishable by death," the Omega Alpha said. "His father was put to death shortly after our Alphas and soldiers heard word of it. His mother was still alive, only barely, and yet she was carrying the boy in her womb. I was only an Omega at the time of finding her, but she was nearly ready to give birth. A Wildborn does not take long to develop, so Tratiki was born within a week of her being impregnated, and his mother died giving birth to him. As a young Wildborn, he was shunned by all Sila until he started fighting back. Every day he fought with our Alphas and Sigmas, defeating them quite easily until he challenged me and I defeated him in combat. It was then that the wild nature that consumed him subsided and he became like every other Sila, fierce and stubborn. That is how I became Omega Alpha, the one who defeated the Wildborn and tamed the feral nature of the beast."

"What would happen if he reverted to his old self?" Dreamen asked. "Would he pose a threat to the Sila?"

"I don't know. Despite my rank and file, I have not been an Omega Alpha for long. It was shortly after the wild nature left him and he came into maturation and gained his Silacon form that I saw the bestial nature was still in him. I had only suppressed it. He recognized that I was his leader, and so I named him to the guardianship to show the people that I was a progressive leader. The Omegas despised my decision, but they did not question my prowess for ridding them of a potential monster."

Silence fell again throughout the war room. The music of the festival could be heard off in the distance. It was starting to get late, but there was still more to discuss.

Octavio was the one to break the silence. "Oh, great Omega Alpha, there is truth to what the Teller of Doom states. Ieava still has a claim to the throne of Strati Polis. If Ieava were to be crowned queen, Tratiki would become her protectorate, establishing the Sila as a people of great loyalty and trust. It would show the people of Stratis that the Sila are ready to take the first step toward unity and cooperation."

The Omega Alpha was baffled at this proposal, but then he grinned maliciously. "The Avia who opposed them would hate this arrangement with all of their being. There would be no end to the assassination attempts."

"But the Sila would have a foothold in Strati Polis, and the Avia would have no choice but to obey this. All we would need is the backing of three of the five houses to support this selection."

"Quite insightful, Octavio," Rekusolus said, with admiration. "You surprise me."

"Thank you, Teller of Doom." Octavio bowed his head humbly. "Your words honor me."

"I agree," the Omega Alpha said. "Your apprentice there has made me reconsider my stance on this matter. I will support the plan you originally stated. The Omegas may not like it, but even they understand the meaning of power and security. The House of the Feral Beast would support this."

"Then let us make a toast to the creation of the Demon Allegiants and the success of the war to come. To the liberation of Stratis by our hands." Rekusolus raised his glass, as did the rest of them.

"Let all those who oppose our survival be crushed under our heels," the Omega Alpha said.

"All those who would heed our call join our effort to defend their families with iron resolve, the skies they call home and the ground they deem sacred," Dreamen said.

"Like the demons they fear, we will sweep across their cities and cleanse those who would see us suffer. While in the guise of demons we will wreak a terrible vengeance upon any who slaughters an Avia, Sila, Wingless, Compa, or Terran for reasons of purity or conquest," Sorice said.

"And create a future for us all, one of a united Stratis and Jormundgard, of Winged and Terrans. Soaring the skies and blazing trails, a world we call Tortragard, our skies and our lands!"

"To Tortragard, to our skies and to our lands!"

Chapter 26: Harbinger

The celebratory creation of the Demon Allegiants never left the boundaries of Silacorlis as the news was announced publicly to the citizens and visitors of the Savage City. The news only seemed to drive celebrants into an even higher euphoric celebration of dancing, music playing, feasting, bar brawling, gambling, and racing. They were enjoying themselves; there was not a person on Silacorlis or on its outlying islands that was not happy for this most momentous day in history, their history.

All except for one, one individual who shared their happiness and wild sense of abandon. He was on the outskirts of the Savage City, where the *Vigilant* and *Legionnaire* were docked. The ships were undergoing necessary maintenance and rearming to prepare for the battles ahead, but only for this night there were very few Winged and Terrans standing guard to bother with. It was Mervieris, and he was looking for someplace to carry out his true mission.

He boarded the *Legionnaire*, roamed the decks, waved to crewmen going about their business and a few Avia from the *Vigilant*. A tour was being held by some Terrans who were showing a few of Sorice's lieutenants around the innards of the *Legionnaire*. His destination was the engine room; he had been there on multiple occasions to inspect the machines and learn all he could from the Terrans who worked them. As he opened a bulkhead to the engine room, he found the entire area was empty; not a whisper or breath could be heard. While checking one last time, he burned the bulkhead shut with his fire and turned to the gigantic mana reactor. It stood before him, a vessel holding an incredible amount of energy. He marveled at the volatile mana source of Jormundgard churning and whipping at its cage, waiting to break free.

He summoned a ball of fire in his hands that slowly grew until it was as tall as he was. It floated in front of him until it began to take the shape of a flat disk made of flames. Then, in the center, the flames began to clear as an image took shape, the image of a woman, someone at least fifteen years older than Mervieris but still fully glowing with youth.

She was a strange one to behold. Her hair was a fiery crimson, in fact, her hair was literally on fire. Her eyes were a dark shade of crimson, her lips were scarlet, and her facial features were wild and exotic like the flame of a burning fire. In her hair she wore a crown with rubies and diamonds and a large flower with red and green petals. The dress she wore smelled of ash, and her armor was made of obsidian stone.

"Oh, great Urfera Fireheart," Mervieris began, "I have news."

The woman in the portrait curtsied with respect to Mervieris, and he bowed in return.

"It is good to see you are well," Urfera said. "It has been so long, I feared you were lost when you escaped through the Neutral Crossing."

"I am alive and well, Your Majesty, but how goes the war, my lady? How are the Ash Knights holding up?"

"It fairs well, my harbinger. The Oceanmind's forces have abandoned the crossing, my minions press the attack, but as you always know, our war is eternal."

Mervieris smiled. "My lady, I have news that might provide a turning point in the war. I have found the power of the Incarnates."

"You have…where is it? Do you have it with you? Do you know who possesses it?" There was excitement in her voice, a tone Mervieris had not heard for some time.

"I do not have it, Your Majesty, but I know where to find it."

Urfera looked displeased with the news, but she regained her composure and allowed for Mervieris to continue.

"The power of the Incarnates exists not in a location; it resides in the hands of these two." He summoned two more flames, and they changed shape into the images of Siphero and Awesha.

Urfera scrutinized the appearance of Siphero and Awesha, the looks upon their faces, their wings, and the fact they were holding hands. She seemed startled to see Siphero's face, but she hid it before Mervieris could ask.

"They possess it. Is there any way for you to take it from them?"

"No, I apologize, my lady, I cannot. Their power is far greater than my own. I would not do it because I do not have a death wish."

The gentle flame surrounding her hair intensified in size; Urfera was cross. "You would disobey my orders, Sir Mervieris? Go against me for the sake of protecting these keepers of the power?"

"I would, my lady, because they have proven they have the fire within them. They are capable innovators and warriors. I have seen them give a portion of the Incarnates power to some of their friends, ones called Urvnic and Nylf."

He caused the flames resembling Siphero and Awesha to change shape into new forms resembling Urvnic and Nylf. Again, Urfera examined them both and saw similar characteristics between them.

"I see similarities between the pairings you have showed me. What are the names of the two worlds and their inhabitants?"

"The world I am in now is the world of Stratis, a world of endless skies, home to the Winged beings who have the power of flight. They live in a feudal-style civilization where the pure seek to destroy the impure. This is the reason a war is about to start."

"What of the other world?"

"The other world is called Jormundgard, a world covered in rock and metal with lakes and deserts and enough mana to flood the entirety of Aquatyer. This land belongs to the Terrans, a species without magic, but one filled with the power of imagination, innovation, and technology. Their technology is far beyond the capabilities of the Winged, but as my friend Siphero told me, they are in a state of constant war. They have no unified leadership and endless competition."

"And these two," Urfera said, and pointed to the flames of Urvnic and Nylf, "is the one called Urvnic from Jormundgard and the one called Nylf from Stratis?"

"That is correct, Your Majesty. In the same regard Siphero is from Jormundgard while Awesha is from Stratis, but their meeting and bonding is what created the power that you seek. They have dedicated themselves to one another as a husband and wife would in the throes of marriage."

Saying those words, Urfera felt a tightness in her chest. She had never known the feeling to dedicate all you are to the existence of another and vice versa.

"My lady," Mervieris asked, "is something the matter?"

She snapped back to his attention and resumed the conversation. "Nothing is wrong, Sir Mervieris. How fairs their war?"

"The faction I have joined has promised to unite both worlds, Jormundgard and Stratis. The leaders of these Demon Allegiants have made it their ultimate goal to end the tyranny of the Grand Clerician and the chaotic wars of the Terrans."

"Ah...a lofty goal, but not impossible." She pondered. "I have a new mission for you, Mervieris."

"What is your will, my lady?" he said, bowing before her, ready to fulfill any request she might have.

"I desire for you to assist, with all your power, in the unification of these two worlds."

"Your Majesty," Mervieris said, "I thought you only wanted me to find and bring you this power of the Incarnates?"

"I still do, but if we can assist the ones who possess this, we will have the leverage to make them give it to us willingly."

"As you wish, Your Majesty," Mervieris said. He disliked this plan. He had come to know Siphero and Awesha. He considered them to be like the Ash Knights he had grown up alongside, but he knew his place; to disobey the queen would be to cast his lot in with the Aquatics.

"I am authorizing the use of all the powers granted to you by your knighthood. Succeed for me, my knight. Your queen demands it of you."

"I will succeed for you, Your Majesty."

"And one more thing," Urfera said, "when you are successful, and you bring me the two with the power of the Incarnates, I will offer you the hand of my daughter in marriage."

Mervieris looked up in surprise. The hand of his queen's daughter? Marry the offspring of an all-powerful sorceress? That was the desire of any knight who served the great Urfera Fireheart. Surely he did not deserve the honor.

"I will not fail you, my queen," he said. "I will succeed for the glory of the Obsidian Legion!"

"Very good, my knight, now go forth and win this victory alongside your comrades. Notify me of any changes in your mission or of your success. I will continue to keep the forces of the Oceanmind at bay. Be victorious, Sir Mervieris."

The portal of fire dissolved into the air as Mervieris returned to his feet.

"I will succeed, my lady," he said to himself, "but I will not succeed the way you intend."

He left the engine room, passing the crewmen of the *Legionnaire*, and returned to his quarters, where he went to sleep on his bunk, the wings of fire on his back disappearing from existence.

"Tomorrow, I shall share the truth with Siphero and Awesha. It will be my first act of defiance."

He drifted into his dreams of a never-ending battle, of an aquatic world filled with angry soldiers and the shadow of a warrior princess, an enigma with a strange connection to him.

Chapter 27: Oath

A couple of days passed by, but Mervieris still remembered the promise he made to himself to tell Siphero and Awesha about his place in their war, deliberately going against what his leader had ordered him to do. He felt he owed this much to Siphero and Awesha. He never thought he would meet either Siphero or Awesha in the Strati Polis, let alone become a trusted comrade of theirs. As he stood on one of the balconies onboard the *Legionnaire* overlooking all of Silacorlis, he pondered how best to tell them.

He saw the Sila, Avia, and Terran factions working together, sharing resources and technologies, training together and preparing for an inevitable war. He even saw a Sila woman with butterfly wings walking hand in hand with a Terran, her long green hair and white dress flapping in the wind, and the Terran, with his graying hair and rust-colored armor, appeared to be crying.

Mervieris thought it was an odd pairing until he looked down at his own hand, remembering the promise Urfera made to him for her daughter's hand in marriage. It was the ultimate prize all Ash Knights strived for in the Obsidian Legion. He didn't actually love the queen's daughter. He followed orders like everyone else, received his knighthood, and became one of many who served the queen. Then he thought about how the Winged and the Terrans were about to fight a war similar to the one between the Ashers and Aquatics.

"No, it's not like that," he said. He felt like he was talking to the queen again, and this time he was speaking his thoughts. "Their war is different. There are individuals here from both peoples that seek a different approach, one where they must strive for a new future. These Demon Allegiants are risking everything to do the impossible. The Obsidian Legion has only ever known warfare, never peace or the desire for unification.

"That's it." Mervieris finally understood in that moment. "I never realized how simple it is. The reason why Ashers and Aquatics have never been able to; no one has come forward who wishes for unification, an end to the warfare."

After having this epiphany, he saw a small bird fly toward him. It was metallic in appearance, carrying in its talons a bottle with a rolled-up piece of paper inside. It dropped the bottle at his feet and landed on the rail next to him, looking at him in an odd way.

Mervieris soon realized that this was the drird that Siphero had built, but it had become lost during their escape to the *Legionnaire*. He had wondered where it went, but now it was right here looking at him and chirping angrily, which seemed to mean, *Take a look in the bottle, idiot.* He picked up the bottle, and the drird immediately flew off, diving between a gap in the clouds and disappearing from sight.

As he pulled the piece of paper out of the bottle, unrolled it, and read the contents, his eyes filled with astonishment. It was addressed to him:

To the Ash Knight in this strange world of skies, I am a supporter, like many from our world who wish to resolve the war between our two warring worlds. The never-ending war of fire and water must come to an end; the forces of Urfera Fireheart and Tregion Oceanmind must end. We have defected from our forces and escaped to the world of the earth. If you desire to act upon our offer, go forth with the chosen defiant that wish to travel to the world of the earth. You will find us in the greatest of their lakes, biding our time, waiting for the moment to speak. I am Farsheva, daughter of the Oceanmind, and I await your arrival.

As he finished the letter, he smiled. "The enemy of my enemy wishes to make me the enemy of my friend." He paused in silence. "I accept."

The letter then changed shape in his hands, the surface becoming a series of symbols and directions. It was a map. Some words at the base of the paper said, *Give this to the one called the Otherworlder.*

Mervieris knew that it meant Siphero; only a Terran could read the map because it was a location in Jormundgard, one of its greatest bodies of water. He rolled up the paper and put it in his satchel, deciding it was time to find Siphero and Awesha. He took off from the deck of the *Legionnaire* and flew in their last known location, determined to tell them the truth behind his existence.

He flew for a couple minutes until he saw Gargran waving to him. He set down next to the old drunkard as he was training with Urvnic, Nylf, and a handful of Terrans and Avia.

"Excuse me, Gargran," he said, "have you by any chance seen Siphero and Awesha? I have something important to share with them."

The old Storm Rider took a rag and wiped the sweat off his face. "I saw them only moments ago, headed to the main pavilion in the Savage City with Dreamen and Rekusolus. That's where you might find them."

"Thank you, Storm Rider," he said, taking off in the direction Gargran had pointed to. He continued for another minute until he reached the main pavilion, where several Sila guards were standing guard with halberds, shields, and swords.

As he approached, the guards stood at attention and asked for the name of the visitor.

"My name is Mervieris, and I am here to talk to Siphero and Awesha. I assisted them in the battle to retake Silacorlis."

The guards moved out of his way to let him pass, and Mervieris entered the building. Inside, Sila were carrying battle plans, delivering messages, and talking among themselves on important matters regarding the coming war. He ignored the vast majority of them as he tried to find the two he needed to speak with.

Siphero and Awesha were in a corner, discussing the already predetermined plans to return to Jormundgard to secure reinforcements while finding a way to convince the leaders of Jormundgard to stop fighting one another and unite, an extremely difficult but not impossible ordeal.

"You get to keep your promise to me, Siphero," Awesha said. "We're going back to your home of Jormundgard."

"Yeah...and dear old once-dead dad is coming along as a chaperone," Siphero huffed. "Can't wait."

"Why are you so concerned about that, Siphero? Do you not trust your father?"

"Sure I do. What I don't trust are the Terran factions we have to meet with and those loyal to the True Allegiants. Just like with Winged, you can never be sure with Terrans. They always have an alternative motive or agenda."

"I'm not worried, Siphero," she said, grasping his hand tightly until he yelped for a release. "I have you."

Siphero grimaced in pain, looking around for anyone to help him, when he saw Mervieris. "Mervieris, what in the Savage City are you doing in the Savage City?"

At the mention of his name, he took a deep breath and strode toward Siphero and Awesha, none of his original charm existent in his personality.

"Siphero, Awesha," he began, "I have something very important to tell you both." He looked around at the Sila going about their business behind him. "I wonder if there is somewhere we can talk in private?"

"Yes, of course," Siphero said.

Awesha and Siphero led Mervieris up a few flights of stairs to a balcony overlooking the main square, where the festival had taken place only days ago, surprised to see how vibrant a city of the Sila was.

They turned to Mervieris, who walked to the balcony and turned to look at them.

"So what is so important to demand our attention, Mervieris?" Awesha asked.

Mervieris did not speak. He stayed silent for a few minutes, looking down at his hands, and remembered the prize if he should succeed in their war, the hand of the queen's daughter, and then looked at his satchel, where the map was. He cleared his mind as Siphero and Awesha continued to look at him curiously.

"I think it's better if I just show you," he said. He raised his arm in front of him, touched a tattoo on it painted with chains, a picture of a flaming avisus with burning wings and a sword wreathed in lava. He focused until Siphero and Awesha saw Mervieris was surrounded in a cocoon of fire. They materialized their weapons in response to this change, as they had never seen Mervieris do this before. When the blazing cocoon subsided, they saw Mervieris had undergone a strange metamorphosis.

The red-haired Winged no longer had wings; he was covered in a set of black and red armor with red streaks, and fires burned in place on his pauldrons. His helm had small antlers on the sides that smelled of ash and soot. On his back was a cape that burned like a real fire and flickered every so often. At his waist was a sword three feet long with a hilt the color of obsidian and glittering with red stones.

To his side stood an avisus, its withers slightly taller than his shoulder, its mane, tail, and hooves burning with small fires while sparks came out of its nose when it snorted. It too wore black and red armor similar to his own. The wings of the avisus would appear every now and then when it neighed or reared up.

Then, Mervieris opened his eyes, and the aura of fire surrounding him subsided as he stepped toward Siphero and Awesha.

"Mervieris, who…are you?" Siphero asked, his shield raised and tesla projector pointed toward the Asher.

Mervieris pulled his sword out of its sheath, the white and black blade gleaming in the sunlight. He thrust it into the sky and planted it into the ground as he kneeled before them.

"I am Mervieris, the Ash Knight, one of many knights loyal to Queen Urfera Fireheart in the Ashlands."

Awesha and Siphero stared at each other and then at Mervieris, who remained in a kneeling position. They had no idea what to say to Mervieris, who had just revealed to them his true self and the fact that he wasn't from either Stratis or Jormundgard. He was a renewed, total stranger to them.

Anticipating their speechlessness, Mervieris rose from his position and sheathed his sword. Allegiant guards from the command center came to the balcony, where they surrounded Mervieris. His avisus reared up while he attempted to calm his companion. Rekusolus, Dreamen, and Sorice joined his company shortly afterward.

"Mervieris," Rekusolus said, the first to speak, "why are you dressed like that, and where are your wings?"

The Ash Knight chuckled as he walked forward, the places where he stepped leaving black soot. Sila soldiers pointed their weapons at him, but they dared not confront him. Once he was five feet in front of Siphero and Awesha, he unsheathed his sword yet again and planted it in the ground, where he knelt with respect to them.

"Upon my honor as a knight," he began, "what I have to say is not for the ears of you tiny Demon Allegiants. I will only speak to the keepers of the Incarnates power, Awesha and Siphero. Any who would dispute my request will meet me on the field with my blade through their innards. Now leave!"

The soldiers were a little shaken as they looked to their leaders, especially the Teller of Doom. Rekusolus considered the request of Mervieris and raised his arm, signaling all soldiers to stand down.

"Very well," Rekusolus said, "I will allow your request to be fulfilled, but how do I know you will not threaten our alliance?"

The Ash Knight surprised them yet again. "I will reveal all to you once I have made my request to Siphero and Awesha. I am risking my life to avert a disaster before it starts; the least you could do is be patient. The information I have to share will open your eyes to obstacles you are barely aware of!"

This news made Rekusolus nod with uncertainty, and he ordered all soldiers present to return to their posts while he, Sorice, and Dreamen stood just outside the balcony area. They were still going to eavesdrop; they had fulfilled Mervieris's request. He knew that they were still listening as he shot a fireball at the ground, which enveloped him, Awesha, and Siphero in a dome of fire. Rekusolus and the others tried to break through the barrier, only to have their weapons melt, get severe burns, or cause projectiles of water to turn into steam.

"What do we do now?" Dreamen said anxiously. "My son is in there! We can't let him be at the mercy of that monster of a knight."

"Let him be," Sorice said to them. "Your son is much stronger than us, and Awesha is much fiercer than him. She would rather die than let Siphero come to harm; that is how deep she cares for him. I have seen it with my own eyes."

"I hope for their sake you are right, Vice Admiral," Dreamen answered.

They watched as the flames enshrouded the three, waiting and wondering what would transpire in the sphere of fire.

Inside the fiery dome, Siphero and Awesha held each other to try and keep from getting singed.

"Do not worry, Siphero, Awesha," Mervieris assured them. "The flames will not harm you. If I wanted to do so, then you would not be here. Now please have a seat."

His armor around him disappeared into smoke, returning him to his nobleman attire, the burning avisus to his left knelt to the ground, where it went to sleep. As he placed his hand in midair, a chair made of brimstone and obsidian appeared, which he seated himself in. Two more chairs appeared in front of Siphero and Awesha, as did a table with a burning rose.

"Please sit," Mervieris repeated himself. "I really don't want to say it again."

Siphero and Awesha took their seats, their wings folding around them, but they continued to hold hands for fear of what might happen.

"Now that we are more comfortable, I would like to tell you both an important truth: I am not from this world. My home is a world that is constantly at war with another world. My world is known as the Ashlands, a world of fire, brimstone, magma, and beautiful, scorched lands as far as the eye can see."

"How is that beautiful?" Awesha spoke up. "Wouldn't a land that is always on fire be barren and uninhabitable?"

"Not necessarily, but would you please let me continue?" Mervieris pouted. Awesha remained silent, and brushed her hair to keep herself busy.

"Anyway," he said, "my home has constantly been at war with the world of Aquatyer, a world made entirely out of water and ruled by a wise and tyrannical man known as Tregion the Oceanmind. For most of my life, I was brought up to believe the people of Aquatyer were the demons of children's nightmares until…recently."

Mervieris pulled out the map the drird had given him, placed it on the table, and pushed it toward Siphero. Siphero grasped the map and took a good look at it, his eyes widening as a result. Awesha stole a peak of the map but couldn't understand what was so important about it. She didn't know any of Jormundgard's geography.

"What is it?" she asked. "Is it something special?"

Siphero looked up and said, "Where did you get this?"

"From some friends who think the same way I do," he said, "people from the other side of my war who want to put an end to it. Do you know where that is in Jormundgard?"

"Yes...yes I do. It's called the Diseased Abyss, the largest dumping ground for refuse and byproducts of our technology. It is usually deserted because the pollution is so bad the area is considered unlivable. Why would these friends of yours go near there?"

"Simple, it's the same way we got here," Mervieris explained. "Do you know why we have been fighting for centuries upon centuries? It is for the control of a special land that houses a device allowing those who control it to cross into other worlds. We call this land the Neutral Crossing."

"So that's why you are here now and those friends you mentioned are in Jormundgard," Awesha deduced. "Both of you used the device to come to our worlds." Then she was gripped with a deep suspicion. "How long have your allies and enemies been coming to our worlds or other worlds, for that matter? And why did you end up in Stratis and not Jormundgard?"

Mervieris frowned and then answered, "It rarely happens on our world, since either side only ever has control of the device I mentioned for more than a few minutes. That is only enough time to send one person, let alone five or ten, through the portal. Even when we have control for the briefest time, the portal does not send us to the world of our choosing. There's something about this world that causes the instability of our departure to Stratis or Jormundgard. Other than that, I have no idea."

"So those friends of yours," Awesha asked, "are you going to meet them?"

"That is my desire, Awesha," he said. "I plan to go to this Diseased Abyss and seek the aid of those who would desire to bring an end to this war. I heard from the higher ups that you, Siphero, and Dreamen are heading to Jormundgard. I would very much wish to come along, to meet these rebels. In return, my queen ordered me to assist you both in your own battle, but she ordered me to capture you both once the battle was over and take the Incarnates power you possess."

Siphero and Awesha felt slightly threatened at this announcement and reached for their weapons, but Mervieris begged them to relax, and they did so.

"So, you are going against the orders of your queen in order to undermine her power and aid the enemy of your enemy, is that about right?" Siphero said sarcastically.

The Ash Knight laughed heartily, the flames around him intensifying only briefly before they returned to their original state. "You never cease to make me laugh, Siphero Antolus, and this is exactly why I am glad I defected from my Urfera. She could never appreciate the delights of the common Winged or Terran, no offense meant to either of you, mind you."

"Well it's good to be appreciated, I guess. So what exactly are you going to do since this queen of yours will find out sooner or later?"

"I've thought it out that far, Siphero, Awesha." He paused for a brief moment, gathering his thoughts. "I will assist you both in your war to reclaim Stratis and Jormundgard from the grasp of these zealots, and I will also help you discover this enemy that Hevros mentioned, the enemy you have been keeping a secret from the others."

Siphero and Awesha's faces filled with surprise and shock. How could Mervieris know about the Incarnates? They never told him, and yet here he was telling them he honestly wanted to assist them in every regard for the small favor of going to that lake.

"How do you know about them?" Awesha said, baffled. "We never mentioned them to—"

Mervieris smiled. "The Incarnates exist on my world too. They have spies and footholds in both our worlds and all other worlds out there. They have been manipulating my queen and those who came before her for hundreds of years. It is knowledge very few have ever acquired."

"So how did you come to know?" Siphero asked. "We were told on a whim by those Archons we mentioned. They have terrible timing."

Mervieris nodded in agreement. "Archons exist in my world too. They are looked at as beings of great knowledge and power. An Archon called Hevros appeared to me one day on the field of battle for the briefest moment. He opened my eyes to the truth about my queen, the war, and my very existence. I have been keeping it a secret ever since."

"Hevros, what a coincidence." Siphero laughed. "That's the name of the Archon that appeared at the time I was born."

Mervieris was the one who was shocked now. "The same Archon that appeared for me also appeared at the time of your birth? There's no way our meeting could be chalked up to a coincidence."

"It is strange," Awesha said, "but I have heard enough of your request, Mervieris." She arose from her seat, it dissolving into ash behind her. "I deem all you have said to be the truth. You trusted us upon our escape from Strati Polis and during the battle with the Aerial Fleet. It is my turn to trust you. Will you trust him, Siphero?"

"Certainly," Siphero said, "even if he's a bit of an ass—a manipulative, noble, and insensitive ass."

Mervieris felt overjoyed as he got up. His armor returned to him as did his sword. He pulled it out of his sheath before the two of them and stuck it in the ground in the same spot as before. Kneeling down, he began to speak binding words. "I, Mervieris, the Ash Knight of the Ashlands, do solemnly swear, I shall serve Siphero and Awesha, with all my power, strength, and resolve in order to see their worlds become united as one. With those who I make this oath to as my witnesses, I do so bind this promise. Once my services are no longer needed, I will stay with them as their friend in their worlds as my new home. This I swear upon the mighty Hevros!"

The flames surrounding them shot up into the air like a pillar as the barrier died down around them. The Sila guards were about to surround Mervieris again when Siphero and Awesha stood in the path of their weapons. None of the guards came any closer. The avisus at Mervieris's side dissolved into flames as it returned to the tattoo on his arm, much to everyone's surprise.

Awesha looked at Siphero, who looked at Mervieris, the Ash Knight. Slowly they put their weapons away while their wings flanked Mervieris protectively.

"Mervieris, despite his annoying personality—"

"Don't forget regal and benevolent appearance," he said.

"And his deceptive reasoning," Awesha said for Siphero, "Mervieris is here at great risk to his well-being. He has shared with us crucial information to our war and has pledged himself to us in return for being allowed to join the Demon Allegiants."

"If any of you so much as scratch his armor, you will have me and my love to deal with." Siphero threatened all there. He didn't like making threats, but Mervieris really was on the sword end of all issues at the moment.

"As much as your sentiment pleases me, Siphero," Mervieris said, "I can keep myself safe far better than the two of you could. These soldiers can't best me on the field of combat. Siphero and Awesha would have a better chance, but no one else does. If you want me, I will be back onboard the *Legionnaire*, preparing to leave."

Then before their eyes, the flaming avisus appeared from beneath where he was standing. The avisus reared up, fire bellowing from it snout. He mounted his avisus and turned, facing the balcony.

"I am not your enemy; only you can decide that," he said. He then kicked his mount's sides, and it jumped off the balcony. Everyone rushed to see where he had gone as he appeared again, the avisus sprouting wings of fire and galloping off in the direction of the *Legionnaire*.

"What does this mean, Siphero, Awesha? What does this bode for our plans?" Rekusolus wondered.

They both watched as Mervieris's trail of fire dissipated in the air.

"It means," Siphero said, "that more than one world is facing a crisis similar to our own."

"And there are those among the forces fighting these wars who desire an end to conflict," Awesha added, "and we have just met one of those defiant few."

Chapter 28: Departure

It took several more days than originally planned for the hullabaloo surrounding Mervieris's true identity to reach every ear in Silacorlis. It sent the continent into an uproar as many questions were directed at the Ash Knight about his involvement in their war. Could he be trusted? What was his true agenda? Why would he swear himself to Siphero and Awesha? And the true question that baffled them all was, how many worlds are there like Stratis and Jormundgard?

Mervieris dismissed any who tried to ask him questions, throwing them off the *Legionnaire* and back onto Silacorlis, making it clear he didn't like being bothered. His friends started to get worried. Gargran went to visit but didn't stay to ask him questions. Gargran knew what it was like to be suspected of disloyalty; it was one of the reason he was named to guardianship. He made himself available as a friend to Mervieris if he wanted to talk.

The others went for ulterior motives, to gauge if he was the same person or a double agent, which led to little success.

The Ash Knight answered no questions until Awesha and Siphero asked him to share what he knew with the rest of the leaders of the Demon Allegiants. He complied because they had asked for his cooperation and he agreed.

He told them all about why he was there, his world, the war he was fighting, about the potential allies present in the Diseased Abyss, and how going against his orders would lead to great consequences if his queen ever found out.

"That is intriguing information," Rekusolus said. "So you are risking your life to fight our war, but your queen doesn't know of your treachery?"

"She does not, but she will figure it out eventually," Mervieris concluded. "So do you trust that I am no longer a threat to your war party?"

The council was silent for several seconds until the Omega Alpha spoke up. "That is a very Sila-like quality to have. You dared go against someone who has their own designs, and you did so despite the consequences. I believe he is worthy of our trust."

The Omega Alpha pointed his weapon into the air in acknowledgment of Mervieris, as did Sorice, Dreamen, Siphero, and Awesha. Rekusolus was the last to do so, but he proudly said, "Welcome to the Demon Allegiants, Ash Knight. Stand as a demon about to destroy the chaos of a long and bloody war."

Everyone in the war room broke into applause, as did Siphero and Awesha and all their friends. Urvnic and Nylf stood near the entrance, applauding to him as well. They thought Mervieris was very daring to do something like this.

Siphero, Awesha, Mervieris, Urvnic, and Nylf left the war room walking side by side. They were all friends, yet the peace they enjoyed was going to be short-lived. As they approached the docks where the *Vigilant* and the *Legionnaire* were tethered, they passed an assembly area where Terrans and Winged were building a vessel of some sort. Terrans were directing the Winged in building the vessel while the Winged were tying it together with binding magic and with the assistance of Terran welding machines and technology.

"What is that?" Mervieris asked. "I've never seen a ship like that, let alone being built by Terrans and Winged."

"Oh that," Urvnic said, taking a smoke of a pipe, "that's a new ship commissioned by our leaders in the Demon Allegiants, the first cooperatively built ship. It will have the mana reactor of a Terran airfortress and the carrying capacity for Terran airblades alongside those skimmer drakes and avisi, but most importantly it will be twice the size of the *Legionnaire* and the *Vigilant* put together."

Siphero and Awesha eyed the *Legionnaire* and the *Vigilant* at the docks and then turned back to the new ship. A ship with the best of both worlds built into it seemed too good to be true, and yet here it was being built right in front of them.

"How long do you think it will take to finish?" Awesha asked. "It seems like they still have a long way to go."

"Not sure," Urvnic said, blowing smoke. "Right now they're working on fusing metal refined through Terran techniques with the wood of Winged sky galleons to make it possible to go into Jormundgard. I'd guess maybe a couple years, since this war will take at least twice or thrice that amount."

Before they could contemplate anything else, Siphero and the others heard a proud roar from above them and saw Tratiki in

Silacon form giving Ieava a ride. They touched down right in front of them. As they embraced and shook hands, Tratiki was the most surprised to see Mervieris wearing his new armor, but he didn't feel like giving him a hard time.

"Siphero, Awesha," Ieava said, "we wanted to tell you the wonderful news."

"What is it?" Siphero asked. "What's so great?"

Ieava blushed heavily, her hand on her stomach, until Nylf and Awesha started crowding around Ieava and congratulating her, while Urvnic and Siphero stood around Tratiki, who appeared to have had a massive weight placed upon his back.

"You're going to be a father, huh, Tratiki," Mervieris deduced. "Now I feel bad for trying to drive the two of you apart all those weeks ago."

"You should be," Tratiki retorted. "But its forgiven now. You're with us, not against us, and now you have to do whatever Siphero and Awesha say."

Mervieris looked at Siphero, who was about to say something, but he interrupted with, "Not a word Siphero, not a word."

"So how did it happen, ya proud papa?" Urvnic elbowed Tratiki.

Tratiki gritted his teeth at Urvnic, who backed off in surrender, but he answered anyway. "It was during the festival. Ieava and I were having such a wonderful time while I was a Silacon, and then I felt a strange connection with her as we returned to our respective chambers. The next day she told me she was sick, and then a couple days later, she started eating more than I eat in a day, and trust me; I eat a lot. We went to the Terran doctors instead of a healer because their medical technology and practices are much better than Winged. The doctors revealed that Ieava had a parasite inside her, but to our surprise they said she was pregnant."

He dropped his shoulders and slouched on a nearby chair while his wings folded around him. Urvnic, Siphero, and Mervieris tried to alleviate him of his troubles, only to make the Sila father even more miserable. Then Tratiki started to laugh, and he laughed loudly and mightily. It took them all by surprise, especially Mervieris. In response they all started laughing and took seats next to each other. Awesha, Ieava, and Nylf returned to those they were bonded with as they all watched the construction of the new ship.

"None of this, none," Tratiki said after a short silence, "would have been possible if not for our friends Siphero and Awesha and their otherworldly connection."

"Here, here," Urvnic agreed.

"Indeed," Mervieris said.

"We have them to thank for making our lives better and bringing us together," Ieava chimed in.

"Nothing would have changed if not for their meeting," Nylf said.

They all grabbed drinks from a passing Cherubim carrying a silver platter. It bowed to them and winked at Awesha. She later realized that Nerv had done this little kindness.

"I would like to make a toast," Siphero said to them all, "a toast that no matter where we go, what trials we face, the connections we forge or wars we fight, we will always be connected by the bonds we have created between us. Distance won't matter. We are always by each other's side. To us—the crusaders of defiance to the status quo!"

They all clinked glasses together and drank deeply. The beverage was nonalcoholic, so no one complained, except for Urvnic. They just wanted to commemorate the moment with something.

As they all settled down, they watched as Winged and Terrans worked hand in hand, complementing the work of each other in building a new flagship for the Demon Allegiants.

"I wonder what that thing is going to be called when it's done?" Nylf asked, "I hope it isn't called the *Ship*."

Urvnic, Siphero, and Mervieris laughed, and they agreed that *Ship* would not be a good name.

"Would you like to know?" a voice said. It was Weltrox, the Alpha Tratiki and Ieava had met back during the battle.

"Sure, what is it, hairy boy?" Urvnic teased.

"Don't aggravate him," Tratiki warned. "He doesn't deserve it." He turned to Weltrox and said, "You may continue, Alpha Weltrox."

"Thank you, Guardian Tratiki. The name was just decided a couple minutes ago." Weltrox cleared his throat. "The ship will be commissioned as the *Crusader of Defiance*."

They were all perplexed that it would be getting a name like that, when they turned their heads to Siphero, who raised his hands in surrender. "Don't look at me; I have nothing to do with this."

"He's right," Weltrox said. "I heard your toast and brought the idea to the Terran foremen who have been scratching their heads for the past several days trying to pick a name."

"It is a name that speaks to us all," Ieava acknowledged. "I approve of the name."

"As do I," Mervieris said. "It tells me we are about to embark on a journey that will change the fate of all our worlds."

"Then the *Crusader of Defiance* it shall be," Weltrox said, before excusing himself.

Siphero, Awesha, and the others continued to hang out together for a few more minutes until Tratiki and Ieava excused themselves too. They had to talk with the Omega Alpha since they had been named as successors to the throne of Strati Polis by the council of Omegas.

"We have so much to do," Ieava said, disappointed. "With our baby adding to it, we are going to be very busy here at Silacorlis, and we might not see you all for some time."

"Don't worry about us, Ieava," Awesha said, holding her hands. "Keep your baby safe and raise it into a beautiful child."

Ieava smiled, a tear rolling down her cheek. Tratiki looked at Siphero and offered his hand.

"A while ago," he said, "this was a custom you told me of. A little odd for a Terran and a Winged to do, but not at all odd for comrades."

Siphero shook Tratiki's hand, and they hugged like brothers would when leaving on a long journey. Tratiki then whispered into Siphero's ear.

"In this war all shall remember the name of Siphero, the Terran Winged."

"Thanks, but you know me. I don't need much, let alone people having to say my name."

"Then I will give you all you need and then pester you for more."

He joined Ieava, and they flew off together, waving good-bye as they went. They headed back toward the palace they had been given for their own purposes as new leaders in the Demon Allegiants.

Urvnic and Nylf were next to excuse themselves; they needed to join Gargran and the Sky Devil platoon, a name Siphero smiled at.

"The old grump is taking us and a few others over to the Stormlands, the place he calls home," Urvnic said. "He says we're going to make excellent leviathan food."

Siphero laughed. "Don't worry. Gargran will keep you safe; he did it for me."

"Of course, I'm sure, but still, Winged and Terrans working and fighting together…I never thought I would see the day. It still feels surreal."

"How can it not?" Awesha said. "I was afraid of Terrans and the other Winged races several months ago, and now I'm with Siphero and you both are my friends. A lot can change in a short time."

"Sure can," Nylf said. "We need to go now. We hope to see you again."

Nylf and Awesha hugged while Siphero and Urvnic did a brotherly handshake.

Urvnic was about to follow Nylf back to Gargran when Siphero stopped him, his face serious. "Keep that bond between you safe. Only tell Gargran, or those you believe can be trusted, or else it could become a huge problem in this war."

Urvnic returned the seriousness. "All right, Siphero, I will keep her and the bond safe."

They left with long good-byes until it was just Siphero, Mervieris, and Awesha watching the *Crusader of Defiance* being built. They remained for a few more minutes until they got bored and left the shipyard, flying the short distance to the edge where the *Legionnaire* was docked. There they saw Stager, Yevere, and Dreamen were preparing for the long journey back to Skyspire, where they would return to Jormundgard. As they touched down, Dreamen looked up and approached them.

"Hey, Father," Siphero said, "are you almost ready to go?"

"Yes, nearly," Dreamen said. "Mervieris, Awesha, could you prepare your beasts for the journey? I need to speak with my son."

Mervieris and Awesha moved past Dreamen, and Awesha tended to Yevere, who was happy to see her. Mervieris spawned his avisus, much to the surprise of those working nearby.

Dreamen returned his gaze to Siphero, who was puzzled that his father wanted to speak with him.

"Siphero," his father began, "I wasn't entirely truthful with you on the *Legionnaire* about the time when your home of Saltdeep was attacked by Winged."

"What do you mean, Dad?" Siphero was confused, but he stayed quiet.

"The real culprits of the attack were a group called the Obsidian Legion."

Siphero was deeply shocked but was quickly gripped with anger toward his father for keeping this from him. "Why didn't you tell me the truth?"

"Please forgive me, Son," his father said. "I wasn't completely sure myself, but I remembered the color of the armor after seeing Mervieris's. I'm sure of it."

"But...Mervieris is my friend. He'd never do something like that."

"I'm sure he didn't, Son, but he probably doesn't know of the consequences his queen's crusade has wrought. Don't fault him for it. Travel with him as he discovers the truth. Help him confront his queen. I'm sure Mervieris will understand."

Siphero stepped back and let that thought sink in. Then he turned away from his father and busied himself by getting Stager ready to go.

"Also, Son," Dreamen said, "I won't be coming with you."

Siphero paused, and said over his shoulder, "Perhaps it is better if you don't come."

Dreamen stared at Siphero's back, sighed heavily, and took off for the *Vigilant*. Siphero silently watched his father fly away. He couldn't shake the feeling that his father had lied to him.

"Is everything all right, Siphero?" Awesha asked. She could sense he was upset about something.

"You're lucky your father always told you what he wanted for you," he said, slightly angered.

He pulled some equipment and fastened it down on Stager's back, and the behemoth seemed like he wanted more weight to test his strength.

Awesha grabbed Siphero's hand and forced him to look into her eyes, her wings shimmering with their rainbow aura.

"At least you have a father who loves you for the person you are and not what you should be." She then kissed him against his will until he gave in and stopped struggling, the light of their bond shining brightly again and drawing the attention of everyone to them.

As the light faded, they all went back to work, and Siphero and Awesha stopped and embraced. "Don't ever think either of us had a happy childhood, Siphero, because we both know the truth."

Siphero felt bad now that Awesha made him feel better. He couldn't be mad any longer. "I'm sorry, Awesha, I…just need some time to cool off. I hate my father for keeping secrets. I hadn't realized that I had a father until a month ago. I still want to get to know him. Thank you for making me see that."

He went back to saddling up Stager and was finished within the hour. Awesha finished with Yevere, and so did Mervieris, with his mount called Pyrus. As they climbed on their mounts, Siphero tossed Mervieris a communication piece and showed him how it worked, and he equipped it beneath his helm.

They gave the cue to fly, and their mounts climbed into the sky and circled several hundred feet above Silacorlis. Siphero never thought he would use the compass he was given back in Skyspire, but those were the instructions Rekusolus had given him. He held the compass out in front of him, and it started turning in all directions. Then a familiar wind swept over him. He knew the wind, the wind that pointed him in the direction of the *Legionnaire* when they had escaped from Strati Polis some months before.

"Pops," he whispered, "you never left me. You've always been with me." He tried to hold back a tear and then said the next best thing: "Take us home, Pops, take us home to Jormundgard."

The wind picked up as the compass stopped spinning and pointed southwest.

"We have our heading; now prepare to enter a slipstream," Siphero said. "It's going to be a little bumpy."

"Wait," Siphero heard in his earpiece. The voice came from a Terran. "Siphero Antolus, we have orders from Rekusolus to accompany you to Skyspire. We need to establish a base in the Air Wastes and reinforce the village."

Siphero, Awesha, and Mervieris turned in their saddles to see as two Claymores took off from an empty field in Silacorlis and joined them in their flight path above Silacorlis. They saw the airblades were loaded with supplies, and several Winged were riding on their backs, some Sila and some Avia.

"All right then," Siphero said, "we will lead the way, so try to stay close. This is going to be a straight shot for Skyspire, no rests or refueling."

"Understood, sir," the voice said. "Awaiting your signal."

Siphero then contacted Mervieris. "Can Pyrus there go into slipstream by chance?"

Mervieris smiled. "Pyrus can do it; he is an avisus after all. All avisi know how to do it."

"All right then," Siphero said, "let's go to Skyspire."

They gave their mounts the cue for slipstream, and they broke the sound barrier with a clap of thunder. The Claymores rode the wake created from the slipstream as they disappeared from sight above Silacorlis, the hopes and dreams of the Demon Allegiants traveling with them.

One Winged stood on a balcony overlooking the city as it cheered and waved to their departing heroes. Siphero, Awesha, and Mervieris and their reinforcements headed in the direction of Jormundgard, the war-torn frontier.

"Stay safe, Sister," Myrvah wished. "Brave this storm and then come home…"

She turned as she faced several Sila guards holding the struggling bodies of Sleghis and Recril, their mouths gagged.

"In your stead, I will make Father and his pawn suffer for what they made you, Siphero, myself, and all the others suffer!"

The Crusade of Defiance will continue…

Appendices

Character Appendix:

Siphero Antolus: A traumatized military engineer and pilot. Son of Dreamen and Straea Antolus.

Awesha: A fiercely independent duchess and bonded to Siphero Antolus.

Nerv: A Cheribim, member of a slave race, Awesha's personal caretaker and servant.

Pops: The Siphero's adopted father, a drunkard and obsessive engineering savant.

Yern: A living portrait who serves Awesha's family.

Recril: Awesha's father and self-appointed chieftain of Skyspire, husband of Ulmafe.

Ulmafe: Awesha's mother and wife of Recril.

Greven: The guard captain of Skyspire.

Querce: One of Greven's guard magi, responsible for ceremonial rites.

Yevere: A skimmer drake and personal flying mount to Awesha.

Stager: An rarity in Stratis, Stager is the name Siphero gave to the forty foot tall behemoth.

Revaal: A blacksmith for the village of Skyspire and the primary employer of Siphero in Skyspire.

Jixve: The elder of Skyspire and considered by the village's inhabitants to be the true leader of the village.

Verrencae: A noblewoman who died in the defense of her people, the Scarred, when the Sangria Legion besieged her home, the Lost Isle. She is the personal Archon of Awesha.

Preduvon: Also known as the Great Defiant, Preduvon is a Wingless Archon who serves as a spirit guide to Siphero and gets him into trouble.

Weeslon: One of many suitors chosen by Awesha's mother and father to be her fiancé. Weeslon is a Bond Scrivener, a Winged born with the inability to form a bond but who has a startling ability to tamper with, break or even overwrite bonds between two Winged.

Losfodel: A Wingless skywhale handler who has a deep-seated disgust for any Winged who remind him of his place in society.

Corty: The name of Losfodel's skywhale.

Cortus: An Engria who serves the king and queen of Strati Polis by settling caste disputes and maintaining order in the polis.

Nylf: A Wingless who was born and raised in the slums of Strati Polis and serves the king and queen of the polis.

Airon: The name of the drird Siphero built while in the Halls of Rulers. It functions just like a real bird except this one is completely mechanical and doesn't need to eat, sleep or relieve itself.

Ieava xin Roncresta: The daughter of the king and queen of Strati Polis and considered to be one of the most pure white wings in all of Stratis.

Tratiki: A Wildborn Sila from the polis called Silacorlis. Bonded to Ieava xin Roncresta.

Mervieris: An Asher from the world of the Ashlands who came to Stratis on a secret mission for his sovereign.

Gargran: A Storm Rider hailing from the remote Storm Polis located in the Stormlands and its chosen guardian.

Jieti the Grand Clerician: The primary overseer of the Sangria Legion and all Bond Scriveners. Jieti is a firm believer in the superiority of white winged Avia. Wife to Cortus.

Octavio: A young historian and scribe who was named to the guardianship by the librarians of the Archo Polis, the learned of the Winged.

Xhe-Zhe: A rare pair of Winged twins from the Far Eastern Polis. Xhe-Zhe share one identity, meaning they speak and act in unison instead of independently.

Dreamen "Drenex" Antolus: The father of Siphero Antolus and former harbinger of the Sangria Legion.

Rekusolus: A former member of the Archo Polis who foresaw a great war between Terrans and Winged and was exiled by his brethren.

Straea Antolus: Siphero's mother and wife to Dreamen. Straea lived all her life in Saltdeep as a farmer outside of any Terran military faction.

Urvnic: A Terran pilot who serves aboard the *Legionnaire* and is assigned to be Nylf's commanding officer.

Weltrox: An Alpha who serves in Silacorlis's army during the siege of Silacorlis by the Aerial Fleet.

Vice Admiral Sorice: The commander of the sky galleon named the *Vigilant* and senior officer of the Aerial Fleet, until Recril was appointed as its new Admiral.

Myrvah: The younger sister of Awesha and bonded to Sleghis.

Sleghis: A Bond Scrivener who forcefully bonded with Myrvah and caused her to go insane.

The Omega Alpha: The grand leader of the Sila who joined the Demon Allegiants with all Sila behind him.

Urfera Fireheart: A sorceress and queen of the Ashers, the people of the Ashlands.

Tregion the Oceanmind: The leader of the Aquatics and also ruler of the Ashland's sister realm called the Aquatyer.

Farsheva: The daughter of the Oceanmind who seeks to end the war her father is fighting using a unified front.

Hevros: An ancient Archon who only ever appears to those who represent great change. He appeared for Dreamen and Straea when Siphero was born.

King and Queen of Strati Polis: Ieava's parents and progressive rulers of Strati Polis. They die at the hands of Jieti and the Sangria Legion.

Incarnates: Mysterious enemies that threaten everything Siphero and Awesha are a part of. Their origin and reason for existence is unclear, but all will be made clear eventually.

Pyrus: The name of Mervieris's fiery avisus.

Lore Appendices

Terran Lore:

Terrans: A race of tenacious earth dwellers who have been fighting each other for one thousand years. As a direct result of their continuous struggles against one another, their militaristic technology has greatly evolved to create monumental engines of destruction while other areas of technology have fallen short.

Jormundgard: The world the Terrans fight over, and where they live and die. Jormundgard is a world of endless earth. Mountains taller than its largest cities dot the horizons. Mesas, canyons, valleys and crevices cover its vast landscapes. The few lakes in Jormundgard are highly contested while others remain underground. Jormundgard is home to a rather volatile form of mana which the Terrans harness to fuel their weapons of war.

Steam Lift: A vertical transit system used to travel up and down cliffs and building interiors with immense speed. Just like an elevator.

Wing Armor: A Skelton prototype Siphero is working on. In a completed state it would allow the user to fly without a cockpit or external equipment related to flight.

Airblades: The Terran equivalent of jet aircraft, known for their incredible speed and versatility.

Mana Catchers: The Terran equivalent of rain catchers except they collect mana.

Mana Batteries: A piece of equipment Terrans use to collect mana, which fuels their smaller vehicles, that is to say, anything short of a Claymore.

Paragon: A prototype Spearhead built by Pops and Siphero, and tested as an experimental vehicle.

Edge Mountains: A region of Jormundgard with tall mountains, smooth mesas and towering plateaus. These mountains are located in northern Jormundgard.

Salvagon: One of the Terran cities in Jormundgard, best known where all of the buildings are built entirely out of scrap and cobbled-together materials.

The Envisioner: The title of the Terran general in charge of military intelligence in the city of Salvagon. One of the seven generals ruling over Jormundgard.

The Air Wastes: The area in the Edge Mountains between Jormundgard and the cloud layer marking the entrance to Stratis.

Drird: A mechanical bird that Siphero builds as one of his many side projects.

Golem: A Terran war machine that is the descendent of the Iron Giant. Standing at a quarter of their height, the Golem is a much safer and versatile weapon of war and a lot easier to maintain.

Ruster Petal: A mutated flower native to the war-torn lands of Jormundgard that is primarily found in the Rustlands.

Rustlands: The site of several Terran world wars, which serves as the greatest reminder to all Terrans that their conflicts have left a lasting scar on their world. The Rustlands are located in the center of Jormundgard.

Deep Drake: An underground dwelling drake that can only be found in Jormundgard, and a very distant cousin of the skimmer drake. Known for their voracious appetite and destructive tendencies.

Airfortress: A versatile flying battleship employed by all the Terran Armies of Jormundgard. It is a troop, aircraft and heavy vehicle transport.

Iron Giants: Apex war machines of Terran design that come in all shapes and sizes, but more often than not resemble humanoids.

Terminus Maximus: The largest city in all of Jormundgard and home to the greatest number of Iron Giants and other mechanized war machines.

Legionnaire: The name of the airfortress under the command of Rekusolus and Dreamen. It is the first airfortress to ever enter Stratis.

True Allegiants: A secretive organization led by a collection of unknown parties, both Terran and Winged who heard tell of Rekusolus's warning of an inevitable Terran and Winged war, and have been readying themselves for more than twenty years for that fateful day.

Mana Blade: A next-generation Terran weapon which uses mana to generate a powerful blade of energy which can cut through anything…or anyone. However, it consumes a lot of power and is still considered an experimental technology.

Skelton: A military exoskeleton that Terrans developed to provide support and further specialize a Terran's role in combat. These combat suits are highly adaptable and come in many shapes and sizes, equipped with different armaments.

Claymore: The troop and vehicle transport of Terran airblade squadrons which can also serve as an assault or heavy bomber.

Saber: The workhorse of the Terran airblade squadron. It serves as a light troop transport, air-to-air dogfighter, and air-to-ground bomber.

Spearhead: The first single piloted airblade of its kind. Specialized for air to air combat, recon and hit and run tactics. Fitted with a Winged compartment to allow for allied Winged to catch a ride.

Mana Reactor: A powerful and dangerous piece of Terran technology that provides power for Terran airfortresses, Iron Giants, and any other massive war machine.

Mana Engine: A small-scale version of the mana reactor which provides thrust or power for Terran airblades and ground vehicles.

Clipper: A Terran anti-aircraft/artillery emplacement capable of firing powerful mana infused laser blasts for siege purposes or highly explosive rounds for anti-aircraft supremacy.

Scrap Rig: A heavy-duty truck-like vehicle meant to transport cargo, salvaged materials or troops in Jormundgard.

Diseased Abyss: A dumping ground for all Terran hazardous byproducts created by their technology. It used to be a deep hole in the ground, but now it has grown to the size of a lake thanks to constant Terran dumping procedures.

Winged Lore:

Winged: A race of free spirited winged beings who live upon floating masses of land in the skies above Jormundgard. For one thousand years, they have lived peacefully in their isolated communities and have built a thriving empire of commerce between one another. Over this period of time, Winged believed those with wings were far superior to those who had less than two, poorly formed or no wings at all. Thus a caste system erupted from their vanity and prejudice which divides them to this day. Some of the upper castes have secretly been killing the lower castes to purify their race.

Stratis: The name of the endless skies above Jormundgard's lands. It is home to the Winged who live in peace and seclusion. Their population centers, villages and animal sanctuaries are separated by massive swaths of open sky and spontaneously turbulent updrafts. This beautiful world houses a deep-seated hatred for those of lower social status.

Cheribim: A slave race of spirits who can only exist if they have a master to serve. They fulfill a variety of tasks like housekeeping, cooking, tending to children and tutoring them. Cheribim choose whom they serve unless they have been ordered to serve a particular person by their highest ranking master. They possess free will, but few have their own identity. Nerv is a Cheribim.

Affinities: A gift of elemental manipulation which certain Winged are born with. By using sheer willpower and understanding of their affinity, Winged evolve this power over time, so that it grows with them as they go through life. Some Winged can even use their affinity as a way means of transportation or flight.

Skyspire: One of many secluded villages in Stratis, near the impenetrable cloud barrier. Unlike the other villages, this one rests on top of the tallest mountain in Jormundgard, which reaches into the lower parts of Stratis.

Magnification Turret: A simple yet underestimating weapon mounted on sky galleons and city walls. It can only be used by Winged with an affinity by focusing their given element through the lenses to create a devastating beam of elemental magic.

The Bond: A Winged's rite of passage, which also requires Winged to initiate the bond with one another in order to survive. If Winged do not initiate a bond, then the mana in their bodies will kill them because the bond regulates and controls the output of mana in a Winged's body.

Keeper of the Wood: A profession which exists within Winged society whereby maidens dedicate themselves to tending the crops and greenery to provide for Winged communities. They are farmers.

Shaper: A type of Winged tradesman who uses either a fire or earth affinity to forge metal into necessary forms. They are metalworkers essentially.

Skimmer Drake: A winged dragon creature used as a traveling mount by only the most daring. They can go into slipstream and are incredibly loyal to their masters. They are native to Stratis.

Slipstream: A mode of transport used by sky galleons, skimmer drakes, avisi and Stager. It is best described as the Mach cone which forms when a flying vehicle breaks the sound barrier.

Delvorza: The natural habitat and birthplace of all skimmer drakes. This is where Awesha tamed Yevere and Siphero befriended Stager.

Ipherim: A region of Stratis that is near Skyspire. A remote wild land where skimmer drakes and avisi run free among the Delvorza mountains.

Drake Pipe: A ritualistic tool a skimmer drake fashions for their rider when a Winged journeys to Delvorza to acquire their mount. Afterwards, it becomes the only means for a Winged to summon their skimmer drake.

Bond Scrivener: The profession of certain Winged who are born without the ability to bond with other Winged. However, they can interfere, break, or even overwrite the bond between Winged. Weeslon and Sleghis are Bond Scriveners.

Sky Knights: A peacekeeping order of knights put together by the king and queen of Strati Polis to serve the Winged community as a police force.

Archon: An astral being that acts as a spirit guide to those whom they have chosen. They assess the strength or uniqueness of a bond and may provide wisdom to its parties. Archons are representative of individuals who have a powerful trait or performed a self-righteous act.

Sky Galleon: The primary vehicle of the Winged Empire used for commerce, civilian transport, and combat.

Avisi/Avisus: A winged horse native to Stratis and heavily domesticated. An avisus can go into slipstreams like skimmer drakes, but they lack the stamina skimmer drakes have.

Behemoth: The species that Stager belongs to. They resemble a minotaur, but their entire body is covered in fur and they have more horns. They communicate by sharing their thoughts through physical contact.

Sila: A caste of animalistic Winged made mostly of shaman, hunters, tribesman, and craftsman who are looked down upon by the Avia and Engria. In terms of wings they have bat, butterfly, insect, drake and other wings with a thin membrane. They hold the middle tier of the Winged caste system.

Avia: A caste of Winged represented and named by their feather-like wings. The white winged Avia occupy the second highest tier of the caste system within Winged society with all other Avia acting as a subordinate group within this caste.

Engria. A caste of Winged with wings made out of fire, lightning or other elements depending on the affinity of the recipient. This caste holds the highest office within Winged society, however, a Winged can only become an Engria if their elemental affinity is incredibly powerful or a previous Engria passes the mantle to one they consider to be worthy of the highest regard.

Compa: A caste of Winged represented by their lack of having two natural wings, or having one natural one and one artificial one, or having two artificial ones. Winged from the Sila and Avia castes and even Wingless with an artificial wing can be in this caste. This caste occupies the second lowest tier in the Winged caste system.

Wingless: The lowest caste of the Winged caste system represented by any Winged who are born without wings or lose their wings through some form of punishment or battlefield wound. Because they belong to the lowest caste, Wingless are shunned, beaten and even killed by Avia. No one cares for the Wingless or even puts them to work. That all changes when the True Allegiants roll into town.

Great Defiant: The title of the infamous Preduvon because of his indomitable will and refusal to submit to Avia superiority.

Lady of the Scarred: The title of the merciful and benevolent Verrencae who used her status as a noble to take in refugees from the poleis who were kicked out by the Avia.

The Lost Isle: The name of Verrencae's home and personal isle which served as a refuge and asylum for any and all refugees whether they be Avia, Sila, Compa or Wingless. It mysteriously disappeared 25 years ago from Stratis, never to be seen again.

The Scarred: The name given to the refugees Verrencae protected from the onslaught of the Sangria Legion and its purification efforts—ethnic genocide of the lower castes.

Sky Polis: A polis renowned for its exceptionally crafted sky galleons and trade goods, which also boasts the mightiest navy in all of Stratis. This is Awesha's home.

Guardians: A nomination given to a paragon of a polis in Stratis. The people of the polis name a guardian every year to be recognized for their outstanding contributions to the Winged Empire and to formally become guardians serving the Winged Empire in whatever way possible.

Otherworlder: A title awarded to Siphero after he is appointed to the guardianship by Jixve, the village elder of Skyspire.

Daughter of Exiles: A title awarded to Awesha after she is appointed to the guardianship by Jixve, village elder of Skyspire.

Skywhales: A whale-like creature which traverses the skies of Stratis in pods or individually under the employ of their handlers.

Rising Wind: A powerful current of air much, stronger than the greatest hurricane-force winds. It is a traveling hazard resembling a continuous upward draft which throws anything that can't resist the current into the upper atmosphere. This weather phenomenon moves across Stratis and can only be traversed by either a sky galleon or a skywhale.

Strati Polis: The capital of the Stratis and the center of the Winged Empire. It is home to the Sangria Legion and the king and queen of the Strati Polis.

Sangria Legion: The military branch of the Winged, which is filled with white wing supremacists and those who hate the other castes. They are led by the Grand Clerician Jieti who trains and employs Bond Scriveners.

Grand Clerician: The highest rank within the Sangria Legion, this ruler oversees the legion's activities, and dictates their actions, but answers to the King and Queen of Strati Polis. Jieti holds this office.

Teller of Doom: A slanderous title the other scholars of the Archo Polis called Rekusolus because he had a vision of the end of days brought on by a war between Winged and Terrans.

Silacorlis: A polis home to a majority of Sila and Silacon, and a refuge for outcasts from the other poleis.

Silacon: A bestial state that only a certain number of Sila can reach. The user becomes a four legged beast with wings and their instincts take over.

Savage City: The capital of Silacorlis and the place where the Omega Alpha resides with his fellow Omegas.

Feral Dance: A wild celebration which occurs in Silacorlis whenever they have important to celebrate. On average the Feral Dance happens ten times a year, but they have also been known to be a reward after a hard fought battle.

Wildborn: A taboo child resulting from a combination of Silacon and Winged parents. A Wildborn is possessed with the wild nature of his or her Silacon parent and an insatiable desire to establish itself in the animal hierarchy. Tratiki is a Wildborn.

Vigilant: The flagship of the Aerial Fleet and commanded by Sorice.

Aerial Fleet: The largest fleet of sky galleons which serves as the Sky Polis's navy. The commander of this fleet was Sorice until he was demoted.

Sigma Alpha and Sigma Omega: Titles given as a reward to outsiders who have contributed greatly to Silacorlis and the Sila. They are made honorary Sila on the spot.

Demon Allegiants: The new name of the True Allegiants after their expedition force allied themselves with Silacorlis, the remnants of the Aerial Fleet, and with any outlying Sila, Compa and Wingless refugees trying to escape the wrath of the Sangria Legion.

Leviathan: An apex predator in Stratis that preys upon sky galleons and skywhales alike. They mostly inhabit the Storm Polis and rarely venture out of it.

Sky Eater: A legendary leviathan several times larger than your average leviathan, said to be the father of them all.

Storm Polis: A polis out in the middle of the Stormlands with a legendary guild of hunters called the Storm Riders. This is where Greven is from.

Stormlands: The most dangerous place in all of Stratis. The Stormlands are home to a never-ending storm which serves as a breeding ground for leviathans and sky whales.

Far Eastern Polis: A center of trade, commerce and corruption within Stratis. The Far Eastern Polis is a hub for trade in exotic goods and trinkets, some of which can only be found in the polis. This polis has the largest Wingless population of all the poleis. This is the birthplace of Xhe-Zhe.

Winged Twins: A pair of Winged born together and can only be found in the Far Eastern Polis. They share one mind and one pair of wings between two bodies. Separating them is a death sentence to both. Xhe-Zhe are Winged Twins.

Archo Polis: A polis home to the most learned scholars and to the wisest elders from across Stratis. The Archo Polis serves as an academy, an archive, a library and a keeper of all history in Stratis, and is open to all regardless of caste superiority. This is where Octavio hails from.

Learned: A group of Winged who watch over and live on the Archo Polis, tending to the archives and the libraries.

Tortragard: The chosen name for a united Stratis and Jormundgard, approved by the Demon Allegiant leadership.

Horn of the Storm Beasts: A legendary horn capable of summoning the king of all leviathans, the Skyeater.

House of the Feral Beast: One of five governing bodies in Stratis that determines the succession to the throne of Strati Polis and the Winged Empire. This house is represented by the Sila leadership of the Omegas and the Omega Alpha.

Other Lore:

Ashlands: The home of the Ashers and the birthplace of Mervieris. It is ruled by Urfera Fireheart, and is a land of molten rivers, volcanic landscapes and obsidian cities.

Ashers: The denizens of the Ashlands.

Aquatics: The citizens of the Aquatyer.

Aquatyer: The home of the Aquatics and the birthplace of Farsheva. It is controlled by Tregion the Oceanmind and is characterized by endless oceans, dark abysses, gigantic creatures and sunken civilizations.

Ash Knight: Mervieris's designated rank in service to Urfera Fireheart.

Obsidian Legion: The army that Mervieris belongs to, which gets its orders directly from Urfera Fireheart.

Crusader of Defiance: The name of a hybrid Terran and Winged sky galleon/airfortress that is only in the developmental stages. It is a cultural exchange project between the two civilizations to create a next-generation weapon of war to put an end to their future wars.

The Sanctum: The void-filled place where Siphero, Awesha and Myrvah meet Hevros, Preduvon and Verrencae.

48330749R00160

Made in the USA
Middletown, DE
15 September 2017